CINDERELLA AT THE B...

He danced smoothly, moving in perfect sync with her body. When the last note floated into the air, he didn't loosen his hold on her even though the song had clearly ended.

The nearness, the warmth, the sheer maleness of him made her dizzy. Her palms felt damp and her brain felt fuzzy, as if she weren't getting enough oxygen.

His voice sounded in her ear, low and rumbly, sending a shiver down her arms. "Do you have any idea what you make me want to do?"

He pulled back enough to look down at her. His eyes were hot. The heat burned its way through her, making her feel as if her bones were melting. Against all wisdom, she found herself breathing the irresistible question. "What?"

The soft warmth of his breath against her ear sent a quiver of pleasure coursing up her spine. "For starters, I want to kiss you."

She looked up at him, unable to speak.

"And unless you tell me you don't want me to, that's exactly what I'm going to do."

"I—" Her lips parted, but no further words came out.

His mouth brushed her ear again as he rocked her to the rhythm. The slow strains of another sultry song reverberated in the night air.

"That didn't sound like a no."

She didn't know if it was the rising notes of the painfully beautiful music or the feel of his breath on her neck that raised goosebumps on her skin. She only knew that she felt helpless to deny the aching need to feel his lips on hers. "It . . . wasn't."

PRINCE CHARMING

ROBIN WELLS

LOVE SPELL BOOKS   NEW YORK CITY

LOVE SPELL®

November 1999

Published by

Dorchester Publishing Co., Inc.
276 Fifth Avenue
New York, NY 10001

ISBN 0-505-52344-2

The name "Love Spell" and its logo are trademarks of Dorchester Publishing Co., Inc.

Printed in the United States of America.

To Ken, my personal Prince Charming.

With thanks to Bill Kinzeler, Gordon Jackson and Gene Giles at American Commercial Barge Line for the towboat tour; Bill McNeal for sharing his many years of accumulated wisdom, lore and life-on-the-river literature; and Captain Jim Calhoun, USCG, ret., for his invaluable information.

PRINCE CHARMING

Chapter One

Josephine Evans scrambled out of her gray Mercedes, her legs wobbling from the shock of the accident, and stared at the smashed front end of her vehicle. Uptown-bound traffic, already thick in this part of New Orleans at rush hour, clotted behind her like Creole cottage cheese, but Josephine was too worried about her damaged car to care.

Oh, dear—the hood looked like an accordian, one of the front tires slanted in at a crazy angle and a puddle of gooey liquid oozed from under the crumpled engine. The car was undrivable—probably even unrepairable. Which meant it was most likely unsalable.

Josephine's spirits sank to the soles of her navy Givenchy pumps. Great, just great—just what she needed on top of all her other money troubles. And since she'd struck the pickup from the rear, the accident was clearly her fault.

"You hurt, lady?"

The late-afternoon sun glared in her eyes so brightly she could barely make out the man climbing out of the black pickup with the dark, tinted windows. He was tall—she could tell that—and muscular. His shoulders were as broad as a linebacker's in full uniform, and his arms were brawny, but his chest tapered to a flat stomach and narrow hips.

"I'm fine. Are you all right?"

"Hell, no, I'm not all right." His voice was a deep, gravelly rumble, as low and ominous as thunder. He stalked to the rear of his vehicle and stared at the bumper. "What in Christ's name have you done to my truck?"

Josephine squinted at him, the light still in her eyes. Backlit by the low-riding sun, he looked like he was on fire. A chill chased through her, despite the unseasonably warm March air. He reminded her of the fiery demons her father used to preach against. His black eyebrows curled like gargoyle wings above coal black eyes, his blue-black hair looked like it hadn't seen a comb in weeks and his face was grizzled with what looked like a week's worth of stubble. The effect was altogether disreputable, completely intimidating and more than a little dangerous.

Josephine backed against the smashed fender of her Mercedes as he moved along the rear of his truck, running his hand along the fender. His palms were large and square and his fingers were long and tanned, and the sight of them made her distinctly uneasy. So did the message emblazoned on the back of his dirty gray T-shirt under the picture of a crawfish: *Suck the Head and Eat the Tail.*

When he turned toward her, his scowl made her grateful for the swarm of Magazine Street traffic slowly surging around them. This was not the kind of man she'd want to encounter on a deserted road.

Not that this location had much to recommend it. She cast an uneasy glance around, taking in the sleazy second-hand clothing shop on the sidewalk behind her, the dingy tavern on the corner and the boarded-up buildings across the street. She was about a mile shy of the upscale antique shops and restaurants the tourists liked to frequent, in a seedy, broken-down neighborhood that smelled of old garbage.

Josephine lifted her chin and pulled herself to her straightest posture, the way she always did whenever she was nervous. *Poise and a gracious manner can overcome any obstacle.* The phrase had been drummed into her at finishing school, and it was one she'd often repeated to her own charm school students. She repeated it silently to herself now, forcing a practiced expression of composure onto her face.

"I'm very sorry I hit you, but you pulled in front of me so suddenly that I didn't have time to stop."

"Like hell! You speeded up when I tried to pass you!"

The venom in his voice made her jump. She inched closer to her bumper as he took a menacing step toward her.

"I know your type," he said with a snarl. "You hoity-toity society broads all think it's your God-given right to barge ahead of everyone else."

Josephine nervously smoothed the jacket of her navy wool suit, trying to smooth her nerves as well, and mentally recited another finishing school axiom: *The more dire the situation, the greater the need to remain calm.* She carefully modulated her voice to a low but firm level. "I'm afraid that you're mistaken. I was trying to hit the brake, and I accidentally hit the accelerator instead."

"Jesus Christ! What's the matter with you? Don't you have the sense God gave a goose?"

Irritation shot through her. He had every right to be upset, but there was no need for him to be insulting. And there was certainly no need for him to take the Lord's name in vain. "I'll thank you to kindly keep God's name out of this. It was an accident, not a deliberate act, I assure you. Besides, it looks like your truck is barely scratched."

"Barely scratched? Hell, lady, it's more scratched than a rat's ass. The bumper's all dented in and the paint job's ruined."

She'd been considering giving him the benefit of the doubt—after all, everyone dressed down on occasion—but this man was clearly every bit as uncouth as he looked. "It's so covered with dirt that I don't see how you can tell," she said stiffly. "But in any event, there's no need to curse at me."

"Oh, no?" He leaned toward her, a vein bulging in his forehead. His eyes were bloodshot, his breath smelled of stale beer and his mouth was curled into what could only be described as a sneer. "What the hell do you think I should be doing? Strangling your scrawny neck?"

Her gaze inadvertently flew to his immense hands, and another shiver chased up her spine. She forced herself to look him in the eye. "There's no need to threaten me, either."

A malevolent gleam lit his face. His lip pulled back in an awful smile. "Sweetheart, that wasn't a threat. If I told you I was going to cart you off to the swamp, snatch the hide right off your sorry, no-driving self, then feed the curly side of your south end to the gators, well, now, *that* might be a threat. Which, come to think of it, isn't a half-bad idea."

Josephine stared at him, aghast. She'd never been talked to so crudely in her entire life. He wasn't hurt, for heaven's sake. It wasn't like the accident thirteen years ago, the accident where . . .

The unbidden memory made her shudder. With long-practiced determination, she thrust it from her mind. She couldn't allow herself to think about that now or she would surely fall to pieces. Her whole world was already falling apart as it was. If she hadn't been so preoccupied with her current troubles, she never would have hit this cretin in the first place—even though he *had* rudely swerved directly into her path.

He was glaring at her belligerently. She glared back, channeling all of her distress into indignation. "You, sir, are the most foulmouthed, ill-tempered, uncouth man I've ever had the displeasure of meeting."

His scowl deepened and his eyes narrowed. "Yeah, well, I'm not exactly charmed to make your acquaintance, either. So what the hell are you going to do about my truck?"

"Your truck? *My* car's the one that's totaled!"

"Yeah, and whose fault is that, huh? Maybe next time you'll be a little more careful about which pedal you're stomping on."

He stormed back to his pickup, extracted a cellular phone and started to punch in a number.

Alarmed, Josephine ran toward him. "What are you doing?"

"What does it look like I'm doing? I'm calling the police."

"What for?"

"To get you ticketed."

"Oh, please, sir—please don't do that!"

His mouth twisted into an expression of disdain. "For some strange reason, my insurance company prefers a police report to just taking my word on these things."

"You don't need to report it. I mean, I'll—I'll pay for the damages." Though how she'd manage, she didn't know. She didn't even know how she was going to pay the phone bill. Or the electric bill. Or buy food, once she'd eaten the last of the Budget Gourmet frozen entrées in the refrigerator that was about to be repossessed.

"Damn right you'll pay."

"Of course I will. Just—please, sir, please don't call the police."

He glared at her, the phone dwarfed by his enormous hand. "What's the matter? Is there a warrant out for your arrest?"

"Of course not!"

"Well, then, why are you so scared of the law?"

"I'm not. It's just that—well . . . " She was embarrassed to say it aloud. It was so irresponsible, and so unlike her. She just hadn't had the 590 dollars last month when the premium was due, but there was no point in telling all that to this man. She swallowed nervously. "I'm—I'm afraid my insurance is expired."

"Oh, good Lord!"

Josephine winced. "Please, sir—don't use the Lord's name in vain like that."

He stared at her, the trace of a smirk playing on his mouth. "Why the hell not?"

She steeled herself against rising to his bait. "Because it's one of the Ten Commandments. 'Thou shalt not take the name of the Lord thy God in vain.' Besides, it's offensive, and being offensive breaks the rules of polite society."

"Oh, Christ. What are you, some kinda friggin' church lady?"

"Well, no, but if you must know, my father was a missionary and it offends me to hear language like that."

"Oh, so you're offended, are you?"

"Yes."

"Well, now, ain't that too dorkin' damn bad."

He seemed to be waiting for her reaction. She tried her best not to give him one, but she must have failed, judging from the mocking smile on his face.

Oh, dear—how she wished she were more like some of her former students! If only she knew how to flirt and smile, to cajole and flatter, she could probably persuade this man to see things her way. But she'd never had the chance to learn those things. She'd wanted to, but her father had never approved of frivolous behavior. The one time she'd behaved indiscreetly, the consequences had been so horrible that she'd never dared try it again.

No, flirtation wasn't an option. She'd have to try appealing to this man's sympathetic side. "Look, sir, if you call

14

the police, they'll take my license for not having any insurance."

"Sounds like a personal problem to me." He raised the phone again.

She should have guessed that he'd have all the sympathy of a serial murderer. The only way to change the mind of a brute like this was to appeal to his self-interest. "If I have to pay for a ticket, it'll only delay my being able to pay for your car repairs."

One of his dark eyebrows lifted. "Are you telling me you're broke?"

Josephine shifted uncomfortably from one high-heeled pump to the other. "I'm saying my financial situation is temporarily a little . . . under the weather." *To put it mildly.* She nervously twisted the strap of her navy Coach handbag. "I always pay my debts, though. It may take me a few weeks, but I'll get you your money."

He eyed her derisively. "Believe it or not, most body shops these days take credit cards."

"I can't use one."

"Why not? Is credit against your daddy's religion?"

"No." *Oh, dear.* She was humiliated beyond words, but she couldn't think of a single explanation to give him other than the truth. "I-I'm afraid my cards are all maxed out."

The information seemed to startle him. His eyes narrowed, and he scanned her from head to toe. Something about the way he looked at her made her think he was not only estimating the cost of her navy suit, but seeing all the way through it to approximate the price of her bra and panties. "Looks like you're dressed for work. You got a job?"

"Well . . . yes." She'd quit her paying job at the public library when Aunt Prudie had gotten sick, but that didn't mean she was unemployed.

"So I'll give you a break. I'll wait till your next paycheck to collect."

"I don't get a paycheck. I'm self-employed."

"Doing what?"

"I operate the New Orleans Academy for Etiquette and Social Graces."

"What the hell is that?"

"Some people refer to it as charm school."

"Charm school." He repeated the words incredulously, his mouth curling into a jeering grin. He shoved his hand in his pocket and extracted a small round can labeled *Redman.* "You mean you teach manners and how to act all la-di-da?"

She watched him open the tin and stuff a wad of what looked like dirt in his mouth. *A lady remains civil under all circumstances,* Josephine reminded herself. She was quivering with the effort to do so now. She lifted her chin. "As the name describes, it's a school for etiquette and social graces. And if I might make an observation, you could do with a few lessons yourself."

His loud bark of a laugh caught her by surprise. "Don' know what makes ya say that."

An enormous brown spit wad narrowly missed her shoe, surprising her even more. She jumped aside, nearly tripping over her own heels in horror. He wiped his mouth with the back of his enormous hand, his chest rumbling with amusement.

"So, Teach, how do ya propose to pay me?" His gaze rolled over her in a lascivious manner. She folded her arms against her chest, alarm surging through her.

Was it her imagination, or had his accent just slipped from a Harry Connick Jr.–sounding New Orleans drawl to a low-class ninth-ward brogue? He was making her more nervous by the minute. "How . . . how much do you suppose it'll cost?"

"I dunno. It's a brand-new truck. Dependin' on what has to be done, I'd guess anywhere from eight to fifteen hundred dollars."

Josephine's heart sank. "I don't have that kind of money."

"Not much of a market for manners these days?" He spit another huge loogie, this one apparently aimed right at her feet, forcing her to jump yet again.

A car behind them honked. The man shot them the finger as casually as Josephine might say "please" or "thank you."

He was a beast. She'd visited zoos on two continents, but she'd never seen a more uncivilized creature. Anger, frustration and a miserable sense of helplessness formed a hard, hot knot in her chest.

"So get your family to loan it to you."

"I don't have any family left." To her embarrassment, her voice cracked and her eyes filled with tears. Oh, dear, this was no time to fall apart! But this seemed like the final straw; Aunt Prudence had been dead for only six weeks, her financial situation had gone from desperate to hopeless and now her car was totaled. To top it all off, this awful man was *expectorating* at her.

The thought helped her to muster a steadying sense of indignation. She wouldn't give this monster the satisfaction of reducing her to tears. Blinking hard, she struggled to rein in her emotions, but one traitorous tear eked out anyway. She furiously wiped it away.

"Ah, Christ, don't cry." He shoved the can back in his pocket and gave an exasperated frown. "Hell. If you promise to stop bawlin', I'll push your piece of junk out of the street."

Willing herself to assume a semblance of composure, Josephine tried for her frostiest, most formal tone. "I am *not* bawling. I would, however, very much appreciate your assistance in moving my car."

"All right, all right. Just wait here and quit your sniveling." He strode around to the driver's side of the Mercedes and opened the door. Reaching in, he steered the car with

17

one hand and pushed with the other, moving it to an empty curbside parking space as if it weighed no more than a bicycle.

He ambled back, his tall, heavily muscled body moving with a feline grace that seemed somehow predatory. She involuntarily jumped out of arm's reach as he approached, pressing her back against the window of the shoddy used-clothing store.

She needn't have worried. Without a word, he strode straight past, hopped in his truck and drove it to the parking space behind her car.

She was being ridiculous, she tried to reassure herself. He wasn't a wild animal, she wasn't a scared rabbit and he wasn't going to pounce. But she wasn't so sure when he slammed his truck door and stalked back down the sidewalk, holding a pen and a crumpled piece of paper.

"Okay. Give me your vital statistics."

Josephine stared. "Excuse me?"

"Come on. I haven't got all day." He pulled a toothpick from the pocket of his jeans and slid it between his lips. The movement drew her attention to his mouth. His bottom lip was full and lush, shockingly sensuous in such a hard, masculine face. "Give me your vitals."

"You want my *measurements?*" she blurted incredulously, her voice thin and alarmed.

He grinned, the toothpick dangling from the corner of his mouth. "Well, sure, darlin', if you're offerin'. But this ain't the tryouts for Miss America. I meant your name, address and phone number."

"Oh. Of course." Heat scorched her cheeks. Why on earth had she asked such an idiotic question? Something about this barbarian made her think about sex. Not that she had a very high opinion of the activity. Her limited experience in sexual matters had convinced her that it was vastly overrated.

He placed one foot on the concrete step of the second-hand store's stoop, smoothed the paper over his thigh and poised the pen above it. "So what's your name?"

"Josephine Evans."

She watched him write it down, unnerved to note that his denim-encased thigh looked as hard as a marble table-top.

"And your address?"

"Seven hundred Poydras Plaza."

His eyes narrowed warily. "That's a business address. Where do you live?"

It seemed unwise to give such personal information to a man who made all of her intuitive warning systems flash "danger" in red blinking lights. "You can reach me at the office at any time." She rapidly gave him the phone number. "If I'm not there, I have a machine on, and I check my messages often."

He shifted the toothpick to the other corner of his mouth. "Well, now, I'm not callin' you a liar, sweetheart, but just to make sure you're who you say you are, you'd better let me take a look at your driver's license."

The distrust in his eyes made Josephine stiffen. "I assure you I'm telling the truth."

"Then you won't mind me seein' that license, will you?"

She couldn't stand to have her character questioned. She'd worked too hard for too long to make sure her reputation was spotless. If she kept her behavior above reproach for enough years, she figured, maybe someday she'd be able to forgive herself for that one, terrible, horrid indiscretion. "I'm sure you don't mean to be so insulting, Mr. . . . "

"Dumanski. Cole Dumanski."

Cole. How appropriate. With his charcoal eyes, coal black hair and pitch-black soul, the name was a perfect fit.

Josephine tilted her head up to an imperious angle, just as she'd seen Aunt Prudie do when she'd wanted to set someone in their place. "Yes, well, Mr. Dumanski, I'm sure you don't mean to be rude, but I'm unaccustomed to having my word doubted."

A nerve jumped in his jaw. "There's a first time for everything, now, isn't there?"

"I beg your pardon?"

Her haughty expression made his blood boil. God, how he hated these better-than-everyone-else, nose-in-the-air New Orleans blueblood types. He'd almost forgotten how much he'd detested them, but seeing that photo of Alexa Armand in this morning's newspaper had stirred up all of the old resentments, all of the old stomach-churning hate.

This dame was just the same. She might be the daughter of a missionary, but he'd bet his life she came from old money just the same. He'd known it the moment he'd gotten trapped behind her in traffic. She'd been driving her old Mercedes the speed of a snail on Valium, oblivious to the traffic bottled up behind her, as if she owned the road. When he'd tried to pass her, she'd sped up. Cole's blood simmered. He wasn't going to let any damned New Orleans rich bitch push him around—not ever again.

With a fierce sense of purpose, he'd gunned the engine and cut in front of her. "Take that," he'd muttered as he slowed for the next stoplight. But his sense of deep, soul-felt satisfaction had been short-lived, abruptly interrupted by the impact of her Mercedes plowing into his rear bumper like a runaway barge.

He glared at her now. "Your type always thinks you're above the rules the rest of us everyday folks play by. Well, I've got news for you, sweetheart—your highfalutin, high-brow ways don't impress me one bit. Now, I don't know if you're leveling with me or not about having money problems, but let's get one thing straight: you're not gonna weasel out of payin' me what you owe me, and you're not gonna leave here until I verify who you are and where I can find you. So you can either give me your driver's license right now, or you can give it to a cop in a few minutes. Which is it gonna be, sweetheart?"

Cole watched the emotions play over the woman's pale face—outrage, indignation, resignation. It wasn't a bad face—not if you liked the ice-queen type. Personally Cole had never cared for it. He liked his women hot-blooded and willing. This one looked like she wouldn't warm up with a blowtorch under her tush.

All the same, she wasn't actually bad-looking. She had a straight nose, a nice mouth and big blue eyes. He couldn't tell much about her hair, slicked back like it was in that god-awful bun.

"All right," she finally conceded. "I'll show you my license. But I'll need to see yours as well."

"Fair enough." Cole dug his wallet out of his back pocket as she unsnapped the neat leather bag on her shoulder, then waited until she'd handed over her license before passing his to her.

He glanced down at the laminated card. Jesus—the photo looked like a prison mug shot. Most women at least tried to smile when they had their picture taken. Was this broad's face capable of forming a pleasant expression?

His gaze flicked from the photo to the information. Josephine L. Evans. Brown hair, blue eyes, twenty-nine years old.

Like the photo, the information on the card didn't really do her justice. Her hair was more blond than it was brown, and her eyes were the color of deep water. He couldn't tell much about how her one hundred and ten pounds were distributed on her five-foot-five frame under that expensive suit, but he'd already noticed her legs. They were long and slender and nicely shaped, with rounded calves and narrow ankles.

He glanced at the address and scowled. Her house was in one of the ritziest neighborhoods in New Orleans, not far from where Alexa had lived.

The thought made his muscles tense. He'd managed to put Alexa out of his mind for most of the last fourteen years, but seeing her picture in this morning's New

Orleans *Times-Picayune* had dredged up all of the old bitterness he'd thought long buried.

He glared at Josephine. "How the hell does a person who lives in Audubon Place manage to have no money?"

He saw her spine stiffen. "My finances are my own concern."

"Not when you owe me money, lady."

Her smooth forehead wrinkled in a frown. "The house belonged to my great-aunt," she explained reluctantly.

"Belonged?"

"She died six weeks ago."

She looked as though she was about to cry again. *Crap.* Nothing made him more uncomfortable than a bawling female. He never knew what to do or say around one. He lowered his voice, hoping to forestall her tears. "So I suppose your money's tied up in probate or something like that?"

"Something like that." She bent her head evasively and carefully began copying the information from his license into an expensive-looking leather notebook, using an Argento pen.

Hell. She claimed to be broke, but she carried a pen-and-paper set worth at least three hundred dollars. He knew because he'd bought his accountants something similar for Christmas.

She suddenly gazed up quizzically. "Your address says the Governor Nichols Street Wharf. Does that mean you live on a boat?"

At least she wasn't stupid. He gave a curt nod. "Yeah. A towboat. I'm captain of *La Chienne Mauvaise.*"

Her head cocked to one side and her brow furrowed. " 'The Bad Dog'? "

" 'The Mean Bitch.' "

Her eyes flew open so wide he couldn't help but laugh. She sure was a stiff-necked little prig. He had to hand it to her, though—there weren't many of these nose-in-the-air, hoity-toity broads who would *admit* to being flat-busted broke, although he suspected more than a few of them were.

A charm school teacher. Didn't that just beat all?

He twirled the toothpick in his mouth and watched her diligently copy down the information from his license. Well, whether she was flat broke or not, he had no use for bluebloods, and this one would bleed indigo if he cut her. There was no way she was going to get away with bashing in his bumper and not paying.

"I'll get an estimate from a body shop, then let you know what you owe."

"All right."

There was no point wasting any more time here. He handed her back her driver's license, shoved the paper into his pocket and turned to go.

"Wait!"

Now what? He slowly pivoted toward her.

Her eyes were distressed, and her throat visibly moved as she swallowed. "D-do you think you could give me a ride?"

He glowered at her. "Look, lady, I'm in a hurry. My boat casts off at dawn, I need to find a cook for the crew before then, and now, thanks to you, I've also got to take my truck to a body shop. Why don't you just grab a cab? That way you and I can just call it a day."

She dropped her gaze to the pavement and fiddled with the purse strap on her shoulder. "Because I, uh, don't have any money on me."

Oh, for the love of bilge water. He started just to shove a few dollars at her, but the concept stuck in his craw. She owed *him* money, by damn.

But he couldn't just go off and leave her. A crime-ridden public housing development was less than two blocks away. In this part of town, an expensive-looking dame like Little Miss Priss here was likely to get robbed, raped or worse.

He didn't know why he should care, except that if she

got killed he'd never have the satisfaction of making her pay him every red cent she owed. "Oh, hell. Come on."

"I really do appreciate this." She ran to catch up with him.

"Yeah, yeah, yeah." He climbed in his truck and inserted his key in the ignition, only to realize she was still standing on the sidewalk beside the passenger-side door.

"What's the matter? Can't get the door open?"

Her face flushed scarlet. "I, uh, was waiting for you to open it."

Was this dame for real? He leaned over the seat and pulled the inside latch, flinging her door open so fast he nearly hit her with it. He glared at her through the opening. "Let me see if I've got this straight. You wreck my truck, you don't have any insurance, you want some kind of easy-payment plan, you mooch a ride home—*and* you expect me to open the door for you?" He muttered a low and ominous oath. "Get your ass in here, sister, before I leave you eating dust."

She scurried into the vehicle and fastened her seat belt. Cole gunned the engine and screeched away from the curb before she'd even finished closing her door.

Her spine grew straight and rigid. "I've apologized for hitting your car, and I fully intend to pay you back. There's no reason to treat me so abominably."

The prissy note in her voice made him again reach for the tin of tobacco he'd purchased for his first mate. Cole personally despised the stuff, but this woman's reaction to it was just too damn satisfying.

Steering the pickup with his knees, he pulled out a pinch and stuffed it in his cheek. The expression of horror on her face made it impossible not to grin. He gave a few open-mouthed chews for added effect. "I don' know what you're talkin' about, sweetheart. I haven't touched your stomach."

"My stomach? I didn't say anything about my stomach."

"Sure you did. You said I've been treatin' you abdominally."

Cole glanced at her from the corner of his eye as he stopped at the Washington Street intersection. He'd never seen a face so transparent. Her eyes telegraphed shock and astonishment before narrowing into displeased comprehension. She exhaled huffily through her nose. "I don't find you at all amusing."

"That's a shame, sweetheart. 'Cause I think you're a downright laugh riot." He turned right and headed toward St. Charles. "Ya know what? It's gotten awfully stuffy in here." Hitting the master control buttons on his door, he lowered her automatic window.

"If you don't mind, I'd prefer to turn on the air—*Oh!*" With a shriek, she flattened herself against the back of the seat as a huge spit wad sailed past her face and out the open window.

Two bright spots flamed on her cheeks. Her hands curled into tight fists in her lap, and her blue eyes snapped with outrage as she turned them on Cole. "You stop that this instant!"

"Or you'll do what?"

The challenge in his voice stopped her short. Or what, indeed? She was still too far from home to walk. Her fingernails dug into her palms in futile rage. "Or—or you're likely to get that nasty stuff all over my clothes," she finished lamely.

He flashed a wicked grin. "Oh, is that all you're worried about? Well, then, you just sit back and relax there, sugar. If I hit you, I'll let you deduct the cleanin' bill from what you owe me."

He was despicable—beyond despicable. He was loathsome, crude, cadlike, detestible, vulgar, contemptible, vile. . . .

She busied herself with silent adjectives, biting her tongue and trying hard to keep from telling him exactly

what she thought of him. Just a few more minutes, she told
herself. Just a few more minutes and he'd be out of her life
forever.

She was grateful when he finally stopped at the red brick
guard station outside the enormous wrought-iron gate that
sequestered Audubon Place from the rest of the world.
Cole slid down his automatic window. "I've got Miss
Josephine Evans here—973 Audubon Place."

It disconcerted her that this horrid man had memorized
her address. She reached for the door handle. "I can walk
from here. Thank you very much for the ride."

Cole clicked a button under his window that snapped
her door locked. "I've brought you this far, sugar," he said,
shoving the toothpick back into his mouth. "Might as well
see you all the way home."

The brute had just locked her in! She stared at him,
speechless, her initial sense of shock giving way to a
moment of fear when she realized his finger was still on
the control button.

But they were sitting right outside the guard station; if
he intended her any harm, surely he wouldn't have brought
her this far. His desire to see her to her door wasn't motivated by chivalry—she was sure he didn't even know the
meaning of the word—but it probably wasn't motivated by
anything sinister, either. He was probably just nosy about
where she lived.

Another car pulled up behind them, and Josephine stiffened. *Oh, dear.* It wouldn't do to create a scene, especially
not with a neighbor watching. Aunt Prudence's strictest
rule had been never to create a public spectacle. Even
though the old lady was dead, Josephine still didn't want to
do anything that would have embarrassed her. As much as
she hated giving this loathsome creature the satisfaction of
getting his way, the easiest course of action was just to go
along with him.

Gritting her teeth, Josephine leaned forward and waved

at the guard. The uniformed man nodded and hit a button. The black scrollwork gate slowly swung open, and Cole drove through.

He eased the pickup along the exclusive private road lined with massive live oaks and royal palms, past the impressively landscaped lawns of the even more impressive mansions. Five hundred yards in, he pulled under a Spanish moss–draped oak, in front of the imposing white-columned home Aunt Prudence had modeled after Jefferson's Monticello.

"Nice little shack you've got here," he remarked dryly.

Josephine placed her hand on the door handle. "Thank you for the ride. Now, if you'd just let me out of here . . ."

"Hey, what's that hanging on your front door?"

She swiveled her head toward the house and saw a bulky metallic object suspended from the knob of the leaded glass door. Pasted to the ornate beveled glass above it was a large orange sign. "I-I don't know."

Cole stretched across and stared out her side window. "Looks like a padlock. And a sheriff's notice."

Josephine's stomach lurched, and for a moment she thought she was going to be sick. Pressing her hand to her belly, she closed her eyes and drew a deep breath.

"Hey, lady—are you okay?"

She opened her eyes to see Cole frowning at her.

"You've gotten awfully pale. You're not going to pass out on me, are you?"

"Of course not." Even to her own ears, her voice lacked conviction. She leaned her head against the headrest. "I'm—I'm suddenly feeling a little ill, that's all."

His dark brows pulled more tightly together. "Has it got anything to do with that junk on your door?"

She averted her eyes and swallowed. Her mouth felt parched. She knew she should get out of the vehicle, walk to the front door and read the sign, but she couldn't seem to find the strength to do it. It was as if her body were preserving all her resources, knowing she'd need every ounce of stamina to deal with the situation once her suspicions were confirmed.

"Want me to go check it out for you?" Cole asked.

Josephine managed a nod. "Please."

Without a word, Cole climbed out of the vehicle and strode to the porch. She watched him go, her head still propped against the tan leather headrest, feeling a strange sense of detachment. She'd lived in the house for the past three years, but it had never felt like home. Not the way she'd always imagined a home should feel, anyway. Come to think of it, she'd never known a place that had. Home should be a place where you felt safe and at ease and loved, a place where you knew you were accepted just as you were.

She'd never known a place like that. She'd spent most of her life in boarding schools. Oh, maybe she'd had a real home when her mother was alive, but she'd died when Josephine was barely five, and try as she might, Josephine could piece together only the barest wisp of a memory of her now.

The only relatives she remembered were her father—a rigid, bitter man, hell-bent on serving a God he blamed for the death of his wife—and Aunt Prudie, a prim, proud matron who played the role of grande dame and arbiter of New Orleans society.

It was probably a good thing Prudie was already gone, Josephine thought, watching Cole study the notice on the door. If she weren't dead already, the current turn of events would have killed her.

Cole disappeared around the side of the house, then emerged on the opposite side a few moments later. He strode back and stuck his head in the open passenger window, resting his forearms on the door. His dark eyes told her nothing.

"Well?" she managed.

"It says your property's been seized by court order."

She'd known that was what the notice was likely to say, but hearing it aloud jarred her all the same. The interior of the pickup seemed to pitch and reel. She grabbed the door handle, needing something to hold on to. "Does—does that mean I'm evicted?"

"Afraid so. It looks like all the entrances are pad-locked."

Despair, strong and terrifying, gripped and shook her. "What am I going to do?"

"Well, I guess you can start by calling the sheriff's office. Or an attorney."

She'd already done both of those things to find out what was likely to happen in the event of foreclosure, but there was no point in explaining that now. Panic was rapidly gaining hold of her. "I mean tonight. Where am I going to stay tonight?"

He lifted his wide shoulders. "Beats me, lady. With a friend, I guess."

But there was no one—no one Josephine could call up and say, "Guess what? I can't afford a hotel, my home has been seized, my car is totaled and I need a place to stay tonight." Josephine had never made friends easily, and Aunt Prudence had discouraged the few fledgling relation-ships she'd attempted.

With her job at the library, weekend work as an etiquette teacher and the increasing care Aunt Prudie's heart condi-tion had demanded, it had been easy to limit her life to home and work. She had dozens of acquaintances and con-tacts, but no one to whom she was really close.

She took a deep gulp of air. "I don't really have any friends."

It was no damn wonder, Cole thought; with an attitude as priggish as hers, even the bluebloods would be hard-pressed to stand her company. Still, this wasn't the time to point that out. The dame seemed to be in a real bind.

"You must have someplace to go. Maybe a neighbor's house?"

"Oh, no, I couldn't bear it. I couldn't stand to face them. Especially not with that—that *notice* on the door." Tears sprang to her eyes. She gave a ragged sniffle, then unsnapped her purse and extracted a monogrammed handkerchief.

Oh, crap. She wasn't going to cry again, was she?

He glanced at his watch. It was getting dark, and he still hadn't found a cook. Blast it all to Hades; this weepy woman wasn't the only one with a pressing problem. He'd checked with all of the maritime employment agencies, and none of them had any cooks available. He'd spent the afternoon visiting every diner and greasy spoon in the French Quarter, asking every short-order hash slinger he saw if he or she would be willing to work on his boat. He'd found no takers, not even for an outrageous sum of money. Everyone, it seemed, had responsibilities that prevented them from just packing up and taking off for four weeks. The chances of finding someone now who'd agree to set sail at dawn were slim to none.

Damn. His crew would mutiny if they had to endure any more of his first mate's cooking. What the hell was he going to do?

Sudden inspiration struck. It wasn't an ideal solution, but it would solve an immediate problem for both of them.

"Hey, there, Josie, I've got an idea."

"Josephine. My name is Josephine," she said stiffly, sniffling into the ridiculously expensive hankie.

He waited until she'd wiped her nose and looked up at him with red-rimmed eyes. As she met his gaze, her chin tilted up imperiously, he experienced a moment of fierce doubt.

He was crazy. He was certain he'd live to regret this. His crew would eat her up and spit her out before the first day was over.

But what else was he going to do? He drew a deep breath, swallowed hard and bit the bullet.

"Josephine, do you know how to cook?"

30

Chapter Two

"What do you mean, can I cook?" Of all the insensitive questions to ask at a time like this, Josephine thought indignantly, this one had to top the list. Life as she knew it had just ceased to exist, yet this Neanderthal's biggest concern was whether she could fix him dinner. If she fixed him a good enough meal, she supposed he was going to offer her the privilege of sleeping with him, too.

She tried to glare at him, but the effect was ruined by the fact that she was crying.

"The question's not as off-the-wall as it seems." He pushed away from the passenger door, walked around the truck and climbed into the driver's seat. His weight made the vehicle lurch, and her pulse did the same as he closed the door, sealing himself inside with her. He intensified her uneasiness by stretching his hand across the back of the seat, resting it unnervingly close to her head.

She must have really come unglued, she thought. Here she was, penniless, homeless and without transportation, yet the thing that bothered her the most at the moment was the proximity of this savage.

That infernal toothpick still dangled from his mouth. He reached up and pulled it out. "I need a cook on my towboat. If you took the job, it would give you a place to stay for the next thirty days and pay you more than enough to reimburse me for my truck repairs. I'll pay you twelve hundred a week."

The suggestion was too bizarre to absorb all at once. She seized on the money issue. "Twelve hundred *dollars?*"

"No, Princess." He gave a sardonic grin. "Mardi Gras beads."

She was so taken aback by the salary that his sarcasm scarcely registered. In her previous job at the public library, her net take-home pay for an entire month wasn't much more than what he was offering for a week.

"If you can spare the time from your charm school, that is."

She glanced at him sharply, trying to determine whether he was making fun of her, but his dark eyes were unreadable.

He draped a forearm across the steering wheel and angled his body toward her. "How'd you end up in a fix like this, anyway?"

She started to tell him she didn't owe him any explanations, but the fact that he'd just offered her a job stopped her. She couldn't afford to eliminate any options right now.

Besides, she thought with a deep sigh of resignation, there was no point in continuing Aunt Prudie's charade of pretending everything was perfectly fine while life crumbled to bits around her.

The thought sent a fresh wave of despair crashing over her. She drew a deep breath, fighting the undertow of emotion, determined not to let it suck her under. It might help to talk about it. Explaining the situation to a stranger might help her make sense of it herself.

She looked away from his face, directing her gaze to the moss-covered limb of the live oak in Aunt Prudie's lawn. "The academy belonged to my aunt. She operated it for fifty-two years, but evidently it hadn't been profitable in a long time. Unfortunately, I didn't know that until a few weeks ago."

"Why didn't you know?"

"Aunt Prudence never discussed finances with me. She said discussing money was coarse."

He muttered something she was glad she couldn't quite hear. Even without the words, the deprecating tone in his voice came through loud and clear.

Josephine's spine straightened defensively. "Besides, I wasn't involved in the day-to-day operation of the academy. I had a full-time job at the public library. I only taught a few classes on evenings and weekends."

"Well, surely you must have had some kind of a clue her business wasn't exactly booming."

Josephine had been berating herself for the exact same thing, which no doubt explained why his remark rankled so. "I probably should have, but I didn't. Aunt Prudence never altered a single aspect of her life. She still employed a gardener, a maid. . . . " She started to add "a cook," then thought better of it. "She insisted on handling all the household bills herself."

"How convenient for you."

The disdain in his voice was galling. She struggled to maintain the pleasant tone of voice she instructed her students to use in difficult situations. "I would have much preferred to have a small place of my own, but Aunt Prudence's heart had been bad for years, and she didn't want to live alone. And not that it's any of your business, but I paid my own way. I turned almost all of my salary over to her every month for room and board."

"So what happened to your job?"

"Aunt Prudie became bedridden a month before she died, so I resigned in order to take care of her and run the academy when spring classes began. I didn't find out until after the library had already hired my replacement that she didn't have a single student registered for the spring semester." Josephine twisted her hands in her lap and stared at the red-tiled roof of the Spanish-style mansion across the street. "And then she died, and that was just the beginning of the surprises Aunt Prudie left behind. I discovered she'd not only run through all the money she'd inherited from her husband, but she'd taken out an enormous mortgage on the house two years ago. She even had a loan out on that car I wrecked. And she'd spent all of the money she'd borrowed."

"On what?"

"Living expenses, evidently. She was making payments on the notes with the very money she'd borrowed."

Cole let out a long, low whistle, shaking his head in disbelief. "Christ. Wasn't much for long-term planning, was she?"

Josephine privately thought the old woman had planned things all too well. She'd lived long enough to run through every penny she had, then died before she'd had to face the consequences.

Josephine shifted uncomfortably on the leather seat. "Her bank account was not only completely empty, but overdrawn. And then two weeks ago, I discovered she was six months behind on the house payments and the bank was threatening foreclosure."

"So you saw this coming?"

Josephine reluctantly nodded. "I moved all my jewelry, most of my clothes and a few of the more expensive paintings into the charm school earlier this week. But I didn't think the bank would foreclose this soon."

"What about the school? Do you owe money on it, too?"

"No. Aunt Prudie didn't own the building. She'd always rented it. I paid off six months' back rent with the last of my personal savings before I discovered the truth of the situation. It's paid up for the next three months."

Cole's dark eyes regarded her incredulously. "Why the hell didn't your aunt do something before things got this bad?"

Because Aunt Prudie was selfish, shortsighted and a master of self-delusion. Josephine edited her thoughts to put her late aunt in as favorable a light as possible. "She probably couldn't face it. It was easier to keep hoping that each semester would be better than the one before. Besides, she probably thought scaling back her lifestyle would make business even worse."

"What do you mean?"

"If people in her social set thought she was having financial problems, they would have started avoiding her. New Orleanians act as if money troubles are contagious."

He gave a derisive snort. "Better to have lost a few phony friends than all of her belongings. Unless she knew she didn't have long to live and didn't care what kind of mess she left behind. Who was she going to leave her estate to, anyway?"

"To me." The words came out soft and small.

"Christ." Cole rubbed his jaw and eyed her quizzically. "Why didn't she at least tell you what shape things were in?"

Why not, indeed? The question had been haunting Josephine. She swallowed hard, then gave him the answer she'd been trying to convince herself to accept. "She was probably trying to protect me. She must have thought the academy's business would pick up and her finances would turn around."

But Josephine didn't buy that for a minute. The old woman had an uncanny ability to delude herself, but even Aunt Prudence couldn't have believed the academy could ever earn enough to pay off the tremendous debts she'd accrued.

No, it was far more likely that Aunt Prudie simply hadn't trusted her. She must have feared that if Josephine knew her money was gone, she'd abandon her.

Which hurt—more than Josephine would have thought possible. Her aunt had been arrogant, snobbish and perpetually fault-finding, but all the same, it hurt to think that her last living relative had had so little faith in her. Had all the years of careful, cautious living, of watching everything she said and did, of overruling her emotions and tamping down all of her personal dreams—had all of it counted for nothing? Had her aunt still judged her character solely on the basis of a single rash act she'd committed in her teens?

Evidently so, Josephine thought glumly. Evidently her aunt still had viewed her as her father had when he'd handed her over to Prudie's care. "Keep a close eye and a short leash on her. She can't be trusted," her father had said.

Josephine swallowed around the hard lump in her throat and blinked back a fresh onslaught of tears. She needed to change the subject fast if she didn't want to break down completely. "Tell me about your boat and this cook's position."

Cole lifted his arm from the steering wheel and turned his palm up. "There's not much to tell. There are six of us—me, my first mate, an engineer, a relief pilot and two deckhands. We push barges up and down the Mississippi. We need someone to cook three meals a day, seven days a week, during a four-week run up to Minneapolis and back. Interested?"

When she'd called her bank this morning, she'd had forty-three dollars in her checking account. She could raise some cash by selling the jewelry she'd inherited from her mother and the paintings she'd stashed at the academy, but that would probably take a while. She was desperate.

But she hated to admit it to this arrogant man. "It depends," she hedged. "What are the living conditions?"

One corner of his mouth lifted in a mirthless smile. "A lot less plush than what you're accustomed to, Princess."

"Would I have a private room?"

"It's called a cabin, and it's probably smaller than your idea of a shower stall. But yeah, the cook has her own."

"What does the boat look like?"

Cole had had just about enough of Little Miss High-and-Mighty's inquisition. "Does your decision hinge on what friggin' color the boat's painted?"

Josephine's blue eyes snapped at him like thin ice. "No, but it might hinge on whether or not you continue to curse at me like a drunken sailor."

This would never work. He'd been out of his mind even to consider it. "You ain't heard nothin' yet, darlin'. Wait'll you hear me an' the boys after a few beers." He let loose a string of particularly explicit examples. "And that's before we get really wound up," he added.

Her response disappointed him. He'd been counting on shock, hopefully even outrage. Instead, she inclined her head like a duchess and regarded him with exaggerated patience, as if he were a puppy who'd just pooped on the floor.

"Are you quite finished? Because if you are, and if you can assure me I won't be subjected to that sort of language again, well, then . . . " She hesitated only long enough to draw an audible breath. "Well, I'll take the job."

She had to be kidding. Cole squinted at her, trying to determine whether she was pulling his leg. "Are you jackin' with me, lady?"

"Jacking?" Her forehead scrunched in confusion, as if she'd never heard the term before.

"You know—jacking around." Comprehension still seemed to elude her. Irritated, he drummed his fingers on the truck's dashboard and tried again. "Jacking. As in jack-ing off."

She shook her head, clearly baffled, as if he were speaking a foreign language.

She didn't have a clue, he realized in amazement. She'd evidently never heard the term before in all of her twenty-nine years. "Hey, have you been locked up in a monastery or somethin'?"

"No." Her voice was prickly and defensive. "What makes you ask a thing like that?"

"I dunno. Maybe the fact that you look like you're in your twenties, but act like you're ninety. How long did you live with this old aunt of yours?"

She pulled herself tighter and taller. "The past three years."

"What did you do before that?"

"I was a teacher."

"Oh, yeah? Where?"

She glanced evasively out the truck window. "At an institution of higher education."

She must mean a college. Now there was an experience from which few people emerged innocent and naive. "Oh, yeah? Which college?"

"It wasn't exactly a college," she hedged. "It was a finishing school in Switzerland."

"Finishing school? What the hell is that?"

"A form of higher education for women that primarily focuses on cultural skills."

Cultural skills. Just what he needed in a cook, he thought scathingly. "What did you teach? Advanced tea pouring?"

Josephine's chin tipped up defensively. "For your information, the curriculum included art history, European history, language and philosophy. It's very similar to the course of study a liberal arts major might pursue here in the United States. I attended the school myself, and I think I got a very well rounded education. After I graduated, I taught etiquette there for six years."

"Etiquette," Cole muttered darkly, shaking his head. "Chri—" He stopped himself in the nick of time. Surely she had *some* experience in the real world. "So where'd you go to high school?"

"I attended an ecumenical boarding school in New England."

"Ecumenical. You mean religious?"

"Well, yes." She folded her fingers in her lap as precisely as military pleats. "But it had an excellent academic program."

"Uh-huh." Good gravy—no wonder she acted like she'd just come out of a time warp. Cole tapped his fingers on the steering wheel. "Sounds like you've led a pretty sheltered life."

Her chin tilted up even higher. "I wouldn't say that."

"Well, I would. You don't even understand normal English."

"That's probably because Aunt Prudence wouldn't allow a television in her home. As a result, I'm sure there are a few phrases in the American lexicon that I'm unfamiliar with, but—"

"You've never seen *television?*" Cole stared at her in amazement.

"Well, of course I've *seen* it. I've just never really *watched* it. Not in the United States, anyway." She unfolded, then refolded her fingers in her lap. "But that doesn't mean I'm not well informed. I've held a job since the day I finished school, and I'm very well-read."

No amount of reading would have prepared this dame for his randy crew of deckhands. "Look—I've, uh, rethought the situation, and I don't think you're exactly suited for life on the river. The crew can be pretty rough, and—"

"Nonsense. I'm sure I can handle it."

Cole was far less confident.

"If you can control your language, that is," she added primly.

That prissy tone of voice raised his hackles like a junkyard dog's. "I can control my language, all right. But I might find it hard to control the urge to strangle you if you don't stop talking to me like I'm some kind of f—" He stopped abruptly, expelled a harsh breath and ran his hand down his face. " . . . frigging two-year-old."

"If you stop acting like one, I'll certainly stop treating you like one."

Cole drew in a deep breath, mentally counted to ten, then stuck the key in the ignition, thinking he'd like to tell this gal where she could stick something else. "All right, lady. If you'll get off your high horse, I'll watch my mouth. But you da—" He stopped abruptly and censored himself. "You'd darn well better know how to cook."

Josephine nodded and gazed out the window. It was a good thing she was a quick learner, she thought. Just because she'd never made anything beyond party garnishes, frozen dinners and an occasional sandwich didn't mean she wasn't capable.

She was capable of doing anything she set her mind to— including living on a boat and putting up with this obnoxious man for the next four weeks. In fact, despite all the warning bells clanging at top volume in her mind, the prospect gave her a tiny bit of a thrill.

She'd never done anything so exciting in her entire life. With Aunt Prudence gone and her world in upheaval, the rules that used to constrain her no longer applied. There was no one to disapprove or warn of dire consequences or threaten her with social and religious ostracism.

No one but her own internal monitor, that was. The restraints she'd imposed upon herself had always been stricter than the restraints imposed by her father or her great-aunt or the strict boarding school staff. She'd held herself carefully in check for thirteen years, ever since the fateful night she'd committed a wild, reckless act that had taken a life and forever changed her own.

As always, the thought caused a painful constriction in her chest. Ever since that night, she'd lived in fear that if she didn't keep a tight enough rein on her behavior, she would again do something rash, would again inadvertently bring harm to someone else. She'd tried to make up for that moment ever since. She'd obeyed every rule of expected behavior, heeded every one of Aunt Prudie's suggestions and followed every accepted convention as if her life depended on it, but nothing seemed to ease her nagging conscience.

The pickup passed through the automatic exit gate and stopped for traffic on St. Charles Avenue. Josephine stared at an approaching streetcar, its single headlight a beacon in the twilit dusk. It rattled past in a pea green and rust red blur, the brightly lit faces of its passengers clearly visible as it clattered toward the end of the line on Carrollton Avenue.

She was already at the end of her line, Josephine reflected. She was at rock bottom. She had no family, no money, no home and no future.

By all rights, this should be one of her darkest moments. But instead of feeling despondent, she felt strangely exhilarated.

For the first time in her life, she was truly free.

"I know the rule is 'ladies first,' but you'd better let me go ahead so I can help you aboard, Princess."

The condescending pet name was driving her crazy. He'd been using it or one of his other phony endearments ever since they'd left her aunt's house. "My name is Josephine," she said frostily.

The lighting on the wharf was dim, but not too dim to see a wicked grin cross his face. "Oh, pardon me. In that case, I guess the proper title is Empress."

He seemed to delight in goading her, and it irritated her no end. Josephine had no idea how to respond, but she'd already figured out that protesting against any of his behavior only made him redouble his efforts.

His driving, for example. On the way to the wharf, he'd cut in and out of traffic at frightening speeds, driving precariously close to other vehicles. When she'd asked him to please stop tailgating, he'd given her a slow grin that had raised goose bumps on her arm, then gunned the engine and driven so close to the faded blue Chevy ahead of him that she'd thought he was trying to crawl into the car's backseat.

But at least he wasn't cursing. And he *had* taken her by her school to let her collect her clothing, and stopped at a Walgreens to let her purchase essential toiletry items. He'd even advanced her a couple of twenties so she could pay for them. He'd also called a tow truck to haul her wrecked vehicle off to a garage. And he *was* giving her a job, she reminded herself—one that would pay her well enough to at least get a toehold on some kind of a future.

The Mississippi River loomed wide and dark at the end of the wooden dock, lapping noisily against the metal hull of the large towboat. Painted blood red and trimmed in black and white, the four-story vessel was completely lacking in beauty or grace. It was angular and boxy, with straight sides, a square nose and a blunt end. Each level was smaller than the one below it, giving it a stacked effect, like a rectangular wedding cake. The only curved lines on the entire boat were the circular portholes and two low, rounded smokestacks near the back.

She watched Cole lunge off the dock and onto the deck. He tossed Josephine's heavy Louis Vuitton suitcase aside as if it weighed no more than a feather, then turned back toward her.

"You'll probably need to hike up your skirt to make it over the bulwark."

"Bulwark?"

"The metal lip on the edge of the boat."

"That little wall thing?"

"Yeah, Empress." His mouth curved into a derisive smirk. "The little wall thing."

Reaching under her jacket, Josephine self-consciously rolled her waistband until her skirt was above her knees, acutely aware of Cole watching her the whole time.

When she finished, he stretched out his arms. "Okay, grab hold and watch your step. I don't want to have to fish you out of the drink."

He grasped her arms instead of her hands, leaving her to do the same. The feel of his biceps under her fingers jolted her. She had no idea a human body could feel so hard and muscular. His arms were so large her hand could fit only halfway around. Drawing a deep gulp of air, she gathered her courage and stepped up, trying not to look down at the water gleaming in the moonlight through the gaping space between the end of the dock and the side of the boat.

Her foot came down, but failed to land on anything solid, and for a fleeting, terrifying moment, she thought she was falling.

The next thing she knew, she was hauled against a chest as hard and warm as sun-baked stone. It smelled of sweat and tobacco, but it wasn't at all unpleasant. On the contrary. It was heady and masculine and distinctly unsettling.

His thick arms had somehow wound around her back. She could feel his thighs, as hard and sturdy as a pair of Greek columns, pressed against her legs. She stood there, her senses shocked and overloaded, glued to him like a fly on flypaper.

"Unless you want to get to know me a whole lot better, Empress, you'd better let go of my neck."

She abruptly dropped her arms and stepped back. His hands slid down to her waist as she pulled away, his thumbs skimming the sides of her breasts, his fingers tracing the shape of her body.

She was glad it was dark, because she felt her face burning. In fact, the brief, accidental intimacy left her burning all over.

He backed away and turned to a black metal door edged in heavy rivets. It groaned as he yanked it open. "I'll help you through the hatch," he said gruffly. "You have to step up, then down."

She hesitantly took his outstretched hand. It was big and rough and warm, as warm as his chest, and his fingers curled around her hand like a crusty French roll around butter, giving her an odd melting sensation in the pit of her stomach.

She wasn't accustomed to physical contact—surely that was why she was so rattled by this man's touch. Her father had been distant, Aunt Prudie had been cold and the teachers at boarding school had been restrained and reserved. She could vaguely remember her mother hugging her and rocking her, but she wasn't sure if the faded, yellowed memories were of actual events or old dreams.

Her experience with men was even more limited. The only man she'd ever seriously dated was Wally Winston, the son of one of Aunt Prudie's friends. Aunt Prudie had urged Josephine to encourage Wally's affections, and to please her aunt, she had—despite the fact that the man bore an unfortunate resemblance to Woody Allen. Josephine had even let things go far enough for Wally to declare her frigid.

She'd accepted the pronouncement without question. After all, the only thing she'd felt during Wally's lovemaking had been a distinct sense of queasiness.

Cole's touch was affecting her stomach, too, Josephine thought distractedly, but in an entirely different manner.

Still holding her hand, he helped her step through the hatch into a narrow metal stairwell flanked by two doors. The space was small and warm, but not warm enough to account for her sudden rise in temperature. Josephine self-consciously dropped Cole's hand, only to realize she was staring at his biceps. Clearing her throat, she forced her eyes away and tried to concentrate on what he was saying.

"This deck houses the engine room and the galley." He gestured to each of the two doors.

"Oh. And where's the kitchen?"

He muttered something under his breath that she felt sure violated his moratorium on swearing. "The galley *is* the kitchen." He jerked one of the doors open impatiently. "Come on. It's in here."

Josephine followed him into a long, narrow room walled with cheap woodlike paneling. The only adornments on the wall were a rusty intercom box and a message-littered bulletin board. A long table with a red-checked plastic tablecloth stapled to it was bolted to the floor by the entrance. The other end of the room contained a none-too-neat kitchen.

Josephine crinkled her nose at the heavy smell of old grease. Not exactly the place for an aesthetically pleasing dining experience, she thought ruefully.

She stared at the steel-topped stove splattered with baked-on spills. Was this the thing she was expected to cook upon?

He noticed her uncertainty. "It's electric. Just like you probably had at home."

Josephine shook her head. "Aunt Prudie had a gas stove. I've never used this kind." It was a completely true statement. Of course, she'd never used Aunt Prudie's stove, either, but she saw no point in telling him so.

"There's nothing to it." He showed her how to turn the burners on and off, and did the same with the oven.

She opened the industrial-size refrigerator and peered inside. It was chock-full of food—dozens of eggs, gallons of milk, huge slabs of cheese, enormous jugs of condiments and heaven only knew what else.

"We've got a week's worth of supplies," Cole said. "The food delivery service just dropped off a batch of groceries."

"What does your crew usually eat for breakfast?"

"Oh, bacon, eggs, pancakes—the usual."

Josephine looked around nervously. "Where are the cookbooks?"

"Cookbooks?" Cole gave scoffing grunt. "We don't eat anything fancy enough to call for a cookbook."

Without some kind of reference material, she was lost. "But—but I need a cookbook. I like to measure things out, follow directions." She could tell by the scowl gathering on his face that she needed to talk fast, before he lost what little patience he had. "I've never cooked without one."

Or with one, either, but now was not the time to break that particular piece of news.

Cole expelled a harsh breath, clearly exasperated. "Okay, okay, I'll find you a blasted cookbook. Anything else you think you'll need, Your Highness?"

The query sounded more like a challenge than a question. She forced her voice into a deliberately calm and cheerful tone, the same tone she advised her charm school students to use whenever they were forced to deal with a difficult person. "I can't think of anything further at the moment, but thank you for asking."

He eyed her warily, then yanked the door open. "Breakfast is at five-thirty. You'll probably want to set your alarm for an hour earlier."

"In the morning?"

He scowled. "I don't know when you and the other fancy pants on Audubon Place eat breakfast, but most of us working folks seem to prefer it then." He snapped off the light and released the door, leaving her to scurry after him to avoid being left behind in the pitch-black room.

He was already halfway up the narrow gray stairs by the time she made it to the stairwell.

"The cabins are up here. Yours and mine are on the right side."

She clambered after him up the clanging metal stairs, regretting the fact that she was wearing heels. He opened a door on the landing and led her down a narrow corridor. "This one is yours." He swung open a door marked *Cook* in red plastic letters and dropped her suitcase on the floor.

She peered inside. The dingy gray room was smaller

than the walk-in closet she'd had at Aunt Prudie's, wide enough to house a bunk and little else. Behind the door was a toilet, a sink and a shower the approximate size of a postage stamp.

"Well, I'll let you get settled."

She was suddenly reluctant for him to leave. "Do you, uh, want me to fix you a sandwich?"

"Nah. But fix yourself anything you want. I'll eat in town."

"You're going to leave me on the boat alone?"

He looked at her oddly. "You got a problem with that?"

"No." Even to her own ears, she sounded less than convincing. She looked around nervously. "It's just that, well—is there some way of locking the door or hatch or whatever it's called? This is a pretty rough part of town, and you never know who might come along. . . ."

Cole shoved an impatient hand through his hair. *Damn.* She was obviously afraid to stay on the boat alone—and the annoying thing about it was that she was probably right. Not because of strangers, though. If any of his crew came back, she'd have good reason to be concerned.

She might not know it, but she wasn't any too safe with him, either. She'd felt awfully damn good when she'd fallen against him. She was hiding a nice pair of breasts under that armorlike jacket—soft, warm, surprisingly full breasts that had nestled against his chest like a pair of soft, warm honeybuns, honeybuns just begging to be tasted.

He suppressed a self-directed oath. He hadn't been able to resist the urge to cop a feel as she'd slipped out of his grasp. He wished he hadn't touched her, though, because now every time he looked at her, he thought about the swell of her breasts and the nip of her waist above that bunchy, rolled-up waistband, and he couldn't help but wonder if she looked as good as she'd felt.

Damn it all to Hades. The last thing he needed was to be lusting after an irritating blueblood socialite. Hadn't his experience with Alexa taught him anything?

47

The thought made him scowl. Damn that photo in the newspaper, he thought sourly. It had dredged up more muck than a shrimp trawler's net. All kinds of long-buried thoughts and feelings had floated to the surface, including, apparently, a penchant for ice-queen society types.

He hadn't had a woman in a good long while, that was the problem. Too long, judging from the effect the Empress here was having on his libido. The brunette bar-maid down at the Porthole Bar and Grill could probably cure what ailed him, but not if he were escorting Little Miss Priss around for the evening.

But he couldn't very well leave her here. He didn't want Junior or Hambone stumbling in half-drunk, scaring her so badly she'd jump overboard.

He eyed her with exasperation. "Are you trying to tell me you want to come with me?"

"I wouldn't dream of forcing my company upon you." She gave him a tight, polite smile. "But if you were to invite me along—which, of course, would be the civilized thing to do—well, then, that would be an entirely different matter."

He gazed at her lips, pressed firmly together in that prim little smile, and wondered what they'd feel like under his. The thought made him pull his eyebrows into a menacing frown. "If you're waiting for an engraved invitation, Empress, you're fresh out of luck. If you want to come with me, be out in the hall in fifteen minutes. If you're not there, I'm leaving without you."

He turned and marched across the hall to a door marked *Captain,* where a long, hot shower offered a welcome respite from an evening that promised all the enjoyment of a root canal.

Chapter Three

"Okay, Empress, here we are. Take your pick."

Josephine stared at the shelf of cookbooks in the chic gourmet shop in Canal Place, an upscale shopping mall on the edge of the French Quarter, too unnerved by the impatient way Cole hovered over her to focus on the titles. The scent of Dial soap and shaving cream radiated from him like body heat, invading her personal space and jarring her senses. She was keenly aware that they were alone in the store except for a pudgy, white-bearded clerk dusting the hanging copper pans in the next aisle.

She sneaked another sidelong glance at Cole, the way she'd been doing ever since he stepped out of his cabin thirty minutes earlier. He'd changed into pressed chinos, a blue cotton shirt and brown leather loafers. With his dark hair combed back and his face freshly shaved, he looked completely different from the unkempt beast she'd run into that afternoon.

He was entirely presentable. No—he was more than that. He was handsome. Not in the usual even-featured way—his nose was slightly crooked, as if it had once been broken—but handsome all the same. There was a stark, rawboned attractiveness about him, tough and rugged, but undeniably appealing.

His beard had hidden some of his strongest features: the deep cleft in his chin, the strong plane of his jaw, the prominent bones of his cheeks. His face was all hard lines and weathered angles, as powerfully drawn as his muscular body.

Despite his attractiveness, there was a hardness about him, about the set of his eyes and his mouth, about his stance and attitude and speech, that made her nerves jump whenever he looked at her. There was nothing vulnerable, nothing soft, nothing penetrable about him. He was completely, uncompromisingly masculine.

He leveled a glance at her that set off an odd fluttering in her chest. Josephine folded her arms, trying to ward off the effect he had on her.

"We haven't got all night. Which one do you want?"

Josephine reached out, plucked a cookbook off the rack and riffled through it. *Oh, mercy*. The recipes all included words like "sear" and "parboil" and "fold in." She had no idea how to do any of those things.

She jammed the book back on the shelf and pulled out another one, opening it to a recipe for seafood gumbo. "Begin by making a rich brown roux," she read. If she knew how to do that, she thought, slamming the book shut in disgust, she'd know enough not to need a recipe in the first place.

A trickle of fear coursed through her. She must be crazy to think she could pull this off. She quickly replaced the book on the bookshelf, hoping Cole wouldn't notice the fact that her hand was shaking, and reminded herself she had no other option. This job offered her a chance to get back on her feet. How hard could cooking be? If she pulled herself together and kept her wits about her, surely she could figure it out.

Under all circumstances, a lady remains poised and calm, she mentally recited. She forced her lips into what she hoped would pass for an offhand smile. "I don't see the cookbook I usually use."

"What's it called?"

She should have known he'd ask. "I'm not sure," she hedged. "But I'd know it if I saw it."

He glowered impatiently. "Well, who wrote it?"

Josephine thought fast. "Martha Stewart."

The rotund clerk in the next aisle looked up, feather duster in hand. "We don't carry any of her cookbooks, ma'am."

"Better pick something else. And make it snappy. I'm starved."

Josephine rapidly scanned the titles. One jumped out at her—*Appetizing Basics*.

Something basic—that was what she needed. She picked up the book and was relieved when the page fell open to a recipe for meatballs.

Meatballs. Now there was a dish she could probably handle. She scanned the directions and was delighted to note that she recognized all the terminology. She smiled up at Cole. "This one ought to do."

"Let's get it, then, and get the fu—" He broke off in midsentence. His scowl told her how it irritated him to modify his speech on her behalf. " . . . the *heck* out of here."

He paid for the book without looking at it, then passed the plastic bag to Josephine and stalked out of the store and into the elegant mall. She trailed after him, struggling to keep up in her heels. He slowed and gave a sexy grin to two smartly dressed women who smiled at him flirtatiously; then he resumed his rapid pace, ignoring the fact that Josephine was running behind him like a puppy on an invisible leash.

The indignity of the situation incensed her. "Could you please slow down?"

"Why? Can't you keep up?"

A lady is polite under all circumstances. Her teeth gritted with the effort, Josephine carefully modulated her voice as she scurried after him. "Your legs are quite a bit longer than mine, and I can't run very well in these shoes."

He didn't slow down until he reached the glass elevator that led to the parking garage. He regarded her coldly, his mouth a tight line of displeasure. "If you're going to work for me, you'd better learn to do things at my pace."

He watched her reaction, noting the way her lips pursed tightly together. On any other woman, the expression might have been a sexy pout, but on Josephine it looked like she'd just bitten into a green plum.

Damn, but she was annoying! The fact that she was screwing up the last chance he'd have to alley cat around for the next four weeks did nothing to foster any feelings of goodwill toward her, either. Nor did the realization that she was the reason his hormones had kicked into sudden overdrive.

The last thought brought a ferocious scowl to his face. He shot her a withering look. "Why didn't you change into some sensible shoes while we were on the boat, anyway?"

"You said we were going out to dinner. I wanted to be dressed appropriately."

His gaze raked over her. She still wore that jacket of navy armor and the same high-buttoned white blouse under it, but she'd traded in her skirt for a pair of matching slacks, managing to hide the only part of her anatomy that had been visible before. He gave a snort.

"Did you say something?" she asked.

"Nothing. Nothing at all, Your Highness."

She probably thought he was taking her to Arnaud's or Antoine's. He couldn't wait to see her face when she walked into the Porthole, an aptly named hole-in-the-wall bar and grill that catered to deckhands and sailors.

He was grinning at the prospect when they reached his truck. Without thinking, he unlocked and opened her door.

"Thank you very much."

Too late, he realized he'd unwittingly done something polite. "Yeah, well, don't get too used to it." Slamming her door with more force than necessary, he strode to the driver's side and hauled his large frame inside.

"What do you have against manners?" she asked as he eased the pickup out of the parking spot.

"Nothing. I've just got a heck of a problem with someone trying to shove them down my throat."

"I hope you don't think that's what I'm trying to do."

"Whyever would I think a thing like that?" he asked sarcastically. Cole threw the truck into gear and barreled through the parking garage, taking the tight turns to the exit at twice the posted speed. He jerked to a halt at the bottom, rolled down his window and paid the attendant, then gunned the engine and roared onto Canal Street.

Beside him, Josephine nervously tightened her seat belt. "I simply thanked you for a courteous act."

"Yeah, and I simply told you not to get used to it. We don't have time for a lot of fancy-schmancy etiquette on a workboat."

"It takes no longer to be polite than to be rude."

"See? There you go again." He made a hard right turn into the French Quarter on Decatur Street, throwing her against the door. She straightened and braced herself, one hand on the dashboard, the other on the seat beside her. She seemed to be struggling to maintain her composure, a fact that pleased him enormously.

How did a person as stuffy as the Empress function in the real world? She seemed as anachronistic as the quaint, balconied buildings he was driving past. He angled a curious glance at her. "Tell me about this charm school of your aunt's. What kind of people sign up for etiquette lessons these days?"

She raised an eyebrow and shot him a pointed look. "Not the people who most desperately need them, obviously."

Cole couldn't keep from grinning. "Why, Empress—if I didn't know how polite you were, I might think you'd just insulted me."

She continued to stare straight ahead, but her profile revealed the shadow of a smile.

"Tell me about the school," he urged.

She cast him a wary glance.

"Come on," he coaxed. "I really want to know."

"Well," she said hesitantly, "we offered classes for children, teens and adults."

"Which did you teach?"

"Mainly the children's classes. Children made Aunt Prudie nervous, but I loved working with them."

Cole was willing to bet that *life* had made Aunt Prudie nervous. He glanced curiously at Josephine in the neon lights of the Hard Rock Café. "What kind of things did you teach?"

"The basics, mostly—writing thank-you notes, standing when an adult enters the room, that sort of thing. But I'd also teach them the ins and outs of fine dining, how to comport themselves in social situations, how to introduce people, and so on."

He braked for a stoplight in front of Jax Brewery and glanced at her again. Her face had softened as she talked. Her eyes had grown large and animated, and her chin had lost its stubborn tilt. She'd evidently enjoyed her work, he thought with surprise. He hadn't thought her capable of enjoying anything.

"What were the adult classes about?" he prompted.

"How to entertain, mostly. We'd also prepare debutantes and their mothers for their season, and Mardi Gras royalty for their reign."

"Mardi Gras royalty?" Cole's eyebrows lifted. "What do they need to know besides how to throw beads and doubloons?"

"Oh, lots of things." She met his gaze, her blue eyes earnest. "The old-line Mardi Gras Krewes have very ritualized traditions. There's a lot of etiquette involved in their balls. It takes a lot of practice to wave a scepter the right way, for example."

"I just bet it does," Cole said wryly. The topic dredged up old, sour memories. Alexa had been obsessed with the whole royalty thing. Cole recalled asking her what she wanted to do after high school.

"Be Queen of Carnival," she'd replied.

With her father's connections and money, the dream hadn't been out of reach. Two years later, Cole had read that Alexa had been named Queen of Rex, the Mardi Gras Krewe that ruled over the annual Fat Tuesday festitivities.

Unfortunately, Cole had been unable to celebrate Mardi Gras that year. He'd been finishing a two-year sentence in a juvenile correction center.

The memory made him scowl. Deliberately pushing it aside, he turned his attention back to Josephine. "So why did the bottom fall out of the charm school business?"

Josephine sighed. "Well, the debutante and Mardi Gras classes were only seasonal, and I'm afraid Aunt Prudie didn't do a very good job of marketing the other courses. She didn't even send out any notices for the spring semester. She must have known her health was failing, that she wouldn't be able to handle it."

Or that she wouldn't be around and it wouldn't be her problem, Cole thought. It sounded as if the old bat had given no thought to Josephine's future at all.

The light changed, and Cole edged the pickup forward. The faint wail of a saxophone grew louder as he approached Jackson Square. "Well, it's probably all for the best."

"What do you mean?"

Cole swerved to avoid a carriage pulled by a horse in a flowered straw hat. "Now you can focus your energies on something relevant."

He could sense her bristling beside him. "I happen to believe that etiquette *is* relevant."

55

"Oh, come on. You're not going to sit there and tell me you think a few more pleases and thank-yous will change the world, are you?"

Her back grew ramrod straight. "As a matter of fact, that's exactly what I think. Good manners are nothing more than common courtesy, and common courtesy is nothing more than respect for others. If there was more respect in the world, it would definitely be a better place."

Just when he'd begun to think there might be a real person under that priggish exterior, she reverted to form. "Christ," Cole muttered.

Both of her eyebrows rose simultaneously. "Excuse me?"

Scowling ferociously, he gripped the steering wheel the way he wished he could grip her neck. "I'm sorry, Your Highness. I meant to say criminy."

He didn't look particularly sorry, Josephine thought. He looked angry. But then, he'd looked hot under the collar the whole time she'd known him.

She cast a quick glance at him, taking in his stiff jaw, his narrowed eyes, the tight curl of his fingers on the steering wheel. He was angry, all right, and he looked like he'd been angry for a good long while. The emotion was too dark, too intense to have been caused solely by the events of the afternoon. She recognized the symptoms. It was the same kind of deep, smoldering anger her father had held against the world, against God, against himself after her mother had died.

She wondered what was behind Cole's anger. She wanted to ask him, but she didn't think he'd take kindly to such a personal question. Besides, it would be rude to pry.

His hard frown was a barrier to further conversation. She sat in awkward silence as he drove past Jackson Square—past the row of horse-drawn carriages, past the tourists watching a white-faced mime and a juggler on stilts, past the blaring horns of a ragtag brass band. She stared out the window at the umbrella-clad tables of Café du Monde, then at the line of produce trucks hunched in the smelly alley behind the French Market. He turned onto Esplanade Avenue, drove three blocks, then abruptly veered left onto Royal Street.

One block farther, and he suddenly jammed on the brakes to claim a parking spot, making the tires scream like banshees. He threw the truck into reverse, then rammed it back so hard Josephine was certain he was about to hit the car behind him. With only inches to spare, he slammed on the brake again, then jerked the vehicle forward, hurling Josephine hard against her seat belt shoulder strap.

"Do you always drive like this?" she said with a gasp.

"Nah." He shot her a wicked grin. "Sometimes I'm not so cautious."

Josephine whipped her eyes away from him, her fingernails biting into her palm. No matter how well he cleaned up, her original appraisal of him had been correct. He was a beast—a beast and a heathen, with a soul as dark as the devil's boots. He was baiting her, deliberately trying to upset her. Well, she wouldn't give him the satisfaction of knowing he'd succeeded.

He killed the engine, then wordlessly climbed out of the pickup. Josephine scrambled out the passenger door and scurried after him. He strode down the sidewalk without a backward glance, walking so rapidly she practically had to run to keep up with him. She straggled behind him down a darkened side street into one the scabbiest sections of the French Quarter, past two staggering, booze-soaked bums and a derelict sleeping in a doorway. She was relieved when he finally stopped.

"What's this?" she asked. They stood in front of a black-painted glass door, outside a building that smelled of urine. There was no sign, no light, nothing at all to indicate what was inside.

"The place where we're having dinner." He opened the door a crack. Raucous laughter and loud music tumbled out into the damp March air.

"But it sounds like . . . like a bar."

"So? They've got a grill, and they know how to cook up a mean rib eye." He threw her a challenging look. "What's the matter? Not ritzy enough for your tastes?"

The man had a chip on his shoulder the size of the Rock of Gibraltar. Well, she'd be darned if she'd let him goad her into trying to knock it off. "No. That's not the case at all."

"So what's the problem?"

It was a bar—that was the problem. She hadn't been in one since she was sixteen, since that awful night when she'd made that unforgivable mistake, when . . .

But she couldn't think about that now. She wouldn't allow herself to. That had happened a lifetime ago, half the continent away. And she certainly wasn't about to explain it to this man now.

She drew herself to her full height and forced a smile. "There's no problem at all. None whatsoever. This place looks absolutely . . . delightful."

He pushed the door farther open, one eyebrow mockingly winging upward. A wave of smoke and bawdy laughter assaulted her. She hesitated, fighting back an onrush of fear. She could handle this, she told herself, drawing a deep breath. This was obviously a test of some kind, and she'd be darned if she'd flunk.

"After you." He bowed and swept his arm in front of him.

She stepped into a room as dark as a movie theater, so dark she was momentarily blinded. It smelled of musty, beer-soured carpeting and thick, acrid smoke.

She gazed around, trying to adjust to the dim lighting, as Cole stepped close behind her. A tattooed, burly man sitting on a bar stool at the right gradually came into focus.

His red-and-white-striped shirt reminded her of prison garb. He caught her looking at him and gave a suggestive wink.

Cole abruptly snaked an arm around her waist. "If you don't want anyone to get the idea you're in here trawling for a playmate," he said in her ear with a growl, "you'd better act like we're together."

His breath against her neck sent a shiver chasing through her, setting off an odd quivering deep in her belly. The heat of his hand on her waist intensified it.

"Hey, Cap'n!"

Josephine followed Cole's gaze to a booth against the wall, where a thin, gray-haired man with a face like a bassett hound waved a red cap. "Who's that?" she asked.

"Henry O'Shea. My first mate." His hand briefly tightened on her hip as he guided her to the booth.

Josephine walked stiffly beside him, trying to keep her bearings. It was alarming, the way his touch affected her. It made it hard to breathe and almost impossible to think. She'd never known anyone so disturbing on so many different levels in all of her life.

Cole waved his free hand toward her when they reached the table. "Henry, this here is Josephine."

The older man smiled, the expression deepening the folds in his face. He had hound-dog jowls, deep circles beneath his eyes, and one continuous gray eyebrow, but his blue eyes were bright and friendly. "Nice ta meetcha."

Cole motioned for her to sit down, then slid into the booth beside her. She was keenly aware of the moment he pulled his arm from her waist, and just as aware of his thigh bumping hers as he scooted in beside her.

"Josephine's our new cook," Cole said.

Henry's smile dissolved into a worried frown. His gaze raked over her. "Gee, Boss—she sure don' meet the three-hundred rule."

Josephine's eyebrows lifted quizzically. "The three-hundred rule? What's that?"

Henry gave a gap-toothed grin. "Just a sayin' in the tow-boat industry. It's best not to hire a female cook unless her weight and her age add up to at least three hundred."

Josephine had heard of age discrimination, but she'd always thought it worked the other way around. "Why not?"

Henry squirmed uneasily, fingering a can of Redman on the table. He looked longingly at his beer. "Well, the crew can get pretty rowdy. Boys bein' boys an' all, well, they tend to give the nice-lookin' girls a hard time, if you know what I mean."

Cole gave a snort. "Nice-looking? Our crew isn't that particular. That last cook was at least a two-eighty-five, and look what they did to her."

Trepidation, cold and clammy, gripped Josephine's stomach. "What did they do?"

Henry picked up his brown bottle of Guinness and took a long swig, avoiding her eyes.

"Might as well tell her," Cole urged. "She's got a right to know what she's getting into."

Henry set down the bottle and sighed. "Well, ma'am, it seems one of the deckhands stole her underwear."

"What?"

"One of the deckhands—Hambone's his name—he, well, he stole all her undies."

"Why on earth would he do a thing like that?"

Henry's blue eyes cut pleadingly to Cole. "Gee, Boss, I don' think this is the kind of thing we ought to be talkin' about in front of a lady."

Thank heavens—at least someone here had an inkling of propriety. Josephine held no such illusions about Cole.

A devilish gleam lit his eyes. "She asked, Henry, and she's got a right to know. Better go ahead and tell her."

The older man cleared his throat, shifted uneasily and delicately looked away. "Well, ma'am, the fact of the matter is he says he likes to sniff 'em."

Josephine's hand flew to her mouth.

Cole let out an enormous guffaw. "That's right—and I was darn glad to hear it. For a while there, I was afraid the dumb lug was wearing them."

Josephine gripped the edge of the greasy Formica table-top, holding on to it like a lifeline. *Oh, dear*. What had she gotten herself into?

"It wasn't entirely Hambone's fault that the cook jumped ship in Natchez, though," Cole was saying. "That episode with Junior was the final straw. I hope you told him to quit believing everything he reads in those porn magazines."

Porn magazines. Dear heavens. It just got worse and worse. These men sounded like sex fiends.

"I tol' him, Cap'n."

She couldn't afford to panic, she told herself sternly. She needed to keep her wits about her and gather as much information as possible. After all, knowledge was strength. She was certain she'd need every ounce of strength she could muster to make it through the next four weeks.

"Who's Junior?"

"He's a deckhand trainee," Cole answered. "Barely eighteen years old, and he doesn't have the sense God gave a goose."

"Now, Boss, he's just still wet behind the ears, that's all," Henry said defensively, placing the tin of tobacco back in the pocket of his red flannel shirt.

"He's all wet, period," Cole said scathingly. "I know you're partial to him because he's young, but if anything like that happens again, I'm putting him off the boat."

She hated to ask, but she needed to know. "What did he do?"

Cole draped an arm across the back of the booth, resting his hand uncomfortably close to her hair. He gave a wolfish smile. "The cook came off duty to find him waiting

61

in her cabin, wearing nothing but a pimple-faced grin and a big old teenage boner."

Boner. It took a moment for the meaning of the unfamiliar term to hit home. When it did, Josephine was chagrined to discover she'd audibly gasped.

"It was jus' a misunderstandin'," Henry explained. "The cook gave him an extra helpin' of oyster stew, and he thought she was sendin' him a love signal. He'd just read an article 'bout how to tell if a gal is int'rested, an', well, he ain't too bright." Henry shot a worried glance at Cole. "I'm 'fraid we're embarrassin' the li'l lady here, Boss."

"The little lady needs to know what she's getting into." Cole's eyes settled on her, his expression hard. "Our crew isn't as refined as the folks she's used to on Audubon Place. If she has any questions about whether or not she can hack it, I need to know now."

She'd rather die than admit she couldn't deal with anything this coarse, crude brute and his gang of cutthroats could dish out. She lifted her head, hoping her cheeks weren't as red as they felt. "The only question in my mind right now is why you don't have better control of your staff."

Cole's eyes narrowed in displeasure. Pleased that she'd hit a nerve, she added a disapproving frown for good measure. "How did Junior happen to have access to the cook's cabin in the first place?"

"She left her door unlocked. If you keep yours fastened, you'll have nothing to worry about. No one will have a key to it except you." Cole's lips curved upward, his eyes gleaming dangerously. "And me, of course."

Josephine's face must have reflected the alarm she felt, for his grin widened into an evil smile. "It's standard maritime procedure. A captain always maintains access to all parts of his vessel. For the safety of his crew, of course."

It certainly did nothing to make *her* feel safe. She was about to say as much, when a stocky middle-aged man came up and slapped Cole on the shoulder. "Hi there, Captain."

Cole glanced up and grinned. "Dirk—hello! How's the *Black Cat* running?"

"Purrin' like a lion with a full belly. In fact, I want to talk to you about extending the charter."

"Sure. Let's grab a beer at the bar." Cole rose. "Order me the usual when the waitress comes by, Henry. And try to keep the Empress here out of trouble until I get back."

"Aye-aye, Cap'n."

Cole turned and strode to the bar without even bothering to glance in her direction.

Josephine's eyes followed him. "Is he always so rude?"

Henry shrugged. "He's been in a bad mood all day. Somethin' in the newspaper upset him this mornin'."

Josephine doubted that such overwhelming rudeness was a one-day aberration in the life of a normally genial person, but Henry's remark piqued her interest. She'd love to know how to upset the man. "Really? What was it?"

Henry took another swig of his beer. "Got no idea. Just know he ripped somethin' out, tore the rest of the paper in half, then lit off the boat without sayin' a word to nobody."

"And here I thought it was just me," Josephine said sardonically.

The bags under Henry's eyes puckered as he grinned. "Well, ma'am, no offense meant, but you do seem to rub him the wrong way."

Josephine smiled back. She liked the old man's frankness. "Believe me, the feeling is entirely mutual." Henry could prove to be a valuable ally. Maybe he could even help her figure out how to deal with the impossible captain. "Have you know Cole long?"

"Ever since he was Junior's age."

"How long ago was that?"

"Let's see—'bout thirteen years ago, when I was workin' for Crescent City Barges. Cole signed on as a deckhand trainee, an' he was greener than Junior. Why, he fell in the drink the first time he tried to lash together a tow

63

of barges." Henry slapped his knee and gave a wheezing cackle. "He had gumption, though. Climbed right out and went right back to work, actin' for all the world as if he weren't wet as a catfish and didn't smell like one, too."

Henry shook his head, his eyes full of admiration. "Yes, sir, I knew from the git-go he had what it took. An' now look at him—not only a full cap'n, but owner of a whole fleet of towboats besides."

Josephine leaned forward, not sure she'd heard him correctly. "Pardon me—did you just say Cole owns some boats?"

"Six of 'em. He cap'ns the *Chienne* and charters out the others. That fella he's talkin' to right now charters one of them." Henry paused and took a swig of beer. "Yes, sir, Cole's got a golden touch when it comes to makin' money. You'd never know it by looking at him, but he's got enough greenbacks to buy and sell half of New Orleans."

The concept of Cole as a businessman astonished her. "From operating his boats?"

"Started out that way. Now most of his money comes from his investments."

Josephine's gaze wafted toward the bar, locking on Cole's broad back. It was hard to accept the fact that the rude Neanderthal she'd hit this afternoon was not only successful, but *intelligent*. "He's an investor?"

Henry's head bobbed vigorously, making his jowls jiggle. "Better'n Donald Trump. He's a right out genius when it comes to playin' the stock market. Knows how to make money hand over fist."

"But . . . how?"

Henry shrugged. "Says he listens to the talk on the wharves about what's not bein' shipped in its usual volume, then invests in it. Says when somethin' is scarce, the price goes up. I don' know all the ins an' outs of it, but I know this—he's made me a right tidy sum. I give him half my pay to invest each week."

"You're kidding."

"Serious as a heart attack. He's got more money than most banks, but you'd never know it. Fact is, he can't stand folks with money. Says they put on airs, think they're better than the rest of us. He 'specially can't stand them New Orleans uptown types." Henry eyed her speculatively. "Did I hear Cole say you wuz from Audubon Place?"

Josephine nodded.

"I gotta say, it's mighty odd, him hiring someone from there to work on his boat. No offense meant, ma'am, but your kind usually makes him act like a cat with a shot of Tabasco up its tail." His bright eyes met hers, his expression frankly curious. "If you don' mind me askin', why in tarnation are you signin' up to cook on a towboat, anyway?"

"It's a complicated story." Josephine drew a long breath, then slowly let it out. The weight of everything she'd lost suddenly came crashing down on her, and her throat thickened with tears. She swallowed hard, determined to choke them back. "The long and the short of it is, I have no place else to go."

Henry reached out and patted her hand, his blue eyes gentle. "Reckon I know well enough what that's like. Most of us on the river ended up here the same way. Must be awful hard on the likes of you, though." Henry shook his head. "It's a long, hard fall from Audubon Place to here."

There was no derision in his face, only sympathy. It was almost more than she could stand. She blinked hard to keep the traitorous tears at bay and steered the conversation back to him.

"How did you come to work on a towboat?"

Henry shrugged. "After my wife died, I had no place else to go, either."

"What did you do before?"

"Worked the oil patch up in east Texas. Had a nice little home in Deadwood. After Hazel passed on, I couldn't stand comin' home to an empty house. I tried a little off-shore work, but I hated all the time off between tours of duty on the rig. Left me too much time with nothin' to do but miss Hazel."

"Don't you get time off on a towboat?"

Henry nodded. "Most of the crew works thirty days on, then fifteen days off. Cole and I live on the *Chienne*, though, so we work all the time. Junior and Hambone are working back-to-back runs this time, too. They lost all their money gamblin' in Baton Rouge, and Cole didn't have the heart to leave 'em shoreside stone-cold broke."

She shot a skeptical glance at Cole's broad back at the bar. "He *has* a heart?"

Henry's face creased in a grin. "A bigger one than he likes most folks to know." He took a long draft of beer, then settled his gaze on her. "I don' imagine you're lookin' to make more than one trip up the river and back."

"No."

"Well, I gotta warn ya—if you're not used to it, four weeks on a boat can seem like a mighty long time. The hours are long, the work's hard and the company leaves a little to be desired."

Josephine gave a tight smile. "So I've been given to understand."

"I'm not tryin' to run you off, mind you. Lord knows, the crew's likely to jump ship if'n they have to endure any more of my grub. Jus' wantin' to tell it like it is, though."

"I appreciate it."

"Okay. Long as you know what you're gettin' into." He took a final pull of his beer. "Well, I sure hope you can cook. The boys are mighty particular about their chow."

Josephine felt a twinge of concern. It rapidly escalated as Cole slid into the booth beside her. She scooted against the wall, her veins inexplicably flooding with adrenaline.

"Speaking of chow, that waitress been by yet?" he asked.

"Not yet," Henry replied.

With a displeased grunt, Cole stuck two fingers in his

mouth and whistled. The ear-piercing shriek made Josephine jump, causing her to lurch against his arm.

Cole angled an amused glance down at her. "Didn't mean to startle you, there, darlin'. Just trying to get the little gal's attention."

Josephine nervously straightened herself and smoothed back a stray wisp of hair. "Well, I hope you don't plan to whistle like that every time you want a meal on the boat."

"Heck, no, darlin'. On my boat, I just help myself to whatever I want."

Josephine's mouth went dry. Surely he was only talking about food.

He stretched his arm out along the back of the booth and gave her a lascivious grin. "As my employee, it'll be your job to anticipate my wants and needs. I'm sure it won't take you long to catch on to my preferences." He leaned forward and lowered his voice, as if he were imparting confidential information. "I happen to have quite an appetite."

For food. Surely he was only talking about food. She hoped and prayed he wasn't talking about anything else.

Josephine shrank back against the corner of the booth, and was relieved when a platinum-haired waitress arrived at the table wearing a tight blue T-shirt that read, *The Porthole*. Both Os were large, round portholes, each of which encircled the tip of a ponderous breast.

Angling a well-cushioned hip at Cole, the blonde smiled widely enough to expose a large wad of chewing gum. "Ya want somethin'?"

"Sure do."

The waitress grinned at Cole as if he were the catch of the day. Josephine fought the urge to roll her eyes. It was positively nauseating, the way women stared at him. She'd noticed it in the mall. She'd also noticed he wasn't above staring back.

Cole gave the waitress a sexy wink. "I'll have the porterhouse—extra rare. Tell the cook just to knock off the horns and wipe the tail." He glanced at Josephine. "You want the same?"

The thought of ingesting a slab of raw meat turned her stomach. "Could I see a menu, please?"

The blonde smacked her gum. "We don't got no menus. All we serve are burgers, rib eyes, and a two-pound porterhouse. What do ya want?"

To wake up and discover this is all a bad dream. Oh, what she'd give to be back in her own home, curled up with a warm TV dinner, a cold glass of Perrier and a good book!

But she no longer had a home. Aunt Prudie's house—along with her stash of Perrier and her last two Budget Gourmet dinners—were now the property of a mortgage company. Life as she knew it no longer existed. She had to carve out a new one, and for the time being, that meant putting up with this obnoxious cretin.

Gritting her teeth, she forced her face into what she hoped was a pleasant expression. "I'll have a rib eye, please, cooked medium-well."

"Want any sauce with that?" the waitress asked.

The question came as a pleasant surprise. Perhaps this establishment wasn't as primitive as it seemed. "Why, yes. Some béarnaise on the side would be nice."

"We don't got none of that."

"No? What do you have?"

Cole turned to Josephine, his eyes gleaming with amusement. "Your choices here, Empress, are Tabasco, ketchup and Heinz Fifty-Seven." His teeth flashed in a blinding smile.

He was horrid, Josephine fumed. Only a black-hearted monster would take such obvious pleasure in humiliating her. And for the next four weeks, she would have to endure his gleeful attempts to get her goat at every turn.

Well, he wouldn't succeed. No matter how much he goaded her, she wouldn't lose her composure, wouldn't lose her temper, wouldn't lose her self-control.

She was afraid, however, that she just might bite off her tongue in the process.

Chapter Four

A tinny buzz jerked Josephine out of a deep, thick sleep. Her radio alarm must be going on the fritz, she thought groggily. An unfamiliar smell, musty and damp, assaulted her nostrils. She wrinkled her nose, making a mental note to tell the maid to change the linens and air out her room.

And then it hit her. This wasn't her room, she wasn't at Prudie's home and she didn't have a maid. Her stomach tightened into a hard, cold knot. She squeezed her eyes shut, trying to cling to the illusion that she was in the familiar four-poster bed, snuggled under a goose-down duvet, waiting for Consuela to bring her a steaming mug of café au lait, but she was unable to sustain the fantasy.

She'd let Consuela and the rest of Aunt Prudie's staff go three weeks ago, when she'd learned the truth about her financial situation. She'd given them each two extra months' pay, even though she could ill afford it.

She certainly hoped they were faring better than she was. No doubt they were; *they,* at least, had marketable job skills. One thing was for sure—they couldn't have ended up with an employer any more boorish than Cole Dumanski.

Opening her eyes with a sigh, she reached out and grabbed the squawking alarm, smashing the knobs behind its glowing green face until it ceased its metallic shriek. The sudden silence jangled her nerves as much as the noise.

But not as much as the dark. Josephine shivered, even though she lay under three blankets. When she'd finally fallen asleep, the cabin had been illuminated by lights shining through the small porthole above the bed. Now it was impossible to tell that the room even had a porthole, much less where it was.

Josephine wrapped her arms tightly around herself, suppressing another shudder. She hated the dark. Memories always bubbled up through it—memories of that black, awful, terrifying night when she'd lain trapped in her overturned car, lain waiting, waiting, helplessly waiting.

Waiting for dawn. Waiting for help. Waiting for someone to tell her why her best friend's hand had grown so cold.

She abruptly sat up, pushed back the covers and thrust herself out of the narrow bed. The floor was gritty and cold beneath her bare feet. She stubbed her right big toe on something as she groped her way to the door. Ignoring the pain, she limped forward and flipped on the light switch.

A bare bulb burst to life, mercifully sending the memories skittering back into the dark recesses of her mind. The tight, panicked feeling in her chest began to loosen its hold. Stumbling back to the bed, Josephine sat down, cradled her injured toe and surveyed her surroundings.

The cabin was grim as a prison cell. Practically everything in it was gray—the walls, the painted metal floor, the door, even the sheets and blankets. At one time the sheets had probably been white, and there was a possibility that the blankets might once have been blue, but life on the towboat had apparently drained them of all color.

Just like life with Aunt Prudie had done to her.

Josephine thrust the unwanted thought aside, deeming it disrespectful, and glanced again at the smudged face of the rusty alarm. Four o'clock. No wonder she felt so awful—she'd had less than two hours' sleep. She'd climbed into bed immediately after Cole and Henry had brought her back to the boat around eleven, but the loud, strange noises of the river had kept her awake. The towboat had shifted and groaned against its mooring until she'd been certain it was about to break apart. Freighters had rumbled past, chains had clanked like the Ghost of Christmas Past and a foghorn had jarred her awake just as she'd finally drifted to sleep.

But the worst noises of all had been human—heavy footsteps, bawdy laughter and a string of vulgarities the likes of which she'd never even imagined. Her heart had pounded wildly as the sounds had grown closer. And then her doorknob had rattled, and her heart had stopped in her chest.

Someone was trying her door.

She'd rapidly assessed her options. It was at least a two-story drop to the river, and the porthole was awfully small. She was seriously considering trying to squeeze herself through it nonetheless when Cole's distinctive voice roared out an order, followed by a vile, ominous threat. The other voices and footsteps rapidly retreated.

Josephine had fallen back against her pillow, limp with relief. Never in a million years had she imagined that a detailed description of castration could sound so sweet.

Never in a hundred million years had she imagined Cole in the role of savior.

He was only looking out for his own interests, of course, she reasoned now, giving her toe a final rub. He couldn't afford to lose a cook or have any of his crew members carted off to jail.

He'd be looking out for his own interests this morning, too, she thought dryly, and the thing he'd be interested in was breakfast. Josephine scrambled to her feet and headed for the shower. She'd set the alarm half an hour earlier than he'd recommended, figuring she'd need some extra time for planning a menu, familiarizing herself with the equipment and locating all the supplies.

Not to mention learning how to cook.

Trepidation, cold and queasy, shimmied up her spine. She fought it down with a silent pep talk.

She was a fast learner. She had a cookbook, and she was good at following instructions. Millions of people prepared meals every day.

How difficult could it be?

A lot more difficult than she'd ever imagined, Josephine thought forlornly twenty minutes later. She stood in the grease-scented galley, trying to keep her beige sweater and matching wool slacks from coming into contact with the dubiously clean green-flecked countertop, and flipped through the pages of the cookbook. She was growing more chagrined by the moment.

Whoever would have guessed that a cookbook named *Appetizing Basics* would contain recipes for nothing but *appetizers?*

A burst of indignation shot through her. How dare they print a book with such a misleading title! She played by the rules, by golly. She worked hard to live up to people's expectations, and she firmly believed the rest of the world should do the same. It wasn't fair. The authors were totally lacking in integrity. It was a low-down, nasty trick, a deliberate deception, and she had half a mind to write the publishing house and tell them exactly how much she resented it.

But that wouldn't help her now. She nervously bit the inside of her lip. She'd have to make do with what she had at hand, and at the moment, this cookbook was all she had.

Coffee—that was what she needed. A good, strong dose of caffeine would help her think more clearly.

A coffeemaker just like the one at Aunt Prudie's school sat on the counter. Thank heavens she knew how to use it. Coffee was the one thing every well-bred New Orleans woman knew how to prepare to perfection. Josephine found a bag of chicory-laced, dark-roasted Columbian in the cupboard and put a pot on to brew, then turned her attention back to the cookbook.

Ceviche. Curry Dip. Pâté de Foie Gras en Aspic. Rumaki . . . None of the listings in the index looked very much like breakfast fare. She needed recipes for things like pancakes and bacon.

She fought down a rising tide of panic. There had to be *something* in here she could use. She was vastly relieved when she finally spotted the heading "Eggs."

Flipping the pages eagerly, she scanned the recipes. *Eggs Cardinal, Pickled Eggs, Stuffed Eggs, Russian Anchovy Eggs . . . Oh, dear.* Every one was a recipe for hard-boiled eggs. Not a single instruction for scrambling or frying anywhere in sight.

Well, there was nothing wrong with hard-cooked eggs, Josephine decided. Cole had said his crew ate eggs for breakfast. He hadn't specified what type.

Josephine searched the cabinets until she located two large pans, then carried them to the sink, turned on the faucet, and splashed a few inches of water in each. Placing them on the stove, she carefully turned on the burners as Cole had shown her.

There. That wasn't so hard. Pleased with herself, she turned back to the book.

There were no recipes for pancakes, but there was a recipe for miniature crepes. Crepes were a lot like pancakes. She'd cook some up and serve them in a stack, and no one would be the wiser.

She scanned the cookbook, looking for a similar solution for bacon. Ah—here was a recipe for Bacon Chutney Canapés. Maybe she could prepare just the bacon part.

"Broil bacon until crisp," she read. "Drain on paper towels."

Hmm. There was a "broil" setting on the oven knob. And she remembered seeing Aunt Prudie's cook place raw bacon on a stack of paper towels.

Grabbing two large plastic platters from a low shelf, she lined them with paper towels, then pulled a package of bacon from the refrigerator. The thought of actually touching the raw meat made her skin crawl, but she saw no way around it. Holding her hand as far away from her body as possible and wrinkling her nose in distaste, she gingerly lifted a strip between her thumb and forefinger.

" 'Morning, Empress."

Josephine jumped, dropping the bacon on top of her beige suede loafer.

Cole strode into the room, wearing a denim shirt a couple of shades lighter than his jeans. He bent and picked the slab of bacon off her feet. The scent of his toothpaste hit her in a heady rush as he straightened. He was standing close, close enough that she could see the individual dark whiskers of his beard. He had a five-o'clock shadow, and it wasn't even four-thirty in the morning.

She'd read somewhere that the thickness of a man's beard was tied to his testosterone level. Wasn't testosterone what regulated sexual function and desire? Cole's must be through the roof.

The thought sent a flush of heat rushing to her cheeks. What was wrong with her? Every time she was around this man, her thoughts ended up in the bedroom. Maybe his testosterone level was somehow affecting *her* hormones. Maybe they exerted some kind of pull, like gravity.

She didn't know. She only knew she was so relieved when he stepped back that it took her a moment to realize he'd placed the fallen bacon on the platter.

She frowned in consternation. "Oh, I can't cook that one now."

"The crew won't mind."

"But it was on the floor!"

Cole shrugged. "The floor's probably cleaner than the pig was. Besides, cooking will kill everything except the taste." He grinned, his white teeth gleaming in sharp relief against his tan skin. "You might want to spray some Lysol on that shoe, though."

Josephine gazed down at her feet in chagrin. The pale suede now sported a dark, greasy smear.

Cole stepped to the sink beside her and began washing his hands. "No point in ruining your good clothes while you're on the boat. Why don't you just wear tennis shoes and jeans?"

"I don't have any."

He shot her a look of sheer amazement.

"Aunt Prudie thought they were vulgar," she added, feeling the need to explain further.

Cole's gaze seemed to go right through her. "The old gal really kept you under her thumb, didn't she?"

Turning her attention back to the bacon, Josephine stiffly yanked another strip from the package. She'd always secretly resented the old woman's controlling ways, but her resentment had made her feel guilty. If she were a better person, the kind of person her father had tried to mold her into, she wouldn't be so mean-spirited. After all, Aunt Prudie had taken over her upbringing after she'd committed that awful, irresponsible act. "My aunt was set in her ways, and I did my best not to upset her, that's all."

"Why?" He shut off the faucet and dried his hands on a dish towel. In the confines of the narrow kitchen, he seemed impossibly tall, improbably hard-muscled and unnervingly close. Josephine was painfully aware of his slightest movement. From the corner of her eye, she watched his tan fingers fold the towel, then drape it across the long faucet. "Afraid she'd leave her inheritance to someone else?"

He was baiting her again. She lifted her chin and shot

him her iciest gaze. "It was a matter of respect—something you and your crew know nothing about, judging from the crude language I heard in the hall last night."

Cole sighed harshly. "I'd hoped you'd slept through that."

Josephine eyed him reprovingly. "A dead person couldn't have slept through that ruckus."

He leaned his hip against the counter and ruefully rubbed his jaw. "The boys had too much to drink last night. They ended up on the wrong side of the deck, and thought your cabin was theirs. I'm sorry." He sounded genuinely penitent. Surprised, she glanced up to find that he looked it, too.

"Did they scare you?" he asked quietly.

Josephine would rather die than admit she'd nearly leaped out the porthole. On the other hand, she couldn't allow him to think such behavior was acceptable. She yanked another strip of the bacon from the package. "It was . . . somewhat alarming."

"Well, don't worry. You're safe on my boat."

She looked up, surprised at the uncharacteristic reassurance. His impossibly sensuous mouth curled in a sexy smile. "I personally guarantee that nothing will happen to you that you don't want to happen."

The remark was clearly suggestive. She started to protest, but her heart was pounding crazily, making her feel flushed and slightly breathless.

He folded his arms across his chest and continued to grin at her. She could see his biceps bulge beneath the denim fabric of his shirt. Flustered, she fastened her eyes back on the bacon and changed the subject. "What are you doing up so early?"

"Getting ready to cast off. Gaston will crank up the engine at any moment."

"Gaston?"

"Our engineer."

"That's an unusual name. Is he French?"

"He speaks it. He's Cajun."

The coffeemaker gurgled as the last drop of water drizzled into the basket. Cole glanced at it. "Hope that coffee tastes as good as it smells."

He reached into a cupboard above Josephine's head and pulled down a large mug with a black plastic lid, the kind commuters used. His arm brushed her shoulder, and she inhaled sharply. The slight contact sent a dizzying buzz of warmth shooting through her, making her strangely light-headed.

"There's the engine now," Cole said.

The engine—thank heavens. For a disoriented moment, Josephine thought the roar in her ears and the shaking under her feet was the result of physical contact with Cole.

The pans on the stove rattled, and the silverware clattered in the drawer. The mechanical roar was so loud she had to raise her voice to be heard over it. "Is it always this loud?"

"It'll get even louder when the propellers kick in. But you'll get used to it."

She watched him take a sip of coffee, apparently unbothered by the shuddering din. His eyebrows flew up in surprise. "Say—this isn't bad."

There was no reason that such faint praise should thrill her so, but it delighted her nonetheless. She watched him take another large swallow, then nod appreciatively. "Quite an improvement over that engine sludge Henry tries to pass off as coffee."

He snapped the black plastic lid on the mug. "Well, I'd better get up to the pilothouse." He ambled to the door, then paused, lifting the cup in a gesture that resembled a salute. "If you can cook as good as you make coffee, this whole arrangement might work out better than I thought."

Josephine turned back to the bacon, her heart pounding faster than normal, her thoughts scattered and confused. She almost preferred Cole's rude behavior to this. When he was rude, at least she had a logical reason for feeling so agitated around him. There was no explanation for her distress when he was nice.

Nice. How rapidly her standards were slipping, she thought wryly. "Not bad" didn't actually qualify as a compliment, and "nothing will happen to you that you don't want to happen" wasn't exactly a carte blanche ticket of security. Instead, it probably implied that anything that happened to her would be her own fault—or at least something she subliminally wanted.

With his colossal ego, she thought indignantly, he probably thought she wanted to sleep with him.

The thought sent a hot shiver chasing up her spine. Alarmed at her reaction, she tried to muster an appropriate sense of outrage as she placed the last strip of bacon on the paper towel, but try as she might, she failed.

She stalked to the sink, turned the faucet on with her elbow and plunged her hands under the running water. Well, she had news for Mr. Cole Dumanski—the only thing she wanted from him was a paycheck at the end of the voyage and to be left alone to do her job in the interim. She didn't care about any of his personal wants or needs or appetites—except for food, of course. And the only reason she cared about that was because she was the kind of person who believed that anything worth doing was worth doing well. It certainly wasn't because she cared about pleasing him or longed for more of his meager praise.

Determined to put him out of her mind, she turned her attention back to breakfast preparations. She might as well go ahead and start the bacon. Studying the oven, she carefully turned it on "broil," then opened the door and thrust the paper-lined plastic tray inside.

This cooking business was a whole lot easier than she'd thought it would be. Smiling to herself, she flipped the pages of the cookbook to the recipe for miniature crepes. She'd known she could handle this job—she could handle anything she put her mind to. She just hadn't known it would be so simple.

* * *

Cole stared out the pilothouse window, absently watching a Lithuanian freighter chug downriver on its way to the Gulf of Mexico, and took a deep draught of coffee, savoring the rich flavor. He'd pegged the Empress as the type who'd brew up a weak, namby-pamby pot, but she'd made it just the way he liked it—strong enough to deliver a jolt, but not so strong it tasted bitter. So far she'd earned two points in her favor—she could make a decent cup of joe, and she hadn't come unglued when Hambone and Junior had nearly broken down her door last night. All in all, it was more than he'd expected from a spoiled New Orleans socialite.

Socialite. Just the thought made him scowl.

Deliberately thrusting her from his mind, he turned his attention back to the river. Usually he loved being in the pilothouse at this time of day—loved watching the first rays of dawn change the water from inky black to rusty brown, hearing the first shrill squawks of the just-awakened gulls, smelling the earthy, musty scent of the water.

But not in New Orleans. Every one of his trips up and down the Mississippi began or ended here, yet each time Cole docked in this city, a suffocating feeling came over him, a feeling of not being able to draw an easy breath. Too much had happened here.

Too much, and not enough. He was haunted by unsettled scores.

Cole turned away, but the pilothouse was walled in windows, and there was no escaping the view. The river was high, twelve feet on the Carrollton Street gauge, which meant that from his vantage point four decks above the water, he could clearly see the French Quarter over the levee. He could make out the hulking, castle-like Jax Brewery building, the three black spires of St. Louis Cathedral, the iron balconies of the Pontalba buildings, the slanted, circular roof of the Aquarium of the Americas. The skyscrapers of the New Orleans Central Business District loomed beyond.

Tourists from all over the world flocked to New Orleans, drawn by the city's quaint charm. Most of them would find this view exquisite. To Cole, however, it had all the appeal of raw tripe.

Well, the sooner he got to work, the sooner he could cast off and leave the city in his towboat's wake. He crossed the room, unlocked the waterproof file cabinet where he kept his important papers and pulled out the captain's log, then settled himself at the oak chart table to make the first entry of the day. But the moment he opened the large leather-bound volume, a newspaper clipping fluttered to the floor.

That blasted picture of Alexa. Damn. He'd ripped it out of the New Orleans *Times-Picayune* yesterday, then stashed it away with the log when Henry had walked in on him. He'd been interrupted before he'd finished reading the article, but he didn't need to read any further than the headline. It had told him all he needed to know. *Alexa Armand to marry Robert McAuley.*

He bent and picked up the ripped scrap of paper, staring down at the familiar smiling face. Alexa Armand—he'd know her anywhere. She'd changed, of course, in the fourteen years since he'd last seen her. Her sleek dark hair now stopped at her shoulders instead of spilling all the way down her back. Her face was thinner, and she'd acquired the veneer of wealth and polish that the New Orleans upper crust wore like a coat of high-gloss boat varnish.

His stomach balled into a hard knot. Gorgeous, tantalizing, coldhearted Alexa—all grown up and more beautiful than ever. And set to marry the son of a bitch who'd framed him, sent him to jail and killed the only mother he'd ever known.

"Somethin' wrong, Cap'n?"

Cole ripped his eyes from the photo as Henry loped into the pilothouse. Crushing the clipping in his hand, Cole rose from the black vinyl stool by the chart table and shoved it loosely in his pocket. "Damn right something's wrong. Your two prized deckhands stumbled in so drunk last night they tried to bunk with the new cook."

Henry ruefully rubbed his grizzled chin and gave a sheepish, brown-toothed grin. "So I heard. But it was an honest mistake, Boss. They didn't mean no harm." The gray-haired man lowered his ropy frame onto the stool Cole had just vacated, pulled out his ever-present tin of chewing tobacco and placed a chaw in his cheek. "How'd she take it?"

"Better than you'd expect. She's still aboard."

Henry chortled. "Where the heck did you find that gal, anyway? Most unlikely-lookin' cook I ever set eyes on." He eased the tin back in the pocket of his blue plaid shirt and cast Cole a speculative look. " 'Specially knowin' how you feel about uptown types."

Cole frowned, his mind still on the newspaper clipping. "She was all I could find. Job applicants weren't exactly beating down the hatch and swarming the deck."

Henry gave a rasping chortle. Cole leveled a stern look at the old man. "I don't want the crew bothering her. Last thing I need is her suing my ass for sexual harrassment."

"Jeez, Boss, I been runnin' the river for nigh on twenty-three years and never heard of a cook doin' nothing like that."

"Well, things aren't like they used to be, and she's not your typical cook. There'd better be no more incidents like last night."

"Aye-aye, Boss. I'll keep the boys on a short leash." Henry peered up at him, his wizened face creased in a frown. "You feelin' all right? You don't look so good."

Cole scowled. "Yeah, well, you're not going to win any beauty crowns yourself."

Henry gave an amused chuckle, but his eyes didn't waver from Cole's face. He studied him in silence for a long moment, chewing thoughtfully. "Did the stock market take a dive or somethin'?"

Cole glanced at him sharply. "No. Why do you ask?"

Henry shrugged. "Well, somethin' in the paper upset you yesterday, an' you been out of sorts ever since." Henry hesitated and cleared his throat. He reached for an old coffee can under the table, spit into it, then wiped his mouth with the back of his hand. "If that somethin' has to do with that money of mine—you know, the money you've invested fer me—well, I just want ya to know it don' make me no never mind. Not much to spend it on, living on the river. An' I wouldn' have it in the first place if it weren' for you." Henry spit again. "So if the market takes a fall or somethin' like that happens, well, it don' much matter. I mean, you shouldn' worry none 'bout tellin' me or nothin'."

Affection for the old man filled Cole's chest, causing a lump of emotion to clog his throat. When he spoke, his voice came out gruffer than usual. "Your money's safe. Nothing's happened to it."

"Well, somethin's botherin' you, an' that's a fact. If it was my money, I wanted to set your mind at ease." Henry's blue eyes rested on him. Cole could feel the warmth in his gaze, feel the depth of his concern. "Hazel used to say it's not good to keep things bottled up inside. I know you're my boss an' all, but we go way back, and you're kinda like the son I never had. Somethin's on your mind, and it might do you good to get it off your chest. I hope ya know there's nothin' you could tell me that would ever make me think any less of ya."

A tender spot ached in the center of Cole's chest. He shot the old man a quick glance, then strode to the captain's chair. "Hey—I'm sorry if I've been rough on you lately." Cole rested a hand on the back of the leather chair, the chair where he sat and guided the boat. He drew a deep breath, let it out and gazed at the river. "Reckon there is something on my mind. Did you ever think of quitting the river, Henry?"

The old man's contiguous eyebrows shot up in surprise. "Nope. What else would I do? I ain't got no hankerin' to sit around twiddlin' my thumbs." Henry squinted at him, his blue eyes sharp and bright in his wizened face. The vertical creases over his bulbous nose deepened as he frowned. "You thinkin' 'bout hangin' up your cap, Cap'n?"

"Maybe. At least for a little while." Cole rubbed his unshaven jaw. "My accountants are urging me to give more time to the investment end of things. I've been feeling mighty restless lately, and I've been wondering if maybe I should take their advice."

Henry spit again into the rusty can and somberly nodded. "Does seem like all you do is work. If you ain't in here, you're at that computer of yours in your cabin or talkin' business on the phone, or doin' all three at the same time. Chartering out five towboats is a full-time job without trying to captain a sixth one at the same time—not to mention watchin' the stock market like ya do. I ain't never met no one so driven to succeed in all my life."

He was driven, all right, Cole thought grimly—but not by a desire to succeed. That aspiration had died with his foster mother fourteen years ago.

The thought of Mom Sawyer sent a spear of pain shooting through his chest. She was the only person who'd ever given a damn about him when he was growing up, the only person Cole had ever really loved. He'd have done anything to make Mom proud. Instead, Cole thought bitterly, he'd broken her heart. She'd died soon after he'd been locked up in that juvenile correction center for a crime he didn't commit.

Anger, hot and acidic, burned in his throat. Cole swallowed hard, struggling to push it back down.

Anger and the need to control it—that was what really drove him.

He had to stay busy, had to stay focused, in order to keep his demons at bay.

Lately, though, it no longer seemed to be working. No matter how many projects he took on or how many hours he put in, the past kept raising its ugly head. A sense of restlessness and dissatisfaction was building inside him like oil pressure in his boat's engine.

And it always got worse when he was in New Orleans. Cole stared out the starboard window, where the slate gray sky was lightening to silver over the city.

When he was here, the memories rose to a fever pitch, festering and creeping to the surface like infected splinters. They tainted his thoughts, they poisoned his dreams, they awakened him in the night with his heart pounding and his skin soaked with sweat.

Maybe he needed to face his demons head-on, he mused. Instead of running from the past, maybe it was time he confronted it. Maybe if he stayed in New Orleans long enough, the city and the memories of all the things that had happened here would lose their power to torment him.

He stared out at a run-down warehouse on the Mississippi's west bank, upstream from Algiers Point. When he'd left New Orleans, he used to dream about moving back when he'd made enough money to somehow exact revenge. If he only had enough money, he used to think, he'd win Alexa's heart, then crush it like a grape under his heel, just as she'd done to him. He'd find a way to get even with all the bastards who'd laughed at him in high school. But most of all, he'd devise a special form of torture for Robert McAuley. He'd discover what the scumbucket wanted more than anything else in the world, let him think it was within his reach, then brutally yank it away.

The thought made Cole thirst for revenge all over again. *Don't think about it,* he told himself. *It's in the past. Leave it alone.* He'd spent the last fourteen years convincing himself to let bygones be bygones, repeatedly reminding himself he had his father's blood in his veins. He'd be damned if he'd repeat his old man's mistakes, and he couldn't trust himself not to repeat them where McAuley was concerned.

All the same, his fingers tightened into a stranglehold on

his coffee mug in the way he wished he could grip McAuley's neck.

"Think you'd be happy as a landlubber?"

Henry's question jerked Cole out of his dark reflection. He took a long swig of coffee. "Well, now, that's a good question."

A damn good question, one that he'd been asking himself a lot lately. Cole watched an oil tanker approach, its deep bow carving a vee out of the muddy water. He didn't know how he'd like living shoreside. But then, he hadn't known how he'd like living on the river, either, when he took the only job he could get when he'd finally gotten out of that juvenile jail.

The only thing he knew for sure was that that damned newspaper photo had stirred up thoughts and feelings he'd thought he'd put behind him. Memories rolled through him like the wake of the passing tanker, along with all the old, familiar bitterness.

Alexa Armand—gorgeous, sexy Alexa. She'd inherited something more valuable than money, something rarer than good looks, something that ensured her entrée into the highest circles of New Orleans society—an aristocratic lineage that could be traced back to the city's antebellum elite and a family history of wealth that went back even farther. In the uppermost echelons of New Orleans society, old money was the only kind that counted.

She had it all, all right—and all because of her name. Through no effort of her own, through nothing but a circumstance of birth, Alexa had acceptance, esteem, a sense of belonging and a name that commanded respect.

For the exact same reason, Cole was an outcast, a misfit, a bad seed with tainted blood. And no amount of money could ever erase the fact.

"You're not really gonna call it quits, are you, Cap'n?"

Henry's words jerked him back to the present. Cole turned to the old man, his heart warming at the worried expression on the old salt's face. Aside from Mom

Sawyer, Henry was the only person in the world he'd ever really trusted.

"Not anytime soon. At least, not entirely." Cole clapped the man on the back. "But if I do decide to charter out the *Chienne.* you and the boys will be part and parcel of the deal. I'll even make sure you get a raise out of it."

Henry grinned. "If you dry-dock yourself, I bet you won't last two months before you're chompin' at the bit to get back to the pilothouse."

"You're probably right, Henry." Cole strode back to the chart table to finish his paperwork.

The intercom suddenly crackled to life. "Hello! Is anyone there?"

Muttering an epithet, Cole stretched forward and punched the button on the interior intercom. "Yeah, Empress. What do you need?"

"Some help." Her voice sounded high and urgent. An even more urgent-sounding alarm shrieked in the background. "The kitchen's on fire."

With sudden, horrible certainty, he recognized the keening wail as the smoke detector. "Leave the galley immediately," he ordered. "I'll be right down."

Cole and Henry stared at each other for a fraction of a second, then simultaneously bolted for the stairs.

Chapter Five

Thick, acrid smoke poured from the oven, burning Josephine's eyes. She slammed the door shut, but smoke kept billowing out. Gray pillars rose from the four burners on the stove, seeped out around the oven hinges and unfurled from underneath.

Josephine reached across and turned off the oven, but the plastic platter of bacon inside continued to blaze behind the closed door, making the appliance eerily resemble a glass-screened fireplace.

The high, thin screech of the smoke detector made it hard to think. Panic choked Josephine's throat. This was all her fault. She had to put out the fire before it spread, before anyone was hurt. *Oh, dear God, please keep anyone from being hurt!* She could stand anything, anything at all, except knowing she'd again injured another person.

It was difficult to see, much less to breathe, and the smoke was steadily getting thicker. She had to act fast. Her gaze fell on the pans of water she was boiling for the eggs.

Snatching one from the stove, she opened the oven door and threw its contents on the burning platter.

The fire sputtered, but refused to die. She grabbed the second pan and repeated the action. The flames hissed angrily. Despair, stifling and dark, pressed down on her chest. The whole towboat would go up in flames, and it was all her fault.

Suddenly Cole burst through the doorway, brandishing a fire extinguisher like a rifle. Smoke curled around him, making him look like a being from the underworld, but Josephine's knees went weak with relief at the sight of him.

"Get out!" he barked, striding rapidly into the narrow galley. Stopping in front of the open oven, he pointed the extinguisher, pulled the pin and fired. White foam shot out, coating the inside of the oven like Maalox on stomach lining.

The fire smothered and died a fizzing white death. Cole punched a button on the hood of the stove, activating the exhaust fan, then crossed the room in four steps and threw open the porthole.

Henry's face appeared in the galley doorway. "Go fetch the fans from the engine room," Cole ordered. "If we blow the smoke out of here fast enough, we'll avoid any smoke damage."

Josephine was seized by a sudden fit of coughing. Before she knew what was happening, she found herself lifted off her feet, tossed over Cole's shoulder and toted out the galley door like a bag of dirty laundry. She tried to protest, but she was coughing too hard to speak. She beat on his broad back, but to no avail. It was as hard and muscled as the flank of a horse, and apparently just as impervious to pain.

He carried her through the hatch to the outside deck, then unceremoniously plopped her on her feet in front of a metal bench. She sank down on it, drawing a deep breath.

The fresh air tasted like heaven. Josephine gulped in a sweet lungful. She coughed, then drew another.

Cole squatted down in front of her, his brow knit, his dark eyes intense. "Breathe," he ordered. "Take a deep breath, then tell me if it hurts."

Josephine did as he directed.

"Does it hurt?" he demanded.

Josephine shook her head. Her eyes were watering and her throat felt as if it had been scrubbed with sandpaper, but breathing was pure pleasure. "I'm okay," she said in a raspy voice. "Are you?"

"Fine." He straightened and loomed over her. His eyes narrowed, and the look of concern she thought she'd seen earlier evaporated so thoroughly she was no longer sure it had been there at all. "I thought I told you to get out of the galley."

"The fire was my fault. I had a responsibility to try to put it out."

"When you're on my boat, your first responsibility is to do as I say."

She stared up at him. "I couldn't just run off and leave it!"

His dark brows hunkered together in an ominous scowl. "Listen up, Empress, and listen good—I can't have someone on my boat who won't obey orders. I need to know I can rely on my crew to carry out my directions, especially in an emergency. If you can't abide by that, then get your stuff and get off my boat right now."

Josephine's fists balled in futile rage. With all her heart, she wished she could do as he suggested. But she couldn't. She had no other place to go. She needed this job, and she had to do whatever it took to keep it. She drew a deep breath, sputtered and coughed again.

"Well?" he demanded.

"Well, what?"

"Do you agree to follow my orders?"

She didn't know why it galled her so. She was used to following directions, to living by the rules. A part of her even acknowledged that his request was reasonable. But another part of her hated to concede anything to this stubborn, arrogant man.

"Oh, all right," she finally mumbled.

"All right what?"

He couldn't make it easy, could he? He had to wring every last shred of dignity from her. Pulling her spine straight, she belligerently glared at him. "All right. From here on out, I promise to obey your every command."

Cole glared back, a nerve twitching in his jaw. "You'd better. Because believe it or not, it's for your own damn good. The safety of my crew comes before everything else. That means that whether either one of us likes it or not, as long as you're on my boat, your safety and welfare are my priority."

She stared out at the dock and the hulking warehouse behind it, emotions rocking through her like the boat on the choppy water. All of her life, she'd longed for someone to make her well-being a priority, to put her needs above concerns for property or position. Why, oh, why, did the first person to do so have to be this coldhearted beast of a man?

"So how did the fire start?" he asked gruffly.

Josephine pulled her gaze back his face. "I was, uh, cooking the bacon."

"In the oven?"

Josephine nodded.

His eyes narrowed suspiciously. "On what?"

She regarded him warily. She didn't like the displeased look on his face or the accusatory tone of his voice. "On broil."

"I meant, what kind of pan was it on? It smelled like burned plastic."

Josephine squirmed. She had the uneasy feeling that

91

anything she said was incriminating evidence that could be used against her. "Well, you saw it," she said defensively. "You put a piece of bacon on it yourself."

He stared at her incredulously. "That was a plastic tray covered with paper towels. Are you telling me you put *that* in the oven?"

Oh, dear. Oh dear, oh dear, oh dear! Cringing inside, she nervously smoothed a stray piece of hair back into her bun. "Well, I'm really not familiar with electric ovens."

"Are you trying to tell me that's the way you usually cook bacon in a *gas* one?" Sarcasm dripped from his voice the way the plastic pan had dripped from the oven rack.

Josephine thought fast. "Umm, no. I'm really not familiar with cooking bacon at all. The, uh, doctors had Aunt Prudie on a low-fat diet." It was perfectly true. Not that the old woman ever followed it, but Cole didn't need that particular piece of information.

He made a low grunting sound and simply stared at her.

She decided to seize the offensive. "Why didn't you say something when you saw how I was fixing it?"

"Because I assumed you were going to cook it in the microwave."

The microwave. Of course. That must be how Aunt Prudie's cook used to prepare it. Josephine lifted her hand to her mouth, mortified to her very soul. "Oh dear," she whispered. "Of course."

Too late, she realized she'd let her composure slip. She rapidly tried to regain it, but Cole was looking at her strangely, as if he could see right through her.

"I'm so sorry!" She sat up straight and tried to act self-possessed. "I was nervous about preparing my first meal for your crew, and—and I guess I just wasn't thinking clearly." She was trying her best to act poised and confident, but it was hard when her bottom lip was trembling. "Are—are you going to fire me?"

Cole gazed at her. *Criminy.* How was he supposed to respond to that? Especially when she looked at him that way—with her eyes all wide and filled with remorse, her lips all parted and wobbling?

She'd nearly burned up his boat, by damn. He'd be well within his rights to hand her her walking papers, or at least chew her out good and proper. But how in Hades was he supposed to do it with those big, contrite baby blues staring straight through him?

Hell. He needed a cook, and she *could* make a decent cup of coffee.

"Everyone's entitled to one mistake," he said gruffly. Shifting uneasily, he jerked his thumb toward the hatch. "Let's get back inside and see if the smoke's cleared out yet."

Drawing a breath of relief, Josephine followed Cole through the hatch into the boat's interior. The man was certainly an enigma, she mused. Given his belligerent behavior yesterday, she'd fully expected him to curse a blue streak and throw her off the boat. It was hard to reconcile the beast of yesterday with the man who'd just said "everyone's entitled to one mistake."

Even more difficult to reconcile was the expression on his face when he'd said it. He'd actually looked human. Maybe even understanding.

An enormous fan blocked the doorway to the galley. Cole picked it up and moved it aside, and Josephine stepped in behind him. The room smelled like a trash incinerator, but the air was free of smoke.

"How do things look?" Cole asked Henry, who was adjusting another fan at the far end of the room.

"Okay, Boss. Nothing's damaged."

A dark-haired man in his early forties stood on the bolted-down dining table, resetting the smoke alarm on the ceiling. He climbed down and turned toward them.

Cole waved a hand in his direction. "Hey, Gaston, this is our new cook. Josephine, this is Gaston Dupuis, the boat's engineer."

The French-speaking man—how nice. The French were

known for their civilized manners. "It's very nice to meet you," she said cordially, reaching out her hand.

Gaston looked down at his grease-streaked hand. To Josephine's horror, he spit on it, wiped it on his shirt, then extended it toward her. "Likewise."

Unless she wanted to be unbearably rude, she had no choice but to take it. Suppressing a shudder, Josephine allowed him to grip her palm and pump it heartily.

"You de one who made dis here mess, cherie? Whatcha do?"

"I— Well, I . . . "

"A dish that was supposed to be oven-safe wasn't, that's all," Cole said quickly. "We need to get some better-quality cookware in here."

Josephine stared at him, amazed that he would rise to her rescue. For the second time this morning, he'd behaved like a true gentleman.

"Is the oven usable?" Cole asked.

"Oh, yeah," Gaston replied. "But it's a helluva mess."

No kidding. Josephine grimaced as she gazed at it. The foam had disintegrated into a nasty brown goo that oozed down the exterior of the oven and puddled in a greasy, viscous pool on the floor. Inside the oven, the filthy slime floated on a bed of charred yellow plastic that now coated the oven bottom and both oven racks.

Cole pulled a butter knife from a drawer, bent down and prodded at the yellow substance. "Looks like the plastic will peel off when it cools. But you've got your work cut out for you, Empress. It's going to take some doing, cleaning this up."

She'd been wondering who handled cleanup duties in the galley. With a feeling of chagrin, she realized she'd just found out.

"Guess we'll all make do with cold cereal this morning." Cole clapped Henry on the back. "Well, come on, men—let's get back to work. Henry, go wake up Hambone and Junior and get them out on the barges. We'll get under way as soon as Pete arrives."

She'd heard of Hambone and Junior, and she'd met Gaston and Henry. Josephine glanced at Cole questioningly. "Who's Pete?"

"The relief pilot."

"We call him the Ghost," Henry volunteered. "We hardly never see him. He spends all his free time holed up in his cabin, watchin' TV and writin' letters to his wife. He's real quiet—he'll go days without sayin' a word to nobody. Since he works when most of the rest of us are sleepin', it's almost like he's invisible."

"What does a relief pilot do?"

"He and I take turns in the pilothouse," Cole said. "Gives me a chance to sleep and take care of other business."

Gaston laughed. *"Comme chassant la cuisiniere, eh?"*

Like chasing the cook. One of the things Josephine had learned at finishing school was French.

Cole shrugged and grinned. *"Peut-être. Si j'aurais de l'ennuie."*

Maybe. If I get bored. Josephine huffed out an indignant breath.

Cole tossed her a sharp-eyed glance. "Speak French, do you, Empress? Well, Gaston, I guess that means we can only talk about her when she's not around." With a sly wink, he strode to the door.

Josephine stared after him angrily as he and the other men filed out of the kitchen. Just as she'd nearly decided there might be a decent side to the man after all, he did something to prove otherwise.

She should have known better than to think he was capable of actual kindness. The only reason he'd covered for her in front of Henry and Gaston was to save face himself. If his crew knew what an idiotic mistake she'd made, Cole would look bad for having hired her.

Filled with indignation, Josephine yanked open cabinet

doors until she located a pair of rubber gloves, some cleaning supplies and a full-length apron. Placing a towel on the floor to kneel on, she knelt down and started mopping up the grimy foam, pretending she was wiping the smug smile right off Cole's face.

She would stop thinking about him, she told herself firmly. She'd concentrate on doing her job and refuse to let him or any of his ruffians get under her skin.

The sudden boom of what sounded like a loudspeaker blared outside the porthole. "Cast off the center line."

Curious, Josephine hurried to the window. Henry stood on the deck, unlooping an enormous rope from a concrete pillar at the end of the dock.

"Cast off the stern line." She recognized Cole's voice. He must be up in the pilothouse, broadcasting instructions to the crew.

"Cast off fore and aft. All gone!"

The engine roared. The floor shifted under her feet. Out the tiny window, an expanse of choppy brown water slowly widened between the dock and boat.

A rush of excitement chased through her. She'd passed the point of no return. For better or for worse, she was committed to making this voyage.

Despite all of her misgivings, a thrill of pleasure shivered up her spine. Finally, finally, at long last, she was about to begin a life on her own. Finally, finally, she had no one to answer to except herself.

And Cole, as long as she was on his boat. With a sigh and a grimace, she turned away from the window and back to the oozing oven.

Half an hour later, Josephine was still on her knees, doing battle with the hardened plastic. She'd just stuck her head in the oven to scrape a recalcitrant strip of melted goo off the burner with a butter knife when a shrill wolf whistle startled her so badly that she hit the crown of her head on the oven ceiling.

Backing out, she looked up to see a pair of scummy-looking men slouched in the galley entrance. The larger, older one had greasy brown hair swept back in a pompadour that exposed a receding hairline and Elvis style sideburns. When he caught her eye, he grinned lasciviously, then lifted his black T-shirt to scratch an enormous, hair-covered belly. The redheaded, ferret-faced youth beside him simultaneously scratched the crotch of his filthy jeans. They looked so much like a pair of mangy dogs that Josephine halfway expected one of one of them to lift a leg.

The larger one widened his grin to show several missing teeth. "Hell*oooo,* there, darlin'."

Oh, dear. This had to be Hambone and Junior, and they were worse than anything she'd imagined. For a moment, she considered crawling in the oven and closing the door behind her.

A warm first greeting sets the tone for all future encounters. Remembering the oft-repeated finishing school advice, Josephine reluctantly scrambled to her feet, peeled off the yellow gloves and forced a pleasant smile. "You must be Hambone and Junior. I'm Josephine." She started to extend her hand, then remembered what had happened with Gaston. She opted to graciously incline her head instead.

Junior turned to Hambone. "She's not near as old or fat as the other cooks."

"No, she ain't. Got a right nice booty on her, too," Hambone remarked, as if she weren't even in the room.

Josephine's smile froze, then faltered. She had no idea why they were discussing her loafers, but she hated being talked about as if she were an inanimate object. She forced a pleasant expression on her face. "If you have something to say about me, I'd prefer that you speak directly to me about it."

"All right. Sure." Hambone elbowed Junior in the ribs.

The skinny youth snickered. Hambone's gaze returned to Josephine. "I like your booty."

"My shoes?"

Hambone cackled. "No, sweetcakes. Your *booty*. You know—your tush."

Dear heavens. Was this man actually talking about her *backside?* From the way Junior was sniggering, she was afraid he was. *Oh, dear*—she must have presented quite a view, bent over and reaching in the oven. She stared at the men, appalled and shocked—all the more so because Hambone was acting for all the world as if he'd just paid her a high compliment.

Her face heated, and she found herself at a loss for words. All she could think to do was pretend the remark had never been made. She started to turn away from them, then whipped back around, not wanting to expose her backside for further examination. At least the front of her was covered by the grime-soaked apron. "Would—would you gentlemen like some coffee?"

"Why, sure, darlin'." Hambone jabbed Junior again and spoke in a loud whisper. "She likes me." Straddling the bench at the dining table, he continued to ogle her as she edged her way backward across the kitchen. "See that?" he muttered to Junior. "She can't take her eyes off me."

Josephine fumbled in the cabinet and pulled down two coffee mugs, searching her mind for something to say. "Do . . . do you take cream and sugar in your coffee?"

"Nah," Hambone replied, scratching his belly again. "Only thing I'd like in it is a hair of the dog that bit me last night, but Cap'n Cole don't allow no booze on the boat."

Thank heavens. Forcing a smile, she turned to Junior, who'd seated himself opposite Hambone. "How about you?"

"I'd, uh, like a little sugar."

Hambone guffawed. "This boy's always ready for a little sugar, if you know what I mean." He gave Josephine a broad wink.

Josephine suppressed a shudder and poured the coffee. She dawdled over it as long as she could, then drew a deep breath, squared her shoulders and carried the mugs to the table.

The moment she set them down, Hambone's hand shot out and grabbed her derriere.

Josephine jumped. "What on earth do you think you're doing?" she demanded, wrenching away.

"Just admirin' your *ass*ets, darlin'," Hambone replied, reaching for her again.

"Stop that immediately!" Pulling herself free, she retreated to the far end of the kitchen. Bracing her arms on the counter, she stood with her backside protectively pressed into a corner.

"Okay, okay. You just wanna talk, huh? Okay, I can dig it." Hambone took a long, loud slurp of coffee, his beady eyes fixed on her over the rim of the brown mug. "So tell me, sweetheart. What kinda panties you wearin'—bikini or thong?"

Henry froze in the galley doorway. He'd intended to have a few words with his men before they met Josephine, but it sounded like he'd arrived too late. The best he could do now was to get her away from them as soon as possible. He cleared his throat and sauntered in. "Good mornin' again, Miz Josephine. I take it you've met Hambone an' Junior. Boys, I hope you've been on your best behavior, 'cause Cap'n Cole said he'd fire the next man who bothered a cook."

Hambone stared guiltily at the tabletop. Junior scratched at the back of his buzz cut.

"Miz Josephine, the cap'n would like you to take him a thermos o' coffee and a bowl of Cheerios. I'll stay down here and get breakfast for the boys whilst you go on up to the pilothouse."

"Oh, certainly." Josephine looked immensely relieved.

She untied the apron and pulled it off, then started opening cabinets and drawers, evidently trying to locate the needed supplies.

"You'll find a tray in the pantry," Henry told her. "There's a thermos on that lower left-hand shelf, an' the bowls are in the right-hand cabinet. There's a little pitcher you can put some milk in right beside 'em."

"Thanks, Henry."

He watched her assemble everything on the black plastic tray, then tossed a few packets of sugar on for good measure. Heaven only knew Cole could use some extra sweetening up. "Now you git on up there an' see if you can git him to eat a good breakfast while I have a little talk with the boys here." Henry frowned in their direction. "I hope you'll excuse them, ma'am, for the noise they made last night, an' for anything insultin' they might have said or done this morning. I know they'd sure appreciate it if you could see fit not to mention it to the cap'n." Henry glared at Hambone and Junior, hoping they'd pick up on his cue and contribute an apology of their own. He didn't really hold out much hope. Neither of the boys was known for his smarts.

"I won't say anything this time." Josephine picked up the tray and shot what looked like a warning glance at Hambone and Junior. "But it had better not happen again."

Henry smiled as he watched her march out the door, her head held high. Something about her reminded him of his late wife Hazel.

She had gumption—that was it. His Hazel had been full of it. A soft smile playing on his lips, Henry let his mind drift back thirty-eight years to the first time he'd set eyes on his wife. She'd been a tiny young thing, delicate and dainty-looking, fresh off the farm and just starting a job as an oil field dispatch operator in Sulphur, Oklahoma. He'd walked into the office to find her kicking the shins of a roustabout twice her size. "An' the next time you get fresh,

I'll kick you where you deserve it," she'd declared. The redneck had beaten a hasty retreat.

The memory made him smile. Yes, sir, Hazel and Josephine were a lot alike. He was certain his Hazel would have taken a shine to her. Josephine might have some funny highfalutin manners, but she had guts, signing on to work a towboat. There was something kind of vulnerable about her, too—something soft, something that contradicted all her stiff, proper ways.

Henry swung back around and glowered at his deckhands. "What do you boys have to say for yourselves?"

"Aw, shucks, Henry, we didn't mean no harm," Hambone whined.

"That's right. We wuz just havin' a little fun."

"Well, you'd better save all your fun for shoreside, or the cap'n will kick your sorry tails overboard. An' I'm gonna tell you a little secret. Even without all the cap'n's threats an' warnings, anyone who messes with Josephine is gonna damn sure wish he never had."

"Whaddaya mean?"

"Well, it's a personal matter, and I really shouldn't be tellin' you," Henry hedged. Josephine would have a fit if she knew what he was about to do. But what she didn't know wouldn't hurt her, and it was for her own good, after all. It was the only way to ensure Hambone and Junior would leave her alone.

"Tell us what?" Hambone demanded.

"Yeah, Henry. What?"

"Well, it's right sad." Henry directed his gaze to the floor and shook his head. If he knew his deckhands, they'd value the information more if they had to wring it out of him. "But I really shouldn' be tellin' you. It's priv'leged info'mation."

"What is?" Junior urged.

"Come on, Henry. Give," Hambone urged.

Henry sighed reluctantly. "Oh, all right. I'll tell you, but

101

you've got to promise not to breathe a word of this to anyone else."

"I promise," Junior vowed solemnly

"Cross my heart and swear on my mother's grave," Hambone said.

Henry resisted the urge to tell Hambone he knew for a fact that his mother was still alive. Instead, he heaved another heavy sigh. "I shouldn' be telling you this, but . . . " He paused melodramatically. "That poor girl's got an untreatable case of the clap."

"Clap?" the deckhands echoed simultaneously.

Henry nodded glumly. "A special kind from the Far East that ain't got no cure. They say it's not so bad for a woman, but if a man catches it . . . " Henry mournfully shook his head.

"What happens?" the deckhands asked simultaneously.

Henry stuck a chaw of tobacco in his cheek and chomped sadly. He gave a long sigh for added effect. "They say it makes his willy shrivel up to nothin'."

"Nothin'?" Junior asked, wide-eyed.

Henry nodded glumly. "Damn near disappears. It just withers away till a man can't even take a leak standin' up."

"Wow," Junior said softly.

"I sure don' want none o' that," Hambone muttered. His sloping forehead creased in a frown. "Say, is it safe for her to be handlin' our food?"

Henry had to bite his lip to keep from grinning. "Oh, yeah—perfec'ly safe. The germs can't live outside the human body. You're not in any danger 'less you mess with her direc'ly."

"Well, I damn sure won't be doin' none o' that," Hambone stated vehemently.

"Me, neither," Junior echoed.

Henry slapped them each on the back. It was a good thing he was standing behind them so they couldn't see his smile. "That's what I was countin' on, boys. That's what I was countin' on."

Josephine hesitated outside the pilothouse door, the wind whipping her hair into disarray, and shivered in the damp, chill air. The inside stairway to the top deck had looked too steep to climb while carrying a tray, so she'd opted for the outside one.

She could see Cole through the window, seated in a brown leather chair behind an enormous control panel, each of his hands on a long, shiny lever. Balancing the tray on one arm, she tentatively tapped on the door.

"Come in," he called, not taking his eyes from the river. Juggling the tray, she tugged open the door.

She was struck by a sense of space and openness the moment she crossed the threshold, even though the room was small and crammed with equipment The pilothouse was walled in windows, exposing a panoramic view in all directions. Out the front windows, a flat fleet of faded green and red barges, four abreast, stretched longer than a football field. From the sides, the banks of the levee rolled down to expose the Kenner Rivertown development. Out the back, muddy water churned in the towboat's wake.

Cole flipped down the arm of his chair and unfolded what looked like an airline tray. He tapped it with his long, brown fingers. "Put my chow here."

Josephine stepped forward and gingerly set down the tray. The scent of smoke from the morning's kitchen fire still clung to him, mingled with the aroma of coffee and something else, something essentially masculine that made her pulse pound erratically. She backed away like a skittish colt and searched for something to say, something that dealt with hard, cold facts, something solid that might anchor her thoughts and rein in the odd, jumpy feeling she got whenever she was around him.

She gestured to the massive control panel. "Looks like

the cockpit of an airplane."

Cole glanced up and nodded. "In some ways, it is. In other ways, it's as simple as the dashboard of a car."

He seemed more at ease here, less on the defensive, than she'd ever seen him. If she could engage him in a nice, neutral conversation, maybe it would dissipate some of the tension between them. "What are those long things you're holding?" she ventured.

"These?" Cole briefly lifted his fingers from the silver levers on either side of his body. "We call them the sticks. I steer with them. They're connected to the rudders."

"What about the handles between them?"

Cole rested a hand on one of them. "They're throttles. Like the gas pedal on a car."

"Oh. Why are there two of them?"

"Because the boat has two engines."

She immediately realized she'd asked an idiotic question, but she detected no derision in his tone. Encouraged, Josephine pointed at a lit screen that looked like a TV to his right. "Is this radar?"

"Yep. And this one's a depth finder." He gestured to another screen suspended above the control panel to his left. "Tells me about the channel up ahead."

"What's the round thing under it?"

"A swing meter. It tells me the rate of turn—whether I'm going straight or not. With a tow this long, it's more valuable than a compass. Especially at night."

He was evidently in his element here. Hoping to prolong his good mood, Josephine looked around for something else to ask about. "What are all the phones for?"

He placed his hand on the one at his right. "This one goes straight to the engine room. I can call any cabin on the boat with the other one, or get an outside line."

Josephine glanced up at two black boxes suspended over his head. "Are those radios?"

"Yep. Two different frequencies. They let me communicate with other vessels on the river." He pointed to a microphone on a long, coiled cord above his head. "And this lets me communicate with anyone on the boat. I used it this morning to tell the deckhand which lines to untie. It's connected to both the ship's intercom and the outside loud-speaker. In an emergency, I can talk to everyone at once."

"I had no idea that piloting a boat was so complex," Josephine murmured, gazing at the equipment. "How do you keep track of everything all at the same time?"

His hands went back to the sticks. "Years of practice, Empress. Years of practice."

Henry had said Cole started out as a deckhand at the age of eighteen. Since then, Cole had somehow managed to earn his captain's license, acquire six boats and become a wealthy investor.

The man was an intriguing jumble of contradictions. Josephine gazed out at the long tow of barges, trying to think of a way to get him to talk about himself. "Henry said you started working on the river when you were as young as Junior."

Cole frowned. "Henry talks too much."

He was starting to withdraw. She could feel it. His very reluctance to talk about anything personal made her all the more curious. "It must have been difficult, working your way up to captain," she ventured.

"Not as hard as a lot of other things I've done." Cole rose from the chair and headed across the room.

Josephine watched in alarm. "Is it safe for you to just get up and leave the driver's seat?"

Cole smiled. "When we're on a straight stretch like this and no other traffic's coming, it is." He strode to the right wall and glanced at three large black machines.

"What are those?" Josephine asked.

"Monitors for the electrical generators. We have two and a backup. The monitor for the bilge-pumping system is also up here, behind the settee."

"The settee? What's that?"

"The best seat in the house." Cole gestured to a tall,

built-in seat that looked like a vinyl-covered sofa on a small stage. "Climb up and give it a try."

He watched her do so, noting the way her slacks molded to her slim, round derriere. The wind had loosened some of her hair from the tight bun at the back of her head, and honey-blond strands spilled around her shoulders in wild abandon. There was something erotic about her unintentional state of disarray. He shoved his hands in the pockets of his jeans and deliberately turned away, disturbed to find himself attracted to her. "So what do you think of the river?"

"Oh, it's beautiful." Her voice was soft and fervent. He glanced over to see her gazing raptly out the front window. "It's almost like it has a spirit—a spirit of determination. Nothing gets in its way, nothing slows it down."

Her response surprised him. He hadn't expected her to see the beauty of the muddy, messy stretch of water. He'd thought a hothouse flower like her would restrict her admiration of nature to landscaped gardens and man-made lily ponds. "Yeah, it's really something, isn't it? It gets even more beautiful once we get beyond Baton Rouge. But there are some great sights along this stretch, too. You'll be able to see Destrehan Plantation in a few minutes if you keep looking over that way."

He pulled his hand from his pocket to point. As he did, the newspaper clipping fluttered out and landed on the settee, right beside Josephine's hand.

Cole's heart jumped to his throat as she picked it up. She glanced at the picture, then looked curiously up at him. "Why, this is Alexa Armand! Her parents were friends of Aunt Prudence's." She glanced back down and scanned the article. "And she's going to marry Robert McAuley. I know him, too—his family always invited Aunt Prudie and me to a ball the night before Mardi Gras." She looked up and met his gaze, her eyes questioning. "Are Alexa and Robert friends of yours?"

Friends? Not exactly the word Cole would choose to

describe his relationship with either one of them. He reached out and snatched the clipping from her hand. "I went to high school with them."

"You went to St. Alban's?" Josephine repeated, her eyes wide.

Oh, hell. He should have figured she'd know that Alexa and Robert had gone to the most elite, most exclusive private high school in the parish. Wadding the clipping into a ball and shoving it back in his pocket, Cole scowled. "I know it's hard to believe that such a hallowed institution would stoop to accept the likes of me, but yeah, I went to St. Alban's. I was the token charity case."

He could see her mind working. "You must have been an awfully good student."

Cole shrugged. "It's like anything else in Louisiana. It isn't what you know; it's who you know. My foster mother used to clean house for the headmaster's mother. She got the old lady to pull a few strings with her son, and—presto—I was in."

"Did you say . . . *foster* mother?" she asked tentatively.

She was fishing—digging for information. A nerve twitched in Cole's jaw. He should have expected as much. These bluebloods always judged a person's worth based on their family connections. Well, if the Empress wanted information about his family, then, by God, he'd give it to her. He'd tell her so much she would wish she'd never asked.

"Yeah, that's right," he said brusquely. "I grew up in the foster care system. My real mom was a junkie, and she abandoned me when I was four. My father died in prison. He was serving a life sentence for murder."

Cole watched her closely, expecting to see the usual reaction—shock, revulsion, fear.

He saw none of it. He pressed forward, determined to wring a reaction out of her. "I served a stint in prison, too, when I was sixteen. It was actually a juvenile correction

107

center, but it was a prison all the same."

She still didn't seem sufficiently shocked. He decided to go further. "It was all thanks to your friend McAuley."

Her eyes grew even larger. "Robert?"

"Yeah, that's right. He framed me. Over Alexa."

Josephine's mouth fell open. Good, Cole thought grimly. He was finally starting to shock her.

"Why?"

"He found out I was secretly seeing her. You see, Alexa had a taste for walking on the wild side." A cold, dark fist of pain clutched around his heart as he thought about it. "Getting it on with a murderer's son was her idea of excitement. She used to do anything and everything with me in private, then pretend she didn't even know me at school."

Josephine's eyes looked as if they were about to bug out. "You dated her?"

Cole's mouth twisted into a mirthless smile. "It wasn't dating—just mating. I wasn't exactly big man on campus. Being seen with the likes of me wouldn't have been good for her image." His gut tightened at the memory. "I had an early morning garbage route to help Mom Sawyer pay the bills, and I used to come to class smelling like the bottom of the corner butcher's trash can." He could still remember the way he'd tried to clean up every morning, changing from his work clothes into his school uniform in a gas station rest room, washing his hands and arms with Lava soap. Despite his best efforts, the horrid, nasty stench of rotting meat would cling to his skin and hair until he got the chance to shower after third-hour PE. "You can imagine how popular that made me with the rich kids at St. Alban's. They used to call me 'Trash Boy.'" His lips stretched in a mirthless grin. "Wouldn't do for word to get around that Alexa Armand was sleeping with Trash Boy, now, would it?"

Instead of the revulsion he'd expected, Josephine's eyes grew disconcertingly soft. She stretched out her hand, her brow furrowed in compassion. "How awful for you."

Oh, hell. Instead of horrifying her, he'd only made her pity him.

The last thing he wanted was pity. He could stand anything but that. He'd seen it dozens of times—on the faces of social workers, teachers, even a few foster parents—and each time he'd lashed out in anger. He'd learned at an early age that people found it hard to feel sorry for someone they actively disliked.

It was a principle he called upon now. "I survived," he said curtly. "And if you want to do the same, you'll haul your tail back to the galley and clean up that mess you made. I'll let you get by with just fixing sandwiches for lunch, but you'd better fix one hell of a dinner tonight. I hired you to cook meals, not set fires and pour out bowls of Cheerios."

She gazed straight at him, her eyes clear and warm as a summer sky. Cole had the eerie sensation she was seeing way too much. With a dark scowl and a mumbled oath, he strode back to the captain's chair, lowered himself into it and placed his hands on the steering levers. His knuckles blanched as he tightened his fingers around the cold metal.

"Well, what are you waiting for?" he barked. "A military escort?"

This time his rudeness didn't seem to bother her. She didn't get all stiff and prickly, and her lips didn't press into that tight, thin line he'd come to expect. She simply rose from the settee, climbed down and left the pilothouse, softly closing the door behind her.

Cole muttered another oath under his breath. He'd meant to upset her with the sordid details of his life, but he was the one who'd ended up with a hard, cold knot in his stomach. Instead of scaring her off, he had the uneasy feeling that he'd inadvertently given her a glimpse of his soul.

Chapter Six

Josephine placed the last carrot stick on the carefully arranged plate of crudités, then nervously glanced at her wristwatch. Twenty-five minutes after six. Henry had told her earlier in the day that the crew would appear at the dinner table at six-thirty sharp.

"An' ya better have supper ready, 'cause they'll be hungry as a pack of rats."

"How many places should I set?" Josephine had asked.

"Five. Six, if ya want to sit and join us. Pete takes over as relief pilot at six o'clock, so you'll have to take his meal up to the pilothouse."

That meant Cole would be dining here in the galley. The thought made Josephine's pulse race. When she'd taken him a sandwich at noon, he'd deliberately kept his eyes on the river. He hadn't looked at her and hadn't spoken, except to mutter a curt "Thanks." He probably regretted telling her so much about his past.

Well, *she* certainly regretted hearing about it, she

thought, lifting the lid on the pan of meatballs simmering on the stove and peering in. Try as she might to keep her thoughts focused on dinner preparations, she couldn't stop thinking about Cole and Alexa Armand.

Anything and everything—that was what Cole had said they'd done together. A hot shiver chased through Josephine. She couldn't begin to imagine all that *anything and everything* might entail, but the possibilities left her flushed and flustered.

Especially since it was disturbingly easy to picture the two of them together. Cole and Alexa must have made a striking couple. Both were tall and attractive, both were arrogantly self-assured, both exuded an air of smoldering sexuality.

The last thought made Josephine accidentally drop the pot lid with a loud clatter. She picked it up and rinsed it in the sink, her thoughts still fastened on Cole and Alexa.

They might be physically well matched, but when it came to social standing, they couldn't have been more different. Alexa's family was the crème de la crème of New Orleans society. Her father owned a giant oil conglomerate and was a descendant of a wealthy antebellum plantation owner. Her mother's family could be traced back to the Marquis de Vaudreuil-Cavagnial, the "Grand Marquis" who had governed Louisiana in the mid-1700s. Alexa had even reigned as the Queen of Rex, the crowning honor for a New Orleans debutante. As a former Queen of Carnival, she was true New Orleans royalty.

It was a role that Alexa had always played to the hilt, Josephine thought, picking up a spoon and turning back to the meatballs. The gorgeous brunette thrived on being the center of attention and commanded it wherever she went. She could walk into a room, any room at all, and every head would turn in her direction. Josephine had spent many an evening sitting on the sidelines with Aunt Prudie, watching Alexa, wondering what it would be like to be in her shoes. How would it feel to be so beautiful, so confident, so desirable that she could have anything—or anyone—she wanted?

Including Cole Dumanski. Josephine distractedly stirred the meatballs, her stomach tightening at the thought. Alexa could have had her pick of any wealthy scion in New Orleans, yet she'd chosen to carry on a secret affair that would have mortified her parents.

Josephine realized she was stirring so hard that she'd smashed two meatballs. She pulled out the spoon and set it on a saucer by the stove. As much as it galled her to admit it, she could understand Alexa's attraction to Cole. Even Josephine wasn't immune to his dark charm, and she was supposedly frigid.

The heat from the stove suddenly seemed oppressive. Josephine replaced the lid on the pan and took a step back, wondering what Cole had meant when he'd said Robert McAuley had framed him. She surmised that the two men had had some kind of disagreement over Alexa. It must have been quite an altercation if Cole had ended up in jail as a result.

She wondered why Cole was keeping the news clipping about their engagement in his pocket. Was he still carrying a torch for Alexa?

The question made Josephine's stomach clench again. She deliberately turned her thoughts away from Alexa to what Cole had told her about his upbringing.

A mother who abandoned him, a father in jail, a childhood spent in foster homes . . . his whole youth sounded like a nightmare, she thought sadly. Even a turn of events that on the surface sounded fortuitous—being admitted to the finest private school in New Orleans—had turned out to be a hardship. It must have been awful on him, being the only have-not in a school full of haves.

The information went a long way toward explaining Cole's antagonism toward her and society in general. Not excusing it, but explaining it.

It was funny, Josephine mused, pulling six plastic Mardi Gras cups from the cabinet. In spite of all of their differences, she and Cole had a lot in common. Both had grown up with missing or emotionally unavailable parents, and both had been thrust into narrow, circumscribed worlds where they felt like outsiders.

The difference was in the way they'd coped. Cole had rebelled. Josephine had conformed.

"What in blazes is all this?" demanded a familiar masculine voice.

Startled, Josephine turned to see Cole looming in the galley doorway. Her heart pounded wildly, but she kept her expression calm. "All what?"

He jabbed his thumb in the direction of the dining table, his face creasing in a scowl. "All this."

Josephine defensively straightened her shoulders. "It's a table set for dinner."

And given the limited resources she'd had available, she thought she'd done an admirable job of it. She'd artfully arranged a cluster of grapes, plums, yellow squash, red peppers and green apples into a centerpiece in the middle of the table. She'd flanked the arrangement with two white utility candles she'd found in the back of a drawer, now flickering in hollowed-out zucchini chunks that she'd turned into candle holders.

Cole snorted. "Looks like you've set up a fruit and vegetable stand. And what the hell is with the sheet?"

Josephine was especially proud of her creativity with the navy bed sheet she'd found wadded up and stuffed in the corner of the galley that housed a small washer and dryer. She'd swagged the sides, gathered the corners with rubber bands and puffed the fabric into large, dramatic poufs. "I couldn't find a tablecloth."

Cole's mouth turned up mockingly. "Something wrong with the plastic one nailed to the table?"

He was baiting her. She wouldn't bite. "It's so much nicer to eat off fresh linen, don't you think?"

His grin was slow and insolent. "I hate to tell you, dar-lin', but you've got us set to eat off fresh polyester."

Irritation flashed through her. She'd worked hard to bring some semblance of civility to this squalid little room. Instead of appreciating her efforts, he was poking fun at her.

"It's still better than eating off stained plastic," she said, tilting her chin at a stubborn angle. "I would think that a man who'd been educated at St. Alban's would have learned to appreciate the amenities of civilized society."

"Well, now, Empress, that's where you're wrong." His voice was a low, lethal rumble. His dark eyes grew even darker. "All I learned to appreciate about fancy manners is that they're usually covering up something ugly. Like this sheet on this here tabletop." He waved a hand at it in a dis-paraging gesture, and strode toward her. "I should have known better than to mention St. Alban's to you. If you know what's good for you, you won't bring it up again." The intensity of Cole's black gaze made Josephine back up against the countertop, her fingers gripping the edge of it.

Footsteps clanked on the metal stairs in the outside hall. Cole turned away, and Josephine breathed a sigh of relief as the galley door burst open.

Henry stepped into the room, his nostrils twitching like a bloodhound's. "Say, supper smells mighty good."

"Thank you, Henry." Relaxing her grip on the counter-top, Josephine graced him with a wide smile that deliber-ately excluded Cole.

"What ya got fixed?" the old man asked.

"Meatballs."

"With spaghetti?"

"No. In pineapple sauce."

"With potatoes?"

"No. With . . . rice." A wave of uneasiness washed through her. The rice, unfortunately, hadn't turned out nearly as well as the meatballs.

"Well, that ought to be good for a change." Henry ambled toward the table, then stopped in midstride and let out a low whistle. "Hey, now! What's the special occasion? Is it someone's birthday or somethin'?"

"No." Josephine struggled to keep her voice from sounding as defensive as she felt. Couldn't anyone simply appreciate a well-dressed table setting without trying to read something into it? She hadn't realized she'd need to justify her efforts to make the table attractive. "I just believe dinner should be an aesthetically pleasing experience, that's all."

Henry scratched his jaw. "Well, I can't say as I know what you're talkin' about, but it looks right fancy."

"Too fancy," Cole said in a growl, lowering himself into the gray folding chair at the head of the table.

"Ah, now, Cap'n," Henry said, seating himself on one of the side benches. "Looks real nice. Miz Josephine musta went to a whole lot of trouble."

Cole gave a throaty grunt. "Let's just hope she went to half as much trouble on the food."

"From the way it smells, I bet she did." Henry picked up the paper towel Josephine had folded beside his plate and tucked it into the front of his shirt. "Hey, we got napkins an' everything!"

"I couldn't find any cloth ones," she apologized. "I couldn't even find any paper napkins."

"That's 'cause we usually just use our shirttails." Henry picked up a fork in one hand and a knife in the other, then looked up expectantly. "Okay. Bring it on!"

Josephine stared at him, taken aback. "Don't you want to wait until the others arrive?"

"Never have before." The clatter of work boots sounded in the hallway, making Henry twist around. "But here they are now."

Hambone and Junior stepped into the room, followed by Gaston. The faint odor of unwashed bodies accompanied them.

Hambone stopped abruptly. His meaty jowls sagged in a frown as he stared at the candles. "Somethin' wrong with the lights in here?"

"No. I just thought dinner would be more enjoyable if we didn't have a bare lightbulb glaring in our eyes." Besides, Josephine hoped the soft lighting would hide some of her culinary shortcomings.

"Where's the food?" Junior asked.

"I'll bring out the first course as soon as everyone's seated," Josephine said.

"First course!" Henry looked around the table, grinning broadly. "Hoo-ee! Did you hear that, boys? Sounds like we're in for some high-class eatin'." The older man's gaze fell on Junior's hands as the scrawny youth sat down beside him and reached for a plastic cup of water. Henry frowned disapprovingly. "Hey, there, son, looks like you forgot to wash your paws. Can't sit down at a purty spread like this with hands like that."

With a muttered oath, Junior rose and headed to the sink. Josephine backed against the countertop, afraid the deckhand would attempt to grope her derriere as Hambone had.

To her surprise, Junior made a wide circle around her. His small, rodentlike eyes fastened on her warily. "Did you wash *your* hands, Miz Josephine?" he asked in his nasally twang.

The question made Josephine's mouth fall open. She rapidly clamped it shut. "Why, yes."

Junior flipped on the faucet and gazed at her, as if he were trying to ascertain whether or not she was lying. "With soap?"

"Of course!"

"Just checkin'." He barely wet his hands, then reached for the dish towel, leaving visible brown streaks on the terry cloth. "Ya know, Cap'n," he said as he loped back to

116

the table, "maybe we ought to put up one of those signs you see in restaurants."

"What signs?" Cole asked.

"The kind tellin' kitchen help they have to wash their hands after goin' to the bathroom. Ya know, to prevent the spread of disease an' such."

Josephine drew in a sharp breath. This depraved, filthy, half-grown boy was worried about *her* sanitary habits? Josephine wasn't sure if she was more outraged or embarrassed.

Her face flooded with heat—and when Cole gazed at her, it grew even hotter. But instead of the mocking amusement she'd expected, he looked almost sympathetic.

"Since when did you turn into Howard Hughes?" he barked at Junior.

The scrawny redhead stared at him blankly. "Who?"

Cole muttered something unintelligible under his breath. "When did you become so blasted concerned about hygiene? If I didn't force you to take a shower every week, your armpits would sprout toadstools."

Junior lowered his gaze, his expression sheepish. Seating himself beside Henry, he ducked behind the older man's back as if it were a shield. "Just seems like a good idea, that's all, since she's handlin' our food an' all."

Cole shot Junior a warning look. "I don't know what's gotten into you, Junior, but I'm a whole lot less worried about Josephine's cleanliness than yours. You owe her an apology for that remark."

"Ah, Boss, I didn' mean nothin'," the gangly redhead whined.

"All the more reason to apologize."

"Sorry," Junior mumbled over his shoulder, not meeting Josephine's gaze.

Cole looked directly at her. "You'll have to excuse Junior, Josephine. The only concern the rest of have about you handling our food is when you're going to let us handle some of it ourselves."

Henry banged his knife and fork on the table. "Now you're talkin'!"

It was hard to imagine Cole in the role of defender and champion, but that was precisely what he seemed to be at the moment. Josephine gazed into his eyes and was struck by the warmth she saw there.

And suddenly she understood why. The taunts he must have suffered about his own hygiene as the result his garbage route must have eaten at his adolescent soul. He was trying to spare her the same indignity.

Josephine stared at him, her heart warming and softening like cake icing in the sun. Somewhere inside the man lurked an unexpected streak of kindness.

But the realization failed to comfort her. For reasons she didn't quite understand, it made Cole seem more dangerous than ever. Josephine picked up the platter of vegetables and carried it to the table, trying hard to act more poised than she felt. "I thought we'd start with crudités."

"Why, I believe Junior already did that, Empress." Cole's hard mouth curved in a sly, mocking grin.

Empress. The title set Josephine's teeth on edge. Good heavens, the man was impossible. One minute he was forcing a deckhand to apologize for insulting her, and the next, he was insulting her himself.

But maybe that was the point, she thought, placing the platter on the table harder than she'd intended. Maybe insulting her was a privilege he was reserving for himself.

She couldn't help but wonder if he was planning to reserve any other privileges. The thought sent a shiver of heat scurrying down her spine, and she quickly retreated to the far end of the galley, needing to increase her distance from him. She watched as the crew passed the plate around.

Henry's jowls drooped in disappointment as he stared at the platter.

"Ah, hell. Vege'bles," Hambone proclaimed.

"An' they ain't even cooked," Junior muttered.

Josephine straightened defensively. "Of course not. They're supposed to be served raw."

Henry gazed down at the plate, apparently looking for something positive to say. "Well, they look real nice. What are the little star things?"

"Cucumber slices." Josephine had called upon every trick she could remember from her ninth-grade garnish-making class. If she could impress them enough with the way the food looked, maybe they wouldn't notice the way it tasted.

"What are the round red flowers?" Hambone inquired.

"Cherry tomatoes." Josephine was particularly proud of the way she'd peeled back the skin to form triangular petals.

Gaston let out a raucous laugh. "Junior, *mon ami*—maybe Josephine is sending you a message like zee last cook."

Junior's forehead furrowed in a confused frown. "Whaddya mean?"

Grinning suggestively, Gaston held up the tomato between his thumb and forefinger. "Flowers . . . cherries . . . Use your imagination, *mon ami*."

Hambone hooted loudly. Gaston tossed the tomato into Junior's lap, which caused the gangly youth to jump as if it were a hot potato. He let out a rude, explosive epithet.

Cole banged his fist on the tabletop. The laughter came to an abrupt halt. "I've warned you once, and I don't intend to warn you again," he said in a growl. "There'll be no swearing and no harassing the cook. And Junior, regardless of what you're reading in those smut magazines of yours, no one's sending you any secret messages."

"Better not be," Junior muttered.

Cole glared around the table, looking each of his shipmates dead in the eye. The men ducked their heads and

119

hunched over their vegetables.

Josephine stood perfectly still, stunned into silence. For the second time in as many minutes, Cole had come to her rescue. But any kindness attached to the fact was rapidly erased by the ferocity of the scowl he directed her way.

"This rabbit food wouldn't fill a gnat's belly."

"It's an appetizer," Josephine said defensively. "It's just supposed to whet your appetite."

One corner of Cole's mouth slid into a lascivious grin. "Why, shucks, Empress. You've already whetted it plenty."

A loud laugh broke the tension at the table. To her chagrin, Josephine felt her face flame. Evidently the rules he set down for others didn't apply to him. He'd just reprimanded Gaston for making a crude joke at her expense, yet *he* felt free to ridicule her at will. What a boorish, autocratic monster. She hoped his crew mutinied against him.

And yet no one seemed the least bit bothered by the double standard. No one but her, that was.

Cole was still looking at her, his gaze disturbingly intent. "Go ahead and bring out the real food."

"Yeah. Where're those meatballs I smelled?" Henry asked.

Hambone gave a gap-toothed snicker. "If you mean the ones that smell real rank, they're between Junior's legs."

The men roared again. Josephine blushed seventeen shades of red. They were Neanderthals—Cro-Magnons! She'd never known the human species could sink so low. She longed to flee the room, but she didn't want to give them the satisfaction.

She would stand her ground and hold her head up high. She'd rise above their degrading remarks. She would focus on her work and ignore their rudeness. The more crassly they behaved, the more politely she would treat them.

Mustering all the dignity she could, Josephine headed to the refrigerator, pulled out two saucers heaped with iceberg lettuce, and returned to the table. She set one in front of Cole and the other in front of Henry.

"What's this?" Cole demanded.

Josephine marched back to the kitchen and retrieved two more identical saucers, which she set in front of Hambone and Gaston. "I couldn't find any salad plates, so I had to make do with saucers." She headed back for the last two salads.

"I'm not asking about the blasted plates. I want to know why you're serving more rabbit food."

Josephine stared at Cole quizzically. Everyone ate salad. Even brutes like these must eat salad, at least occasionally. Surely Cole couldn't be upset about what she was serving, so he must be upset about how she was serving it.

She set a saucer before Junior, then inclined her head in a polite smile. "I'm sorry. I assumed you'd want American service, but if you'd prefer European, why, I'll be happy to bring out the salads after the entrée."

Cole's eyes narrowed, displeasure shooting from their dark depths. "Are you mockin' me, Empress?"

"Why, no. I—I—" A feeling of panic swept over Josephine. *Oh, dear.* She was crazy, thinking she could pull this off. She was completely out of her element. She knew little about cooking, nothing about the eating habits of towboat crews, and even less about how to deal with this frightful man. The harder she tried to please him, the angrier he seemed to get. Josephine threw a pleading glance at Henry, hoping for help.

"We like our food all brought out at the same time," the older man explained. "An' we don't use saucers and salad plates an' such. We eat everything off one big plate."

"I see." Josephine didn't see at all, but she'd rather die than admit it. It all sounded dreadfully messy. "And what style of service would you prefer?"

Henry's brow wrinkled in confusion. "Huh?"

"Plated, formal or family-style?"

Cole muttered something dire under his breath.

Henry cut a worried glance at his boss. "Whaddya mean?"

121

"Do you want me to serve everyone's plate from the kitchen, bring the serving platters around and hold them while you serve yourselves, or place the serving platters on the table and let you pass them?"

Cole drummed his fingers impatiently on the table. Henry cast him an anxious look, as if he were a volcano about to blow. "I'll tell ya what, Miz Josephine—jes' bring ever'thin' out and let each fella fend for hisself."

Josephine glanced nervously at Cole. "All right. Could you tell me where the serving dishes are kept?"

"We ain't got none," Henry said. "The other cooks always jes' put the pots and pans on the table."

Josephine opened her mouth to protest, then abruptly shut it. *When in the land of the troglodytes, do as the troglodytes.* If these barbarians wanted to eat in dog food bowls off the floor, why, that was exactly how she'd serve them.

Retreating to the far end of the galley, she sorted through the assortment of garnishes she'd prepared, selected a delicate lemon curl, and dropped it into the middle of the pot of meatballs. With as much dignity as possible, she lifted the cheap aluminum pan from the stove and carried it to the table. She placed it directly in front of Cole as if it were a sterling platter.

He peered into the pan suspiciously, as if he halfway suspected it was filled with snakes. Josephine was gratified to see his eyebrows rise in surprise.

"Say—these actually look pretty good."

A rush of pleasure coursed through her. She'd followed the recipe exactly, and to her delight, the meatballs had turned out looking exactly like the picture in the cookbook.

Henry craned his neck and peeked in the pot. "Looks dee-licious, Miz Josie!" Sniffing appreciatively, he rubbed his hands together. "Now, where's that rice that's supposed to go with it?"

The rice. Josephine winced. The rice was a whole other

story. "I'll—I'll get it." Returning to the stove, she gingerly poked a spoon at the slimy, glutinous mass in the bottom of another battered pan. *Oh, dear.* She'd tried to follow the directions on the bag of rice, but she'd been preoccupied with thoughts of Cole and Alexa, and she'd lost count of how many cups of water she'd put in. The flour she'd added to thicken the watery rice hadn't helped much, either. Now it looked like congealed paste.

Maybe some spices would help its appearance. Grabbing a box of dried parsley off the shelf, she covered the top with a heavy layer of the dull green seasoning. There—that was better. She tossed on some paprika for added effect. *Oh, good!* The spices were even sopping up some of the extra liquid. A little yellow should make the dish look more distinctive. She sprinkled on a handful of dry mustard, then artfully placed three carrot curls in the corner.

She carried the pan to the table with what she hoped was an air of nonchalance and set it as far away from Cole as possible, hoping he'd stay preoccupied with the meatballs.

"Yum. These are great!" Henry popped another meatball in his mouth with his fingers. Pineapple sauce glistened on his chin. "What else ya got cooked up there, Josephine?"

"Hot rolls." She hoped no one would notice that the heat-and-serve rolls were missing their upper and lower crusts, which she'd whacked off with a butcher knife after burning them to a crisp. She'd swaddled what was left of the rolls like mummies in a dish towel, hoping that the amount of handling required to get at them might serve as an excuse for their misshapen appearance.

"Anything else?"

"Green beans." Although they weren't exactly green now. The only recipe for green beans in her appetizer cookbook was for batter-fried ones. She hadn't had the fresh beans the recipe called for, so she'd substituted the canned kind. And since everyone knew fried foods weren't healthy, she'd tried baking them instead. Unfortunately, the resulting batter-dipped beans had resembled soggy cigarettes. To improve their appearance, she'd liberally sprinkled them with black pepper, then drowned the whole thing in soy sauce.

She placed several lemon twists atop the limp, brownish-black green beans, telling herself the dish wasn't really that bad. It was innovative, that was what it was. Heaven only knew she'd been served some atrocious dishes by supposedly outstanding chefs, and all she'd ever heard were raves and compliments. She'd give the beans a fancy name and act as if she were serving haute cuisine.

Carrying the pan of beans in one hand and the plate of mummified rolls in the other, she marched to the table and seated herself at the empty seat opposite Cole.

Hambone stared into the pan of rice. "What the hell is this?"

"Seasoned rice."

"What's all that colored stuff?"

"That's the seasoning."

"Sure is a lot of it." Hambone squinted down at the dish, then looked up at her. "Why's it all mushy-like?"

Josephine thought fast. "It's creamed."

"Creamed?" Hambone gave a leering grin. "Ya mean like Junior's—Ow!" He cast an injured look at Henry. "Why'd ya kick me?"

"To make you shut your trap. Save your randy comments till later."

"Ah, hell. I wasn't gonna say nothin' harassin'."

"You weren't about to say anything too all-fired refined, either. Now shut up and pass some of that fancy rice down this way."

Hambone plopped an enormous amount of the multicolored rice onto his plate, then handed the pan to Henry.

Across the table, Junior struggled with the rolls. He finally unwrapped them, only to have them spill all over the floor.

Josephine was grateful for an excuse to dispose of them. She rose from her chair.

Henry waved his hand at her. "Keep your seat, there, Josephine. Junior can pick 'em up." Henry wiped his meatball-filled mouth with the back of his hand. "A little dirt won't hurt the taste."

Josephine shuddered as the gangly youth snatched the rolls off the nasty linoleum, plucking four of them from approximately the same spot where the raw bacon had fallen that morning. As germ-laden as the floor no doubt was, it probably wasn't half the health hazard of Junior's grimy hands. Josephine sank back into her chair, a wave of nausea rising in her throat.

Cole watched the proceedings from the end of the table. "Mighty funny-looking rolls, Empress."

The deprecating tone of his voice made her spine stiffen. "They're supposed to look like that."

Cole's eyebrows rose mockingly. "Oh, yeah?"

"Yes." Josephine thought fast. "They're called '*Coeurs du Pain.*' "

"Hearts of bread?"

"That's right."

"Like artichoke hearts?"

"Exactly."

"Uh-huh." His eyes narrowed. She had the uneasy sensation he wasn't fooled a bit.

She picked up her fork and poised it over her salad, but she was too nervous to eat. Her stomach knotted as she watched the beans make their way to Junior, then to Henry, then to Cole.

The captain stared down into the pot, then lifted his gaze to hers, one black eyebrow riding high on his forehead. "And what, pray tell, are these?"

Josephine's palms grew damp. *The greater the tension, the more poised the lady.* She lifted her chin. "Blackened Green Beans *Chinoiserie.*"

"Is that a fact?"

Oh, dear. He wasn't buying it. She lifted her head and imitated Aunt Prudie's most imperious tone, the one she'd always used whenever anyone questioned her on anything. "It's Cajun-Asian cuisine. It's all the rage at the better restaurants."

Cole's expression was stony. "By 'better,' I assume you mean snobbier."

She was quaking inside. To hide it, Josephine pulled her back even straighter. "I'm referring to restaurants where cuisine is considered an art form."

Cole spooned a heap of the unsightly brown mess onto his plate. "Let me see if I've got this straight. Are you telling me this here is art?"

She looked at the distasteful mound of slimy green beans. *Oh, dear.* It was too late to back down now.

She was spared from answering by a loud fit of coughing across the table. All eyes turned to Henry, who seemed to be gasping for breath. His face was red and his eyes bulged like double hernias.

Josephine's hand flew to her chest. "He's choking!"

"Looks to me like he just bit into some bad food." Cole reached over and gave the old man a hard slap on the back. Henry spat a wad of beans into his napkin, then grabbed his plastic cup of water and drained it. "Thanks, Cap'n," he said in a raspy voice. Reaching in front of Junior, he grabbed the youth's cup and drained it, as well.

"Ugh!"

Josephine whipped her head in the direction of the sound to see Gaston spew an enormous mouthful of rice directly onto his plate. Then, as she watched in horror, the swarthy man stuck out his tongue and wiped it with his napkin. "Tastes like *merde!*"

Cole slung a pointed look at Josephine, his eyes blazing darts of anger. "Culinary art, huh?"

"Well, taste is a very individual thing, and—"

"Individual, my ass. This food is inedible."

126

Henry finished draining Junior's water, then cast Josephine a sympathetic glance. "The meatballs are good," he bravely volunteered, his voice a thick rasp.

"Thank you, Henry," Josephine replied. Her only recourse was to try to bluff her way out of the situation. Tilting her head at a regal angle, she shot Cole Aunt Prudie's most disapproving look, then pointedly turned back to Henry. "I'm glad to see someone here has a sophisticated palate."

Sophisticated palate? The words made the hair on the back of Cole's neck stand up. Was this highbrow dame making fun of him? By damn, he wouldn't stand for it. He remembered all too well the last time he'd heard that phrase. It was the first time one of her kind had mocked him, and he'd burn in hell before he'd let it happen again.

It had been his first week at St. Alban's. Robert McAuley's parents had invited the entire junior class—about fifty students—to a get-acquainted party at their uptown mansion. At Mom Sawyer's urging, Cole had gone.

"It'll help you make friends and fit in," she'd urged.

Nothing about him had fit in, from his home-cut hair to his Kmart sneakers. After an hour of standing alone in the enormous living room, he'd been relieved when McAuley and a gang of his friends had approached him. After a minute or two of small talk, McAuley had offered to fix him a plate from the dining room buffet. He'd returned and handed him a tidbit of toast with something fishy-smelling smeared on it. "Try the smoked salmon. It's delicious," he'd urged.

Cole had fallen for it like a country rube. In his mind's eye, he could still hear the laughter echoing through the room. Everyone, it seemed, was in on the joke. And they'd all found it hilarious that McAuley had tricked him into eating cat food.

A nerve twitched in Cole's jaw as he glared at Josephine. "Just what the hell are you trying to pull?"

Her face grew white. "I-I'm not trying to pull anything."

He started to call her a liar, but something in her eyes stopped him. There was nothing mocking, nothing insincere in their wide blue depths—just worry and agitation.

"I-I was just trying to fix a pleasant dinner."

Cole leaned forward, both elbows on the table. "Well, you failed. Miserably. So let me tell you how it's going to be in the future." He leveled a dark glower at her. "Forget about fancy-schmancy, artsy cuisine. On this boat, we don't care what food looks like or what it's called. We only care how it tastes. We want plain, straightforward, real, honest-to-goodness food. Do you understand?"

Josephine nodded.

Cole shoved away the pots of rice and beans with his forearm. "Now get rid of all this mess and bring us some more of those meatballs."

Josephine visibly swallowed. "That's . . . that's all there is."

"That little dab is all you made?"

"The recipe said it would serve ten."

"Hell. That wouldn't serve ten pygmies." Cole shook his head in disgust. "Bring us a loaf of bread, a jar of mustard and some cold cuts. And be snappy about it."

Josephine scurried to her feet.

"Give her a break, Boss," Henry said in a low voice. "She don' know our tastes."

"Well, she's going to learn, or she's going to be put off the boat." Cole spoke to Henry, but his words were addressed to Josephine. "This is a workboat, not a luxury liner. Everyone pulls his own weight. If she can't cook food we can eat, she'll be replaced."

The look he tossed her was unyieldingly stern as she approached to pick up the pans. "You have until Natchez. We'll dock there tomorrow afternoon."

Chapter Seven

"Thanks for staying behind and helping me clean up the dinner dishes, Henry." *And showing me how to load the dishwasher*, Josephine silently added, carefully placing the last of the plastic cups into the top rack of the dishwasher as the old man had shown her. Doing the dishes this way was a whole lot easier than washing them by hand as she'd done after breakfast and lunch.

Henry leaned against the counter and reached into his shirt pocket. "I don' mind. Reminds me of how things were when Hazel was alive." Pulling out a tin of tobacco, he opened the lid. "We had a lot of good times in the kitchen."

Josephine studied the grizzled man as she dried her hands on a dish towel. "You must miss her."

A far-off look clouded Henry's eyes. He nodded somberly. "She's been gone twenty-three years, and not a day goes by that I don' wish she was here."

Josephine's heart turned over. "She was a lucky woman, having someone love her like that."

129

Henry gave a bashful smile. "Shucks, I was the lucky one."

"How long were you two married?"

"Fifteen years. Best years of my life."

"Have you ever thought about marrying again?"

"Nah." Henry pinched a wad of tobacco and stuffed it into his jaw.

"Why not?" Josephine pressed.

Henry snapped the lid on the small, flat tin and shoved it back in the pocket of his flannel shirt. "Won' never be 'nother woman like Hazel. 'Asides, who's likely to put up with the likes of me?" As if he were anxious to change the subject, Henry bent down, pulled a box of dishwashing detergent from under the sink and passed it to Josephine. "Here ya go."

She gazed at the green box uncertainly. "What do I do with this?"

"Pour some in here." Henry pointed to the cup in the open dishwasher door and eyed her curiously. "Ya never loaded a dishwasher before?"

"Not this kind." Josephine poured the dry soap where he indicated, avoiding his gaze.

"Well, I'll show ya how to turn it on." He closed the door, flipped the lock and turned the knob. The machine rumbled to life.

She gave him a grateful smile. "Thanks, Henry. I don't know what I'd do without your help."

Henry straightened and grinned. "Hey, it's in my bes' interest. I don' want you to lose your job, 'cause I hate havin' to do all this stuff myself."

Anxiety tightened Josephine's chest. "Would Cole really put me off the boat in Natchez?"

The way Henry's eyes cut away told her all she needed to know. Josephine's shoulders slumped forward, and she heaved a heavy sigh.

"Look—all ya have to do is stick to fixin' simple food,"

Henry told her. "Don' cook us any more of that there *hat cue-sine* or whatever you call it. We're just workin' folks. Don't try to impress us with a bunch of fancy grub."

"I wasn't trying to impress anyone. I was just trying to serve a nice dinner."

"I know ya was. But the cap'n don' like nothin' that reeks of high society. He's awful touchy 'bout rich folks an' their ways an' all."

Josephine sighed. "Seems to me he's awfully touchy, period."

Henry reached out and awkwardly patted her shoulder. "Well, don' let him scare you. His bark is worse than his bite."

Josephine was far from convinced.

Henry gave her a lopsided smile that she knew was meant to be encouraging. "Ever'thin' will be all right, Miz Josie. The cap'n's always fair. Even if worse comes to worst an' he puts ya off the boat, he'll pay ya for the days you worked and give ya bus fare back to New Orleans."

"I'm afraid two days' wages won't be much help." Not when she was facing life without a car, a job or a place to live, she thought dismally.

"Well, all ya have to do is cook a couple of good meals, an' ya won' have anythin' to worry about."

That was easier said than done. Besides, Josephine thought glumly, the captain disliked her so intensely that he'd probably find fault with her if she cooked like Betty Crocker. Unless she could figure out a way to change his attitude toward her, she was sunk.

Her thoughts were interrupted by the creak of the galley door. She turned around to see Hambone and Junior saunter in.

Dismay flooded Josephine's chest. "Don't tell me they're hungry again," she said in a low voice to Henry.

The old man cackled. "Prob'ly so, but you don' have to worry about it. They'll jus' help themselves to some chips an' nuts an' such." He pointed to a dusty TV mounted on the wall in the fashion one might expect to see in a third-rate hotel. "They're here to watch the big fight."

Josephine gazed up at the TV. She'd noticed it earlier, but it was so filthy she'd assumed it didn't work. "You get television reception out here on the river?"

"Oh, yeah. Cap'n's got a state-of-the-art satellite dish on top o' the boat that picks up all kinds of channels."

Hambone reached up and grabbed the remote control from the top of the TV, exposing a large stained circle in the armpit of his dirty T-shirt. A second later, the image of a topless woman riding a motorcycle filled the screen.

"All right!" Junior yelled.

Grinning like a jack-o'-lantern, Hambone lowered himself onto the bench at the dining table, never taking his eyes from the woman's bare chest.

Josephine couldn't take her eyes away, either. She'd never seen anything so immense in her life. The poor woman was practically deformed. Josephine stared, open-mouthed, as the woman's enormous breasts surged upward as she raced over a speed bump.

Henry cut her a sheepish look and smiled apologetically. " 'Course, some of the channels are raunchier than others." He strode to the table, snatched the remote control from Hambone's fist and changed the channel. "There's a lady present," he chided. "If ya wanna look at that kinda stuff, go to your cabin and read a magazine."

"Aw, Henry," Junior whined.

"It's time for the fight, anyway." Henry surfed through the channels, stopping on the image of a heavyset man climbing through the ropes of a boxing ring. Junior settled himself on the bench beside Hambone. Henry started to sit in the chair Cole had occupied at dinner, then paused halfway down. "Wanna join us?" he asked Josephine. "It's supposed to be a good fight. Mad Dog there in the black cape splintered his last opponent's jaw, and the other guy's known for breakin' noses."

The thought of watching two men smash in each other's faces was about as appealing as the prospect of spending time in the company of Hambone and Junior. Josephine shook her head. "Thank you, Henry, but I believe I'll take a stroll around the deck." Hanging the dishcloth over the faucet, she headed to the door. She had the uneasy sensation that several pairs of eyes followed her.

"She's sure got a nice booty," Hambone remarked in a loud whisper.

"Yeah, but you know what *else* she's got," Junior muttered. "Like Henry said, we best not be messin' with her."

Josephine couldn't repress a smile. Bless Henry's heart—he must have told Hambone and Junior that she had some kind of weapon and wouldn't hesitate to use it. That must be why the deckhands had kept their distance since this morning.

She stepped into the cool, dark night, closing the hatch behind her. She could handle Hambone, Junior and even Gaston. She genuinely liked Henry, and Pete was not a problem. She'd met the large, silent man when she'd taken his dinner to the pilothouse, and he hadn't even pulled his eyes away from the river.

No, the captain was the only crew member who worried her. And he worried her practically to death.

The boat lurched to the left, making her grab the lever of the closed hatch. There was no railing around the edge of the deck, nothing to keep her from falling into the river except for the knee-high metal bulwark. Groping the side of the boat, she slowly made her way to the long bench where Cole had carried her after the fire.

The memory of his arms around her made her shiver. It was most disconcerting, the way she kept having these carnal thoughts about him! Deliberately turning her attention to the scenery, Josephine lowered herself to the bench and gazed out at the night. She inhaled deeply, savoring the musty scent of the river and the peaceful quiet of the night. In spite of the roar of the boat engine, she could hear water sloshing against the side of the boat, hear the wind whistling past her ears. She watched the lights beyond the levee, enjoying the sensation of movement.

It felt good to finally be going somewhere. It seemed as if she'd been in a holding pattern for years, as if her whole life up till now had been in a long, tedious wait. The problem was, she'd never known exactly what it was she was waiting for. She still didn't know. She knew only that at long last, things finally seemed to be under way.

Too bad they were going in a strictly downhill direction, Josephine thought ruefully. Unless she drastically improved her cooking skills or managed to change Cole's opinion of her, she'd be set ashore in Natchez.

A knot of fear formed in her chest. She needed the money she'd earn from this job in order to be able to start a new life. She had to figure out a way to stay. She'd pore over that cookbook before she went to bed, she thought determinedly, and she'd get up two hours early to start fixing breakfast. And the next time she saw Cole, she'd try everything she could think of to establish some kind of rapport with him.

The wind whipped at Josephine's hair, loosening strands from the neatly coiled bun. She tucked a wisp behind her ear and gazed out at the night. For a few moments, she wanted to forget about Cole Dumanski, forget about all her inadequacies, forget about the sad state of her financial affairs. For a few moments, she wanted to lose herself in the sheer pleasure of drifting through the night.

The bright lights of a two-story, white clapboard house beyond the levee caught her eye. As a child, she used to look at houses and imagine what it would be like to live there—to be part of a real family, the kind where people laughed and hugged and lived together. She'd been at boarding schools practically her whole life. A home of her own, a home where she was wanted and belonged, had always been her fondest dream. It still was, she thought wistfully.

She watched smoke float into the night sky from the house's chimney and let her imagination float with it. The little window under the eaves might be a nursery. Maybe the lady of the house had just rocked her baby to sleep. Maybe she'd tucked the infant gently into a cozy crib, kissed the child's soft cheek, then joined her husband in front of the fire in the living room.

The room would be dark except for the leaping flames in the hearth. The man would put his arm around the woman and draw her close. She would turn, and the man would claim her lips in a hot, possessive kiss. He'd have dark eyes and thick black hair, and his arms would feel as muscled and hard as tree trunks around her.

With a start, Josephine realized the man in her fantasy was Cole. The realization made her stiffen.

Cole was hardly the domestic type, she scolded herself. Instead of spinning ridiculous fantasies about him, she needed to be figuring out how to convince him to let her keep her job.

A gust of cold wind whipped down the deck, loosening another strand of her hair. She wrapped her arms around herself and rubbed her upper arms. She was freezing, but she wasn't ready to go back inside. Maybe the back of the boat would provide some protection from the wind.

She rose from the bench and carefully made her way down the deck. As she neared the end, she heard a loud clink, followed by a deep grunt. Startled, she stopped and peered around the corner. The deck was flooded with light from the deck above, and the sight illuminated there made her heart catch in her throat.

Cole—wearing nothing but a pair of brief navy shorts, straining under the weight of an enormous barbell. Her stomach fluttered madly. *Dear heavens*. She'd seen pictures of muscular men in the beefcake calendars some of her students used to sneak into the finishing school dormi-

135

tory, but she'd never seen anything like this.

She stared, unable to pull her eyes away, as he hoisted the barbell over his head, his arms extended. The man was all muscle. His pectorals bunched and his biceps bulged. His thighs, his stomach and his calves looked as if they'd been carved from stone. He looked like Atlas holding up the world.

Even more intimidating than his physique, however, was the look of absolute, unwavering determination on his face.

A shiver chased through her as she watched. After long seconds, he lowered the barbell, letting it fall with a heavy thud. Josephine stared, mesmerized by the way his muscles rippled. She watched as he strode to a complicated-looking weight machine and adjusted the weights on it. She continued to gaze at him as he walked toward her and pulled a towel off a bench near where she stood. Too late, she realized he was less than three feet away from her. She started to turn and flee, but before she could, he looked up.

His forehead immediately furrowed. "What are you doing out here?"

Heat rushed to Josephine's face. She felt like a Peeping Tom who'd just been caught. "I—I'm sorry. I didn't mean to interrupt you." She again turned to leave.

Cole reached out and grabbed her arm, his face lined in a scowl. "When I ask you a question, I expect you to answer."

His hand felt like a manacle around her. "I-I just thought I'd get some fresh air. I didn't know you were out here. I didn't mean to bother you."

He released his grip on her arm. The warmth of his hand on her skin remained. So did his dark frown.

The dislike on his face was so intense she could feel it. She had to do something to change his opinion of him, and fast. A piece of charm school advice flashed in her mind: *The fastest way to establish rapport with a new acquaintance is to inquire about his or her interests.* She flashed her most congenial smile. "I didn't know you lifted weights."

He mopped his face with the towel and lifted a brawny shoulder in a shrug. "It's a way of letting off steam. It can get physically confining, being cooped up on the boat." His eyes raked her over. "Do you work out?"

Josephine felt as if he were looking straight through her clothes, evaluating the condition of her body. Alarm crackled through her, making her want to turn and run to her cabin. There was something dangerous about this man, about this whole situation. She remembered the look of determination on his face when he'd lifted the barbell.

He was used to getting whatever he wanted. What if he decided he wanted *her*?

The thought made her belly quiver. She was being ridiculous, she told herself sternly. The man seemed to hate her guts. She forced her thoughts back to the question he'd just posed.

"I've never worked out on weights, but Aunt Prudie had a treadmill. I used to walk three miles a day on that."

Cole pulled the towel around his neck. "We don't have one of those, but I let the crew use the weight machine."

Josephine gazed at it uncertainly. "I have no idea how it works."

"It adjusts to work out different muscle groups. If you're still aboard after Natchez, I'll show you." Tossing the towel back on the metal bench, he adjusted something at the front of the machine, then climbed onto the seat, grabbed some pulleys and began doing something that looked like rowing exercises.

If you're still aboard after Natchez. It didn't sound like he expected her to make the cut. Desperation seized her. She couldn't let him fire her. She'd try harder to get him talking. "Were you involved in athletics at school?" she ventured.

Cole's mouth curved into a sardonic grin. "Yeah, Empress. I was first string on the St. Alban's garbage-lifting team."

Chagrin poured through her. Swallowing hard, she tried again. "When did you start lifting weights?"

"In jail."

Oh, dear. She was striking out all around. She didn't know what to do except press forward. "Was it a required activity, or did you take it up as a hobby?"

For a long moment, she thought he wasn't going to answer. "At first it was just a way to pass time, but then I discovered being in shape helped me hold my own," he finally said, never interrupting the rhythmic clink of the weights. "I was skinny as a rail when I went in there."

She watched his arm muscles constrict and bulge as he pulled on the pulleys. "It's hard to imagine you that way."

His chest pectorals undulated hypnotically. "Yeah, well, I used to be a real beanpole. In fact, 'Beanpole' was one of the more flattering names I used to be called at good ol' St. Alban's."

There was nothing beanlike about him now, Josephine thought, her mouth suddenly dry. She forced her eyes away from the dark curls on his chest and searched for something to say. "Sounds like you really hated going there."

Cole's expression suddenly grew closed. "Your friends didn't exactly make it a picnic for me."

Your friends—he must mean Alexa and Robert. If she could get him to open up and tell her what they'd done, maybe it would help dispel his anger. At the very least, maybe it would help him see how unfair it was to hold her responsible for their actions. "You said Robert framed you."

"Yeah."

"What did he do?"

Cole stopped rowing. Sliding off the machine, he grabbed the towel and whipped it around his neck.

"It's not something I talk about."

"Why not?"

"Because it's in the past." Besides, it was too futile, too

138

frustrating. Cole's hand tightened on the towel. Talking about it only filled him with rage—hot, hungry, voracious rage, an all-consuming rage that ate him from the inside out.

But hell—he was feeling that rage right now anyhow. By God, it wouldn't hurt the Empress to know what kind of people she'd been palling around with. He turned and looked at her through narrowed eyes. "It's not pretty. Are you sure you want to hear it?"

"I'm sure." She lowered herself on top of the capstan and primly crossed her legs.

She looked like Little Miss Muffet on a tuffet, seated so prissily on the giant stool the crew used for winding line. Well, the earful he was about to give her was likely to knock her right off it. Damned if he wouldn't take some satisfaction in doing just that.

"It all started right after Mardi Gras my junior year." Cole's voice was flat and emotionless, but his insides churned like the towboat's wake. He strode toward the railing that surrounded the aft deck, the only railing on the boat, and gazed down at the boiling water. "Alexa dropped a note in my lap during fifth-hour English. 'Meet me in Audubon Park tonight,' it said. 'Eight-thirty by the Nashville Street entrance. Don't tell anyone.' " His mouth pressed in a hard line. "That last part was underlined."

"Did you go?" Josephine asked.

Cole gave a mirthless grin. "You don't know much about sixteen-year-old boys, darlin', if you have to ask a question like that."

He was gratified to see a look of embarrassment color her face. "Did you keep it quiet?" she asked.

"Who was I going to tell? Alexa was the most popular girl at school, and I was Beanpole the Trash Boy. No one would have believed me."

"What about your foster mother?"

Cole shook his head. "Mom Sawyer worked on the night janitorial staff in the skyscraper Alexa's father owned.

She'd have been worried sick if she'd known I was foolin' around with her boss's daughter, and I never wanted to do anything to worry Mom. She was the only person who ever gave a damn about me." He turned and leaned against the railing, his eyes on the right shore, his thoughts drifting back.

"What happened?"

"Alexa showed up carrying a folded blanket, and she led me to a tiny gardener's shack hidden in a thick stand of azalea bushes. She pushed aside some branches, and there was an unlocked door. The building was so small we had to bend down to go into it. It had evidently been used to store equipment. It had a concrete floor, and it was completely empty."

Cole raked a hand through his hair, remembering. He could still see the way the soft light from a nearby street lamp had filtered through the leaf-shrouded window, could still smell the way Alexa's perfume had mingled with the musty scent of the closed-up little building.

"How did you find this place?" he'd asked Alexa.

She'd tossed her dark hair over her shoulder in that flirtatious way she had. "I used to play here all the time when I was little. I'd hide in here if I wanted to get rid of a nanny."

"Get rid of one? What do you mean?"

"My parents would fire any nanny who lost track of me. So if one of them wouldn't let me have my way, I'd hide in here, and voilà." Alexa waved a dismissive hand.

Cole had immediately thought of Mom Sawyer, working the night shift at Alexa's father's building, struggling to make ends meet. It would have devastated her to lose her job. Alexa's nannies must have been in similar situations.

"Didn't it bother you, getting them fired?" he'd asked.

"Why should it?"

"Because they probably have bills to pay and families to feed."

"That isn't *my* problem."

The indifference in her voice had sent prickles of alarm coursing up his spine. He'd started to say something, but Alexa was stretching out on the blanket, her pert breasts thrusting upward, and the words had frozen in his throat.

"Come here," she'd murmured, reaching out her arms.

The way her breasts had strained against the fabric of her white schoolgirl's blouse had swept all coherent thought from his mind. He'd pushed his uneasiness aside and let her draw him into a kiss that had revved his teenage hormones to a loud roar.

That had been his second mistake, he thought now, staring out at the water. His first was agreeing to meet Alexa in the park in the first place.

"What happened in the shack?" Josephine asked.

Cole shot her an amused look. "What do you think happened, Empress?"

Her lips parted, clamped shut, then parted again. Her eyes grew wide.

Cole grinned.

Josephine's brows pulled together. "Just like that? You didn't go to dinner or a movie or anything? You just . . . "

There was something immensely satisfying about shocking this prim bluestocking. Cole's grin widened. "What's the matter, Empress? Didn't we fulfill all the etiquette requirements for polite fornication?"

Even in the dim lighting of the aft deck, he could see her color. Her neck moved as she swallowed. "It just seems awfully fast, that's all."

Cole couldn't help but laugh. "You have no idea how fast, Empress. After all, I was just a sixteen-year-old boy."

And Alexa had had the skills of an experienced call girl. Cole rubbed his forehead with the towel, remembering the way Alexa had worked him into a lather.

"I've seen you looking at me," she'd purred, easing herself onto her side and splaying her fingers across his chest.

141

"Do you like what you see?"

Had he ever. He'd given a nervous smile and nodded, acutely aware of Alexa's thumb stroking his nipple through his cotton shirt. His body had immediately responded.

"Would you like to see more?" Her fingers moved down his chest and across his stomach, stopping just above his crotch.

All he could manage was another speechless nod.

"You can look, but don't touch." She withdrew her hand and slowly unbuttoned her blouse, moving with the deliberate seductiveness of a professional stripper. Cole's mouth had gone dry as she'd eased the white cotton from her shoulders, revealing two dusky nipples pointing through the sheer fabric of a lacy pink bra. Slowly, slowly, she'd unfastened the clasp, releasing her full, white breasts to his gaze.

Then she'd slowly unzipped the green-and-blue plaid skirt, the one she wore shorter and tighter than any of the other girls at school, until she was wearing only a tiny wisp of sheer pink panties. By the time she'd wriggled out of them, he'd spent himself in his jeans.

Cole had been embarrassed, but Alexa had been pleased. "Now you can touch."

Cole's confusion must have registered on his face, because she'd given a husky laugh. "I like it to last," she'd explained.

So Cole had touched—and stroked and kissed and nibbled as Alexa did the same to him.

Josephine's voice again broke into his thoughts. "Weren't you afraid someone would catch you?"

Cole grinned lasciviously. "My thoughts were on other things."

"But . . . but what about Alexa?"

"She was pretty busy, too."

"But getting caught would have ruined her chances to be

Queen of Rex. I don't understand why she'd take such a risk."

I just bet you don't. Cole's eyes raked over Josephine, taking in her tightly pulled-back hair, her shapeless jacket, her stiff posture. *But I'd sure like to show you.*

The thought annoyed him. Josephine wasn't his type at all. He went for hot-blooded women, not icy schoolmarms.

Only problem was, he was beginning to suspect that underneath all those layers of proper clothes and proper behavior, Miss Josephine Evans wasn't icy at all. He remembered the way she'd clung when she'd fallen against him while getting on the boat. His fingers tightened on the railing.

"It's hard to imagine Alexa being so reckless," she murmured, her eyes wide and fascinated.

For such a proper young woman, Josephine sure was interested in off-color behavior. Well, if she wanted to know more, he'd damn sure tell her.

"I'll let you in on a little secret about Alexa," Cole said brusquely. "Danger excited her."

He rubbed his jaw, remembering. He'd been poised above her that first night, eager and panting, aching for entrance to paradise. Alexa had teasingly pulled her thighs together.

"Tell me something before we go any further." Her voice had been a sultry murmur. "Is it true that your father's a murderer?"

Cole's heart had frozen in his chest. Mom Sawyer had gone to great lengths to keep his father's identity a secret. Cole had used his given name, Collin, and was even enrolled at school under Mom's last name to avoid being connected in any way with the murderer whose name he bore. "Where did you hear that?"

"In the school office. I overheard Sister Magdalena telling one of the other nuns." Alexa lifted her hips, rubbing herself against him in a way that made his blood roar.

"I think it's soooo exciting." She squirmed intimately against him. "Is it true?"

His teenage body had throbbed with need. "Yeah, it's true."

Alexa's soft thighs had parted, and he'd thrust his way to hot, slick completion.

Josephine's voice cut through the memory. "How long did you and Alexa go out together?"

Cole gave a derisive snort. "We never went out, Empress. We just screwed."

Cole heard her sharp intake of breath. If she thought that was shocking, Cole thought darkly, wait till she heard the full truth about her high-society friend. He pressed on, his voice hard.

"Sorry if it offends you, Empress, but that's the way it was. The way Alexa insisted on it being. At school, she used to pretend she didn't even know me."

Josephine stared at him, her eyes wide.

"It was play by her rules, or don't play at all. I had to wait for her to pass me a note, telling me when to meet her in the park." A bitter taste crept into Cole's mouth. "She held all the cards, and her deck just kept getting larger and larger. Every time we'd meet, she'd ask questions about my life. She wanted to hear all the dirt about me—the details of my father's crime, how many foster homes I'd lived in, and so on. Pretty soon she knew just about everything about me, but she'd never tell me anything about herself. And at school, she acted like I was invisible."

"That must have hurt," Josephine said softly.

Hurt didn't begin to describe it. The first few times after he'd been with Alexa, he'd floated home, certain there was nothing he couldn't do, nothing he couldn't be. If he could have Alexa Armand, he could have anything at all. He'd been certain that he loved her, and he'd been desperate for her to feel the same.

So each time he met her in the park, he gave away a little more of himself, naively interpreting her curiosity as concern, blindly hoping her interest meant she cared for him. And each time, he'd almost manage to convince himself she did, because his revelations were always followed by torrid, almost violent sex.

But each time afterward, she'd leave him as dispassionately as if he were a paid employee, then completely ignore him the next day.

It had started to eat at his soul. "I started pressing her to go out with me in public after about three months," Cole found himself saying. "That's when she wanted to call things off. Her little 'meet me' notes stopped coming. I tried to phone her, but she wouldn't take my calls. I went to her house to see her, but the maid wouldn't let me in. So one day I blew up and cornered her in the hall at school, right in front of Robert McAuley and some other kids. She finally agreed to meet me that night in the park." Cole turned and faced the water again, his fingers tightly coiled on the railing.

"Of course, she stood me up. I should have known she'd only agreed to get rid of me, but hope springs eternal in the heart of a lovesick boy." His mouth twisted sardonically. "I waited two hours, but she never came."

He could still remember the way he'd felt, as if someone had cut him open and ripped out his heart. He'd tried to tell himself that he should be grateful for the time he'd had with her, thankful that Alexa had ever given him the time of day, but try as he might, he hadn't felt grateful. He'd felt wounded to the depths of his soul.

"On the way home, I ran into McAuley. He'd overheard part of my conversation with Alexa, and he'd shown up to taunt me. 'Jesus, Trash Boy,' he said, 'don't you know when someone's putting you on? Do you really think a girl like Alexa would ever have anything to do with the likes of you?' One thing led to another, and we ended up in a fist-fight."

Cole's muscles tensed as he stared out at the dark river, remembering. He remembered how the air had smelled, full of night jasmine and magnolias, so sweet it hurt. He could almost hear the crack of his fist smashing into McAuley's face, almost feel the pain in his knuckles, almost see the heavy redhead sprawled on the ground. But the memory he recalled most clearly was the vicious, almost overwhelming urge to throw himself on top of McAuley and beat him into oblivion.

It had taken all of Cole's self-control to turn and walk away, but he'd made himself do it. He'd been afraid of what he'd do if he stayed. He'd been afraid of the rage in his chest, afraid that the bad blood he'd inherited from his father would overpower him, afraid that once he started beating McAuley, he wouldn't be able to stop.

"Were either of you hurt?" Josephine asked.

"We banged each other up pretty good. We both got black eyes, and I bloodied McAuley's nose."

"What did your foster mother say when you came home with a black eye?"

"She worked the night shift, so she wasn't there. I crawled into bed and fell asleep." The memories were coming faster now, growing more intense, more painful. "The next thing I knew, Mom was shaking me awake. 'There're people here, and they want to ask you some questions,' she said.

"I could barely open my eyes—the right one was nearly swollen shut. But something in Mom's voice jerked me awake real fast, so I sat up and squinted." Cole's chest grew heavy as the memories flooded in like water on a sinking ship. "Three cops were standing in my bedroom. And right behind them were McAuley and his father."

He started to sweat again. Cole ran the towel over his face. "I'll never forget the way McAuley pointed at me. 'See?' he said. 'I told you I gave him a black eye when I grabbed away his gun.'

" 'Gun?' I said. 'What the hell are you talking about?'

"The oldest cop, a big guy with a big potbelly, looked at me like I was the scum of the earth. 'Young Mr. McAuley here says you held him up at gunpoint in Audubon Park tonight. Says you took his wallet and his watch. He told us you wore a ski mask, but he recognized your voice and your shoes.' "

"Oh, how awful," Josephine said softly.

"I'll never forget the way McAuley just stood there and smirked. I wanted to kill the lousy SOB. Mom and a policeman had to restrain me." Cole's heart was pounding hard just thinking about it. "See, the one thing Mom had begged me to promise when I went to live with her was that I'd never get in trouble with the law. I'd promised I wouldn't. Hell, the last thing I wanted was to be like my old man. And here was this jerk trying to set me up." Cole shook his head, the old anger bubbling in his chest. He drew a breath and continued.

"That fat old cop narrowed his eyes until he looked like a mole. 'If you've got nothing to hide, then you won't mind if we search the house,' he said.

" 'Go right ahead,' I told him.

"I stood by Mom against the wall while they searched my room. I knew I hadn't done anything, so I wasn't worried. I had my arm around Mom, trying to reassure her. I remember that she was trembling."

Cole had been trembling, too, he recalled, but not with fear. He remembered standing there in nothing but his jockey shorts, vibrating with anger, impotent to do anything about it.

"I remember thinking it was all going to be okay. They'd find nothing, and they'd leave." Cole's muscles tensed. "And then they lifted the mattress."

Even after all this time, the memory made it hard to breathe. He swallowed hard. "On top of the old, yellowed box spring lay a bright red ski mask, a brown leather wallet, a gold watch and a gun."

"Oh, no," Josephine said with a gasp.

"Oh, yes." Cole's voice was hard.

"What did you do?"

"What could I do? I'd been framed. I remember feeling like I couldn't breathe, like I was about to puke."

"Did you tell them you didn't put those things there?"

"Oh, yeah, I told them. But who do you think they believed—the son of one of the wealthiest, most influential men in town, or the son of a convicted murderer?"

Josephine's fingers covered her mouth. "Oh, Cole. How awful."

"It was awful, all right. And you know what was the worst part? The look on Mom's face."

He'd never forget that until the day he died. Mom was the only person who'd ever believed in him, and he'd let her down. The pain in her eyes had sucked the air from his lungs and all the goodness from his soul.

"We're going to have to take you in, boy," Cole remembered the taller officer saying.

Cole had gazed pleadingly at Mom. "I didn't do it. I swear it! I didn't do anything!"

What happened next was now a jumble of disjointed impressions—the cold metal of the handcuffs on his wrists, the sickening clink as they locked into place, the struggle to pull on a pair of pants with his hands cuffed together, the drone of an officer's voice reading him his rights.

But as he was led away, a police officer on either side of him, two things had registered clearly, two things that were destined to haunt him forever—McAuley's vicious grin, and Mom's gray, grief-stricken face.

"That was the last time I ever saw Mom," Cole said grimly. "She died of a heart attack three days later. Because I wasn't a blood relative, they wouldn't even let me go to her funeral." He stood abruptly and stared out at the water. "McAuley killed her. She was one of the best people who ever lived, and McAuley killed her."

McAuley had killed something inside of Cole, too, Josephine thought somberly, her heart aching with sympathy. Cole had promised Mom Sawyer he'd never get in trouble with the law. It must have crushed his soul to know she'd died thinking he'd broken his word.

Josephine rose from her seat on the capstan, wanting to comfort him, not knowing how. His broad back was turned toward her. She reached out her hand to touch him, then let it drop at her side. "You served time for something you didn't do."

Cole remained as still as a statue. "I didn't even fight it. My court-appointed attorney advised me not to. He said I didn't stand a prayer if it went to trial, that I'd get out sooner if I just pled guilty and took a reduced sentence. I would have fought it with everything I had if Mom had been alive, but after she died, it just didn't seem to matter."

No wonder he was angry and bitter, Josephine thought soberly. No wonder he hated McAuley. No wonder he held a grudge against all New Orleanians with position and money.

"The only thing that kept me going during the two years I was in that hellhole was thinking about McAuley and how I was going to get even."

"Hatred always hurts the one who feels it more than the one it's directed at," Josephine said softly.

"Maybe that's because I haven't sufficiently directed it at McAuley yet."

Josephine watched him for a long, silent moment. "Are you planning to?"

He didn't answer. He continued to stare out at the river. When he turned around, his dark eyes were mocking. "I bet I know what you're about to say. 'Revenge is mine, saith the Lord.' "

The words had been running through Josephine's mind, but she had no urge to say them aloud. She'd had the Good Word shoved down her throat too many times ever to want to force-feed it to someone else. "It's not up to me to tell you what to do," she said softly.

Cole gave a coarse laugh. "Damn right. But that hasn't stopped you so far." He looked above her head at the lights of an approaching towboat, his eyes hard, his expression distant. "The way I see it, the Lord has had fourteen long years to even the score, and he hasn't lifted a finger. Maybe it's time I took matters into my own hands."

The approaching boat gave a short blast of its horn, breaking the quiet. Cole slung the towel over one shoulder and turned toward the stern. "Well, if you'll excuse me, Empress, I believe I've have had all the pleasant chitchat about our mutual friends that I can stand for one evening."

He stalked off into the shadows, the white towel gleaming against his tanned skin. Josephine watched him go, her heart filled with an odd pain and a strange, unnamed longing.

Chapter Eight

Henry hit the remote control, blackening the TV screen, then stood up and stretched. "That was the most disappointin' fight I've seen in a while."

"Yeah. No one was unconscious for more than a just few minutes." Hambone scooted back on the bench, dragging Junior with him.

The scrawny teenager shuffled to his feet, nodding agreement. "No teeth knocked out, no ears bitten off, nothin.' Hardly any blood at all."

"Well, that's the way it goes sometimes." Henry gave a mournful shake of his head, then looked at the beefy man. "Hambone, you're on the night shift, so you might as well get to work. Check the lines on the tow every hour. The cap'n says the top deck needs paintin', so get it scraped and primed. Mop all the decks, too, and clean off the portholes. By the time the sun comes up in the mornin', I want to be blinded by the shine."

"Aw, Henry. What's the point in cleanin' everythin' up when it's just gonna get dirty all over again?"

151

Henry had often thought the same thing himself, but Cole insisted on maintaining the exterior of the boat, the wheelhouse and the captain's cabin in tiptop order. "That's how the cap'n wants it, so that's how it's gonna be."

Hambone gave a long sigh. Henry picked up the coffee can that served as his portable spittoon and started for the door.

"Hey, Henry," Hambone called.

The old man paused and turned back around.

"I been thinkin' about what you said about the cook."

It was always a dangerous thing when Hambone got to thinking. Henry frowned. "What do you mean?"

"You know, 'bout her havin' that incurable clap and all. I was just wondering if maybe you was putting us on."

Henry froze. "Now, why would you think a thing like that?"

Hambone shrugged a lumpy shoulder. "I dunno. I just never heard nothin' 'bout no incurable clap before."

"Me, neither," Junior chimed in. "None of my magazines ever mentioned it."

"Hell, Junior, you don't know if they mentioned it or not," Henry scoffed. "In order to know a thing like that, you'd have to read the articles, not just look at the pictures."

"I *do* read 'em! I always read the letters from the horny women in the Nympho's Corner."

"He does." Hambone nodded solemnly. "Sometimes he reads 'em aloud to me."

"Hell, those aren't real letters from real women." Henry spit in his coffee can. "That stuff's all made up. It's prob'ly written by some drag queen in Brooklyn wearin' panty hose and a feather boa."

"That's not so!" Junior's chin jutted out stubbornly. He reminded Henry of a kid not yet ready to stop believing in Santa Claus.

Henry lifted his shoulders. "Look, you can believe what

you want. Don' make no never mind to me." He again started for the door.

"So *were* you puttin' us on?" Hambone persisted. "'Bout Miz Josephine, I mean."

Damn. Henry affected a wounded look. "Here I am, doin' my best to look out for you boys, and this is the thanks I get? If I didn't know better, I'd think you were doubtin' my word."

Hambone shifted uncomfortably. "I didn' mean to insult you or nothin'. I was just wonderin' how you came to know a thing like that. I mean, it's not the sort of thing a lady like her seems likely to just up and say."

Henry scratched his chin, thinking fast. "It was, uh, in her medical records."

"Medical records?" Hambone's forehead creased. "Since when did the captain start requirin' medical records?"

"You know he makes me give all crew members drug tests." Cole had never asked him to test the cooks, but the deckhands had no way of knowing that. "When Josephine took hers, she had to list all the medications she takes. She ev'dently takes somethin' to control her condition. It don' cure it, mind you, but it keeps her from havin' symptoms."

"Ohhh." Hambone nodded wisely, as if the explanation made perfect sense. "An' the captain's not worried?"

Hell. He didn't want Junior and Hambone relayin' this whopper to the cap'n. Cole was bristly as a prickly pear where Josephine was concerned, and there was no telling how he might take it. Henry ran a hand nervously across his chin whiskers. "I didn't tell him, and I don't want you to, either. It's my job to handle things like this, and there's no need to bother him about it."

Hambone knit his forehead, as if he were thinking hard.

Henry frowned. "Ya look like you're about to strain your brain, son. What's on your mind?"

"Nothin'. I was just wonderin' if her underwear's contagious."

Henry narrowed his eyes. "Now lookee here, Hambone, if you're plannin' to steal any of her undies, I swear I'm gonna—"

"Oh, I wasn't plannin' that." The innocent look Hambone tried to affect wouldn't have fooled a newborn. "I was just wonderin' 'bout the, uh—uh, laundry. You know, if it's safe for her to wash her stuff in the same machine we use."

Henry shot him a knowing glance. "You got nothin' to worry about, seein' as how you never change your clothes, let alone wash 'em."

"I sometimes do," Junior piped up.

Henry cast him a doubtful look.

"Well, I do." Junior's almost nonexistent jaw jutted out defensively. "I wash my clothes every four weeks, right before we dock back in New Orleans. So I need to know if the washer's safe."

The old man scowled. "Hell, yes, it's safe. Everything about her is perfec'ly safe long as you don' mess with her directly. Now, if you two chuckleheads are through askin' stupid questions, I'm gonna take my tired ol' bones to bed." Henry shuffled out the door, but not before he glimpsed another thoughtful look on Hambone's face. He pulled the door closed behind him and shook his head. It was always a bad sign when Hambone got to thinking.

Josephine stared into the large bowl the next morning, her brows creased in a frown. After her experience trying to thicken the rice last night, she knew better than to veer from the written instructions. She was exactly following the recipe for crepes, hoping to pass them off as pancakes, but the batter looked awfully runny.

She couldn't afford any more culinary disasters. She needed to cook a delicious breakfast and a scrumptious lunch in order to keep this job, and she intended to do just that.

Keeping the job had come to mean more to her than money. She knew it was irrational, but she wanted to prove to Cole that she could do it. There was no logical reason why she should care, no reason why Cole's opinion of her should matter in the least, but it did.

A psychologist would probably say she had a deep-seated need for approval because she'd never gotten it from Prudie or her father, she thought glumly. Both of them had gone to their graves with a low opinion of her.

And Cole's opinion seemed even lower. For some reason, it stirred a desire within her for vindication. She wanted to prove to him that she was reliable, competent and trustworthy. By proving it to him, maybe she could finally prove it to herself.

There was only one problem, she thought forlornly: she wasn't any of those things. Not when it came to cooking, anyway.

Well, that was all the more reason to do her level best, she thought with determination. Wiping her hands on a dish towel, she consulted the cookbook. *Grease and heat pan. Drop two tablespoons of batter into pan. Tilt pan quickly to cover bottom. Turn crepe and brown other side.*

Josephine pulled on a worn brown oven mitt and set to work. It took her five tries before she managed to turn a crepe without ruining it, but at last she managed. Her chest swelled with pride as she finally slid a respectable-looking crepe onto a serving plate.

Her smile rapidly faded into a worried frown. It was a great-looking crepe, but a lousy-looking pancake. It was as thin as a sheet of paper.

Well, she'd make a whole lot of them, pile them high and hope no one noticed. The problem was, it was going to take about a million crepes to make a sizable stack, and it was already five-thirty. She'd better use two pans and cook them two at a time.

At least the bacon was already prepared, she thought, bending and retrieving another skillet from the cabinet. She'd cooked two dozen slabs in the microwave, and she was proud of the way they'd turned out. After burning the first batch, she'd checked the next plateful every few seconds until they were done.

The eggs should be nearly done, too. She'd put three dozen in the largest pan she could find and covered them with water and a lid. They'd been boiling for the last half-hour.

Josephine set the second pan of crepes on the stove just as the door banged open. Hambone stepped into the galley, his missing teeth giving him a jack-o-lantern grin. "Mornin'."

"Good morning."

He hitched his pants and strutted into the room as if he were God's gift to women. "How ya feelin' this morning?"

It was an odd question, but it seemed well-intended. Josephine managed a pleasant smile. "Fine, thank you. And you?"

"Whew! I'm beat." Hambone seated himself at the dining table. His jeans rode down to expose a disgusting amount of cheek and cleavage. "Been workin' the night shift."

Josephine averted her eyes from the repulsive sight and focused on flipping the crepes. "I didn't know you worked shifts."

"Oh, yeah. Junior or me is on duty pretty much 'round the clock. We knock off for meals and for a few hours here and there if we're not pickin' up a load of barges or nothin', but otherwise, one or the other of us is always takin' care of things."

Josephine slid a crepe out of the pan, searching her mind for something to say. "Do you usually take the night shift?"

Hambone nodded. "Keeps me in shape for when I'm shoreside."

"In shape?"

He winked suggestively. "For stayin' up all night makin' the ladies happy, if you know what I mean."

Dear heavens. Josephine concentrated on evenly distributing a fresh layer of batter in the pan, wishing she'd never asked.

"I bet you miss that," Hambone remarked.

The pan froze in Josephine's hand. "I beg your pardon?"

Hambone's leer widened. "I bet you miss—you know—being with a man."

Respond to an overly personal inquiry with icy incredulity. The offending party will usually realize that the question was inappropriate and change the subject. The old charm school advice flitted through Josephine's mind. "I'm sure I don't know what you mean," she said in her frostiest tone.

"Oh, sure ya do. Getting some. Getting it on. Bangin'. Ballin'. Screwin'. F—"

Josephine abruptly raised her free hand like a crossing guard halting traffic. "I get the picture." The concept of appropriate behavior was completely lost on this thick-wit. So was the use of subtlety. "My personal life is not a topic for discussion."

Hambone ran dirty fingers through the side of his greased-back pompadour. "Now, now, ain't no point in getting all prickly. There's not much about the people on this here boat that I don't find out."

"Is that a fact?"

"Yep." He nodded earnestly. "And I just happen to know you got somethin' that makes men keep their distance."

He must mean the weapon Henry had evidently told him she had. Relief flooded Josephine's chest. If Hambone thought she was armed and dangerous, he must intend to keep his distance. She placed the skillet on the burner and picked up the other one. "Henry told you about that?"

Hambone nodded. "Me an' Junior. But ya don't need to worry. Your secret's safe. We won't tell the captain."

Josephine gave a weak smile. The captain must have a rule prohibiting guns on board. "Well, thank you. I'm glad to hear it."

"Yer welcome. An' I want you to know I admire you for dealin' with your problem, an' for takin' such good care of yourself."

It was unexpectedly kind remark. Perhaps she'd misjudged the man. She gave him a tentative smile. "Why, thank you."

"An' if you ever get lonely and want to, you know . . . just talk, well, I'm always ready and willing." His expression was eager, almost puppyish.

Her heart softened toward him. "Why, Hambone, that's a very kind offer."

"So you'll take me up on it?"

He wasn't someone she'd ever choose as a confidant, but she didn't want to hurt his feelings. Not when he looked so anxious for her friendship. "Of course. We can talk anytime you want."

Hambone gained an extra chin as he grinned. "Oh, wow! This'll be great." He ran his tongue over his thick lips and leaned forward. "It'll be like phone sex, only without the phone."

Josephine stared at him, too shocked to speak. What on earth was this savage talking about?

Hambone's gaze raked over her as if he were a hungry dog and she were a raw T-bone. He looked as though he might start drooling at any moment. "Mebbe we could even take off our clothes and watch each other while we talk."

Alarm flew through every fiber of her being.

"The only thing you'll be watching, Hambone, is your mouth," sounded a deep voice from the door.

Cole—thank heavens. Josephine's knees nearly buckled

with relief as the tall captain stalked into the room, a black scowl creasing his face. She watched as he yanked Hambone to his feet by the front of his shirt.

"If I hear you talking that way to Josephine or any other woman on my boat again, I'll throw you overboard with the anchor wrapped around your neck."

The color drained from Hambone's face until he was as pale as the flour in the batter. "We was just talkin', Boss," he whined. "I wasn't botherin' her."

"Well, you were definitely bothering *me*. Have I made myself clear?" Cole demanded.

Hambone's head jerked up and down like a puppet's on a string.

Cole loosened his grip so suddenly the heavy man nearly fell over. "I believe you still have half an hour left on your shift."

Without any delay, Hambone scrambled out the door.

Cole turned to Josephine. "What happened?"

Josephine realized she was pressed against the corner of the counter. She stepped forward, her hand still pressed against her throat. "I—I'm not exactly sure. Hambone said he wanted to talk to me, and the next thing I knew, he was suggesting . . . " Her voice trailed off. She couldn't bring herself to repeat the lewd suggestion.

Cole smiled. "Phoneless phone sex. I heard."

Josephine smoothed a stray wisp of hair from her face. "I don't know why . . . I mean, I don't know what . . . "

Cole's grin widened as he crossed the room. "I'll be happy to explain it to you, Empress. Phone sex is a very graphic conversation, where two people describe what they'd like to do to each other, usually while they're—"

Josephine's face flamed hotter. "I know what it is," she snapped.

"You do?"

"Of course. My life hasn't been *that* sheltered."

"Oh, really?" One of Cole's dark eyebrows lifted.

His attitude irritated the heck out her. She met his gaze

with a coolness she didn't feel. "Really." She tilted her chin to a haughty angle. "I was about to say, when you so rudely interrupted me, that I don't know why Hambone thought I would be receptive to such a lewd suggestion."

"I don't, either." Cole's lips curled into a taunting grin. "But what really surprises me is that he didn't suggest something a little more, uh, interactive."

A hot shiver chased up her spine, but she refused to let him know how badly he was rattling her. She lifted her head. "You're no better than Hambone."

Cole's smile lazily widened "Oh, yes, I am, Empress. I'm much better." His gaze roamed over her, lingering on her chest. She fought the urge to fold her arms across her navy cashmere sweater. "For one thing, I'd never attempt to seduce a woman who didn't want to be seduced."

Oh, dear. Was he implying that he thought she wanted to be seduced, or that he thought she didn't? Either way, the remark was distinctly disturbing.

An even more upsetting meaning hit her a second later. *Dear heavens*—maybe he could tell she was frigid. For some reason, the possibility that he knew of her inadequacy upset her most of all.

She gazed at him, her heart pounding, and tried to come up with a witty, indignant retort, but her tongue seemed stuck to the roof of her mouth. The way Cole was looking at her made it hard to think. He seemed to be staring right through her, filling her with a strange, tense heat. She could swear she even smelled smoke.

Smoke. Her gaze darted to the stove. "Oh, dear!" She dashed over and grabbed the handle of one of the burning crepe pans. Too late, she realized she'd forgotten the oven mitt.

"Oww!" She yelped, dropping the pan.

Cole was instantly beside her, turning off the burner and steering her to the sink. "Are you all right?"

"Y-yes. It's just a little burn on my finger."

"Put it in cold water." He flipped on the faucet. "Hold it

there while I get some ice."

He pulled a plastic bag from out of a kitchen drawer, dropped some ice cubes from the freezer in it, then returned to her side.

"Let me see your hand."

Josephine turned toward him. He gently took her hand and examined the red welt on the side of her index finger. "Looks like it might make a blister. Better put this on it for a while."

He pressed the ice to her hand, his touch light and surprisingly gentle. His forehead brushed the top of her head as he looked down at her finger. He was so close that Josephine could feel his breath on her face.

She suddenly felt light-headed and weak. Not because of the burn—it was just a little spot, no larger in circumference than a pencil eraser—but because of Cole. He was so close, so very close. Josephine could smell the clean, soapy scent of his neck, feel the heat emanating from his chest. Every nerve ending in her body suddenly felt alive and sensitized and stimulated.

She glanced up and caught him staring down at her. Their eyes locked and held. A current, deep and hot and thrilling, charged between them like electricity through a buried power line.

Josephine couldn't breathe, and she couldn't look away. She could only watch him watch her. His gaze fell to her mouth. Her thoughts grew dim and foggy, and her heart pounded against her ribs. *Oh, dear Lord. What would she do if he kissed her?* The thought alarmed her.

A second thought quickly followed, this one even more alarming. *Oh, dear Lord. What would she do if he didn't?*

She felt as if she were melting from the inside out. She felt hot and flushed and feverish. She was burning to be kissed, burning to feel the heat of his body pressed against her own.

She swayed toward him, her body moving like a compass needle to true north. He leaned nearer, his eyes heavy-lidded and full of desire. Josephine's eyelids fluttered closed.

"Here." Cole abruptly shoved the bag of ice into her hands and stepped back.

Good grief, he thought, crossing the kitchen in long strides, had he completely taken leave of his senses? He'd been about to kiss her. Even now, standing a good five feet away from her, he was tempted.

Dadblast it, he thought, jerking open a cabinet and yanking out a chipped coffee mug. The last thing he wanted was to get involved with a snooty blueblood broad. Hadn't he learned anything from his experience with Alexa?

Evidently not, he thought with disgust, filling the cup with steaming coffee. He'd spilled his guts to Josephine last night, telling her things he hadn't even let himself think about in years. Just as he'd done with Alexa all those years ago.

He set the pot back on the burner. He was behaving like an idiot, he thought darkly. And as for Josephine : . . Hell, he didn't know what her game was. He knew she was desperate for money and needed to keep her job, but she didn't seem worldly enough to fake the look he'd just seen on her face. Her eyes had all but begged him to kiss her. The heat he'd felt radiating from her big baby blues had lit a fire in him like he hadn't felt in years.

Damn it, her eyes were still smoldering. "There's a first-aid kit on the top shelf of the cupboard if you need a bandage," he said gruffly, taking a punishing gulp of coffee. He looked around for a distraction, for something, anything to focus on besides the woman who was making his jeans uncomfortably tight.

His eyes lit on the burned pan on the stove. "What the hell were you cooking? Tortillas?"

"No. Pancakes."

Cole picked up the plate of cooked crepes beside the stove and frowned. "You call these pancakes? They look more like communion wafers."

Josephine's back straightened. "They're thin, but they're delicious with melted butter and syrup."

"I don't have time to wait for enough of those to make a meal." He headed to the pantry, pulled out a loaf of Wonder bread and undid the twist tie. "I'll make some toast. What else have you got cooked?"

"Bacon and eggs. I'll fix you a plate."

Cole extracted two slices of bread and put them in the toaster as Josephine uncovered a platter of bacon. He glanced over. The bacon actually looked pretty good, he thought begrudgingly. And it smelled delicious.

He watched her daintily lift three pieces with a fork and place them on a plate. "Where are the eggs?" he asked.

"On the back of the stove."

Cole stared at an enormous pot that looked like a turkey roaster. "What kind of eggs did you fix in a pot like that?"

"Hard-boiled ones."

"Yuck. Scramble a couple for me, would you?"

"I . . . I can't."

Cole looked at her strangely. "Why not?"

"Because I boiled them all."

"*All* of them? Every egg on the boat?"

Josephine nodded.

He knit his brow in a hard frown. "What the hell for? Are you planning an Easter egg hunt?" Cole strode to the stove, lifted the lid on the enormous pot and peered in. The sight inside made him take a step back. "Good Lord, woman. What did you do to them?"

Setting the plate on the counter, Josephine quickly stepped beside him and looked in. Her eyebrows flew high in alarm and her shoulders sagged forward, but she promptly pulled them back to her normal ramrod posture. "They . . . they're just a little cracked. It shouldn't affect the taste."

"A little cracked?" Cole stared at the mangled mess.

163

Hardened egg whites bulged through the cracks like hemorrhoids, and pieces of shell floated through the water like flotsam. "They look like you've been using them for batting practice."

Josephine stiffened and stepped back. "Well, then, it's a good thing looks don't matter."

Cole's eyes narrowed as he regarded her. "What the hell are you talking about?"

"Last night you told me not to worry what the food looked like."

Was this insufferable dame trying to teach him some kind of a lesson? He eyed her suspiciously. "Are you saying you did this on purpose?"

Josephine blinked. "What?"

"Don't play innocent. Did you deliberately do this to prove your point?"

Josephine's wide eyes grew wider. "Why, no. I-I can't imagine why you'd think that."

A nerve twitched in his jaw. "Because, Empress, you either did it on purpose, or you don't know enough about cooking to boil an egg. Now which is it?"

For a moment she looked like a deer caught in headlights; then her chin tilted up and her eyes took on the haughty look she'd worn after she'd wrecked his truck. "I won't dignify such rudeness with a response. You already seem to have everything all figured out."

Cole's jaw clenched so tightly he could hardly speak. "The only thing I have figured out, Empress, is that I never should have hired you in the first place." Picking up his coffee mug in one hand and a fistful of bacon in the other, he stalked toward the door, then stopped and glowered at her. "You've got one more meal to prove you can cook. And if anything—I mean *anything*—is wrong with it, I'm putting you off the boat at Natchez."

She was in big trouble, Josephine thought gloomily five hours later. Instead of ingratiating herself with Cole, she'd managed only to alienate him further.

But she hadn't had much of a choice. Cole had been about to see through her. She couldn't very well admit she didn't know how to boil an egg, could she?

Sighing, she stared at the pots simmering on the stove and prayed that this meal would pass muster.

Figuring that nothing succeeded like success, she'd made another batch of the meatballs Cole had liked last night. To disguise the similarity, she was serving them with spaghetti, but she'd had no idea how to make spaghetti sauce.

Fortunately, inspiration had struck. Ketchup. It was made from tomatoes, it was red and it was about the right consistency. If she heated an economy-size jar of ketchup, it ought to pass for marinara sauce.

The spaghetti itself, however, was another problem. She hadn't known how much to cook, or how long to cook it. The directions simply said "cook to taste." Wanting to hedge her bets, she'd kept adding pasta at regular time intervals. Some of the spaghetti had cooked for more than an hour, while some of it had boiled for only a few minutes. All of it had hardened into an enormous, gooey ball. What wasn't stuck to the bottom of the pan was stuck together. Hopefully the meatballs and sauce would hide its rather unappetizing appearance.

The salad she'd made looked delicious, but she wasn't sure about the garlic bread. She'd found a large bag of fresh garlic in the cupboard. Not knowing how much to use, she'd mashed seven entire bulbs and thickly smeared the paste on slices of French bread. It didn't look quite right, but it smelled enticing as it warmed in the oven.

"Hey, Empress." A familiar low voice boomed through the kitchen intercom, making Josephine jump. "I'm getting hungry up here. Bring my lunch up to the pilothouse."

The heathen didn't even have the courtesy to use the word *please.* Resisting the urge to tell him as much,

Josephine punched the button and forced a calm voice. "The rest of the crew hasn't eaten yet. Shouldn't I wait and serve them before I leave the kitchen?"

"Nah. They don't sit down together at lunch like they do at dinner. They'll straggle in one at a time over the course of the next hour. Just set out some plates, leave the food warming on the stove and they'll serve themselves."

Josephine's heart sank. She'd hoped to get Henry to take the plate up to Cole so she wouldn't have to face him, but the older man was nowhere to be seen.

"I can't wait to see what you've fixed, Empress." Cole's voice was a silky and dangerous purr.

He was taunting her. A shiver of trepidation raced through her. "I-I'll fix you a plate and come right up."

Josephine's hands shook as she cut off a hunk of the nearly solid spaghetti. She did her best to hide it under a heaping helping of warmed ketchup and meatballs, then added a generous serving of salad and two slices of the highly fragrant bread.

Her heart pounded as she climbed the stairs. It beat even harder when she reached the wheelhouse door and saw Cole through the window. Seated in his captain's chair, he looked larger than life and completely intimidating.

He seemed to sense her presence. Without taking his eyes from the river, he motioned her in. Drawing a deep breath, Josephine opened the door and stepped inside.

Cole still didn't look at her. He flipped out the tray holder in the arm of his chair. "Set it right here."

He still couldn't bring himself to say the word *please,* Josephine thought irritably. Knowing Cole, he was probably deliberately withholding the word just to upset her. Well, she wouldn't let him. She placed the tray where he indicated and gave him a brilliant smile. "I hope you like it," she said pleasantly. "It's spaghetti and meatballs."

"Meatballs *again?*"

Inwardly Josephine winced. Outwardly she displayed

the calm of Lake Placid. "You seemed to like them last night."

She turned to go.

He stopped her with a look. "What's your hurry, Empress? Sit down while I do a taste test."

She swallowed hard, knowing she had no choice but to comply. With as much dignity as possible, she climbed to the settee. Her pulse pounded in her throat as he speared his fork into the spaghetti and twirled. To her chagrin, the entire serving of spaghetti spun on his plate like a rotating tire.

He lifted a dark eyebrow and shot her a questioning glance. *Oh, dear.* She needed this job more than she'd ever needed anything in her life. She'd never find another job that would pay so much in such a short amount of time. She silently crossed her fingers as he picked up his knife, cut off a forkful and placed it in his mouth.

He stopped in midchew. "Tastes like ketchup."

"Oh, really?"

"Yeah. Really." Criminy, it was awful. It was all Cole could do to gag it down. By damn, it *was* ketchup! He took a big bite of bread to chase away the sickly sweet taste.

It chased it, all right.

"Holy cat balls," he said with a gasp. His tongue was on fire. His eyes watered, his nose ran, and his mouth felt like the inside of an incinerator. He grabbed the plastic cup of water on his tray and downed it in one gulp. "What did you do to the bread?"

"I put garlic on it."

Had she ever. He reached for his morning coffee cup and swilled down the cold contents. Thank God he was navigating a straight stretch of river with no oncoming traffic, he thought, gasping for breath.

Dadblast the woman! She'd lied to him. She was no more of a cook than he was a ballerina. He swiveled toward her, as inflamed by anger as he was by the garlic.

167

She was perched on the settee, her back straight as the crease in a Coast Guard officer's trousers. He opened his mouth, ready to tell her where to go and how to get there, and then he noticed her hands. They were primly folded in her lap, her fingers tightly laced together. And they were trembling.

Oh, hell—from the look on her face, she might be about to cry. Her skin was a ghostly shade of white, and her eyes were as large and round as blue balloons. He was stabbed by an unexpected jolt of pity.

Damn—she'd lied because she needed the job. He'd done the same thing when he'd applied for his first job on a towboat, claiming experience he hadn't had in order to get hired. She was simply struggling to get by, the same as he'd done.

The thought took the wind out of the sails of his anger, which irritated him immensely. He was much more comfortable around her when he was angry.

Still, it had taken a lot of guts for her to bluff her way aboard, and he had to admit he admired her for it. The least he could do was let her down easy. He ran a hand down his face and blew out a hard breath. "Look, Josephine—this whole situation just isn't going to work."

She clenched her hands until her knuckles whitened. "I'll do better. I promise."

Cole shook his head and turned his attention back to the river. "There's no point in dragging this out. I think it's best for everyone concerned if you just get off the boat at Natchez. I'll pay you for the days you've worked. Hell, I'll even throw in an extra day's pay. And I'll give you bus fare back to New Orleans."

"Don't fire me. Please." She rose from the settee, dragged the stool under the chart table toward the captain's chair and sat down beside him. "I can do better. I just need a new cookbook. You see, the one I have doesn't really have very good recipes, and . . . "

The pleading note in her voice was hard to resist. He

steeled himself against it. "You selected that book your-self," he said coldly.

"I know. But I didn't look at it very carefully in the store, and . . . "

He raised his hand. "I'm sorry, Josephine, but your cooking is even worse than Henry's."

"I really, really need this job."

"And I really, really need a good cook." He stared straight ahead, not wanting to see the pleading look in her eyes. "The only thing the crew on a towboat has to look forward to is its meals. Take that away, and I've got a group of unhappy men who do a half-assed job and won't sign on for the next tour of duty."

He couldn't keep from sneaking a sideways glance at her. He immediately regretted it. Her woeful expression made him feel like an ogre. He exhaled an exasperated breath. "Look, Josephine, you're not cut out to be a cook. You'll be happier doing something else."

"There's nothing else I can do," she said woefully. "I don't have any real job skills."

She was right. She was like a hothouse flower who couldn't survive in the outside world. She was well traveled, highly educated, expensively dressed and exquisitely mannered, but she was completely unequipped to support herself. She'd been taught a bunch of archaic skills that had no meaning in the real world.

A dangerous stab of pity assaulted his heart.

Cole groped for anything that might encourage her. "Sure you do. You said you used to work in a library."

She stared out at the river, her eyes bleak. "And I hated it. I used to feel like one of the books—lifeless and dusty and stuck on the shelf."

The forlorn note in her voice made his chest feel hot and tight. "You'll find something else."

She looked at him hopefully. "Maybe there's something else I could do here on your boat."

Cole shook his head. "I already have a full crew."

"There's got to be something I could do."

She *was* desperate. The fact tugged at heartstrings he didn't know he had, making him immensely uneasy. *Damn it.* She needed a reality check, and evidently so did he. He wasn't doing either of them any favors by playing the nice guy. "Can you lash a barge and check the lines, or supervise the deckhands who do?"

"Well, no."

"Do you have a pilot's license I don't know about?"

"Of course not."

"Do you know how to repair an engine?"

She silently shook her head.

"The only job that leaves is cook, and we both know you can't handle that."

A glum silence followed. "I could clean and sweep and paint," she said at length.

"About as good as you can cook, I'll bet." Cole gave a look meant to intimidate her. "I'm not in the market for a maid, but if I were, you'd be the last person I'd hire."

She stared silently out the window, then suddenly turned toward him. "I know something I could do for you."

Didn't the woman ever give up? "I've told you, Josephine. The boat is fully staffed."

"I'm not talking about a staff position. I'm talking about a personal service I could perform. It's something you desperately need, whether you want to admit it or not."

Oh, dear Lord. Was she suggesting what he thought she was suggesting? He glanced over at her, and she boldly met his gaze.

He turned his eyes back to the river and swallowed hard. Damn it, but the idea was tempting. From where she was sitting, he could smell the faint scent of her perfume. It must be charged with sexual pheromones or erotic ions or something, because the soft scent was driving him crazy. He remembered all too well how her body had felt when he'd carried her from the galley after the fire. More than anything, he'd like to carry her like that to his bed.

He didn't know what it was about her, but the thought of peeling off all the layers of her expensive, high-necked clothes made him ache to do just that. Maybe it was because it was so unlikely ever to happen. Maybe he was turned on by her inaccessibility. Maybe she represented all he'd been denied as a teenager.

Maybe. But the real reason, he suspected, was his growing certainty that underneath all of her clothes and manners and oh-so-proper demeanor lurked an explosively passionate woman.

Whatever the reason, he only knew that he wanted her as he hadn't wanted a woman in ages.

But not like this. Not because she needed money.

He slanted a slow grin at her. "Hey, I'm real flattered, sugar, but the crew would be likely to get awfully jealous if I kept your, uh, personal services all to myself."

She breezily waved her hand. "Oh, I could do them, too. That wouldn't be a problem."

Cole's mouth fell open. His stomach tightened like a fist around a baseball. "It sure as hell would be," he said gruffly.

It already was, just thinking about it. His fingers tensed on the metal steering stick. It was downright painful, hearing the Empress demean herself like this. He cast an uneasy glance at her. "Look, I'll tell you what—you're evidently in a worse financial bind than I realized. I'll loan you an extra five hundred dollars when we get to Natchez, but I've got to pass on your offer. Nothing like that is going to take place on my boat."

"I was afraid you'd say that." She breathed a soulful sigh. "In my experience, the people who need it the most are always the most reluctant to sign up for it."

She couldn't have surprised him more if she'd hit him upside the head with a two-by-four. "What do you mean, in your *experience?* You mean you've done this before?"

She looked at him strangely, as if he'd lost his mind. "Well, sure. I used to make a living at it."

Either she'd lied about a lot more than cooking, or their wires were seriously crossed. He leaned forward. "What the hell are you talking about?"

Her exquisitely shaped eyebrows knit together. "Etiquette lessons, of course. What did you *think* we were talking about?"

Etiquette lessons. He threw back his head and laughed, an unexplained sense of relief flooding his veins. "Never mind."

"It's nothing to laugh at," Josephine said reproachfully. "The lack of social facility can be a serious handicap. It's unfair and it's very unfortunate, but people discriminate against those who appear ill-bred."

"You're tellin' me, Empress."

Her expression was deadly serious. "Well, I can help you with that."

"I don't just appear ill-bred, Empress." Cole's mouth twisted in a wry smile. "I *am* ill-bred. The gene pool doesn't get any lower than the offspring of a junkie whore and a murderer."

He thought she would recoil at that, but she didn't. "There's no excuse for unrefined behavior. Anyone can learn to conduct himself properly. If you chose to, you could have the manners of a prince."

"A *prince?*"

Josephine nodded.

An idea hatched in Cole's mind, an idea so farfetched that it made him shake his head. He stared out the river as the idea grew.

It was insane. It was bizarre.

It was the perfect solution.

It would never work.

But if it did, it would be the most satisfying way he could ever imagine of getting back at Robert and Alexa and all the other high-society deadbeats who'd ever looked down their noses at him.

Best of all, if it failed, he didn't stand to lose a thing—

except maybe his sanity from having to put up with the Empress for the rest of this voyage.

Maybe even that wouldn't be so bad, he mused. Given a little more time and proximity, maybe he'd have a chance to find out if he was right about the passion he suspected lay under Josephine's prim exterior. One thing was for certain: keeping her aboard would ensure that the voyage wouldn't be a dull one.

He glanced over at her. Her shoulders were more rounded than he'd ever seen them, and her eyes held a sad, defeated look. Against his will, his heart softened toward her.

What the hell. She desperately needed a job, and her charm course might give him a once-in-a-lifetime opportunity to settle an old score that had haunted him for years.

"Etiquette lessons, huh?"

She nodded, her lips pressed tightly together. She was obviously braced for rejection.

It was nuts. He was nuts. He was certain he'd live to regret it. All the same, a feeling of anticipation pulsed through him, along with a sense of excitement he hadn't felt in years.

His lips pulled into a grin. "All right, Empress. Consider yourself hired."

Chapter Nine

Henry closed the door to the pilothouse behind him. "I just saw Josephine down in the galley, an' she said she's gonna stay aboard and give us etiquette lessons."

Cole's eyes remained steadfastly on the river. "That's right."

Henry squinted in the early afternoon sun, trying to read the captain's expression. He didn't look like he was pulling some kind of a joke. "What the hell's goin' on?"

Cole lifted his shoulders in a casual shrug. "I figured I could stand a little polishing up, that's all. It'll help me in my business dealings."

Henry frowned. "The way you're makin' money hand over fist, don' seem to me that you need any help."

"Well, you never know. It might come in handy on down the road. And while I'm at it, I thought I'd let her shine up the rest of you as well. Won't hurt any of us to learn a few manners."

There was a lot more to this than Cole was letting on. The way he kept his eyes fixed on the river was a dead

174

giveaway he was up to something. Henry pondered the situation as he reached in his shirt pocket for his can of tobacco. On the one hand, he was glad Josephine wouldn't be out of a job, because the poor girl needed the work. On the other hand, he wasn't sure remaining on the boat was in Josephine's best interest.

Or in anyone's best interest, when it got right down to it. "So who's gonna cook for us?"

"I just hired a new cook over the phone. She'll come aboard in Natchez." Cole glanced over at him. "She's Earl's cousin."

Earl was one of the relief deckhands. "Are you sure this gal can cook?"

Cole nodded. "Earl swore to it. Said she used to own a truck stop on Highway One in Nachitoches."

"What happened? She git closed down for givin' somebody a case of ptomaine or somethin'?"

"Nah. A new stretch of interstate went in two years ago and her business dried up. She's been the cook at a diner in Natchez ever since, but Earl says she doesn't get along with the owner. Besides, she's always wanted to travel."

The wheelhouse door creaked open. Henry turned to see Josephine enter, carefully carrying a steaming mug. "Here's the coffee you requested."

Cole reached out his hand. "Thanks."

Josephine passed it to him, then stood behind his chair, gazing out at the view. "Looks like we're coming into a city."

Cole nodded. "We're just outside Natchez."

"Are you getting ready to park?"

Henry chortled at her choice of words. Even Cole smiled. "Dock, Empress. You park a car, dock a boat. Although what we're going to do is kind of like double parking. We won't pull up to the shore. We'll stop in the river and a towboat will push some more barges out to us."

"What are you picking up?"

"Four loads of steel. And a new cook." Cole shot a

glance over his shoulder. "You need to go pack your stuff."

Josephine's face took on a stricken look. "I-I thought we'd agreed I'd stay aboard."

"You are, but you're switching cabins."

"Where ya movin' her, Boss?" Henry asked.

"In with me."

The silence that followed was thick as Hambone's skull.

"With you!" Josephine finally exclaimed, staring at Cole as if he'd lost his mind.

Cole nodded. "There's a perfectly good bunk that pulls out above my bed. No one's using it. You can sleep up there."

Josephine turned to Henry, her eyes wide and alarmed.

Henry cleared his throat. "Hey, now, Cap'n—I don't think that's such a good idea. Why don't I bunk with you and let Josephine have my cabin?"

Cole shook his head. "No way. You know you snore like a freight train."

Josephine cast another pleading look at Henry. Against his better judgment, he went to bat for her again. "Ah, come on, Boss. Josephine's a lady, and she's kinda led a sheltered life an' all. You could take the cook's cabin and let the two women share yours."

Cole's voice took on an irritated edge. "I'm not giving up my quarters. I need access to my computer and files and fax machine. Besides, I'm not the big bad wolf. She's got nothing to worry about."

Henry scratched his jaw. "Well, it just don' look right."

Cole brow plowed into a furrow. "So who's looking?"

Henry shifted uncomfortably. "Well, the boys might think . . . I mean, they'll get the idea that you two are . . . "

Cole's eyebrows rose challengingly. "So? Josephine will be safer if they think exactly that."

"But they ain't been botherin' her none, Boss."

"Oh, yes, they have. I caught Hambone bothering her plenty just this morning."

Dadblast that boy! Henry would have to give him a piece of his mind. "But, Boss—"

"Look, if it'll make you feel any better, I'll give you my word, Henry." He cast a sideways glance at Josephine. "I won't lay a hand on her unless she lays a hand on me first."

Josephine sucked in an audible gasp of air.

Cole turned his attention to the depth gauge. "And if Josephine has a problem with this arrangement, why, then, she's more than welcome to get off the boat in Natchez."

There was no mistaking the challenge in his words. Cole probably hoped she'd do just that, Josephine thought indignantly. He was probably having second thoughts about letting her stay aboard, and this was his way of trying to run her off.

Well, he was in for a surprise. She had no idea what had prompted him to take her up on her offer of etiquette lesson, but she'd felt like a death-row prisoner who'd received a last-minute reprieve. Staying on the boat meant she could earn enough money to make a fresh start, and she wasn't going to let him scare her out of the opportunity. Besides, it would give her the chance to prove to herself that she wasn't as incompetent as she feared.

She directed a pleasant smile at the first mate. "Don't worry, Henry. I'm sure the captain is a man of his word. If he says he'll conduct himself as a gentleman, why, I'm certain that's exactly what he'll do." She turned to Cole, giving him the same cheerful grin. "I appreciate your hospitality. Now, if you'll be so kind as to give me the key to your cabin—I suppose I should say *our* cabin, shouldn't I?—why, I'll go move my things."

A muscle twitched in Cole's jaw. "It's not locked, Empress. No one on this boat ever walks into my cabin uninvited." His lips tilted in a challenging smile. "Why, I imagine that if someone were in there screaming and yelling bloody murder, no one would walk through the door without my say-so." He turned to the old man. "Isn't that right, Henry?"

Henry swallowed hard, his expression one of pure misery. "I reckon that's so, Cap'n."

The barbarian was deliberately trying to frighten her. Well, she'd be darned if she'd let him. She gave a composed smile. "Excellent. That means I'll be perfectly safe, doesn't it?"

She sure didn't *feel* perfectly safe, Josephine thought two hours later, setting her suitcase down in the hall and staring at the door marked *Captain.* She felt about as safe as a rabbit hopping into a den of lions.

She wished she knew why Cole had so abruptly agreed to take etiquette lessons. Before she could find out, their conversation had been interrupted by Gaston, who'd sauntered into the wheelhouse to discuss something about one of the engines with Cole.

"We'll talk about this later," Cole had told her. When he'd buzzed her on the intercom an hour later and asked her to bring a cup of coffee up to the pilothouse, she'd thought she was finally about to get some answers, but by the time she'd climbed the stairs, Henry had been there. Whatever Cole's reasons, he didn't seem to want to discuss them in front of his crew.

She supposed she'd find out soon enough. Drawing a deep breath, she opened the door, picked up her bag and stepped inside. The door closed behind her with a solid thud.

Josephine set her bag on the floor and looked around. The cabin was as uncompromisingly masculine as Cole. The floor was teak, the walls were paneled in mahogany, and the furnishings, most of which were built-in and custom-made, were a deep, rich cherry. Henry had told her that a master carpenter had outfitted the captain's quarters to Cole's specifications. The room was neat as a pin and far more spacious than she would have imagined. Everything in it was simple, clean-lined and oversize.

Especially the bed. Instead of a narrow single mattress, Cole's cabin featured a king-size bed built into the far corner of the room. It was covered with an expensive plaid comforter in shades of burgundy, deep green and blue, and had a number of tailored pillows tossed against the built-in headboard.

Against the wall above the bed, built into the rich woodwork so well it would have gone unnoticed if she hadn't known to look for it, was what looked like the outline of a narrow, horizontal Murphy bed. Two discreet wooden handles were tucked into grooves in the wood.

Her mouth went dry at the thought of sleeping directly over Cole. He would know every time she turned over, every time she drew a breath. She found it hard to draw one now, just thinking about it.

She deliberately turned away, forcing herself to examine the rest of the room. A leather armchair sat in the corner. A heavy cherry desk and cordovan leather chair squatted against the far wall, under a porthole covered with a navy window shade. The desk was empty except for a computer, a mouse pad, a brass file holder and a fax machine. Josephine ran her hand over the back of the chair, inhaling the rich leather scent, then crossed to the heavy bureau against the other wall.

Slowly, tentatively, she pulled open the middle drawer and found it filled with neatly folded clothes. Clean T-shirts, crisp jeans and tidily paired socks were lined up with military precision.

Josephine ran her hand across the soft fabric of a gray T-shirt. For such a rough-hewn heathen, Cole took surprisingly good care of his things. But then, from what she knew about his past, it made sense that he would. He'd been raised without many possessions, so he'd probably developed the habit of taking good care of the few things he had.

The thought sent a dangerous, tender ache edging into

Josephine's heart. Hoping to thwart it, Josephine closed the drawer and marched into the bathroom.

It was tiled in white and scrupulously clean. Twice the size of the bath in the cook's cabin, it was still extremely small. The tiny counter held only a razor and a can of shaving cream. Josephine picked it up, pulled off the lid and sniffed. It smelled like Cole's face.

An erotic shiver buzzed through her, shocking her with its intensity. The reality of her situation settled in hard. She was in Cole's quarters—the rooms where he bathed and dressed and slept. She would discover intimate details about him, such as how long he stayed in the shower, what kind of toothpaste he used, and what he wore—or didn't wear—to bed. She would find out if he snored or talked in his sleep.

And he would discover the same about her. A rush of alarm and something that felt suspiciously like excitement pulsed through her.

"Hey, Empress." Cole's voice thundered through the intercom like the voice of God.

Josephine jumped as if she'd been poked with a cattle prod.

"The intercom's by the door. Press the button and let me know if you're there."

On shaky legs, Josephine crossed the room to the small brown box. "I-I'm here."

"You can stash your stuff in the bottom two drawers of my dresser. Just move my things up to the top drawers. And there's some extra room in the closet and the bathroom medicine chest if you need it."

Josphine's mouth went dry. "Okay. Thank you."

"The tow's lashed together and the new cook's aboard, so I'm gonna shove on upriver. As soon as you get settled in, come up to the pilothouse and we'll get these lessons under way."

Josephine couldn't help but wonder what else he intended to get under way. He'd said he wouldn't lay a hand on her unless she laid a hand on him first, but she didn't know if he could be trusted.

Or was it herself she doubted?

"All right, Empress. Teach me some charm."

Josephine tightly folded her hands in her lap and stared out the pilothouse windshield. Cole had insisted that she pull up a chair beside the captain's. In order to fit behind the instrument panel with him, she'd had to pull her chair close to his, and she was sitting so near she could smell his shaving cream—the same shaving cream she'd seen in his bathroom just a few minutes earlier.

She tried to force her thoughts away from him and onto the reason she was here. "Well, first I need to know what you're hoping to get out these lessons."

Cole shot her a displeased look. "What do you think I'm hoping to get—an extra belly button?"

They were certainly off to an auspicious beginning. "When I taught etiquette classes before, they were usually geared to a specific purpose. I was either preparing young women for their debut, instructing them in the art of entertaining, teaching children table manners and comportment, or educating young men about social protocol and ballroom dancing."

"Ballroom dancing?" Cole's eyebrows rose incredulously. "You teach ballroom dancing?"

He made it sound as if she'd just confessed to mugging little old ladies. Josephine laced her fingers nervously together. "Just the basics," she said defensively. "Nothing fancy. Just enough so that my students can successfully navigate a dance floor."

"Hell," he muttered.

Under the circumstances, Josephine thought it best to overlook his lapse into profanity. "So what, exactly, do you want to learn?"

"Everything."

Josephine's surprise must have registered on her face,

because he pulled his brow into a vicious scowl. "You said you could teach me to act like a friggin' prince, and that's what I want you to do."

One lapse could be overlooked, but two required action. "No, I didn't," she said archly. "I've never used the word *frigging* in my life."

"Well, you have now." He shot her an amused glance. "But if you like, I'll rephrase the statement. I want to know how to act like a prince."

"I . . . see." She didn't at all. "Is there some special occasion you're preparing for?"

"Yeah. I guess you might say there is."

He was being deliberately obtuse. She drew a deep breath and willed her features not to show her growing irritation. "It would be helpful if you'd share that information with me."

"You're going to hound me till I do, aren't you?"

Patience is a virtue, she reminded herself. "Well, I can't give you what you're looking for until I know what it is."

"Okay, I'll tell you." He riveted her with a steely gaze. "But this is just between us. Not one word to anyone, do you understand? If you breathe a word of this, you'll be off the boat before you can ask why."

Pulling her spine straight against the back of the chair, she met his menacing gaze as coolly as possible. "You don't have to threaten me. I always respect my students' confidentiality."

He stared at her for a long moment, then gave a curt nod, apparently satisfied. "One other thing—I don't want to hear a lecture, and I don't want you to try to talk me out of it. In fact, I don't want to hear one word—not one *syllable*—of disapproval. Have I made myself clear?"

"Perfectly."

"All right." He drew a deep breath and exhaled it, then turned his eyes back to the water. "I intend to steal Alexa Armand away from Robert McAuley."

Josephine's heart gave a painful thud. "But—"

"Not one word of disapproval," Cole warned.

"But they're engaged!"

"That's the whole point." Cole's mouth settled into a grim line. "I intend to break their engagement."

Josephine stared at him, dumbfounded. Her body froze, but her insides churned with turmoil.

Alexa Armand. After all this time, she still had a hold on Cole's heart. Something that felt miserably like jealousy clutched at her chest.

She wasn't jealous. She couldn't be jealous. She certainly didn't want Cole for herself.

Did she?

Of course not.

No, she was simply jealous of Alexa Armand's power to provoke such timeless passion in a man, she told herself. What would it be like to be that kind of woman—for just one day, for just one hour? What would it be like to be so beautiful, so desirable, that a man like Cole would scheme to win her?

She would never know. Josephine stared out the window, swamped by old feelings of inferiority and insufficiency. The only lover she'd ever known had declared her frigid. Cole evidently saw her as so undesirable that he had moved her into his cabin with no apparent ulterior motive at all.

Well, thank goodness, she tried to tell herself. She should be grateful that Cole didn't have any designs on her.

But she didn't feel grateful. Not at all. She felt strangely disappointed and hollow.

"I-I don't really understand what you want me to help you do," she finally said.

"Like I said. I want you to help me impersonate a prince."

Had he lost his mind?

Cole glanced over and grinned. "Better close your mouth, Empress, before you catch a fly."

Josephine wound her fingers tightly together. "Perhaps you'd better explain."

Cole leaned back in his leather chair. "It takes a lot to impress Alexa, but she's always been impressed with royalty. Back in high school, it was the Mardi Gras variety, but I'd bet my bottom dollar there's nothing she'd like better than to be a real-life titled princess. So if she thought I was a prince, I think she'd dump McAuley for me in a second."

It was the craziest thing Josephine had ever heard. "But she knows you!"

Cole shook his head. "I used Mom's last name when I enrolled at St. Alban's so no one would know about my father. His trial made him pretty notorious, and I had the lousy luck of being named after him. I didn't even go by my nickname of Cole. I was known as Collin Sawyer."

"But Alexa will recognize you."

"I doubt it. I've changed a lot in fourteen years. My nose has been broken twice and I'm no longer as skinny as a scarecrow. I've run into several people who used to know me back then, and not one of them ever recognized me."

He spoke so calmly that the insane plan almost sounded rational. "But . . . but a prince has to be the prince of something. Of someplace. Where are you going to say you're from?"

"Romania."

"Won't that be pretty easy to check out? And how will you explain that you don't have a foreign accent?"

Cole smiled. "That's easy. Princess Iliana of Romania had six children. She moved them to the United States after her deportation from Communist Romania. I could easily be one of her descendants born and raised in America."

"But—but . . . " Josephine's head reeled. "How do you know this?"

"I was researching an investment prospect and ran across it on the Internet."

"You have a computer connected to the Internet?"

"Not on the boat. At my accountant's office in New Orleans. When I'm on the river, they look up anything I request and fax it to me over a cell phone."

"But—but . . . " It was a preposterous scheme. There had to be a reason it wouldn't, *couldn't* work. "Isn't it illegal to impersonate someone?"

Cole grinned. "That's the best part. I'm not going to be impersonating anyone."

Was the man completely out of his mind? Josephine shook her head. "You've lost me."

Cole glanced at the radar screen. "I'm not going to actually *say* I'm a prince. That's the beauty of the plan. I intend to start a rumor and let the gossip mill take it from there." He stretched his hand across the back of her chair. His hand felt dangerously close to her neck. "All I have to do is get the right people whispering that I'm a prince who wants to remain incognito. If anyone asks me if I'm a prince, well, I'll deny it. Since I supposedly want to be anonymous, my denials will only strengthen the rumors."

Josephine realized her mouth was hanging open. She abruptly snapped it shut. "Let me see if I have this straight. You're going to impersonate a prince by denying that you are one?"

"That's right." Cole flashed her a blazing grin. "Pretty brilliant, huh?"

"Pretty crazy," Josephine muttered. "But so crazy, it just might work."

Cole's teeth gleamed as he laughed, making Josephine's heart unaccountably jump. She must be as insane as he was, because she was starting to think it might actually be possible. He was good-looking enough to pass for a prince. And heaven only knew he had the arrogance and self-confidence. With the right clothes and manners, he just might pull it off. "How long do you intend to keep up the charade?"

He shrugged. "As long as it takes."

As long as it took to woo and win Alexa. Josephine's heart twisted strangely in her chest. "Alexa will eventually have to learn the truth, you know," she said quietly.

"So? By then I will have ruined the wedding plans, humiliated McAuley and made fools of everyone who bought into the story."

"So this is about revenge." For some reason, the thought lifted Josephine's spirits.

"What did you think it was about? True love?" Cole gave a scoffing snort. "There's no such thing. But there *is* such a thing as settling old debts, and I've been waiting for years to settle this one." His eyes took on a distant look. "When I was locked in jail, the only thing that kept me going was the thought that one day I'd get even. One day, when Robert least expected it, I was going to find out what he wanted more than anything in the world and take it away from him."

His eyes glittered brightly as looked over at her. "And that day has come. Robert always carried a torch for Alexa. Even back in high school, he followed her around like a lovelorn puppy, waiting for her to toss him some crumb of attention."

It was true, Josephine mused. She noticed the same phenomenon at every social event she'd ever attended with the two of them. "But what about her? Your plan is going to hurt her, too."

"It didn't bother *her* to hurt *me*."

Were his feelings for Alexa as callous as they sounded? For some reason, Josephine found herself fervently hoping they were. But she couldn't help but wonder if his air of indifference was hiding deeper, more tender feelings. "What exactly are you hoping to do?"

"Sweep Alexa off her feet. Then get her to tell Robert that she and I are lovers, and she's breaking their engagement."

Lovers. He intended to take Alexa to bed. The thought made her throat dry and tight. "Then what?"

Cole shrugged. "I'm not sure how long I'll string it out. Maybe I'll ask Alexa to marry me and let her make a big deal out of our engagement. And then . . . " Cole's eyes glittered darkly. "And then I'll announce to McAuley and Alexa and the whole world exactly who I am. Not a prince at all, but Trash Boy—the same sorry SOB Alexa refused to acknowledge, the same lowlife McAuley didn't think twice about framing." His mouth curved into a cruel smile. "I'll make fools of them all."

Josephine repressed a shiver. It was wrong. Revenge was always wrong. Yet after all that Cole had told her, she could understand why he wanted it so badly. She could sympathize, even empathize.

But could she help him do it?

Cole seemed to read her mind. He turned toward her and caught her gaze. When he spoke, his voice was soft as suede. "And you're going to make it all possible."

The intent look in his eyes made her heart flutter. Oh, why did he have to affect her so? If she had any other option, any at all, she would refuse. She would run as far from Cole and the dangerous feelings he stirred in her as she possibly could.

Wouldn't she? Suddenly she wasn't so sure.

Ever since she was sixteen, her entire existence had been predicated on trying to make up for her horrible mistake. She'd tried her best to follow all the rules of good behavior, but suddenly no rules seemed to apply. She was beginning to wonder if they ever had.

No amount of good behavior had ever assuaged her guilt. She was beginning to see that it never would, because nothing could alter the truth—the truth was as hard and cold and immutable as her best friend's tomb: her friend was dead, and she was to blame.

Cole must feel the same way about Mom Sawyer's death. He, too, must be tortured by a sense of responsibility. In his case, though, the responsibility rightfully rested on someone else's shoulders.

Up ahead the river curved sharply, and she couldn't see what was around the bend. Cole pulled on the throttle, picking up speed, confidently steering into the great unknown. He steadied the towboat's course and checked the swing meter, then turned his eyes toward her. "You *are* going to help, Josephine." The glint of resolve in his eyes told her he would not be denied.

But then, she was no longer sure she wanted to deny him anything.

Maybe evening the score would bring him peace. She knew what it was like to long for inner calm, to want to silence the relentless clamor of a stricken conscience.

She drew a deep breath and nodded, her heart pounding against her ribs like the wings of a bird against its cage.

"Good." Cole gave a satisfied smile. "Now let's get to work. By the time we get back to New Orleans, I expect you to have turned me into a regular Prince Charming."

Chapter Ten

Henry listed to the side like a capsizing boat under the weight of the hot pink duffel bag. The captain had asked him to show the new cook around and help her get settled, and he'd already carried two of her bags to her cabin. She'd insisted on bringing this one to the galley.

His shoulder ached as he lugged the enormous satchel through the galley door. "What ya got in here—rocks?"

"Brought some of my own pots and pans."

"Hell, we got plenty of those."

"Don't imagine they're as good as mine." Fanny Jarvis followed Henry into the business end of the galley, planted her hands on her ample hips and looked around. Henry leaned against the wall, reached in his pocket for his ever-present can of tobacco and watched her.

Merciful days, but the woman had a chest on her! She wore a baggy blue plaid flannel shirt with the shirttails hanging out, but even in that god-awful getup, it was impossible not to notice her breasts. They were the big,

189

soft, bouncy kind—the kind where the cleavage probably started just below the collarbone.

If it weren't for her chest, though, Henry might have mistaken her for a man. Her salt-and-pepper hair was cut short and slicked back from her face, she didn't wear a lick of makeup and she moved her short, stocky frame with all the grace of a longshoreman. The fact that she was wearing a pair of loose-fitting khakis and heavy work boots didn't help any, either.

She was probably one of those women who didn't like men. Well, that was just as well. That meant Junior and Hambone would most likely leave her alone. She was too old for them, anyway. Henry guessed that she was about five years younger than he was—somewhere in her early fifties.

He watched her lumber to the oven and open the door. She bent down and inspected the inside, then made a har-rumphing sound. Slamming the oven closed, she turned her attention to the stove. Henry stuffed a wad of tobacco in his cheek as she removed one of the burners and checked the pan underneath. Good grief, the way the woman was going over the kitchen, he'd have thought she was considering buying the boat.

She opened the refrigerator and surveyed the contents. Henry watched her pull a small notepad from the back pocket of her pants, jot a few things down, then move on to the cupboard. She inspected it shelf by shelf, scribbling as she went.

Now she was looking at the walls and the cabinets. Hell, this could take all day. "Findin' ever'thin' ya need?"

She turned around, and Henry found his gaze riveted to her breasts.

He was disappointed when Fanny folded her arms across her chest. Henry hauled his gaze up to see her bushy eyebrows pull into a frown. "I'm finding that this place is a mess. I thought a first mate's job was to keep everything on a boat shipshape."

Henry abruptly straightened, surprised by the unexpected personal attack. "Hey, now—the kitchen's the cook's domain."

Fanny shot him a reproachful look. "Hmmph. The captain told me over the phone that *you* were the cook on most of the last run."

Henry rubbed the back of his head. This bossy old broad had some nerve. "Hell, it ain't so bad. The oven was cleaned real recent, and Josephine was real good 'bout washing off the stove and countertop."

"I'm not talking about those. I'm talking about the floor and the walls and the refrigerator and the front of the cabinets." Fanny ran a finger across the front of the flatware drawer, smearing a line in the dark woodwork. She held up a greasy finger. "The place looks like it hasn't gotten a thorough cleaning in fifteen years. No wonder it smells like a grease factory."

"Well, it's all yours now. You think it needs cleanin', you're welcome to clean it." He turned to leave.

"Not so fast, Bub."

Who the heck is she callin' Bub? Henry whirled around. "You talkin' to me?" He pointed at his chest.

"You bet I am."

Henry glared at her. "My name's Henry."

"I'm not on first-name terms with anyone tryin' to sneak off and get out of work."

"I wasn't sneakin'! An' it so happens I've got my own work to do."

She placed her hands on her hips. "Well, then, you need to get a couple of your men in here. I was hired as a cook, not a janitor, and I'm not fixing a lick of food in this sty until it's gotten a good going-over with some scouring powder and elbow grease."

Who did she think she was, tellin' him what to do? Henry narrowed his eyes. "Now wait just a cotton-pickin' minute—"

191

"No, *you* wait a minute," Fanny interrupted. "I won't cook in a kitchen that wouldn't pass a health inspection."

Henry could feel his blood pressure rising. "Is that so?"

"You bet your skinny backside."

Henry's temper flared. "You'll do what you're told, or you won't work on this boat."

The stubborn look on Fanny's round face reminded Henry of a bull terrier. "I'll do what I'm told if the captain does the telling. I didn't hire on to be bossed about by the likes of you."

A vein throbbed in Henry's temple. "Well, we'll just see what the cap'n has to say about this!"

"Say about what, Henry?" said a familiar voice.

Henry whipped around to see Cole enter the room.

Fanny bustled over. "You must be the captain. I recognize your voice from our phone conversation. I'm Fanny Jarvis, the new cook." She stuck out her hand.

Cole took it. "Cole Dumanski. Welcome aboard." He cast a questioning glance at Henry, then looked back at Fanny. "Is Henry giving you a hard time about something?"

"Nothing that I can't handle." She turned her back to Henry in what the old man was sure was a deliberate snub. "Would you care for a homemade cookie?"

Cole's eyebrows rose high. "You've already made cookies?"

"I made them last night and brought them with me. If you'll unzip the top of that bag by your feet, Henry, you'll find them in that plastic container right on top."

Henry had no choice but to comply, although it irritated the heck out of him to take orders from the woman. Suppressing a scowl, Henry dug in the bag and located a square blue container. Pulling up the lid, he helped himself to a cookie and passed the rest to Cole.

The captain looked down at the cookies in his hand. "Chocolate chip. My favorite." He pulled one out and took a large bite. "Say, these are great!"

Fanny smiled. "Glad you like 'em."

Henry bit into his. He had to admit, it was the best thing he'd tasted in a long time.

Cole set the container on the counter and polished off his cookie. "I wanted to let you know that you'll be cooking for one more person than I told you on the phone."

"You've got a new crew member?"

Cole rubbed his jaw. "Not new, exactly. The former cook is staying aboard. She's, uh, going to be giving us all etiquette lessons."

Henry took a certain mean-spirited satisfaction in the look of shock that flitted over the cook's face.

"Etiquette?" Fanny asked. "You mean manners?"

Cole nodded. "Josephine used to be a charm school teacher, and I figured some polishing up wouldn't hurt me in my business dealings. While she's at it, she's going to give the whole crew pointers at mealtime."

"Well, then, I'll set another place at the table."

She probably thought Josephine was Cole's mistress, Henry realized. Well, he couldn't blame her. If he didn't know the girl, he'd think so, too. It was all mighty odd, especially considering the sleeping arrangements.

Fanny pulled a folded piece of paper out of her shirt pocket and passed it to Cole. "I worked up a week's worth of menus last night. See what you think."

Cole set the container of cookies on the counter and glanced down. "Fried chicken, corn bread, okra with tomatoes and homemade apple pie . . . Pot roast with vegetables, homemade rolls, fudge brownies . . . Smothered pork chops, mashed potatoes, green bean casserole and peach cobbler . . ." He looked up and grinned at Henry. "Sounds like we've hit the chow-time jackpot."

Henry avoided answering by reaching for another cookie. Cole gazed at him quizzically, then helped himself as well to another cookie. "Everything sounds great, Fanny. And if these cookies are an example of your cooking, we're in for some mighty fine eating."

Fanny's round face beamed. "Thank you, sir. I've already checked the supplies and made a list of what I'll need, just like you asked when we talked on the phone."

"Good. Just give it to Henry. He'll order it from our supplier and they'll bring it all to us on a boat upriver." He turned to Henry. "Josephine's in my cabin drawing up a list of things she'll need for our etiquette lessons. Be sure and get her list, too, before you call." Cole grabbed another cookie and turned to go.

"There's one more thing I need to discuss with you, Captain," Fanny piped up.

Cole stopped and swiveled back toward her. "Yes?"

"It's about the condition of the kitchen."

"It's called a galley," Henry said with a scowl.

His correction failed to faze her. "Galley, kitchen—whatever you want to call it, the place is filthy. The floors, walls and cabinets are just slick with dirt." She ran her finger across a drawer and showed it to Cole, just as she'd done to Henry.

Dadblast her! Henry took a step forward. "I tol' her that keepin' the galley clean is the cook's job, Boss."

Fanny shot him a disapproving look. "I don't mind keeping it clean, but getting it clean in the first place is going to be quite a job. If I'd let the kitchen of my truck stop get in this condition, the board of health would have shut me down. This place needs a thorough scouring, and I'm not going to have the time to clean it *and* cook three meals a day."

Cole nodded. "I hadn't realized it was this bad. With all the turnover we've had in cooks, I guess I've let it slip through the cracks. Henry, get Hambone and Junior in here ASAP. Fanny will tell you what she wants them to do."

"I'd like to tell her what *she* can do," Henry muttered under his breath.

Cole looked at him so sharply that Henry was half-afraid he'd heard him. The captain moved toward the door.

"Glad to have you aboard, ma'am. If you need anything, Henry will be happy to help you."

I'd be happy to strangle her, that's what I'd be happy to do. Henry's jaw clenched as he watched Cole saunter out the door. He waited until he heard the captain's footsteps clang on the metal stairs, then turned to Fanny. "That was real slick, the way you managed to pull that off," he ground out.

Fanny squatted down and pulled out a can of scouring powder from the cabinet under the sink. "Pull what off?"

"Talkin' the cap'n into lettin' ya use my deckhands. Don' think I didn' see the way you buttered him up with cookies and got his mouth to waterin' with all your fancy menus before you sprung it on him."

Straightening, Fanny poured a generous amount of cleanser in the sink, sending up a small pale cloud. "I didn't spring anything on anyone. I just explained the situation and let him decide how to handle it."

Who did she think she was fooling, acting all innocent? Henry's hands clenched at his sides. "Are you denyin' you set it all up?"

"I'm not denying anything." Her voice was maddeningly calm.

The woman was more irritating than a burr in his undershorts. The fact that he couldn't seem to keep his eyes off her breasts only aggravated him all the more. What the Sam Hill was the matter with him? He was starting to act as bad as Hambone and Junior, he thought with disgust. If he didn't watch out, the next thing he knew, he'd be buying those magazines.

He frowned so hard his face hurt. "Well, don' be thinkin' you can try it on me, 'cause it damn sure won't work."

Fanny strode to the far counter and picked up the cookie container. "I wasn't planning to. It would be a waste of good cookies, trying to sweeten up an old sourpuss like

195

you." Looking him dead in the eye, she gave the lid a loud snap, stalked back across the kitchen and placed the container high in a cabinet beside the sink.

Henry's fingers curled and uncurled at his sides as she picked up a sponge and set to work on the sink. He knew it was childish, but he had a hankering to march over there and help himself to a cookie, just to show her she couldn't cut him off.

He settled for shooting her a lethal glare. "You callin' me a sourpuss?"

She refused to look up, so the glare was wasted. "I call 'em as I see 'em. And speaking of calling, aren't you supposed to be calling your deckhands in here?"

There were a few choice words he'd like to call her, by damn. One of them was on the tip of his tongue when he recalled the warning look Cole had sent him.

With a mighty effort, Henry snapped his mouth closed and marched to the door. Just before he slammed it behind him, he thought he heard her give a soft chortle.

Henry's mood seemed no better when he walked back through the door fifteen minutes later with two deckhands in tow. Fanny continued scrubbing the lower cabinets, pretending not to notice the way the first mate scowled the moment he set eyes on her.

Well, that was just fine. She wanted him to dislike her. She'd learned long ago that the easiest way to deal with a chest-ogling man like Henry was to tick him off right off the bat. When it came to fending off stares and lewd remarks, the best defense was a fast offense.

She'd been coping with men who couldn't see beyond her bust line ever since her breasts had started developing at the age of twelve. For some reason, they all seemed to think that just because her chest was large, her brain was small and her morals were loose. Even worse, a lot of them acted as if the size of her breasts affected her hearing. It was unbelievable how many men made rude remarks in

front of her as if she weren't even present. Fanny knew
that other women paid good money to surgically acquire
what she had in overabundance, but as far as she was concerned, a chest like hers was a curse and an embarrassment.

Of course, things would have been different if she were
pretty. Men fell all over themselves trying to impress the
pretty gals. There was power in beauty. But there was no
power at all in being big-chested and homely, and Fanny
knew she was homely. Her nose was too big, her lips were
too thin and her jaw was too square. She was the kind of
woman who would have faded into the background if
she'd had a normal physique, but her oversize bust made
her the center of unwanted attention. To avoid it, she
downplayed her feminity as much as possible. Life was
easier if she looked and acted like one of the boys—a boy
with a tough, don't-give-me-any-guff, I'm-in-control-here
attitude.

Fanny straightened as Henry and the two younger men
stopped in the middle of the room.

"This here's the new cook," Henry announced ungra-
ciously. "She'll tell ya what she wants ya to do." He turned
on his heel and stalked off, leaving Fanny alone with the
two deckhands.

They were two of the sorriest excuses for human beings
she'd ever set eyes on. The older one looked like a sleazy
Elvis impersonator and the other one reminded her of a
skinny, teenage mole. Between the two of them, they
didn't look like they had enough smarts to tell time.

"It's nice to meet you," Fanny said pleasantly. "My
name's Fanny."

The younger one gave a buck-toothed grin and elbowed
his buddy. "Ya hear that? She said Fanny!"

The heavyset Elvis lug snickered.

Fanny marched around the counter, walked right up to
the young punk and poked him in the chest with her index
finger. "That's right—my name's Fanny. I'm named after

my grandmother. It's a good name, a perfectly respectable name, and I don't want to hear any flak about it. Do you understand me?"

Junior took a step back, his eyes wide. "Y-yes."

"Yes what?"

"Uh—yes, ma'am."

She turned to Hambone, her hands on her hips, and gave her most menacing scowl. "And while we're on the subject, let's get a few other things straight. I don't take kindly to smart mouths, and I've got a pretty bad temper. If you don't want to find saltpeter or somethin' a whole lot worse in your food, you won't make any rude remarks or jokes at my expense. There's ways of doctorin' a person's food that make 'em sick to dying, and no one but the person who did it would ever know what happened. Have I made myself clear?"

The potbellied Elvis swallowed visibly. "Y-yes'm."

She turned to the ferret-faced younger one. He nodded so hard he looked in danger of whiplash.

"Good." She gave a satisfied smile. "You treat me right, and I'll do the same by you. I'm a hell of a good cook and I know how to keep a man's stomach happy. Now, what are your names?"

"I'm Hambone." The large one hooked his thumb at the younger man. "An' this here's Junior."

"Hambone and Junior." With names like that, they had no business making fun of hers. Fanny grinned. "Nice to meet you. You all watch your mouths, and we'll get along just fine." Fanny strode back around the counter. "Would you two fellas like some homemade cookies before we get to work?"

Junior's eyes lit up like a Christmas tree. "Cookies! What kind?"

"Chocolate chip and peanut butter."

He narrowed his already narrow eyes until they were only slits. "Did you put anything in 'em?"

"Nothin' that won't make your mouth happy. The captain and Henry both ate some."

Junior visibly relaxed. "In that case, can I have one of each?"

"You bet." Smiling, Fanny fetched the cookies. The two men helped themselves.

Hambone crammed an entire chocolate chip one in his mouth, then rolled his eyes in ecstasy. "Umm. Is all your cookin' this good?"

"Hear tell it is."

"All right!" Junior exclaimed. " 'Bout time we had some real food around here."

"Yeah." Crumbs dribbled from Hambone's mouth onto the top of his protruding stomach. "The last cook like to starved us to death."

"You mean Josephine?" Fanny asked.

Junior nodded. "Her cookin' was way too fancy."

"I don't know about fancy, but it was sure lousy!" Hambone seconded.

"Well, she's evidently not lousy at other things." Junior cast a sly glance at Hambone.

Hambone's eyebrows rose. "Whatcha mean?"

"While you were out checkin' the tow, Gaston tol' me he saw her movin' her stuff into the captain's cabin."

"Get out!"

"That's what he said. Said she's stayin' aboard to give us charm lessons or something."

"You're puttin' me on!" Hambone exclaimed.

"Am not." Junior made the sign of the cross over his chest. "I swear it."

Hambone looked at Fanny. "You know anything about this?"

Fanny hadn't known about the rooming arrangements, but she'd guessed as much. She hadn't bought the captain's cockamamie story for a minute. "The captain said he wants to learn etiquette and protocol to help him with his business dealings. While he's at it, we're all going to learn with him. Josephine is supposed to give us lessons at dinner."

"Manners? Why the heck do we need to learn about those?" Hambone asked.

Fanny had been wondering the same thing, but as she watched Junior excavate a nostril, she decided it might not be such a bad idea after all. "Can't hurt. Might even help you boys with the ladies."

Hambone puffed out his chest. "Hey, I don't need no help in that department."

Fanny could barely suppress her grin. "I'm sure you don't."

Hambone's eyes suddenly grew wide. He turned to Junior. "Say—do you think the captain knows about Josephine's condition?"

"Henry said he didn't. Remember? He tol' us it was a secret."

Hambone's forehead wrinkled, as if he were thinking hard. "Yeah. He wouldn't be havin' her move in with him if he knew."

Fanny's curiosity got the better of her. "Knew what?"

Junior leaned forward eagerly. "Henry says Josephine's got an awful disease that's got no cure. Any man who, uh, fools around with her will catch it, too."

Hambone kicked Junior on the shin.

"Ow!" Junior grabbed his leg and scowled at Hambone. "Whatcha do that for?"

"You weren't supposed to tell. It's a secret, stupid!"

"Oh, dear." Fanny's mind filled with thoughts of AIDS and hepatitis. "If this gal's got somethin' contagious, surely she'd tell a man before puttin' him at risk."

Hambone shook his head. "I don' know. I heard she don't got no money or place to stay, so she wouldn't be likely to say anything that could get her throwed off the boat."

Fanny frowned. This was serious business. "Someone's got to warn the captain," she said decisively.

Hambone took a step back, shook his head and threw his hands in the air. "Don' look at me. I'm not even supposed to know. Henry said the stuff in her med'cal records is confidential."

"So why did he tell the likes of you?" Fanny demanded.

Hambone and Junior looked at each other and shrugged.

A wave of anger burned through Fanny. How dare that gossipy little twerp of a first mate leak privileged information to entertain these two, but keep it a secret from the captain? Especially when he was putting his boss's life in danger. "Well, it seems to me Henry ought to be the one to do the telling."

Hambone and Junior nodded.

"Hambone, go find Henry and make him tell the captain right now," Fanny ordered. "You tell him that if he doesn't, you'll do it yourself."

"I can't do that!" Hambone whined.

"Well, then, tell him *I'll* tell the captain if he doesn't."

"But we weren't supposed to tell *you!*" Hambone's meaty face twisted in anguish. "He'll fire us."

"No, he won't. The captain outranks Henry, and it's his life you're tryin' to save. You don't have to worry about being fired." But Henry darn well might, Fanny thought heatedly. She'd be glad to see it happen. She'd never met a man so worthless in all her life.

"I'll tell you what," Fanny said decisively. "You take me to Henry, and I'll handle things." The worthless cur was just the type to pull a fast one. She wouldn't put it past the man to say he'd tell the captain, then do no such thing. Her lips pressed into a stubborn line. "Yes, sir, I think I ought to be standin' right behind him when he has his little talk with the captain. That way I can make sure Henry tells him all the facts."

She prodded Hambone in the ribs. "Come on. Let's get

goin' before it's too late. The captain said that girl was in his cabin, and I bet you dollars to doughnuts that's where he was headed, too. No tellin' what they're doin' right now."

Cole found Josephine seated at his desk when he let himself into his cabin. She tore her gaze away from the piece of paper in front of her and looked up, her eyes wide. Her cheeks promptly reddened.

Good. As much as she tried to pretend otherwise, she wasn't indifferent to him. He closed the door behind him. "Got your list finished?"

Josephine scooted back the leather chair and rose, handing him the paper. "Yes. Here it is."

Cole scanned the neat column of items. "Salad forks, soup spoons, seafood forks, intermezzo spoons . . ." Cole's brows rose quizzically. "What the hell is an intermezzo?"

"Something you eat between courses to cleanse the palate. Usually sorbet."

"Hell. Is all this really necessary?"

"A prince would know how to use all of these utensils. You'll need to know how to use them, too, if you're invited to a formal dinner."

She had him there. Sighing deeply, he folded the list and put it in the pocket of his denim shirt. "Okay. I'll give it to Henry." He looked around, but didn't see any of her belongings. "Did you get settled in all right?"

"Yes. But I was, ah, wondering about my bed." The color in her cheeks deepened.

So she was thinking about bedtime already. Cole suppressed a grin. "It pulls down from the wall."

"I figured out that much. But how do I reach it?"

"You have to stand on my bed." Kicking off his shoes, Cole climbed to the middle of his mattress and reached up for the recessed handle in the paneled wall. With a loud creak, a narrow Murphy bed pulled down.

"I'll get you some sheets and blankets." Climbing down, Cole strode to the closet and pulled some linens from a bottom shelf. He returned to find Josephine carefully removing her imported leather loafers. He climbed back on the bed and reached out his hand. She hesitantly took it and stepped up beside him onto the king-size bed.

The mattress creaked seductively. Her hand felt small and warm in his palm. He reluctantly released it and handed her one of the sheets.

She awkwardly unfolded it and spread it over the chest-high mattress.

"You're going to have to climb up on the mattress in order to tuck in the sheet on the far side," Cole said.

"Okay."

"I'll give you a boost." Grabbing her around the waist, he hoisted her up. He was unprepared for the impact the warm weight of her body would have on his libido. He could feel the flare of her hips, the curve of her rib cage, the brush of her breasts against his chest. Desire, hot and instant, poured through him. He held her longer than necessary before setting her on the upper mattress.

She gazed down, her lips slightly parted. Her eyes held a vaguely stunned expression. So she'd felt it, too.

She pulled at her sweater, evidently trying to collect herself. "Th-thank you."

Cole couldn't keep from grinning. "My pleasure."

A shiver of alarm chased up Josephine's spine as she gazed into his face. Something had transpired between them during the few seconds she'd been in his arms, something electric and erotic, something that felt far from finished. It was the same thing she'd felt when she'd fallen into his arms climbing aboard the boat—a feeling of inevitability. And now he was looking at her as if she were a bowl of milk and he were a hungry tomcat.

She crawled to the far side of the narrow mattress and grasped the sheet with shaking hands. Dear Lord, but this man kept her off balance! From the moment he'd walked in the room, she'd found it hard to breathe and even harder to form a coherent thought.

She was keenly aware that he was watching her every move. She nervously shoved the sheet under the edges of the mattress as best she could—a difficult feat, considering that she was kneeling on top of it.

"I've got this side," Cole said. "Pull the back corner tight, Empress."

She awkwardly tried to follow his directions, but she didn't have a clue what she was doing. She tugged and pulled and tugged until the sheet at last lay flat.

"Ready for the top sheet?" He unfurled a dingy gray sheet and flapped it open. She jabbed it under the bottom of the mattress as quickly as possible.

"Here's a blanket." He tossed up a lightweight blue one. "Tuck it in at the bottom, and we'll smooth it out from down here."

"Can I have two? I tend to get cold at night."

"That's the only blanket I've got. If you get cold, you can always climb down and crawl in bed with me." He gave a wolfish grin. "I promise I'll keep you nice and warm."

He was teasing—just making a joke. All the same, her heart pounded madly. A frightening, thrilling energy zinged back and forth between them, filling the room with a heady tension. She struggled hard not to look as shaken as she felt. "You're all too kind," she said dryly. "But I'd prefer another blanket."

"Are you sure?" His mouth looked alarmingly sexy as it curved into a grin.

Josephine found it difficult to pull her eyes away. "Quite."

He gave a low laugh. "Okay. I'll ask Henry to see if he can find another in the storeroom. If he can't, I'll have him order one." He held out his arms. "Ready to come down?"

She wasn't ready to touch him again. "I-I think I can make it by myself."

"Whatever you say." He stepped out of her way, but not off the mattress. Josephine scooted to the edge of the Murphy bed and dangled her legs over the side. She pushed off, only to lose her balance and topple directly onto Cole.

The momentum of her fall pushed them both over, and the next thing she knew, he lay beneath her on the king-size mattress. His thighs were as hard as concrete columns, his chest like sun-warmed cement. His breath was warm on her neck, and his beard prickled her cheek. The faint scent of his shaving cream filled her senses.

She intended to sit up and apologize, she sincerely did, but the moment she raised her head enough to see his face, her senses went spinning helplessly out of control. His black eyes gleamed in the afternoon light filtering through the porthole, telegraphing something that left her shaken and aching with unknown need.

She felt his hands move around her back, his fingers on her bare skin just above her waist, where her gray cashmere sweater had come untucked from the waistband of her black wool slacks.

Slowly, slowly, his fingers crept higher under the sweater, blazing a trail of heat up her back. His dark eyes locked on hers, somehow mesmerizing her, holding her gaze against her will.

And then she had no will—or hers became his. Her gaze shifted to his mouth, and suddenly all that mattered was getting close, then closer.

She felt his fingers in her hair, felt his hand urging her face toward his. And the next thing she knew, she found herself pressing her lips to his.

Soft. The thought filtered vaguely through a haze of rapid-fire sensations. His mouth had looked so hard, but his lips were surprisingly soft. And gentle.

And agile. Slanting his mouth beneath hers, he drew her bottom lip between his and suckled.

Hot chills of pleasure shot through her. She'd never imagined a kiss could simultaneously affect so many parts on her body. Heat tingled to the tips of her breasts, the pit of her stomach, the apex of her thighs.

Cole somehow moved closer, adjusting the alignment of their bodies so that she lay between his legs. She heard a groan and realized, as if from a distance, that it had escaped from her own lips. Cole responded with low growl. Angling his mouth over hers, he deepened the kiss.

Oh, dear heavens—she was on fire. She instinctively moved against him, wanting to get closer, wanting more, not even sure exactly what it was she wanted, but wanting it with all her being. Never, ever before had she felt anything so intense, so consuming, so urgent.

His fingers slipped up her back, under her sweater, to the back of her bra. He deftly unsnapped it. His fingers slid over her bare skin, skimming down her back toward the sides of her breasts. Josephine shifted, aching for his touch. Slowly, tantalizingly, his fingers moved forward, and then—

A loud knock sounded at the door. "Excuse me, Cap'n, but I've got to talk to you." Henry's voice was muffled but audible through the thick door.

Oh, mercy, what am I doing? Josephine stiffened, feeling as if a magic carpet suddenly had been yanked out from under her.

Cole tightened his grip on her, holding her in place. "Later, Henry," he barked.

Josephine tried to pull away, but Cole's arm was like a vise. She heard other voices in the hallway; then Henry apologetically cleared his throat. "Sorry, Cap'n, but I need to talk to you now."

"I said *later*."

"I'm afraid it's urgent, sir." This time the voice was female.

With a heavy sigh, Cole released Josephine. Dazed and

disoriented, she rolled off him. Her stomach quaked as she watched him rise and pause to adjust the fit of his jeans.

"This had better be good," he thundered as he strode toward the door. With a murderous look in his eye, he yanked it open.

Chapter Eleven

"What the hell do you want?" Cole demanded.

Henry nervously glanced behind him. Hambone and Junior cowered in the hallway behind Fanny. The woman stood with her arms folded, the look on her face just as fierce as the captain's.

Henry swallowed hard. Lord have mercy, but they had him between a rock and a hard spot! If he told Hambone and Junior that he'd lied to them, he'd never get a lick of work out of them again They weren't too bright, but they were awfully loyal, and they wouldn't take kindly to being misled. If he didn't tell them the truth, though, that old battle-ax of a cook was going to spout off to the captain that Josephine had incurable VD.

Henry twisted his gnarled fingers together miserably. "There's, uh, somethin' I gotta tell ya, Cap'n. Can I come in and talk to ya in private?"

"No."

Cole stepped forward, blocking the doorway with his

body, but not before Henry got a glimpse into the cabin. His jaw dropped. *Great balls of fire*—Fanny was right! Josephine was sittin' in the middle of the captain's bed, furiously fussin' with the back of her sweater, as if she were trying to fasten her bra or something. The bed was all messed up and rumpled, and so was Josephine's hair. The tidy bun she always kept her hair skinned back into had come all undone, and blond hair spilled halfway down her back.

Henry forced his gaze back to Cole. "I really need to talk to ya, Cap'n. One-on-one. It's kinda, uh, personal."

Cole's gaze coldly swept the hallway. "Looks like you brought quite a gallery of spectators for a personal conversation." His eyes landed on Fanny and the deckhands behind her. "Am I right to assume that all of you know what this is about?"

"Yes, sir," Fanny affirmed. Hambone and Junior nodded, their heads bobbing like corks on the water.

Cole's eyes cut back to Henry. "Since everyone but me seems to know what this urgent matter is, I see no reason not to just go ahead and speak your mind."

"But it, uh, concerns someone else." Henry nervously tried to peer around Cole's shoulder.

Cole turned and followed his gaze. His brows lifted as he turned back around. "You mean Josephine?"

Swallowing again, Henry reluctantly nodded.

Cole's eyes narrowed, and his voice took on a steely tone. "Now, listen, I didn't expect you all to jump for joy at the prospect of etiquette lessons, but I hardly think it qualifies as urgent business. I'll see you all at dinner." He started to close the door.

Fanny stepped up beside Henry. "We're not here about the lessons. We're here about your health."

Cole's brows rode up. "My health?"

Fanny stared challengingly at Henry. "You gonna tell him, or should I?"

Cole opened the door wider and leaned one hand against the frame, his fingers impatiently drumming on the door-jamb. "Tell me what?"

Henry couldn't bring himself to look the captain in the eye. "Well, uh, it seems that I, uh . . . " He shoved his hands in his pockets, wishing the floor would just open up and let him sink to the bottom of the river. "Ya see, I tol' Hambone an' Junior . . . "

"Henry tol' us Josephine's got some kind of incurable clap," Junior interjected eagerly. "An' we're afraid you're gonna get it, now that she's moved into your cabin and all."

Cole stared at Junior as if he'd lost his mind. "He told you *what?*"

"She's got some kind of Far East clap. It's not too bad for a woman, but it makes a man's stallionhood shrivel up till it damn near disappears."

"Stallionhood?" Cole turned his incredulous gaze to Henry.

"Well, that isn't exactly how Henry put it. I'm tryin' to use a polite term because Miz Fanny is present, an' that's what they call it in my magazines." Junior blinked earnestly. "Anyhow, whatever you want to call it, Henry says it gets so teensy a man's gotta sit down to go pee."

Henry swallowed miserably. Fanny stared at Junior as if he'd just sprouted a second head, then poked Hambone hard with her elbow. "I thought it was AIDS or some kind of hepatitis," she muttered.

Hambone rubbed his side. "Nah. Junior's tellin' it just like Henry said."

All eyes turned to Henry. He gave a sheepish shrug and ventured a look at the captain. He was relieved to note a glimmer of amusement in his eyes.

Cole's hand tightened on the door frame. "I appreciate your concern, men, but I don't think you have anything to worry about."

Junior took a step forward. "But Henry said—"

Cole cut him off abruptly. "I don't care what he said. It's not true."

Hambone and Junior stared at each other, then back at Cole.

Junior's eyes grew round with disbelief. "Ya mean Henry made it up?"

"He *lied* to us?" Hambone's voice sounded wounded.

Henry twisted his fingers together and stared at the floor. "Well, ya see, boys, I—"

"Henry didn't lie to you," said a soft voice behind Cole.

Henry jerked up his head as Josephine appeared in the doorway beside the captain. "I lied to Henry."

"What?" Junior and Hambone chorused. Fanny stared from Josephine to Henry and back again. Cole gazed at her, his brows raised in surprise.

Josephine shot an encouraging smile to Henry, hoping he'd play along. "I'd been told that the crew on this boat was somewhat"—she hesitated, searching for the right word—"*flirtatious*. Quite frankly, I wasn't in the market for romance, so I figured if I told Henry I had a horrible disease, why, everyone would leave me alone."

"So ya *don't* got nothin'?" Hambone's eyes glittered eagerly.

Cole quickly snaked his arm around Josephine's shoulders. "Of course not. But don't get any ideas." He hauled her tight against his side. A shiver chased through her as the side of her breast pressed against his chest. "She's off-limits. And I don't want to hear of anyone giving Fanny here any flak, either. Have I made myself clear?"

Junior and Hambone bobbed their heads.

"Good. Now get back to work." Pulling Josephine with him, he stepped back and firmly closed the door.

Josephine's stomach quivered as she found herself again alone with Cole. Slipping away from his side, she moved to the desk, putting it between them. She was acutely aware of his gaze following her.

"That was damn decent of you."

She pretended a keen interest in the brass file holder. "What was?"

"Taking the heat off Henry. He got himself in quite a spot, telling that whopper to his deckhands. Thanks for bailing him out."

"I don't know what you're talking about."

"The hell you don't."

Josephine hated to admit that he could see through her so readily. She eyed him challengingly. "How do you know I didn't tell that story to Henry?"

Cole lowered himself onto the corner of the desk, a slow smile spreading across his face. "That little detail about the shrinking stallionhood was a pretty good clue. It didn't sound like the kind of symptom you'd be likely to come up with."

He had her there. Disconcerted by the dangerous gleam in his eye, Josephine looked down, only to be even more rattled by the sight of his muscular thigh on the polished cherry wood.

She turned away and moved toward the porthole. "Henry obviously concocted that story to protect me. The least I could do was return the favor."

"You're full of surprises, Empress." Cole rose and followed her. "Not many women would call it a favor, having a story like that circulated about them."

"Henry meant well."

"So intentions are more important than actions?"

"No. Well, not exactly. I mean, actions count, too, of course, but . . . " She was babbling. She couldn't think straight when he was standing this close to her. Dear heavens—she couldn't think of anything except the fact that he'd kissed her, and that he looked like he was about to again.

What the heck were they even discussing? Oh, yes—intentions. She was tempted to ask what *his* intentions were, but she was afraid of the answer. She drew a deep breath and folded her arms across her chest. "Look—we need to talk about what happened earlier."

"You mean when I did this?" He bent down and softly claimed her mouth. The gentleness of it rocked her as much as the kiss itself. He eased closer and then, heaven help her—she was melting. Her joints went soft and liquid, and her arms fell to her sides as he drew her into his embrace. She was falling again, tumbling into a sweet, unknown place, just as she had earlier on his bed.

His bed. The thought penetrated the heady fog closing in around her mind. That was where all of this was heading. She grasped her last remaining shred of willpower and pulled back. "I . . . I can't."

His hands tightened on her back. "Sure you can."

"You promised you'd be a gentleman!"

"I'd never promise anything so unlikely." He gave a seductive smile. "I said I wouldn't touch you unless you touched me first. And you did." He ran a finger down her cheek. "You kissed me, remember?"

Oh, dear heavens. Had she really? She couldn't remember who had first kissed whom. She'd fallen on top of him and looked into his eyes and then the next thing she knew . . .

She abruptly pulled out of his reach. "It was an accident."

His lips curved in a most annoying smile.

She planted her hands on her hips. "Look. I agreed to teach you etiquette, not become your sex toy."

His eyebrows rose in amusement. "You really have a way with words, Empress." He stepped toward her, a hot glitter in his dark eyes. "If you're worried the situation will be one-sided, you should know that I'm a firm believer in equal opportunity. I'll be *your* sex toy in return." He traced a finger slowly, enticingly down the side of her neck, making her heart thud wildly. His voice was a low, sensuous rumble. "If you'll play nice with me, I promise to play very, very nice with you."

A shiver of heat pulsed through her. He bent his head and brushed her throat with his lips, tracing the path his fingers had just blazed. His beard rasped deliciously against her skin, and she felt herself going under, drowning in a whirlpool of sensations.

She forced herself to draw away. "I—I don't go in for recreational sex."

Cole gave her an impatient look. "You're holding out for the procreational kind?"

The remark was a perfect reminder of why she needed to keep her distance from this man. She straightened her back. "I just don't think sex should be casual," she said stiffly.

"So I'll wear a tuxedo." His lips tilted in a charming grin.

"Very funny." It *was* rather amusing, but Josephine would rather die than admit it.

"Let me guess," he said dryly. "You have to delude yourself into thinking you've found love everlasting before you'll go to bed with a man."

Josephine felt herself blush hotly. She wouldn't dignify the speculation with a reply. She turned toward the porthole and gazed out the window.

"Yep, you're the kind who wants to hear the *L* word, all right," he said, rising from the desk and following her. "So tell me, Empress, have you been in love with all the men you've slept with?"

All the men! He made it sound as if she'd bedded the entire seventh fleet and half of the eighth. Josephine turned indignantly toward him. "For your information, there's just been one."

Dear heavens—why had she told him that? From his smug smile, she'd evidently given him the very information he'd been after.

"Well, since you don't go in for recreational sex, things must have been serious between you and this lucky gentleman." Cole placed his hand on the wall behind her and leaned close. "How long did you two date?"

Josephine turned away. He placed his other arm against the wall, pinning her in place.

"Might as well tell me, Empress." His voice was low and silky. "I can be mighty persistent."

Josephine's heart clamored loudly in her chest. He was standing too close for her to think clearly. If she told him what he wanted to know, maybe he would back off and leave her alone. "About a year and a half."

"Why didn't you two get married?"

"We, uh, discovered we weren't really in love."

"But you'd thought you were?"

She could smell his clean scent, almost feel the heat of his body. "I thought I might fall in love with him," Josephine said defensively.

"Ah. And what gave you that impression?"

"Well, his mother was a friend of my aunt's, and he was entirely suitable, and—"

"*Suitable?*" Cole stepped back and dropped his arms, gazing at her incredulously. "You went to bed with a man because he was *suitable?*"

Josephine skittered away. Why was she even discussing this topic with this man? She crossed the room and stood behind the armchair, drawing herself to her straightest posture. "My personal life is none of your business."

"Sure it is. At least it's about to be."

"No, it's not." She needed to clear the air on this matter, and the only way to do it was to confront it head-on. "That kiss was an accident. It's not going to happen again."

"That was no accident, and you know it. That was the result of mutual physical attraction—damned powerful physical attraction. So let's reach an understanding here, Empress. I don't believe in hearts and flowers and love and

215

any of that other happily-ever-after nonsense, and I won't pretend I do. If you want to fool around, well, you just let me know." He sank down on the edge of his bed. "If you're not interested, I'll leave you alone. But don't go giving me a bunch of mixed signals. Not in this room." He stared at her for a moment; then his eyes took on a devilish glimmer. "Now around the crew . . . " He slowly rubbed his jaw. "Well, that's a whole other matter."

Josephine didn't like the direction this conversation was headed. "What do you mean?"

"I mean Hambone was harassing you this morning, even when he thought you were a carrier of the dreaded shrinking stallion disease. Can you imagine how obnoxious he'll be now that he knows you aren't?"

An uneasy feeling gripped Josephine's belly. "I'll just stay out of his way."

"Junior's even worse. And I wouldn't trust Gaston with a five-hundred-pound nun. You can't avoid the whole crew."

Josephine's back drew as straight as the pilothouse steering stick. "I can take care of myself."

Cole woefully shook his head. "I'd be tempted to let you try, Empress, if we were only talking about *your* safety. Unfortunately, we're not. If the crew starts competing among themselves and showing off to gain your attention, it could create a dangerous situation. Hambone and Junior might start acting like big shots out on the barges, and Gaston might pick a fight with them just so he can beat 'em up."

Cole thought the crew might fight over *her?* She knew it would be a completely undesirable turn of events, but she couldn't help but feel a small thrill of pride at the idea.

Cole leaned forward. "As long as everyone thinks you and I are a cozy couple, well, all of them will leave you alone, and everyone will stay nice and safe."

She'd seen the way the new cook had looked at her, as if

she were some kind of troublemaking trollop. And she hated to have Henry think she'd sold her soul.

She suspected that Cole was exaggerating the situation to serve his own dark purposes, but he'd managed to find her weak button. She'd do anything to avoid putting someone else in danger. If there was a chance that the crew would recklessly show off to impress her, she had no choice.

She gave a defeated sigh. "What do I have to do?"

Cole smiled like a fox who'd just cornered a chicken. "Just follow my lead, Empress. Just follow my lead."

Fanny checked the simmering pan of tomatoes and okra, wiped an almost invisible smudge off the stove and looked around the galley with satisfaction. In the past three hours, she'd supervised the cleaning of the kitchen and made a meal guaranteed to please even the most ravenous male appetite. The potatoes were mashed, the gravy made and the chicken fried, and it was still twenty minutes until dinnertime.

She lifted the lid on the cream gravy and poured in an extra dollop of milk just as Henry walked through the door. Fanny automatically stiffened with dislike.

"Smells mighty good in here," he remarked.

"Hmph." Fanny kept right on stirring the gravy.

Henry ambled past the dining table toward the counter. "Ah, c'mon, there, Fanny. I'm tryin' to make peace here."

"Save your breath."

Henry's can of tobacco clunked loudly as he slammed it on the counter. "Now, listen up, missy, an' listen good. If anyone has a right to be mad, it's me. That was a low-down, damn fool stunt you pulled, draggin' ever'body up to the captain's quarters just to embarrass Josephine."

"It wasn' Josephine I was tryin' to embarrass."

Henry's face turned so red Fanny halfway expected to see steam shoot out of his ears. *Good.* She'd gotten his

217

goat, just as she had intended. "I was making sure that your loudmouthed self didn't weasel out of telling the captain the truth," she added.

Henry's hands clenched and unclenched at his sides. "You don't even know what the truth is!"

"You evidently don't, either. But that didn't stop you from spreading all kinds of tales all over the place, you gossipy old varmint."

"You've got some nerve! If you'd kept your busybody *be*-hind out of things that are none of your concern, none of this would have happened in the first place."

"Well, well, well." The captain's amused voice interrupted from the doorway. "I'm glad to see you two hitting it off so well."

Fanny whipped around to see Cole sauntering into the galley, his hand on the waist of the woman she'd glimpsed earlier in his room. So this was Josephine. Fanny had expected her to tease her blond locks into a big-haired 'do and slather on an inch of makeup like the tootsies who rode with some of the truckers, but Josephine was the most unfloozy-looking female she'd ever seen. She looked like she'd come straight from an old lady's tea party. Her hair was slicked back in a prim knot, she wore pearls with her expensive sweater twin set and her makeup was so discreet that Fanny wasn't sure if she was wearing any or not. Even odder was the fact that the woman seemed to be trying to keep as much distance as possible between herself and the captain, while the captain seemed equally determined to keep her clamped to his side. Most of the truckers' babes she'd seen were practically superglued to their meal tickets.

Cole guided her to the kitchen counter. "Henry, if you'll quit arguing with Fanny for a moment, I'd like to properly introduce her to Josephine."

"It's a pleasure to meet you," Josephine said with a smile.

Flustered, Fanny dropped the spoon into the gravy. She quickly grabbed another one and fished it out, splattering gravy all over her shirt and the floor in the process.

"Don' know why you made my boys scrub the kitchen if you're gonna smear it up like that," Henry said with a snarl.

Fanny shot him an angry glare. "That was an accident. I'll clean it up."

"I'll help." Josephine slipped out of Cole's grasp, rounded the counter and pulled several paper towels off the roller attached under the cabinet. Before Fanny knew what had happened, the genteel blonde was on her knees, wiping the floor. "Kitchens certainly are messy places, aren't they? Why, I seem to get covered with food from head to toe every time I step into one."

It was impossible to imagine this impeccable woman in such a condition. Fanny knew she was exaggerating to make her feel better. But oddly enough, it did.

"There. All done." Josephine rose to her feet and tossed the paper towels in the trash. Fanny continued to mop her flannel shirt.

Josephine peered in the pans and clasped her hands together. "Oh, this looks wonderful! Nothing I cooked ever turned out looking this good."

"You can say that again," the captain muttered.

Josephine stiffened at the remark. A pink stain spread across her cheeks. "I—I'll set the table," she volunteered.

Fanny nodded. "Thanks."

The captain's eyes followed Josephine as she extracted the flatware from the drawer, his gaze both annoyed and hungry. Fascinated, Fanny watched him from the corner of her eye as she pretended to check the okra. What was the deal with these two? The tension between them was thicker than a good gumbo.

Nothing about the situation was what she'd expected. Fanny had figured Josephine would be a brassy gal with

219

tight clothes and a snooty attitude. What with the manners lessons and all, she'd fully expected a real prima donna. She sure hadn't thought she'd be *nice*.

Fanny stirred the gravy, eyeing Josephine curiously. "I hear you'll be teaching us etiquette lessons at dinner."

"That's right. I thought I'd start by reviewing basic table manners."

Henry made a loud snorting sound.

Fanny shot him a heated glare. "Maybe you should start out with something even more basic, like how not to bray like a jackass."

Cole laughed, then strode across the galley and clapped Henry on the shoulder. "Looks like we've got a few minutes before dinner's ready. Why don't you and I go see how Gaston is coming with that problem in the fuel line?"

"Sure thing." Henry's brow lowered in dislike as he glanced at Fanny. "I need a change of scene, anyhow."

Clutching an enormous handful of flatware, Josephine paused in the kitchen and watched the men leave. "Good heavens. I wonder what's wrong with Henry?"

"He's personality-challenged, if you ask me." *Not to mention big-mouthed and obnoxious,* Fanny silently added, opening the oven and peering in at the corn bread.

"I've never seen him act so rude." The silverware clattered as Josephine set it on the counter. "Out of everyone on the boat, he's the only one who's treated me decently."

Fanny looked at her in surprise. "What about the captain?"

Josephine turned to the cabinet and began extracting plates. "He's the worst of all."

Her voice held a note of despair that made Fanny's brow furrow with concern. Closing the oven door, she turned toward the younger woman, noting the tight lines around her eyes. Fanny rapidly looked her over. Josephine didn't have any visible bruises, but then she was covered from neck to foot by her expensive sweater and slacks. "Is he abusin' you, honey?" she asked gently.

Josephine's brows rose in surprise. "Oh, no, it's nothing like that." She met Fanny's gaze and gave her an awkward smile, then turned back to the cabinet, loading a set of saucers on top of the plates. "He's just rude and ill-tempered, that's all."

"Well, that's still not good. They had a show about emotional abuse on one of the TV talk shows last week. Do you ever watch those?"

"I don't watch much television," Josephine admitted.

"Well, they had a doctor on there, and he said emotional abuse could be just as bad as the physical kind. Said if a woman's in a relationship like that, she needs to get out pronto."

"Cole and I aren't in a relationship."

"I'm afraid I'm not following you."

"I mean we don't . . . I mean we're not . . . " Josephine drew a deep breath. "There's nothing physical between us."

Right. Fanny placed her hands on her hips and cocked her head to the side. "Look, honey, I know it's none of my business, but this is a pretty small boat, and it's hard not to notice where folks are sleeping. You're stayin' in his cabin, aren't you?"

Josephine's fair skin flushed to the roots of her hair. She set down the stack of plates with a clatter. "I'm staying in his cabin, but we have separate beds."

If it made her feel better to lie about the situation, then Fanny wouldn't push her. She bent down and searched a low cabinet until she found a dish she could press into service as a gravy bowl. "Well, like I said, it's none of my business."

"It's not like you think. Really." Josephine's face was earnest as she gazed down at Fanny. "There weren't any other sleeping accomodations. Besides, the crew tends to give women a hard time, and Cole thought there would be less trouble if they think I'm his girlfriend."

Her eyes held a convincing sincerity. Fanny recalled the

odd look on Cole's face as he'd watched Josephine and the unusual tension between them. Maybe they weren't lovers. At least, not yet. The situation certainly was interesting.

Josephine piled the silverware on top of the saucers, then picked the whole stack up and headed to the dining table. "We're going to act like we're a couple in front of the crew, but we're not. The truth is Cole doesn't even like me."

Oh, he likes you, all right. Fanny thought, watching the younger woman move to the other side of the room. *And from the way you looked at him, you like him right back.* She'd bet her first paycheck they wouldn't be pretending the opposite for long. "Why do you think he doesn't like you?"

"He dislikes anyone from uptown New Orleans, and that's where I lived before my aunt died. He thinks we're all a bunch of rich, arrogant snobs." Josephine's lips twisted in a wry smile. "Of course, that's like the pot calling the kettle black. I've never met a more arrogant man in my life." She carefully laid five pieces of flatware at a table setting. "I wish Cole could be more like Henry."

"That old gossipy goat?" Fanny scowled. "I can't believe you'd say that, after the way he gabbed all over the boat about your so-called disease." She lifted the pan of gravy off the stove, then grinned. " 'Course, you must have had his number right off the bat. That was pretty clever of you, making up that wild story and telling it to old Motor Mouth."

Josephine set down another fork. "I didn't make up that story."

Fanny froze, the gravy pan suspended in midair. "But you said you did."

"I just said that to cover for Henry."

Fanny's brows knit in consternation. "What do you mean?"

Josephine looked up. "Henry made up that story so the

crew would leave me alone. He was trying to protect me."

Henry had invented that tale out of kindness? Fanny plopped the pan back down on the stove and frowned.

Oh, dear. She'd been wrong about the old goat—dead wrong. She hated it when people made unfair assumptions about her, but she'd done that very thing to Henry. She'd assumed he was a low-life cad just because he'd looked at her chest a little overlong. She'd wanted to believe the worst of him, so she had.

The insight made Fanny wince. She looked up to find Josephine regarding her curiously.

"You don't care for Henry, do you?" Josephine asked.

Fanny picked up the pan again and sighed. "I guess we got off on the wrong foot."

"What happened?"

Fanny resumed pouring the cream gravy into the white casserole dish. She glanced at Josephine from the corner of her eye. "He, uh, looked at my breasts."

It was Josephine's turn to stop and stare.

Fanny picked up a wooden spoon. "I know it sounds stupid, but when I catch a man ogling my chest, I get real testy." The spoon scraped loudly against the metal bottom of the pan. "I've been self-conscious about being big busted ever since I was a girl. Just because I have big breasts, men act like I'm easy or dumb or both. I learned a long time ago that if I lash out at 'em early on, it tends to keep them in line. So when I caught Henry looking at me all pop-eyed, I let him have it." She placed the empty pan in the sink and turned on the water. "Then when Hambone and Junior said you might give the captain an incurable illness and Henry didn't want him warned, well, I guess I was just ready to think the worst of the old coot." She picked up a gray oven mitt and sighed. "Now I guess I'll have to apologize and try to make peace with the old lech."

Josephine couldn't help but smile. "That shouldn't be hard." She watched the older woman open the oven and pull out a pan of perfectly baked corn muffins. "When he gets a taste of your cooking, I imagine he'll forgive just about anything."

"I hope so. I hate to eat crow." The buxom woman reached in and pulled out a second pan.

Josephine grinned as she laid out another place setting. "Doesn't look like that's what you're serving." She breathed deeply, inhaling the fragrant steam. "Mmm. Where did you learn to cook like this?"

"From my grandmother, back in Tennessee. She raised me and my four brothers after my mother died."

Josephine carefully set down a knife. "I lost my mom when I was young, too."

Fanny looked across the room, her eyes filled with warmth. "I'm sorry to hear it, honey." The two women silently regarded each other for a moment, a bond forming between them. "Did you live with your dad?"

Josephine shook her head. "I lived at a boarding school in New England."

"I thought you said you lived in uptown New Orleans."

"I moved there three years ago. I had a great-aunt who ran a charm school. She developed health problems, so I moved in with her and helped out with her school."

"What did you do before?"

"I taught etiquette at a finishing school in Switzerland."

Fanny let out a low whistle. "So how the heck did you end up cooking on a towboat?"

"My aunt died and I needed a job. I didn't know the first thing about cooking, but I thought I could fake my way through it." She gave a sheepish grin. "There's a lot more to cooking than I thought."

"Don't feel bad. I'm just as lost when it comes to manners. Grandma knew how to cook, but she didn' know much beyond 'please' and 'thank you.' " Fanny smiled, her eyes filled with admiration. "It took a lot of guts, signing on and trying to bluff your way along. I admire a

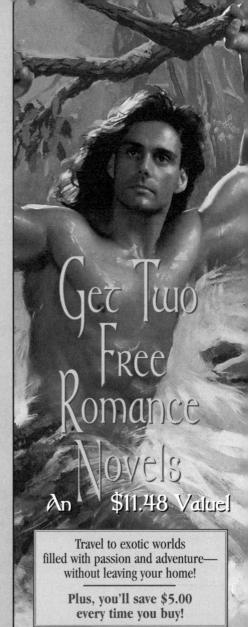

Thrill to the most sensual, adventure-filled Romances on the market today...

FROM LOVE SPELL BOOK

As a home subscriber to the Love Sp
Romance Book Club, you'll enjoy the best
today's BRAND-NEW Time Travel, Futurist
Legendary Lovers, Perfect Heroes and oth
genre romance fiction. For five years, Lo
Spell has brought you the award-winnir
high-quality authors you know and love
read. Each Love Spell romance will swe
you away to a world of high adventure...a
intimate romance. Discover for yourself
the passion and excitement millions of rea
ers thrill to each and every month.

Save $5.00 Each Time You Buy!

Every other month, the Love Spell Romance
Book Club brings you four brand-new titles
from Love Spell Books. EACH PACKAGE WILL
SAVE YOU AT LEAST $5.00 FROM THE BOOK-
STORE PRICE! And you'll never miss a new title
with our convenient home delivery service.

Here's how we do it: Each package will carry
a FREE 10-DAY EXAMINATION privilege. At
the end of that time, if you decide to keep
your books, simply pay the low invoice price
of $17.96, no shipping or handling charges
added. HOME DELIVERY IS ALWAYS FREE.
With today's top romance novels selling for
$5.99 and higher, our price SAVES YOU AT
LEAST $5.00 with each shipment.

AND YOUR FIRST TWO-BOOK SHIP-MENT IS TOTALLY FREE!

IT'S A BARGAIN YOU CAN'T BEAT! A SUPER $11.48 Valu

Love Spell ✦ A Division of Dorchester Publishing Co., Inc.

Get Two Books Totally
F R E E —
An $11.48 Value!

▼ Tear Here and Mail Your FREE Book Card Today! ▼

PLEASE RUSH
MY TWO FREE
BOOKS TO ME
RIGHT AWAY!

Love Spell Romance Book Club
P.O. Box 6613
Edison, NJ 08818-6613

woman with guts."

A sensation of warmth spread through Josephine's chest. She had the feeling she'd just made a true friend.

"I'll bet it took even more guts to talk the captain into takin' manners lessons. How in blazes did you do that?"

Josephine hesitated, remembering Cole's instructions to keep his plans quiet. "He has quite a few business interests. He thought it might make him more at ease in social settings."

"Well, my hat's off to you." Fanny added some salt to the okra. "An' I'm lookin' forward to your lessons. If you want, I can repay the favor by teachin' you how to cook."

The warm feeling in Josephine's chest expanded. "I'd like that very much."

"Well, it only seems fair. Besides, I like havin' company in the kitchen." Fanny smiled generously, then glanced at her watch. "Oh, my, we'd better quit gabbing and get dinner on the table! The men will be here any moment."

Josephine stood by the counter as the men straggled into the dining room, clutching her damp palms stiffly together. She'd already failed as a cook. She couldn't fail at this as well.

But she'd never seen a more unlikely-looking bunch of etiquette students in her life. Their clothing alone violated all the rules of polite behavior. Hambone's faded plaid shirt was torn and dirty, Junior's black T-shirt had stains and dark underarm circles, Gaston's gray sweatshirt was covered with grease and reeked of sweat, and Henry's work shirt sported a tobacco stain on the right pocket. To her dismay, she noted that Henry was toting his coffee-can spittoon to the table. She watched in amazed horror as the men slumped onto the benches around the table.

Cole's sudden earsplitting whistle made Josephine jump. "Okay, men. As you all know, we're going to be learning about manners at dinner. I expect all of you to listen to Josephine and do as she says."

"Ah, Boss. Whatta we gotta do this for?" Hambone moaned.

"Yeah," Junior muttered.

"I'm wondering zee same thing, *Capitaine*," Gaston muttered.

"I'll name some reasons and you can take your pick. Number one." Cole lifted his thumb. "Not everyone I do business with is a river rat, and I don't like looking like an ignorant clodhopper. Acquiring a little polish will help me in my business dealings." He lifted his index finger. "Number two: I believe in taking advantage of opportunity when it comes along, and we happen to have an etiquette teacher here in our midst. And number three: I'm one generous son of a bitch. Instead of hoarding this font of knowledge all to myself, I'm offering each of you the opportunity to better yourselves."

"What if we don't want to?" Junior said.

Cole eyed him sternly. "Well, then, I'll take that as an indication that you don't want to work on this boat."

"Ah, Cap'n," Hambone said with a moan.

Cole leaned forward, his hands on the table, his eyes hard. "Now listen up. Manners have to be practiced, and I'm not gonna be practicing genteel politeness on you jerks only to have you act like a bunch of rude rednecks in return. We're in this together." He sank down in his chair with an air of finality and motioned toward Josephine. "All right, Empress. You're on."

It was not the most glowing of introductions. Josephine drew a deep breath, trying to still the quaking inside.

It would be a lot easier to concentrate if Cole weren't looking at her that way, she thought. He was staring at her boldly, an amused half smile on his lips. She couldn't help but think about the way those lips had felt on hers. Judging from the way he was looking at her, he was thinking the same thing.

He'd said he'd wait for her signal. The arrogant man

probably thought she'd throw herself at him before the night was over. Well, by George, if that was what he thought, he had another think coming. She wasn't sure exactly how that kiss had happened, but she was certainly not going to let it happen again.

Haughtily lifting her head, she gave her best imitation of Aunt Prudie's most intimidating schoolroom demeanor. "Good evening. As the captain explained, I'll be giving a course in etiquette during the dinner hour. Can anyone tell me why etiquette is important?"

The question was met with silence. "Guess no one thinks it is," Hambone said at length.

The other men snickered.

Josephine refused to be thrown off balance. "Etiquette is really nothing more than showing kindness and consideration for others. Knowing how to behave appropriately in social situations helps everyone feel more at ease."

"I feel plenty at ease already." Hambone sniggered.

"Me, too," Junior agreed.

They certainly *looked* at ease, Josephine silently admitted. Hambone sat sprawled with his elbows on the table, his low-riding jeans exposing a large expanse of hairy backside. Junior slumped forward, casually noodling his nostril with his pinky. Gaston tilted back in his chair, his feet propped against the nailed-down leg of the table, while Henry busily tucked a napkin into the neck of his shirt. Only Fanny and Cole showed any sense of decorum at all.

"There's a difference between making yourself comfortable and seeing to the comfort of others around you," Josephine said firmly. "Most people are ill at ease when they're forced to watch behavior that is disrespectful, disgusting or ignorant."

"Hey, Junior, she's talkin' to you!" Hambone elbowed the young man's ribs, causing the youth to ram his finger all the way up his nose.

"Ow!"

Josephine averted her eyes from the repellent spectacle. "I'm talking to everyone in this room. Now, I would like for all of you to please stand up."

"Oh, man," grumbled Junior.

"What for?" asked Hambone.

"We jes' set down," complained Henry.

"You heard her," Cole ordered, rising from his chair. "On your feet."

Satisfaction, warm and gratifying, stole through Josephine's chest. It felt good to have Cole following *her* instructions for a change.

She waited until all the men had followed the captain's example. "As I'm sure you know, gentlemen not only show certain courtesies to each other, but special courtesies to women. In a social setting, such as a meal, they also show special consideration to their host and hostess. For our purposes here, Cole will be the host, and I'll assume the role of hostess."

Gaston winked and nudged Junior. "I think she means mistress, *mon ami,* don't you?" he said in an audible whisper.

Josephine's cheeks heated, but she refused to bow to embarrassment. She turned a steely gaze on Gaston. "It's very rude to exclude other people from your conversation. If you have something to say, please say it loudly enough for the whole group to hear."

Gaston winked again at Junior, making the youth chortle. "It was a private joke, *chérie.*"

Josephine stared him down. "Private jokes are inappropriate at a dinner setting. So is any type of derogatory remark about another person."

"Especially about Josephine." Cole's voice, cold as an Antarctic front, chilled the room. "You will treat her with respect and cooperate with these lessons, or you will be put off the boat." He glared around the table. "No one is indispensable. *No one.* I will not put up with insubordination. Does everyone understand?"

228

The crew nodded, their eyes on the table.

"All right." Cole inclined his head at Josephine. "Please continue."

He was standing up for her. She didn't know why that fact should fill her stomach with an odd fluttery sensation or why it should make her face heat more than Gaston's rude remark had, but it did. She drew a deep, steadying breath.

"As I was saying, Cole is the host, and I will serve as hostess. The host is always seated at the head of the table, with the female guest of honor on his right. Fanny, would you please move to the seat at Cole's right?"

"But that's my seat!" Henry complained.

"Not anymore," Cole replied.

Fanny lumbered over to the spot indicated as Henry glowered at her.

"The male guest of honor always sits at the right of the hostess," Josephine continued. "Henry, would you come sit by me, please?"

"My pleasure, Miz Josie." Henry threw Fanny a smug look, as if he'd somehow bested her.

"Can we sit yet?" Hambone asked.

"In a moment. First, I'd like for you all to move around to the back of your chairs."

"Looks like we're gonna play ring-around-the-rosy," Junior muttered. He gasped as Hambone's elbow landed in his scrawny ribs.

"What's the matter with you? Ya wanna get put off the boat?" Hambone scolded in a loud whisper.

Josephine chose to ignore the exchange. "Before we begin our meal, let me explain the duties of a dinner guest. First of all, guests should show up at the table looking presentable. That means clean clothing, tucked-in shirts, well-groomed hair and clean-shaven faces. It also means clean hands. A gentleman pays particular attention to the cleanliness of his fingernails. I know this is our first lesson, so I'll excuse everyone's appearance today. But if you show up in disarray again, I'm afraid I'll have to ask you to return to your cabin to make the necessary adjustments."

A round of low moans and grumbles circled the table.

"*Now* can we sit down and eat?" Hambone asked.

"In just a minute, Hambone. And for the record, it's impolite to show impatience with the host or hostess."

Hambone heaved a loud sigh.

"That includes sighing, finger tapping or fidgeting." Josephine looked sternly at Gaston, Hambone and Junior, each of whom were committing one or more of the named offenses. "The reason I asked you to remain standing is because it's customary for the host to direct guests to their seats." She looked at Cole, and felt a shiver chase through her at the intense way he was gazing back. "Would you like to direct anyone to another place?"

Yeah, I'd like to direct you onto my lap, he thought. Cole pushed the thought away and shook his head. "No."

"In that case, the appropriate protocol is to wait for the host or hostess to invite you to sit down. Once the invitation is issued, it is customary for the male guest of honor to pull out the hostess's chair. The male host will usually assist the female guest of honor with her seat. Any questions?"

Yeah. Why do you act so cool when you kiss so hot?

He watched her look around the group. Her gaze rapidly jumped over him, then darted back. She was the very picture of composure, except for the way she tried to avoid looking at him.

"Since this is our first lesson, I'll give the signal tonight." She glanced nervously at Cole. "If that's all right with you, of course."

Cole gave a slow grin. "I'm eagerly awaiting your signal, Empress."

He was gratified to see her cheeks color. It was insane, the way this prim-lipped schoolmarm turned him on. She somehow managed to aggravate him beyond words while

230

simultaneously arousing him almost beyond endurance. He was starting to get hard just watching her.

She smiled around the table. "Won't you please be seated?"

Cole gratefully sank into his chair as his men did the same.

"Captain, aren't you forgetting something?" Josephine prompted.

I haven't forgotten a thing. I remember exactly how your mouth opened under mine and how that sweet body of yours squirmed against me as if you were trying to crawl into my skin.

"You're supposed to help Fanny," she reminded him.

I'd rather help myself. To you.

And I will, too, Cole silently vowed, rising to his feet and pulling out the bench for the cook. He'd promised to follow Josephine's lead in the romance department, but he hadn't promised not to try to influence her decision. He could hardly wait to get her alone again to put his powers of persuasion to work.

Chapter Twelve

"Hi there, Captain!" Fanny cheerily called an hour later.

Josephine looked up to see Cole striding back into the galley. She tensed at the sight of him, accidentally rattling the plates she was helping Fanny load into the dishwasher. Cole had disappeared with the rest of the crew after dessert, saying he was headed up to the pilothouse, and Josephine had been relieved to see him go. Every time she'd glanced at the end of the table during dinner, his dark eyes had been fixed on her, and she'd found it difficult to think about anything except the way his mouth had felt on hers.

Fanny smiled brightly at Cole. "Josephine's helping me clean up. We're just about finished."

"So I see." Cole leaned a hip against the counter. "Thanks again, Fanny, for the excellent dinner." He turned a pointed gaze to Josephine. "And thank *you,* Empress, for a very informative etiquette lesson."

The unexpected praise rattled Josephine. She pulled the box of detergent from under the sink, trying hard to act unaffected by his presence. "You and Fanny are good students. I'm afraid I can't say the same, though, about the rest of the crew."

Fanny chuckled. "From what I saw, it's a step up for those boys not to eat with their hands. I never saw a more uncouth band of hooligans in my life." She wagged her head. "I thought truckers were unrefined, but these guys made them look like pinky-lifting tea sippers. They were shoveling in their food so fast I was afraid they were going to bite their own hands."

Cole laughed, his white teeth flashing. "That's their way of complimenting your cooking."

Fanny shrugged modestly. "Ah, well, I was lucky enough to have a grandma teach me how. I've offered to do the same for Josephine, if it's all right with you."

Cole glanced at Josephine. "Fine with me. But I don't think the Empress is interested in cooking lessons."

"It so happens I'm very interested," Josephine said stiffly, irritated that Cole thought he could speak for her. She turned to Fanny with a smile. "Can we start at breakfast?"

"Sure. You might want to wait till lunch, though. Breakfast comes around at a mighty early hour." Fanny straightened and dusted her hands together as if she were wiping off invisible dirt. "Well, if it's okay with you two, I think I'll go to my cabin."

"It's fine with us." Cole ambled toward Josephine. Before she knew what had happened, she found herself encircled by his arm. "In fact, we're about to do the same. Right, honey?"

Josephine's heart pounded so hard she found it difficult to form a coherent thought, much less a response. She longed to tell Cole that Fanny knew the truth and there was no reason to pretend they were a couple in front of her, but she didn't think Cole would appreciate her having shared that information. She managed to nod and smile lamely.

Fanny regarded them curiously. "All right, then. I'll go unpack and settle in. I'll see you both in the morning."

The room suddenly seemed uncomfortably warm and small as the door closed behind the cook. Josephine tried to draw away from Cole's side. "There's no need to act affectionate now that no one's around."

Instead of dropping his arm, Cole tightened it. "You never know who might be right around the corner." His fingers curled softly on her upper arm, stroking the skin on the sensitive underside in a way that sent shivers up her spine. She strongly suspected his plan to pretend that they were lovers was nothing more than an excuse to taunt her, but it would do no good to say so.

His fingers slid slowly up her arm. "If you're going to get up before dawn for cooking lessons, maybe we'd better turn in early as well."

Turn in—oh, dear. The thought of going to bed made her light-headed. Josephine's mind raced. "You, uh, promised to show me how that exercise machine worked."

Cole gave a lazy smile. "You feel like exercising? Why, sure, sugar. I could go for a little workout myself." He gave her arm another squeeze. "Let's go change clothes."

Josephine balked. "I, uh, don't have anything to change into."

Cole ran his gaze over her cashmere sweater and wool slacks. "I'll loan you a T-shirt and some drawstring shorts."

The thought of wearing Cole's clothing struck her as disturbingly intimate. So did the idea of accompanying him to his cabin to change into them.

He moved his fingers on her arm in that alarmingly sensual way again. "Come on."

She had no choice but to go with him. Why, oh, why had she let him bully her into sharing his cabin? Because he'd threatened to leave her in Natchez, that was why, and she hadn't doubted for a second that he would have done exactly that.

Besides, she'd thought he was bluffing. As much as he seemed to despise her, she hadn't thought he'd want her constantly underfoot. Something had shifted in his attitude toward her, something that had changed all the dynamics between them.

Something had shifted, all right, she thought ruefully. She'd shifted herself right on top of him and kissed him like a lust-crazed bimbo.

She bit her lip in chagrin as he led her through the darkened hallway. She didn't know what had gotten into her, behaving in such a shameless fashion. Just as upsetting was the way she seemed unable to put it out of her mind. She couldn't look at him without her gaze sliding to his mouth. At dinner, she'd been in the middle of explaining the correct way to hold a knife when her gaze had fallen on his lush lower lip, and she'd completely lost her train of thought. Then he'd curled his mouth into a knowing smile, and her stomach had sunk with the certainty that he could somehow read her thoughts.

She only hoped he couldn't read them now. He opened the door, stepped back and swept his hand forward. "After you."

"Thank you." She entered his cabin, her stomach quaking. If she praised his efforts to behave politely, perhaps it would encourage him to continue his gentlemanly conduct. "You know, your manners are rapidly improving. You not only did well at dinner, but you opened that door for me just now as if you'd been doing it all your life."

His gaze moved over her. "I'm a quick learner when I've got motivation."

"Motivation?"

His sensuous mouth curved into a rakish angle. "Getting you alone in my cabin."

Oh, dear. He could turn the most innocent remark into something suggestive. She moved as far away from him as possible and smiled brightly. "Well, I'm ready to switch roles and let *you* teach *me* about that exercise machine."

"I can think of a few other things I'd rather teach you."

He was doing it again. She was relieved when he turned to the dresser, opened a drawer and pulled out a white T-shirt. He tossed it to her, and she caught it awkwardly against her chest. He opened another drawer and pulled out a pair of navy shorts.

"Here you go," he said, passing them to her as well.

She froze and stared as he started unbuttoning his denim shirt.

His eyebrow lifted. "Something wrong?"

He loved to upset her. As long as he thought he was succeeding, he would only continue to do so. She wouldn't let on that she was the least bit bothered by the fact that he was taking off his clothes right in front of her. "Of course not."

"Good." He peeled off the shirt and threw it on the bed, his bronze biceps bulging. Josephine's mouth went dry. *Good heavens*—he was gorgeous. Dark hair curled across his muscular chest, narrowing to a line that bisected the hard muscles of his stomach.

He reached for the button on his jeans.

Josephine swallowed convulsively. Dear Lord—he wasn't going to strip naked right in front of her, was he?

The hiss of his zipper answered her question. Hugging the shorts and shirt to her chest, she whipped around and gestured awkwardly toward the bathroom. "I'll, uh, go change in there."

She fled to the safety of the tiny, white-tiled room and locked the door behind her. She peeled off her sweater, only to remember she was wearing a black bra. Great, she thought dismally—it was going to be clearly visible under the white cotton T-shirt. The last thing she wanted to do was to show off her underwear, but she couldn't bring herself to sashay back into his bedroom and pull out another bra right in front of him. She guessed she'd just go braless. She scrambled out of the undergarment and into the shorts and shirt, then silently counted to two hundred, giving Cole plenty of time to get fully dressed before she stepped out.

He eyed her appreciatively when she emerged. "I never knew my clothes could look so good."

He looked awfully good, too, in a loose white muscle shirt and black nylon shorts. They stood there, looking at each other for a moment, sexual energy gathering in the air between them like electricity in a storm cloud.

She needed to get out of there before lightning struck. She flashed an overly bright smile. "Let's head on up."

Cole opened the door, gesturing toward it. "After you."

Her stomach fluttered. Dear heavens, but the man made her nervous! Directing the topic back to manners seemed like a good way to keep their relationship on safe ground, and she desperately felt the need for safety.

"You're doing very well, remembering courtesies to ladies," she remarked as she walked through the door he was holding.

"It's easy to remember I'm around a lady when you're dressed like this." His voice was low and warm, and it sent a current of heat racing through her belly. "You've got a great pair of legs."

The remark startled her so much she froze in her tracks.

He gave a slow grin. "No one ever told you that before?"

She considered lying, but she figured her reaction had already given away the truth. She shook her head, then rapidly resumed walking down the hallway.

He strode beside her. "Not even that guy you dated for a year and a half?"

She shook her head again.

"He must have been blind. What was his name?"

"Wally."

"Wally?" Cole's voice held a distinct note of amusement. "Your lover was a guy named *Wally?*"

She had no interest in defending Wally, but Cole's attitude rankled. "A person's name has nothing to do with what a person is really like."

"Maybe not, but it can sure determine whether or not a person is *suitable,* can't it?"

Josephine bit her bottom lip. Why had she ever even mentioned Wally, much less tried to explain her involvement with him? Especially since she didn't quite understand it herself. The unfortunate liaison had been a combination of desperation, curiosity and blind hopefulness that love would follow romance. Not that anything she'd ever done with Wally had seemed the least bit romantic. "I thought we were talking about first names."

"You're right, Empress. We were. And for your information, first names and nicknames say an awful lot about a person." He clattered down the stairwell, leaving Josephine to follow.

"Wally is short for Wallace," she said when they reached the next deck. "He's named after his grandfather. It doesn't mean anything."

"It means he's a wimp. If he were any kind of man, he wouldn't answer to a name that sounds like it belongs to an overweight walrus."

It was rude to be argumentative, but she couldn't resist a retort. "You told me you were called Trash Boy. Did *your* nickname fit?"

"At the time, I guess it did."

Good heavens, but he was stubborn! Not to mention irritating. And provoking. "If nicknames are so significant, suppose you explain why you call me Empress."

His lip hooked into a smug smile. "You mean aside from the fact that you act like one?"

He was truly insufferable. She lifted her chin. "Yes. Aside from that."

He leaned down and looked directly into her eyes. "Because you insist on being called Josephine—not Jo or Josie or something more approachable."

The remark was delivered in such a straightforward manner that it took Josephine aback. She stood staring after him as he turned away and opened the hatch.

"My . . . my father insisted everyone address me by my complete name," she found herself saying as she stepped up and over the high threshold into the cool night air.

"Why?"

Why indeed? Josephine gazed out at the lapping water, not wanting to speak ill of the dead, but not knowing how to talk about her father otherwise. "He was somewhat . . . rigid." *To put it mildly.* "He said it was my proper name, the name he and Mom had given me, and that's what I should be called. He believed it was important to do things correctly."

"Sounds like a control freak."

It would be disrespectful to agree aloud, so Josephine remained silent.

"What did you call him?"

"Father. I once called him Dad, and he sent me to bed without any supper."

"Sounds like a real nice guy," Cole said wryly. "Did you always do what he wanted?"

"Most of the time." Except for once, she thought guiltily. Steering her mind away from the painful memory, she gripped the side of the boat and made her way down the open deck.

Cole walked beside her. "Was your father the one with the family connections and money?"

"No. That was Mom."

Cole glanced at her in the dim light. "Was she rigid like your old man?"

Josephine shook her head. "She died when I was five, so I don't remember a lot about her, but I do recall she was kind and caring and affectionate."

"At least you remember something," Cole said. "I don't remember anything about my mom." His mouth twisted into a humorless smile. "Although from what I've heard about her, it's just as well."

A pang of sympathy, warm and strong, shot through Josephine.

"Tell me what you remember about yours," Cole urged.

Josephine carefully navigated her way around the metal bench. "I only have one really clear memory. I guess I was about four, and Mom and Dad and I were in New Orleans, visiting Aunt Prudie. Mom and my father took me to the Audubon Zoo. Mom was wearing a pale yellow dress, and I remember thinking how it matched her hair, and how her hair matched the sunshine, and how her laughter somehow matched it, too." Josephine smiled. "I remember my parents were on either side of me, each holding my hand and swinging me in the air between them. It's the only memory I have of my father ever laughing." Josephine rounded the corner to the back deck. "Prudie said he changed after Mom died. She said he thought God was punishing him."

"For what?"

"For planning to leave the mission field." Josephine pushed a strand of hair out of her face. "When I was little, Dad ran a mission in Central America. Mom wanted to raise me in the United States, so when I was big enough to go to school, she talked Dad into accepting a job with Aunt Prudie's husband in New Orleans. But before we could move, Mom caught a fever and died. Dad thought it was God's way of making him stay."

"Nice concept of God he had there," Cole said dryly. "What kind of missionary work did he do?"

"Religious education and health care. He organized teams of health care workers and other volunteers who'd spend their vacations helping the underprivileged. That's how he met Mom. She came to work as a volunteer, and she never left."

"What happened after she died?"

"He sent me to a religious girls' school in Maine, and he stayed in Central America. He came and visited me twice a year, but he never let me come visit him. I guess he was afraid I'd get sick like Mom."

Cole watched her wrap her arms around herself and stare out at the dark sky. She looked small and alone, and an unexpected rush of sympathy poured through him. From the sound of things, she'd grown up almost an orphan. He turned his gaze up to the sky and watched thin, wispy clouds scud by, whitewashing the inky night.

"It's quite a leap from a religious school in New England to a finishing school in Switzerland. How did that happen?"

"It's a long story," she said evasively.

"I've got time."

"I really don't want to get into it."

Her refusal to answer whetted Cole's curiosity. He decided to try another tactic. "How does a missionary happen to have enough money to pay for a fancy finishing school?"

Josephine looked up, her eyes earnest. "Oh, Father didn't pay for it. Mom left me a trust fund. Aunt Prudie took it over after Father disown—" She stopped abruptly. Pressing her lips together, she looked away.

"After your father what?"

"Nothing."

He stared at her. "You were about to say disowned, weren't you?"

She blinked hard and looked away.

"Why the hell did your father disown you?"

"I-I can't talk about it."

"You mean you won't."

"That's right." She tilted her chin up obstinately, but she still refused to meet his gaze.

Curiosity was burning a hole in him. "Ah, come on, Empress. It's the most interesting thing you've told me about yourself."

She walked across the deck to the railing. The light from the upper deck was dim, but not so dim that he couldn't see the lines of pain etched around her mouth. "I made a mistake, okay?" Her voice was tight and tremulous. "It hurts to think about it, much less talk about it."

If anyone knew about mistakes that hurt, it was Cole. He immediately felt chagrined. "Hey, I didn't mean to upset you. It's just hard to imagine you ever getting in any kind of trouble, that's all."

"Oh, I got in trouble, all right." The wind caught Josephine's voice, making her sound far away even though she was less than a foot in front of him. "My father called me the devil's own handmaiden."

"No kidding?" He looked at her with renewed respect. Maybe he could pry some more information out of her if he tried a different tack. "This school you went to—was it strict?"

"To say the least." She turned toward him and gave a rueful smile. "Chewing gum was against the rules because it was considered a hedonistic pleasure."

Cole shook his head. "Wow."

Josephine's smile faded. "Father thought the place was too lenient."

It was a wonder the Empress had any spunk left at all, after an upbringing like that. Cole watched her tuck a loose strand of hair behind her ear, his chest strangely tight. The wind blew the shirt against her back, freeing strands of silvery-blond hair from her topknot and outlining the ridge of her spine. She looked so slight, so vulnerable.

She turned and motioned toward the exercise machine. "I thought you were going to show me how this thing works."

Cole rubbed his jaw, unsettled to be caught staring at her, unsettled by the unexpected tenderness he felt toward her. "Well, I don't know if I should."

"What do you mean?"

He gave a rakish grin. "It might not be wise to help the devil's own handmaiden pump up."

She smiled, just as he'd hoped she would. "I never should have told you that."

"I'm glad you did. It makes you seem more human."

Her forehead knit. Her eyes grew defensive. "I didn't seem human before?"

She'd felt plenty human in his bed that afternoon, but he didn't think she'd appreciate hearing that. "Let's just say it's good to know you have some chinks in your armor."

"What do you mean, my armor?"

"Well, you've got to admit, you're a little stiff-necked."

"Stiff-necked? Exactly what do you mean by that?"

Criminy. Why had he ever opened his big mouth? "You're a little too . . . proper. Too controlled."

"You'd prefer it if I were improper and out of control?"

He grinned. "Sure sounds like a lot more fun."

She stared at him for a moment, then surprised him with a laugh. He smiled back at her, and something crackled in the air between them—something bright and hot, something that sent an unexpected warmth creeping into his chest.

"It might help if you'd let me call you something besides Josephine," he found himself saying.

She looked away, her expression almost shy. "Okay."

He felt the oddest stab of emotion, of something that felt suspiciously like tenderness. "All right, then—Jo."

Her gaze flicked back to his. "Make it Josie, please."

Just when he thought that high, inpenetrable wall around her was about to crumble, she reverted to form. He frowned in irritation. "There you go again."

"There I go with what?"

"Being stiff-necked. Insisting on calling all the shots."

"It's not that." She awkwardly looked down at her fingers. "It's just—I had a good friend who used to call me Jo. She—she died, and now every time I hear it, I . . . " Her voice trailed off and she looked away. She never talked about Lauren. What on earth had prompted her to mention her now? She was telling this man far too much about herself.

Cole reached out and placed his hand on her back. The

243

touch was gentle, and when she glanced up, his eyes were warm and sympathetic. "Hey, I'm sorry. Josie it is."

Josie. Hearing him call her that made her feel somehow freer and lighter. Her pulse quickened.

She turned away and gestured toward the exercise machine. "How do I operate that gizmo?"

"Let me adjust it and I'll show you."

He walked to the machine, crouched down and twisted a knob that lowered the long, padded bench. Moving to the front of the machine, he flipped forward a metal plate, then adjusted two pulleys. "All right. Sit down and straddle the bench, facing the machine."

She did as he requested. To her consternation, he straddled the bench behind her. His chest pressed against her back, his arms on either side of hers. He leaned forward and grabbed the pulleys, aligning his body even closer with hers. "Put your feet on that metal plate in front."

Awkwardly she complied. His muscled thighs swung up beside hers, leaving her trapped by both his arms and legs. "Make sure your knees are flexed. Ready?"

Josephine numbly nodded, so keenly aware of the hard masculine body behind and around her that she could scarcely think.

"Pull with your arms like this." He smoothly pulled the pulleys, and the seat went gliding forward. Josephine found her legs bent in front of her.

"Now push back with your legs." Cole smoothly pushed off the metal plate, causing the seat to glide back. "See? It's a simple back-and-forth motion. Pull with your arms, push with your feet." He handed her the pulleys and climbed off the seat behind her. "You try it."

She swallowed hard, aware of his eyes on her, and awkwardly tugged on the pulleys. The bench shot forward so rapidly that she slid off.

Cole's strong hands were immediately under her arms, lifting her back on the bench. "You need to relax. Keep your knees bent. Try again."

Frowning in concentration, Josephine pulled again.

"Good," Cole said approvingly. "Atta girl!"

Atta girl. An odd feeling of warmth poured through Josephine. All of her life she'd longed for someone to encourage her, to cheer her on, to be in her corner rooting for her. All of her life, she'd longed for an *atta girl.*

How ironic that this hard-boiled towboat captain should be the first to give her one.

The thought disconcerted her. She jerked on the pulleys and once more shot off the bench, this time landing hard on the metal deck.

Cole grinned in amusement, and Josephine found herself grinning back. "Maybe we should start with an exercise where the seat doesn't move." He adjusted the pulleys again, then knelt beside her and tightened a knob under the bench. "Swing your legs around and face the other direction."

She did as he ordered. To her discomfiture, he straddled the end of the bench and sat facing her. His black shorts rode high on his muscle-bound thighs. She had a hard time keeping her eyes averted.

"Grab the pulleys behind you," he instructed.

Josephine stretched back and tried to reach them, but couldn't. Cole leaned forward, his chest pressing against her breasts. She gave a sharp intake of breath, feeling her nipples harden.

Cole slowly leaned back and handed her the pulleys. "All right. Pull them forward."

She awkwardly complied, all too aware that she wasn't wearing a bra and his eyes were fixed on the front of her T-shirt.

He was directly in her line of vision. She looked to the side and tried to focus on the shore beyond the river, but the lights were a mesmerizing blur. Her thoughts became a blur, too. The only thing that seemed real was the man seated inches away from her, his dark eyes fastened on her breasts.

"Relax. You're way too tense." He placed his hands on the tops of her shoulders and kneaded her muscles. The contact of his hands on her skin made her tense up all the more.

"You need to loosen up. Just relax and go with the pull."

He *was* talking about the exercise machine, wasn't he? Because she was certain that an entirely different sort of pull was being exerted on her. Her throat convulsed as she swallowed.

"Don't fight it, Josie." His voice was a low murmur.

Josie—he'd used that name again. A flash of heat raced through her stomach. She gave another awkward pull.

"That's it," he said. "Relax and take it easy."

His touch was anything but relaxing. Tension coiled all through her. The pulleys clanked loudly as she released them too suddenly. "Sorry," she mumbled.

"Easy does it. You don't want to rush it." He leaned forward and retrieved the pulleys for her again, once more brushing his chest against hers. Josephine's hands tightened on the handles as he passed them to her, her nerves ready to snap.

"Take it slow, Josie." His mouth lifted in a sultry smile. "Pretend you're making love with Wally."

"In that case, I'd already be finished." The words were out before she knew it. She stared at him, her face heating.

Cole's eyes widened in surprise; then he burst into a hearty laugh.

She was mortified. The remark was totally out of character. She didn't know what had prompted her to say such an outrageous, revealing thing. "I-I'm sorry. I shouldn't have said that," she stammered.

Cole was devastatingly handsome when he smiled. "Why not?"

"It—it wasn't kind."

"Was it true?"

Josephine couldn't meet his eyes. Rising from his seat,

he leaned forward and took the pulleys from her hands, releasing them back to the machine. Then he sat back down, his knees touching hers, his hands again on her shoulders. She could feel the heat of his gaze up on her. "That Wally was a real loser, wasn't he?"

Josephine shrugged.

His fingers curled on her shoulders. "Sounds to me like you've had a mighty poor experience in the romance department."

Oh, dear! This was getting far too personal. She needed to pull back, to put him in his place. "My experience isn't any of your business."

"I'd like to make it mine." He slid closer, moving his hands up the back of her neck, into her hair. His touch made her feel dizzy and disoriented, as if she'd had too much champagne. Her breath caught in her throat and her heart pounded wildly.

His eyes were dark and hypnotic, his gaze compelling. He seemed to pull her forward, like a magnet would steel shavings.

She ought to get up. She ought to walk away. She ought to . . .

She ought to kiss him. Her body angled toward his, as if pulled by gravity. Her eyes seemed to be closing of their own volition.

And then she was in his arms, and his mouth was just as she remembered, just as thrilling and demanding. This was nothing like the slobbery pecks she'd endured from Wally. This was different—far, far different, as far removed from anything in her previous experience as the thin crescent moon overhead.

This was a man who knew what he wanted, a man who knew how to make her want it, too. Her arms wound around Cole's neck. He leaned against her, pressing her back, and before she knew what was happening, he'd stretched her out on the bench. She lay beneath him, spraddled, her head and torso resting on the padded leather. He leaned over her, warm and strong and man-scented. "Josie," he murmured.

And suddenly, that was who she was. She was no longer Josephine, fettered and tied by inhibitions. She was Josie, the woman she'd always longed to be, the woman locked away in her deepest being.

Cole's mouth slanted over hers, his kiss deepening. She curled her fingers into his shirt, feeling the heat radiating from him, drawing that heat into herself. All thoughts, all reason evaporated in the face of the fire flaring within her.

She gave a little moan and shifted. His pelvis aligned with hers, and she reflexively moved under him. She opened her eyes to see his dark, smoldering gaze gleaming back.

His mouth claimed hers again, then slid down her neck. Softly, gently, his lips moved back up to her mouth as his hand skimmed her side. His fingers moved over each rib, moved slowly, slowly toward her aching breasts. She thought she would die of need before his hands lightly traced the undersides, then the upper sides, then firmly cupped them both.

She arched her back, leaning into his palms. His thumbs flicked against her nipples through the soft cotton. Pleasure, sharp and hot, pulsed through her. She strained to get closer, to get more. She wrapped her legs around his and heard him groan in her ear.

She was caught up in a whirlwind of sensation—the sweet saltiness of his mouth, the warmth of his hands, the weight of his body. The world seemed to be spinning faster, heat seemed to encompass her, and light seemed to pulsate from the innermost parts of her being. She could swear she even heard music. It seemed to pour from the sky—thundering, old-fashioned music, growing increasingly louder and shriller. Strangely enough, it sounded like a calliope.

"Damn," Cole muttered, pulling back.

Josephine opened her eyes. *Oh, dear heavens*—it *was* a calliope! An enormous, brightly lit paddle wheeler rose out of the water less than twenty yards to the left. To her mortification, a large group of senior citizens lined the railings, staring right at them. A white-haired woman pointed in their direction, and her warbly voice carried across the water as she shouted to be heard over the blasting music. "Is that one person or two, George?"

"I think it's two. Looks like a couple spooning to me," came the reply.

"Let me see," sounded another voice eagerly.

Dozens of wrinkled faces craned in their direction. Cole rapidly pulled Josephine upright on the bench and stood in front of her, shielding her from the curious eyes. "They'll be gone in a moment," he said, bending over her shoulder.

It was one of the longest moments of Josephine's life. She sat perfectly still, humiliated beyond belief, as Cole blocked her from the stares of the elderly tourists.

The calliope finally faded into the distance along with the enormous passenger vessel, but Josephine's sense of despair failed to fade with it. How could she have allowed herself to get so completely carried away? She'd long ago promised herself that she'd never let her emotions overrule her head again.

Every modicum of common sense within her told her that getting involved with Cole was a disastrous idea. There was no possibility of a future. He was cold-bloodedly planning to seduce Alexa Armand. How could she sleep with him, knowing she was helping him prepare to seduce another woman?

Especially when she was so inexperienced in the ways of lovemaking. A lump formed in her throat. He was probably laughing to himself at the eager way she'd naively responded to his kiss.

Cole sank beside her on the padded bench. "Sorry for

the interruption." He placed a warm hand on her thigh. "Now where were we?" His voice was low and seductive, his gaze hard to resist.

She *had* to resist. Josephine stood on wobbly legs. "I-I'd like to go inside."

"Good idea." His eyes held a sexy, lazy gleam that made her stomach tighten. He looped an arm around her waist.

It took all of her strength to pull away. "No."

"No what?"

"Just—no. I can't do this."

"Damn it, Josie—what's the deal with you?"

"There's no deal. I just think this is a bad idea, that's all."

"You didn't seem to think so a few moments ago."

She swallowed hard. "I—we got carried away."

"So?"

"So . . . I don't think it's a good idea."

"There's nothing to think about, sweetheart. I want you and you want me."

She couldn't deny it. Not after the way she'd responded to him. She locked her gaze on the river.

"Why are you taking something so simple and turning it into something complicated?"

It wasn't simple. Nothing about this man was simple, and nothing about the mixed-up, churning way he made her feel inside was simple, either. She settled for raising her shoulders in a helpless shrug.

"You're sending out more mixed signals than a monkey at a Morse code machine, Josie."

"I'm sorry," she muttered softly.

Sorry? Dadblast it—how was he supposed to respond to that? What the hell did this dame expect him to do? He ran a hand through his hair and blew out a hard, exasperated breath. "I've never taken a woman against her will, Josephine, and I won't start now. If you're trying to goad me into playing some kind of roughhouse sex game, you're flat out of luck."

She looked up, her expression shocked. "I'm not playing a sex game!"

"Could have fooled me."

The hum of the towboat engine throbbed in the silence between them. She stared down at her fingers. "Under the, uh, circumstances, don't you think it would be better if I slept somewhere else?"

"And just where would that be? The only extra bed on the boat is in my cabin." He wasn't going to make this easy for her, by damn. "Besides, it's in your best interest for the crew to think you and I are an item."

He stepped closer to her, so close he could smell the soft scent of her perfume. The scent teased his nostrils, and he briefly wondered who was punishing whom. He lowered his voice to a low, ominous tone. "No, sugar, if you're staying on the boat, you're staying with me. But don't you worry that pretty little head of yours. I won't lay a finger on you when we're alone in the cabin until you tell me you're good and ready."

"I'll never be ready!"

Liar. You already are.

His face must have given away his thoughts, because her forehead furrowed furiously. "You are the most colossally arrogant man I've ever met."

"I'm not arrogant, sweetheart." He looked straight into her blue, blue eyes. "Just honest with myself. I suggest you give it a try."

Chapter Thirteen

Fanny was mixing a bowl of biscuit dough when Josephine walked into the galley the next morning. The older woman looked up and grinned. "Well, good mornin'! I didn't expect you to be up this early."

"I wanted to take you up on your offer of cooking lessons."

Fanny dumped the dough out on the floured counter, her eyes on Josephine. "Maybe you should have waited till lunch. You look mighty tired."

Josephine rubbed a spot on her aching forehead. "I didn't sleep very well."

To say the least. Even though she'd been exhausted, she'd barely slept at all. She'd been too busy replaying the events of the night like a continuous tape in her mind. Never in her life had she felt anything like the hot, quivering sensations Cole had stirred within her. She'd read about such things in romance novels, of course, but she'd figured the descriptions were grossly overstated or that she was incapable of feeling what other women felt. Nothing

252

she'd experienced with Wally had ever hinted at the possibility of anything so overwhelming.

Overwhelming—that was the word for it, all right. Cole had completely overwhelmed her common sense and good judgment. It was mortifying, knowing that he had that power over her. Even more mortifying was the thought of how much she'd enjoyed it. In plain view of a steamboat full of passengers, no less!

She must have temporarily taken leave of her senses. Whenever she was around Cole, she hardly recognized her emotions as her own. He made her feel unsettled and restless and confused.

Not to mention attracted. She'd never felt more attracted to a man, despite the fact that he was the most galling individual she'd ever encountered. He'd even had the nerve to lecture her about self-honesty!

After the paddle wheeler had rolled past, she'd escaped to his cabin, and he'd gone to the pilothouse to take care of some paperwork. She'd pulled up the shade over the porthole to let in some light from the upper deck, then crawled into the bunk and pulled the covers to her chin, hoping for the blissful mindlessness of sleep, but it had eluded her. To her chagrin, she'd been wide-awake when the door had creaked open around midnight.

Cole. Her heart had pounded traitorously as she'd heard him enter and close the door behind him. She'd lain perfectly still, her face to the wall, feigning sleep and listening to his movements. The sound of a zipper and the rustle of fabric had told her he was shedding his clothes right in the middle of cabin, just as he'd done earlier. She'd heard the soft padding of bare feet, the closing of the bathroom door, and the wet pounding of the shower.

When he finally emerged from the bathroom, soap-scented steam wafted out with him. She'd heard the flap of covers being lifted, then the creak of his mattress below her. Thank heavens—he'd gone to bed without giving her the slightest notice. She knew she should have felt relieved, but instead she'd felt a strange tinge of disappointment.

The bed had creaked again, directly below her. She'd wondered if he were naked. Barbarian that he was, he probably slept in the nude. The thought had sent a feverish chill chasing through her, but she'd made herself lie quietly. At least she'd fooled him into thinking she was asleep. She hadn't been able to fool him on any other score.

She had finally begun to relax her taut muscles when his voice rumbled through the darkened room. "You can go to sleep now, Empress. Sweet dreams."

What an utterly infuriating man! Her hands had tensed into tight fists, but she hadn't given him the satisfaction of a response. His deep, even breathing had filled the cabin a short time later, irritating her all the more. It was unfair that he should be able to sleep so peacefully when his mere presence in the room made her so hot and edgy.

She'd been enormously relieved when he'd risen, dressed and quietly left the room at five. She'd gotten up soon after.

Fanny's voice brought her back to the moment. "Can't say I'm surprised you didn't get much sleep."

Josephine frowned. "What do you mean?"

Fanny's lip pulled in a knowing grin. "Just figured the captain wouldn't give you much rest, that's all."

Josephine watched the cook rub flour on the wooden rolling pin. "What are you trying to say, Fanny?"

"Why, nothin'." Fanny expertly wheeled the rolling pin over the ball of dough. "But after I got all unpacked last night, I took a little stroll around the boat." She cut a sly glance at Josephine. "I walked all over the outside deck, from the front to the very back."

Josephine's stomach tightened. She tried to keep her voice casual. "What time was that?"

"About the time that paddle wheeler cruised by."

Josephine felt a flood of heat wash over her face. "You saw us."

"Now, now, don't be embarrassed." She reached out and patted Josephine's hand with her flour-covered palm. "I only saw enough to know that things aren't exactly platonic between you and the captain."

"But they are! I mean, what you saw is all that happened."

Fanny's eyebrows rose. "I can't imagine the captain's any too pleased with that."

"Well, that's just too bad." Josephine turned and pulled a coffee mug out of the counter. "I signed on as his etiquette teacher, not his paramour."

Fanny resumed rolling the dough, her mouth upturned in a smile. "Well, I've got to tell you, honey, I'd have a hard time refusing that man anything."

Josephine turned and stared at the older woman, the empty mug in her hand.

Fanny grinned. "He's a hunk and a half. Don't tell me you haven't noticed."

"Well, he's nice-looking, if that's what you mean," Josephine said begrudgingly.

"He darn sure is. And intelligent. And personable. And unattached." Fanny gently turned the dough on the counter.

"He's also rude and arrogant, and he has the biggest chip on his shoulder I've ever seen."

Fanny's grin widened. "All I'm sayin' is a gal could do a whole lot worse than a man like the captain." She reached up, pulled a juice glass out of the cupboard and placed it rim-down on the dough, using it as a biscuit cutter. "Lord knows I'm not much qualified to give advice in the romance department, but I do know this—love is darned hard to come by. I've always regretted not marrying and having a family of my own."

"Cole's not in the market for love and marriage!"

"None of 'em are, honey." She placed the cut biscuits on a baking sheet. "Not at first, anyway."

Josie was about to reply that Cole never would be when Henry sauntered into the galley, clutching his ever-present coffee-can spittoon.

He scowled at Fanny. "I came to fetch a thermos of coffee for the cap'n."

Fanny wiped her hands nervously on her large white apron. "Josephine, will you handle that? Henry and I need to have a little talk."

Josephine glanced at the older woman, noting the agitated way she was wadding the remaining dough back into a hard ball. "Of course."

Henry spit into his coffee can. "I got nothin' to say to the likes of you."

"Maybe not, but you have some listening to do."

Josephine grabbed a thermos from the bottom cabinet, filled it with steaming coffee, then quickly headed for the door.

Fanny waited until she heard the latch click, then drew a deep, steadying breath and glanced up at Henry.

His face creased in a dark scowl. "Well?"

Fanny picked up the rolling pin and began flattening the ball of dough, avoiding his eyes. "I, er, owe you an apology."

"Damn right ya do." Henry spit again. "Ya gonna give me one?"

Fanny pressed the dough harder than necessary. "That's what I'm trying to do right now."

He plopped his coffee can on the counter. "Well, what's stoppin' ya?"

This was the most impossible man she'd ever met in her life. "You are, you old coot!"

The snarl on Henry's mouth eased, then evaporated. She was surprised to see the corner of his mouth curl up. "My wife used to call me the very same thing."

"With good reason, no doubt."

Henry's smile widened. Fanny wondered why she'd never noticed the vivid blue of his eyes before. She cleared her throat. "You and I . . . we kinda got off to a bad start. I'm sorry for my part in that. I apologize for anything unkind I might have said or done."

Henry took so long to respond that she was beginning to wonder if he ever would. "Apology accepted," he finally mumbled. "An' I reckon I owe you one of my own."

Relief flooded Fanny's chest. Her head bobbed curtly. "Okay."

"Okay." Henry awkwardly shoved his hands in his pants, then pulled them out again. He picked up his spittoon, then placed it back on the counter. Fanny continued to roll the dough, even though it was already far too thin.

"Do you, uh, ever play poker?" he asked.

"Sure do."

"Ya any good?"

Fanny glanced up. "Don't mean to brag, but I bought an extra refrigerator for my café with the poker winnings I hustled off my customers."

"Is that a fact?" Henry grinned. "No one on this boat likes to play 'cept me an' the cap'n, and he never seems to have any spare time. Mebbe you an' I can get up a game this evenin' after dinner."

"All right. But I hope you're not a sore loser."

Henry swaggered around the counter and pulled a mug from the cabinet. "You don' have to worry 'bout that. Only thing you need to know is I'm a right cocky winner."

Fanny smiled. "I just bet you are. But that won't be a problem, 'cause you're not gonna win."

Henry lifted the coffeepot off the burner, grinning hugely. He wasn't at all bad-looking when he smiled, Fanny thought with a little jolt of surprise. In fact, something about him was rather appealing.

He sloshed some coffee in his mug. "Better watch your mouth, woman. You'll be eating those words before the night is over."

Fanny chortled. "I'm none too worried."

Their eyes caught and held. "Speakin' of eatin', are those fresh biscuits you're makin'?"

"Sure are. If you come back in twenty minutes, there'll be some sausage and redeye gravy to go with them." She slid the pan of biscuits into the oven. "How do you like your eggs?"

"Over easy." Henry replaced the pot on the burner, his blue eyes bright. "Ya know, Miz Fanny, you and me might just get along after all."

"Hmph. Let's see if you still think so after a few rounds of seven-card stud."

He ambled for the door, his face creased in a smile. "Hope you're as good at losin' as you are at talkin'."

"You'd best be hopin' the same for yourself."

Henry hesitated at the door, still grinning widely. Fanny felt a jolt of sexual awareness. She reflexively folded her arms across her chest, even though his gaze was fixed on her face.

"Have a good mornin'."

He pulled the door closed behind him. It wasn't until he'd already left the room that Fanny realized that this time, she was the one who'd been doing the staring.

Hambone frowned at the slab of pie Fanny set before him a week later. "Hey—you didn't give me near as much dessert as you gave Henry!"

"It's impolite to comment on the size of servings," Josephine said from the end of the table.

"Well, I want some more pie."

Josephine fixed him with a patient gaze. "Can you think of a more polite way to phrase that request?"

Hambone rolled his eyes and gave an exasperated sigh. "Would you *please* gimme some more apple pie?"

"That's much better." Josephine smiled approvingly. "But you need to wait until everyone has had a first serving before you ask for seconds. And if you're a guest in someone's home or in a formal dining situation, you shouldn't ask at all, but wait for seconds to be offered."

"There're too many rules to this manners business," Hambone complained. "There's no way a person can remember them all."

"It's just a matter of practice," Josephine said. "The more you practice, the better you become."

"I can think of lots of things I'd rather be practicin'." Hambone's thick lips curled in a lascivious grin. "Like what you and the cap'n are practicin' in his cabin."

Junior hooted. Gaston gave a raucous laugh. Even Henry smiled.

"We'll have no more of that kind of talk," Cole said sternly. He glanced at the end of the table, and took a vicious pleasure in the fact that Josephine's face was flushed, her expression distinctly uncomfortable. *Good. By damn, she* should *be uncomfortable*. He'd been uncomfortable ever since she'd boarded the boat.

But especially since she'd moved into his cabin. He hated the way he lay awake at night, listening to her toss and turn above him. He spent half the night cursing himself for ever having the bright idea of making her move in with him, and the other half wondering why the hell he'd made that rash promise not to lay a finger on her. He ached to just pull her into his bed and do everything the crew thought they were doing anyway.

The memory of how she'd felt and smelled and tasted that night on the deck had been driving him crazy all week. Not to mention the memory of the way she'd responded. The way she'd wrapped her legs around him and moved against him had nearly sent him over the edge. Even after a week, just thinking about it could make him hard.

He rubbed his jaw irritably. She wouldn't be worth the aggravation if she weren't doing such a good job preparing him to get back at McAuley. Despite how she bothered him personally, she was helping him achieve his goal. She wasn't just teaching him etiquette—she was giving him a crash course in upper-crust culture. He was learning about art, architecture and antiques. She was teaching him about wines, whiskeys and even cigars. She was coaching him on elocution, acquainting him with European customs and phrases, and drilling him on common, everyday courtesies until they were becoming second nature. She was doing exactly what he'd hired her to do, and doing a better job of it than he'd ever imagined. She was providing him with the means to hurt the man responsible for Mom's death.

The thought sent a deep ripple of satisfaction straight to his gut. It was the thought that soothed him in the middle of the night, the thought that energized him in the morning, the thought that made him apply himself to learning what he'd always considered shallow, useless information. He was learning what he needed to know to enter McAuley's world and shatter it all to bits. That was more than worth a few sleepless nights or an overwrought libido.

"That was a right delicious meal, Fanny." Henry leaned back in his chair and patted his stomach. "Apple pie happens to be my favorite."

Fanny slid another slice onto Hambone's already empty plate. "That's what I heard. Glad you liked it."

"You wouldn't by any chance be tryin' to butter me up so's I'll let you pick the type of poker we play tonight, would ya?"

"Now why would I do that? I've whupped you good at five-card draw, second-hand fling and seven-card stud."

"And I won back every penny on Low Chicago," Henry retorted.

Fanny flipped her wrist dismissively. "You got a lucky hand. But if it'll make you feel any better, *you* can decide the game tonight."

"All right." Henry grinned. "How 'bout Mexican Armpit?"

"Never heard of it."

"Sounds a little hairy to me," Junior said. Hambone and Gaston snickered.

"It's a right good game," Henry said. "I'll help you clean up these dishes; then I'll show you."

Cole looked around, noting that Hambone had already wolfed down his second piece of pie. He pushed back his chair. "Fanny, that was another excellent dinner."

He looked at Josephine, waiting for her to confirm it was time to end the meal. She met his gaze, then quickly looked away. Just the slightest glance made her skittish these days. *Well, good.* She was the one who insisted on keeping their relationship platonic, so it was only fair that she should be as uncomfortable around him as he was around her.

"Fanny, it was wonderful," Josephine said. "Gentlemen, you're doing an excellent job with your manners." She rose from her chair, signaling that the men were free to leave the table.

Cole sauntered toward her as she picked up her dessert plate and started to gather the one to her left. "Let Henry do that."

"If I help, too, it'll get done twice as fast."

"You've got other work to do."

Josephine looked at him. "I do?"

"You haven't begun to teach me how to dance yet."

Josephine's eyes widened. "I didn't think you were interested."

"Oh, I'm interested, all right."

She shot him a warning look. "In *dancing*."

He grinned. "In that, too."

"You made fun of it when I mentioned it."

"I've thought it over. It's a skill I'm likely to need. As I recall, Alexa took dance lessons in high school."

Josephine stiffly nodded. "She's an excellent dancer."

"Well, then, we'd better get to it. I've got a CD player in my cabin. I'll bring it up to the aft deck and meet you in there in five minutes."

Josephine stood in the breeze on the back of the boat, her arms wrapped tightly around herself. She was unsure if it was the breeze off the water or the prospect of dancing with Cole that was causing her to shiver.

She stared out at a passing freighter. That was what life seemed to be doing to her—silently passing by, slipping slowly but surely around the bend. The trip was almost halfway over. She needed to be thinking about her future, about how she was going to support herself once she returned to New Orleans. But instead of making plans, she was spending all of her time thinking about Cole.

He was far more complex than she'd initially thought. Under his rough, tough exterior, he had a tortured soul and a surprisingly decent heart. He also had a razor-sharp wit, a quick mind and an innate sense of fairness. His crew regarded him with respect, and Josephine was surprised to realize that she'd begun to do the same. The more time she spent around him, the more drawn to him she became. There was an intensity about him that somehow seemed to be burning its way inside her.

She sensed his presence before she saw him. He came striding around the corner, a boom box in his left hand, a large leather case in the other. Her palms grew damp at the sight of him.

He stopped beside her near the railing. "What kind of music do you want?"

"Something slow and easy."

"Here. Take your pick." He opened the leather box. She had to lean close to peer into it. As she did, she smelled a musky, slightly spicy scent.

After-shave. He'd applied after-shave. The thought that he'd done it just for her made her knees feel oddly weak.

She tried to focus on the music selection. "You must have a hundred CDs in here!"

"I like music."

"So I see." She thumbed through the stack and was surprised at the variety. Sinatra, Professor Longhair, the Stones, the Boston Symphony . . . He evidently had very eclectic tastes. The fact that he appreciated a variety of music added a disturbing new depth to his character.

"Let's try this one." He picked out a CD, inserted it in the player, and punched a button. A soft, lush melody filled the air. "What do you think?"

"Very nice."

He held out his arms and gave a jaunty grin. "Okay, Teach. I'm all yours."

Would that you were. The thought ricocheted through her mind like a stray bullet, shattering her equilibrium. Why on earth would she think a thing like that? She had the uneasy feeling that her heart had just given her an insight she wasn't prepared to explore.

Resolutely forcing her thoughts to the task at hand, she drew a deep breath. "We'll start with the basic waltz. The rhythm is right, left, right, pause; left, right, left, pause."

"Sounds simple enough."

"The first thing you need to do is take hold of my right hand and place your left on my waist."

He stepped close. "Like this?"

She could hardly breathe. He overwhelmed her senses when he was this close. His hand was warm. His chest was hard. He smelled of after-shave and soap. She thought she could hear his heart beating, then realized it was her own pulse drumming in her ears. "That's . . . fine." Her voice sounded strange and strangled. "Now step forward on your right foot."

He advanced toward her. She stepped back, but she miscalculated how large a step he would take. His pelvis bumped against hers and his chest flattened her breasts.

She rapidly drew away.

He took another large step forward, again pressing close against her. "Am I going too fast?"

"Yes! No. I mean, you're too . . . "

He took another rhythmic step forward, aligning his body even more intimately against hers. "Close?"

"A—a little," she conceded.

"I dance better when I can feel my partner's response. Am I making you uncomfortable?"

It was a trick question. If she said yes, he was sure to accuse her of being stiff-necked again. "Of course not. But I'm trying to teach you how to behave in polite society, and some women might find such proximity"—she searched desperately for the right word—" . . . intimidating."

"I won't be dancing with anyone who feels that way."

Josephine nodded, her throat tight. *Stupid,* she silently berated herself. *Of course he won't. He'll be dancing with Alexa.* How could she forget for a minute that she was preparing him to seduce Alexa?

Alexa would have no silly qualms about dancing too close. The hauntingly romantic music swelled, and the knot in Josephine's throat swelled, as well. "Maybe I'd better take the lead."

"I've been hoping you would."

Alexa, she was sure, would have the perfect rejoinder. Alexa would know how to flirt and playfully banter, not stand there tongue-tied with no idea how to respond. For lack of a better idea, Josephine focused on the lesson.

"I'm going to step forward three times, then pause. One, two, three, pause. See if you can follow."

He followed her smoothly, moving in perfect sync. With each step, he managed to inch still closer. By the time the last note floated into the air, she was no longer sure who was leading whom, although she strongly suspected he had taken over. He didn't loosen his hold on her even though the song had clearly ended.

She drew a deep breath and made an effort to at least pretend she was still in charge. "You did very well. Would you like to lead on the next song?"

His hand moved low on her back as the strains of "Smoke Gets in Your Eyes" filled the night. "If you promise to follow."

She took a desperate stab at a lighthearted response. "It depends on where you're going."

"I know where I'd like to take you."

The nearness, the warmth, the sheer maleness of him made her dizzy. Her palms felt damp and her brain felt fuzzy, as if she weren't getting enough oxygen.

His voice sounded in her ear, low and rumbly, sending a shiver down her arms. "Do you have any idea what you make me want to do?"

He pulled back enough to look down at her. His eyes were hot. The heat burned its way through her, making her feel as if her bones were melting. Against all wisdom, she found herself breathing the irresistible question. "What?"

His lips brushed against her ear. The soft warmth of his breath sent a quiver of pleasure coursing up her spine. "For starters, I want to kiss you."

She looked up at him, unable to speak.

"And unless you tell me you don't want me to, that's exactly what I'm going to do."

"I—" Her lips parted, but no further words came out.

His mouth brushed her ear again as he spun her around. "That didn't sound like a no."

She didn't know if it was the rising notes of the painfully beautiful music or the feel of his breath on her neck that raised goose bumps on her skin. She knew only that she felt helpless to deny the aching need to again feel his lips on hers. "It . . . wasn't."

"Josie." He lowered his head. The kiss started soft and sure, but rapidly deepened. His hand released hers, and she found her arm winding around his neck as he embraced her in a glove-tight fit. His lips moved over her mouth, the kiss gaining force and momentum. She felt his hands skim over her back, felt his hands cup her bottom. She groaned as he pressed her to him. She could feel the hard proof of his desire, could feel the answering, aching melting deep within her. She rocked against him, melding herself to him. She gradually grew aware that the song had ended.

"Let's go back to my cabin," he whispered.

She wanted to. Oh, how she wanted to! Every fiber of her being wanted to.

"Let me make love to you," he whispered.

Love? The word hit her like a bucket of cold water. All of the little insights she'd had earlier, all of the tender, confused feelings budding inside of her—they all burst into the foreground of her consciousness with sudden, startling clarity.

Dear heavens—she was falling in love with him.

But he didn't love her. He was using her to get Alexa. She pulled back. "No."

His hands ran up her spine, then down again to her bottom. "You know you want to."

"Wanting has nothing to do with it." She had to look away. She didn't have the strength to resist his smoldering gaze. "You don't . . . you aren't . . . we're not . . . " The lump in her throat felt like a boulder. Placing her hands against his chest, she firmly but gently pushed him away. "The only reason I'm here is to help you seduce Alexa. It's one thing to ask me to help you practice manners and dancing. It's entirely another to expect me to help you practice your skills in the bedroom."

Cole stared at her blankly. "Where did you get a crazy idea like that?"

"It's not so crazy."

"That's not at all what all this is about!"

"But that's what would be happening all the same, isn't it?" She pulled away. Despite all her efforts, her voice was thick with emotion. "I'm going to the cabin. Please don't follow me." She turned and hurried away before the tears brimming in her eyes started to fall.

Chapter Fourteen

It was well after midnight when Cole quietly opened the door to his cabin. He'd contemplated spending the night in the engine room, but Gaston was up late working on the backup generator.

He paused in the doorway, listening to Josephine's deep, regular breathing. *Thank God*—she was asleep. The only thing worse than sleeping in the same room with Josephine was lying awake in the same room with her. He silently slipped through the door and quietly removed his clothing in the soft light from the upper deck that filtered through the unshaded porthole. The metal button of his jeans clinked as it hit the floor. He paused, but the sound didn't disturb her rhythmic breathing.

Too bad he was such a stickler for maritime law, he thought ruefully, pulling down the shade over the porthole. He'd give anything for a long, hard snort of whiskey—anything to dull his senses, to blunt the memory of how warm and seductive her body had felt against his, to blot out the haunted look she'd worn when she'd brought up the topic of Alexa.

He yanked back the covers to his bed and crawled in. Josephine stirred restlessly above him, sighing out a breathy moan.

The sound reminded him of the way she'd responded when he'd kissed her. He punched his pillow into a hard ball and turned over, his face to the wall. Damn it, he couldn't remember when he'd wanted a woman so badly. The more time he spent around her, the more appealing she grew. Lately he'd started to notice little enchanting details about her—the prisms of green around the center of her blue eyes, the varied shades of gold in her hair, the slender elegance of her neck.

Damn it all to hell—why did she have to make everything so complicated? By bringing up Alexa, Josephine had managed to make his attraction to her sound somehow sordid. Couldn't she see that one had nothing to do with the other?

The bed above him creaked. He heard her give another groan, and wondered what—or who—she was dreaming about. From her comment about Wally, he'd wager it wasn't her former beau.

A bloodcurdling scream ripped through the silence, scattering his thoughts like buckshot. Cole boated upright. "Josephine! What's the matters?"

Another scream, this one higher-pitched and more terrifying, shrieked through the dark room. Cole scrambled to his feet, stood on his bed and peered into the upper bunk. It was pitch-black, too dark to see anything. She screamed again, a long, agonizing scream, loud and gut-wrenching. He reached toward the sound. His hand landed on hot, wet skin.

Her cheek. She was crying.

"Josie—wake up! Everything's okay." His hand moved to her hair. "You're having a dream."

Rapid, ragged breathing replaced the scream. "Cole?" she said with a gasp.

"Yes, sweetheart."

"It—it's so dark!"

"I know, sweetheart. But everything's all right."

"I ha-hate the dark."

"Well, then, I'll turn on a light. You stay right there."

He strode to the bathroom, grabbed a towel off the towel rack and wrapped it around his waist, then flipped the switch by the door. Soft yellow light poured into the room.

He headed back to the bunk to find that she'd eased herself down. She sat on the edge of his bed, her arms wrapped around herself. Her face was as pale as her white muslin nightgown, and she was visibly trembling.

Sitting down beside her, Cole wrapped his arm around her shoulders and pulled her against him. "Must have been some dream you were having."

Josephine's head bobbed jerkily.

"Want to talk about it?"

"No. I—I have it a lot."

"The same dream?"

Again, she nodded.

"What's it about?"

She drew a deep, ragged breath and slowly let it out. "The—the dark," she finally murmured.

"It's why you hate the dark?"

"Sort of." She drew a deep, shaky breath.

"It might help to talk about it," Cole said softly.

"I never talk about it."

"Maybe that's why you keep having the dream." He rubbed his hand up and down her arm. "Come on. Pretend I'm a world-class shrink." He stroked an imaginary beard and adopted an Austrian accent. "Dr. Freud is here to help."

He was relieved when she gave a shaky laugh. "Tell me," he coaxed. "I told you all my dark secrets."

"This one is really dark."

"So let's bring it out and shed a little light on it." His hand continued rubbing her sleeve. "Whatever it is, you'll feel better if you get it off your chest."

"That's where it feels like it is, all right. On my chest." She touched a spot directly between her breasts. "It feels like it's sitting right here, making it hard to breathe."

Cole felt his own chest grow tight. "Is it something that actually happened to you?"

"Yes."

An odd, irrational fear grabbed his gut. "Were you raped?" He kept his voice low and calm, but his stomach was churning.

"No."

Inexplicable relief flooded through him.

"It might have been better if I had been." Her voice was small and despondent. "At least then my best friend might still be alive."

"Why don't you start at the beginning," he prompted softly.

The beginning. Josephine swallowed. How many, many times had she replayed it all in her mind, wishing she'd followed the rules, wishing she hadn't made the rash decision that had set the whole nightmare into action?

She let out a long sigh, a sigh that felt like it came from the very center of her being, and the words started pouring out. "I was nearly sixteen. School was out for the summer, and most of the girls had gone home. Just me and my best friend, Lauren, were left in the dorm."

"Why were you two still there?"

Josephine gazed down at her lap. "Neither of us really had a place to go. Dad wouldn't let me visit him at his mission in Central America. Lauren's parents were off in New Zealand or somewhere. They were always traveling. They never had time for her."

"So what happened?"

"We'd seen an ad in the newspaper that said a rock band

was going to be playing at a nearby roadhouse. It was against the rules, but Lauren was determined to go. She wanted me to go with her. I tried to talk her out of it, but she was determined. She said she'd go alone if I didn't go with her, and I—well, I gave in."

Josephine squeezed her eyes together, her throat thick with regret. Dear Lord, how could she have been so stupid, so naive? At the time, the only thing she'd worried about was getting caught.

"We waited until the headmistress was asleep; then we sneaked out. Lauren drove her car. It was about half an hour away, and it was nearly midnight when we got there."

Josephine could remember walking into the crowded, smoky bar as if it were yesterday. She and Lauren had been wearing makeup, something the school strictly forbade, and they'd both been dressed in short skirts— another thing the school didn't permit. Josephine remembered feeling so grown-up, so worldly.

"The place was packed," Josephine continued. "There were no empty tables, no places to sit, so we felt really lucky when a group of men invited us to join them at their table. One of them—a red-haired, thirtyish man with a thick hillbilly-sounding accent—kept buying us drinks. Lauren drank them all. I didn't drink anything, because I was going to be the driver on the way back. Lauren had given me her keys." She pulled her mouth into a tight, mirthless smile. "Besides, I didn't need a drink to feel intoxicated. I'd never been in a bar, never heard live rock music, never been asked to dance. It was great fun at first. But then . . . " She drew a deep breath and hesitated.

Cole looked down at her. "Let me guess. The party got a little rough."

Josephine nodded. "Especially the man with Lauren. He was all over her, and she was trying to get away, but she was pretty tipsy. His buddies just cheered him on. When he dragged her outside, I tried to stop him, but he just brushed me aside. I finally jumped on his back. It startled him, and he turned Lauren loose. I yelled at her to run to the car. And then he started in on me."

She shuddered. In her mind's eye, she could still smell his whiskey-scented breath, still feel his dirty fingers groping at her breast. "You jealous, sweetheart?" the man had jeered. "You want some, too?" The other men had laughed. The red-haired monster had smirked and thrown his friends a lewd wink. "No need to fight over us, little girl. There's more than enough for both o'you. Right, fellas?"

"Right!" they'd chorused drunkenly.

A shiver chased through Josephine at the memory. She ran her tongue over her dry lips and continued the story. "Another group of people came out in the parking lot just then. The interruption gave me a chance to break free. I ran to the car and Lauren threw the door open for me. I started the engine and pulled away as fast as I could, but the men were already piling into a run-down van. The next thing I knew, they were chasing us."

Josephine's heart raced as the memories of that awful night came flooding back. "The road was rough and deserted, and it had started to rain. The men were right on my bumper. Then they started to go around, like they were trying to run me off the road. 'Drive faster! Drive faster!' Lauren screamed. So I did. I knew that if they caught us, they'd . . . " Her voice fell off.

Cole didn't have to ask what the men intended. He tightened his hold on her. "What happened?"

"They were right behind us, and I was driving too fast. We were way out of the city limits—out in the middle of nowhere. There was a sharp turn in the road, and I took it too fast. The next thing I knew, the car was spinning, and then we were falling. We shot over an embankment and rolled and rolled."

"Were you hurt?"

"My left arm and leg were broken, and I had a concussion. I was pinned beneath the steering wheel. I called out to Lauren, but she didn't answer. I groped around with my good arm and found her hand." Josephine's voice broke. Tears filled her eyes. "I squeezed it really tight, but she didn't respond. And then I saw a flashlight at the top of the hill and heard some voices. It was the men from the bar. One of them said we must be dead. Another one wanted to come see. He said . . . " Josephine swallowed around a painful lump. "He said they could still . . . " She drew a breath and tried again. "He said if we were dead, we wouldn't put up a fight."

"Jesus," Cole muttered.

"One of the other men cursed him out and asked if he wanted to charged with murder. The next thing I knew, their tires were squealing, and then it was quiet, except for the rain on the car."

She wrapped her arms around herself and shivered. Cole ran his hand up and down her arm. "It was dark—so very dark. There were no stars, no moon, no houses or street-lights. Nothing. Nothing but darkness."

She briefly buried her face in her hands, then sniffed loudly and gazed up at the ceiling. "I kept talking to Lauren. I kept telling her it was going to be all right, that some-one would find us, that it would all be okay. I hung on to her hand and I talked and I prayed. I told God that if he got me out of that mess I'd never disobey again. I promised I'd do everything I was supposed to do. I kept praying and talking and hanging on to Lauren's hand, and her fingers kept getting colder and colder and colder.

"Finally, just before dawn, the police came. One of the policemen had a big flashlight, and he shined it in the windshield. I looked over at the seat beside me, and I could see Lauren. And I could see that she . . . "

A sob burst from her chest. Cole gathered her into his arms. "It's all right," he said softly.

"No, it's not. Nothing's ever been all right ever since. And I keep having this dream." Her hair swung forward, covering her face in a blond veil. "I'm in the dark. I can't see anything, and I don't know where I am, and I can't move. I'm scared, but I keep thinking if I just hang on, just wait, that daylight will come and everything will be all right. And then a light flashes on and I can see, and what I see is worse than anything I imagined in the dark. It's Lauren's face, and she's . . . she's . . . " Her voice dissolved in sobs.

Cole pulled her against him. "It was an accident, Josie."

She looked up at him, her eyes large and tortured. "It was my fault."

"If it was anyone's fault, it was the fault of those animals chasing you."

She shook her head. "It was my fault for being irresponsible. My father said so."

Something she'd told him earlier clicked in Cole's mind. He stroked her hair. "Was this why your father disowned you?"

Josephine nodded miserably. "He said I was a lost cause. He called Aunt Prudie and told her he was turning my mother's trust fund and my upbringing over to her." She pressed her hand to her mouth, but not in time to muffle the sob that seemed to erupt from her very soul.

A nerve jumped in Cole's jaw. "I thought religion was supposed to be about forgiveness."

Josephine plucked at a piece of her gown, twisting the fabric in her lap into a wad. "Aunt Prudie said my father couldn't forgive himself for my mother's death. She said he couldn't deal with the fact that I looked so much like my mother. She said he felt responsible for her death, and seeing me always made him feel guilty."

"So he judged you the way he thought he was being judged?"

She lifted her shoulders. "Or maybe just the way he judged himself."

Cole frowned. "And you bought into his warped view of things?"

She gave another feeble shrug and looked away.

Something deep in Cole's chest shifted, filling him with an odd ache. No wonder the Empress was so rigid. She'd been trying to keep the promises she'd made in her foxhole prayer ever since, trying to prove to God and herself that she deserved to be alive.

He searched his soul for a way to help her, searched his heart for a key to help her open her self-imposed prison. "Know what I think?"

"What?"

"I think you showed a lot of loyalty and courage. You saved your tipsy friend from being dragged off in the parking lot, and you were doing your best to save her hide again when you had an accident. An *accident.*" He turned more fully toward her and lifted her hands. "An *accident,* Josie. It wasn't something you intentionally did."

"I'm still responsible."

"You didn't make your friend go with you that night. You said she planned to go alone if you wouldn't go with her. Sounds to me like *she* coerced *you.*" Cole pressed Josephine's fingers, wishing he could press his conviction into her soul. "Placing blame won't change what happened. You need to quit beating yourself up over it."

There was a long pause, then a plaintive, whispered word. "How?"

Cole desperately searched his mind, longing to give her an answer. "Do you think Lauren would want you to feel like this? Would she have wanted you this miserable and guilty?"

"N-no."

"Why not?"

Josie looked up, her eyes wet. "She was kind. She was a friend. She wouldn't have wished me ill." She lowered her head. "She wouldn't have wanted me to end up like my father."

"And yet that's just what you're doing, isn't it?"

Josephine didn't answer.

"It is, isn't it?"

"Yes." The word came out soft and low, borne on a sob. "I-I never thought of it like that."

He lifted a hand to her face. Warmth and something else, something that felt suspiciously like tenderness, radiated through his chest. "I thought you grew up a pampered hothouse flower." He dragged his finger down her cheek. "Turns out you're a tough little weed like me."

"A . . . weed?"

He nodded. "We had to scrape by without anyone tending us. We had to push our way out of hard, rocky soil. But we survived."

Their eyes caught and held, and a current passed between them—a current as deep as the ocean, charged with their very souls. The warmth in Cole's chest heated and expanded. Heat flowed to every point of physical contact—her thigh against his, his hand on her shoulder. Time seemed to stand still as she slowly raised her hand and touched his face, her eyes still riveted on his.

He took her hand, her smooth, warm hand, and pressed her palm to his lips. He felt her tremble, but her eyes never wavered. And then he heard his name on her lips.

"Cole."

It took all of his self-restraint not to pull her into his arms. He'd promised he wouldn't initiate anything physical when they were alone, but he was aching to feel her against him.

She moved with excruciating slowness, as if she were moving through water. She turned more fully toward him, reached her other arm around his neck, then placed her hand in his hair. She leaned close, then closer, all the while exerting a gentle pressure on his head, until her lips touched his.

Her lips were warm and soft, like velvet. She parted them eagerly, and then he could constrain himself no longer.

With a guttural growl, he hauled her against him and

deepened the kiss, exploring the wet silk of her mouth. She shifted closer, straining against him. Arousal, hot and hard, shot through him like a flaming arrow. With a hungry groan, he pulled her down on the bed.

She lay on top of him, her hands in his hair, her mouth on his, her breasts pressing against his bare chest through the thin muslin of her gown. He could no longer bear to have it between them. He grabbed a handful of fabric and eased it up her back, up, up, up until his hand fell on the soft, bare skin of her thigh. She moaned against him, and he rolled her over until she lay sprawled beneath him.

"I want to see you," he said. He slowly undid the tiny pearl buttons that ran down the front of her gown, his lips tracing the skin that his fingers uncovered. By the third button, she was breathing hard. By the fourth, she was gasping.

The fifth button bared her breasts. Full and lush, they were tipped with taut pink buds that tightened when he took one in his mouth. Her head rolled from side to side on the pillow as he laved the nipple with his tongue.

Cole had never felt so inflamed with desire. He forced himself to move slowly. "You're beautiful," he whispered, moving his lips through the valley between her breasts, then claiming the other rose-tinged peak. "So beautiful."

She groaned and writhed beneath him. "Oh, please . . . " She whispered. "Please . . . "

"Tell me what you want," he murmured, slowly undoing another button of her gown. His mouth pressed a kiss to the underside of her breast, his tongue tracing the curve where her bosom met her rib. "Tell me. You can tell me anything."

She murmured and shifted beneath him, and for a heart-stopping moment he thought she was trying to pull away. He froze and gazed down. "Do you want me to stop?"

"No. I want you to take off your towel," she whispered. Her eyes were soft and shimmering. She reached for the tucked terry cloth at his waist. Another jolt of desire shot through him. She was so responsive, so hot, so full of passion. . . .

So different from the way she'd been earlier that very evening.

The thought hit Cole like a bucket of ice water. His hand closed over hers as the towel loosened. He drew a deep breath and expelled it harshly. "I think we'd better call a halt to things."

She looked up, her eyes dazed. "You don't want to . . . ?"

"Oh, I want to, all right," he said in a growl. "One more tug on that towel and you'll find out just how much I want to."

"So why—"

"Because you told me no earlier this evening, damnit. I don't want to take advantage of you when you're all upset." He reluctantly refastened one of her buttons, then rolled away. "I won't have you full of regrets in the morning because we got carried away tonight."

He swung his legs to the floor and gripped the loosened towel. He felt her hand slide down his naked spine.

"I won't have any regrets," she whispered softly.

She sure wasn't making this easy. A nerve jumped in his jaw. "Make me this offer on a night when you haven't just been sobbing on my shoulder and I'll take you up on it in a New York minute. But for right now, I'm going to take a cold shower and head up to the pilothouse." He rose and tried to rewrap the towel around his waist, but his erection snagged it like a towel hook. Clutching the towel in front of him, he marched bare-assed to the bathroom.

Damn, damn and double damn. Damnit it all to Hades and back! He wanted Josephine more than he could remember ever wanting another woman in his whole life, but not like this. Not when she was distressed and confused and in need of comfort.

He didn't believe in love, didn't believe in happily ever

after, and he didn't believe in letting a woman think otherwise. There was something in the air between him and Josephine tonight that seemed downright dangerous—some kind of chemistry or emotion or kindred-spirit sort of thing. He couldn't quite put his finger on it, but whatever it was, it made the hair stand up on the back of his neck.

Intimacy—that was it. Damnit, it wouldn't be right to have sex with a woman he felt this close and connected with!

He shut the bathroom door, only to realize that he'd just shut off Josephine's only source of light. He wound the towel around his waist and jerked the door back open. "Sorry. I didn't mean to leave you in the dark." He strode to his desk and snapped on the brass lamp.

"Thank you." She was still in his bed, her thin white gown unbuttoned nearly to her waist, her blond hair loose and mussed and floating around her shoulders. He'd expected her blue eyes to register hurt or confusion or maybe embarrassment, but her gaze was direct, her expression soft, and her mouth curved in a gentle smile. "That was very kind."

Kind. Now there was a word he'd never heard applied to himself. Kind of an SOB, kind of a slave driver, kind of a bastard, yes, but never just *kind.*

Kind. Hell, he'd never wanted to be kind. Kind people were patsies. Kind people got kicked around and walked over. Kind people were easy prey in this dog-eat-dog world.

Kindness meant weakness. Silently cursing himself for exhibiting either, he strode back to the bathroom and closed the door. Flinging the towel on the floor, he stepped into the shower and set the water on its most frigid setting. Icy needles of water hammered down at him, but not hard enough to drive away the uneasy feeling that Josephine was overhauling more of him than just his manners.

Chapter Fifteen

"So what's goin' on between you and the captain?" Fanny asked five mornings later as Josephine helped prepare breakfast in the galley.

Josephine looked up from the bowl of biscuit dough she was stirring and smiled. "I've been wanting to ask the same thing about you and Henry. He's been hovering around you so much I haven't had a chance to talk to you alone in nearly a week. Where is he this morning?"

Fanny placed a sausage patty in the cold cast-iron skillet. "He and the deckhands were up half the night messing with the barges. They have to unlash 'em and relash 'em time and again, what with us goin' through all these locks and dams. But don't go and try to change the subject on me. I asked about you and the captain first." She placed the skillet on the stove and turned on the burner. "He seems different around you."

"What do you mean?"

"Well, it's hard to say, exactly." Fanny leaned her hip against the counter. "I just sense a change, that's all. He doesn't tease you as much, for one thing." Fanny's gaze locked on her. "Has anything . . . happened?"

Josephine plopped the biscuit dough out on the counter, remembering too late that she was supposed to flour it first. She reached for the copper canister of flour. "Almost."

"Almost? Goodness, girl, you were at 'almost' when I boarded the boat two weeks ago! I didn't figure the captain for the kind of man who'd be happy to stay at 'almost' for any length of time."

Josephine scattered a handful of flour on the countertop. "I didn't say he was happy about it."

Fanny chuckled.

Josephine smiled back. She genuinely liked the older woman, and she needed to confide in someone. "Things almost changed a few nights ago," she admitted.

Fanny lifted her eyebrows. "And?"

Josephine sighed. "He stopped at the last moment."

"*He* stopped?"

Josephine nodded. The next thing she knew, the words were tumbling out of her mouth in a hurried jumble. "I'd told him no earlier in the evening, and then I had a nightmare and he comforted me, and . . . oh, Fanny, he was so sweet and kind! And then things kind of took on a life of their own, and just when I'd decided I definitely wanted to, he said he didn't want to take advantage of me when I was upset and emotional." Tears welled up in Josephine's eyes. "Oh, Fanny—I'm afraid I've fallen in love with him!"

Fanny was immediately beside her, an arm around her shoulder. "There, there, child. That's not so awful."

"Yes, it is." Josephine wiped her eyes, only to realize she'd just smudged flour all over her face. Fanny handed her a paper towel. Josephine dabbed at her cheeks with the coarse paper. "You don't know the full story about why he wants etiquette lessons."

Fanny cocked her head to the side and placed one hand

on her hip. "So are you gonna tell me, or do I have to drag it out of you?"

"I'm not supposed to tell anyone."

Fanny snorted. "Tellin' me is the same as tellin' no one. My lips are sealed tighter than the hull of this boat."

Josephine felt as she'd burst if she didn't confide in someone. She drew a deep, ragged breath. "He wants to win the heart of a woman in New Orleans."

Fanny's eyes grew large and round. "He's in love with another woman?"

Josephine shook her head. "He doesn't love her. At least, I'm pretty sure he doesn't. From what I can tell, he doesn't even like her."

Fanny flipped a knob on the stove, shifted the skillet to a cold burner, then took Josephine by the elbow. "Come on over to the table," she said firmly. "I want you to sit down and tell me everything, starting at the very beginning."

"What about breakfast?"

Fanny waved her hand. "I expect the men to be late this morning. If they're not, it won't kill the big oafs to wait a few minutes."

Fanny led her to the table, and before she knew it, Josephine was pouring out the whole story—Cole's background, his plan to get even with Robert McAuley, the story behind her recurring dream, how Cole had urged her to stop blaming herself for the accident.

Fanny shook her head sympathetically. "The captain's right, you know," she said softly. "Beatin' yourself up over somethin' you can't change just makes you another victim. Honey, there's not a person alive who doesn't regret somethin' or other that he or she's done. Your friend got the two of you in a bad situation, and you were doing your best to get out of it."

Fanny rested her hand on Josephine's tightly held ones, her eyes bright with conviction. "The only thing that's unforgivable is a person's unwillingness to accept forgiveness."

Fanny's words landed on Josephine's heart like a soothing balm. She looked into her friend's eyes. "Cole asked if I thought Lauren would have blamed me."

"And what did you say?"

"I think she would have forgiven me. And you know what else?"

"What, honey?"

"Regardless of what my father thought, I think God's got to be at least as kind and forgiving as Lauren. So if Lauren can forgive me and God can forgive me, well, maybe I'm supposed to forgive myself, too."

"Hear, hear!" Fanny gave Josephine's hand another pat, then lifted her coffee cup approvingly.

Josephine gave wistful smile. "All my life, I've lived in this tight little box of rules. I used to think that if I just behaved well enough, I'd be loved. After the accident, I gave up on being loved, but I figured that if I followed the rules, at least I wouldn't hurt anyone else."

"Oh, honey," Fanny said softly, her brown eyes moist with sympathy.

"Except for going to that roadhouse with Lauren, I've never ventured out or taken any risks. And you know what? I'm tired of living like that." Straightening, Josephine thumped her palm on the table. "From here on out, I'm going to go after what I want."

"Good for you!" Fanny grinned broadly and patted her on the back. "So what do you want?"

Josephine hesitated. "Oh, I've got a whole laundry list of things."

"What's at the top of your list?"

It was a little frightening, putting it into words. Josephine drew a deep breath. "Cole."

Fanny's eyes widened along with her smile. "My, my, my!"

Josephine grinned, suddenly feeling shy. "I've never felt this way about anyone. Underneath all his rough exterior and all his bluff and bluster, he's . . . well, he's just wonderful."

"Plus he's smart as a whip, built like Arnold Schwarzenegger and sexy as hell."

"That, too." Josephine's smile broadened for a moment, then faded. She leaned forward and regarded her friend somberly. "I'm not going to kid myself about things, though. I know there's no future with him. Cole's told me he doesn't believe in love."

"I think he cares for you," Fanny said gently.

Josephine looked away. "Not in a permanent kind of way. But it's enough that I care for him."

Concern shone in Fanny's brown eyes. "Is it?"

Josephine nodded, a lump forming in her throat. "I've been giving this a lot of thought. I'm nearly thirty years old, and I've never felt this way in my life. I don't think it's likely I'll ever feel this way again. I've got two weeks left to discover what it's like to be with a man I love. And I'm going to go for it."

"Aren't you afraid you'll get hurt?"

Josephine looked up at the older woman. "I'm more afraid of dying without ever really living."

"But what about this other woman?"

A lump formed in Josephine's throat. "I won't allow myself to think about that. Cole doesn't love her. That's enough."

"Is it?" Fanny asked again, her eyes troubled.

"It'll have to be." Josephine swallowed resolutely. "It's all I've got."

Fanny regarded her in silence for a long moment. "So what are you going to do?"

"Seduce him."

"Oh, my!" Fanny fanned herself with her hand, as if the room had suddenly grown too warm. Her face creased in a broad grin. "What have you got in mind?"

"Well, we dock in Minneapolis tomorrow, and I'll get a paycheck. The first thing I'm going to do is buy some clothes that don't look like they were handpicked by Aunt Prudie. And then I'm going to take myself to a lingerie store and a beauty parlor and the makeup counter of a department store. And when I get Cole alone in the cabin tomorrow night, I'm not going to take no for an answer."

Fanny shook her head, her eyes sparkling. "The poor man doesn't stand a chance!"

"I hope not." Josie looked at her friend, then suddenly reached out and touched her arm. "Why don't you come shopping with me? You can pull the same thing on Henry."

"On Henry?" Fanny's wide cheeks flushed scarlet. "Oh, no. Things aren't that way between us. He doesn't see me as anything but a poker buddy."

"Well, then, let's do something to change that."

"But he's still in love with his late wife. And even if he weren't, I'm not his type."

"What makes you say that?"

"He showed me a picture of Hazel, an' I'm nothin' like her. She was petite and blond and real sweet-lookin'. I'm a big, loud, busty old broad."

"And he's crazy about you," Josephine said with a warm smile. "He wouldn't be spending all this time in your company if he weren't." She reached out and patted her friend's hand. "I've seen you two together. There's something going on."

Fanny shook her head and sighed. "The only thing going on is a lot of wishful thinking on my part."

Josephine smiled triumphantly. "I knew it! I knew you were falling in love with him."

Fanny looked ruefully down at her large flannel shirt. "Lot of good it'll do me. He thinks of me as one of the guys." Fanny sighed and shook her head. "And to think I started out mad at him for lookin' at my chest. Now I might as well not even have one."

"You need to stop hiding under your clothes. And it wouldn't hurt to start wearing a little makeup and do something softer with your hair."

Fanny's expression grew wistful. "Do you really think he might notice me differently?"

"I most certainly do!"

"But don't you think it'll be kind of obvious, if I come back to the boat all dolled up?"

Josephine reassuringly patted Fanny's hand. "If we both come back that way, it'll just look like we went on a shopping spree and treated ourselves to makeovers. You can always tell Henry I bullied you into it."

Fanny's smile was uncertain, but her eyes burned with a glimmer of hope. "I don't know that it'll work, but I guess it can't hurt to try."

Josephine smiled. "By the time we're through, Cole and Henry won't know what hit them."

"What's the hell's goin' on with Fanny?" Henry asked Cole the next afternoon.

Cole looked up from the paychecks he was signing and squinted against the afternoon sun gleaming through the pilothouse windows. "What do you mean?"

Henry lowered his ropy frame into his favorite chair and pulled out his tin of tobacco. "Have you seen her since she came back from that shoppin' spree with Josephine? She's wearin' lipstick an' earrings an' her hair's all different. But that ain't the worst of it. She's got on some kinda outfit that's all fitted to show off her chest!"

Cole looked up, his lip curled in amusement. "You don't say?"

"I do say! I dang near dropped my jaw when I saw her. She said she and Josie had been shoppin', and Josie talked her into a makeover."

"So how does she look?"

"Good." Henry scowled darkly. "Real good."

"So what's the problem?"

"Hell, I don' know." He shoved a chaw of tobacco in his mouth. "How'm I supposed to concentrate on cards when she's sittin' across from me lookin' like that?"

"Maybe you should concentrate a little more on her and a little less on poker."

Henry narrowed his eyes. "You know I haven't been with a woman since Hazel died."

"Well, maybe it's time you did."

Henry shook his head. "Won' never be 'nother woman like Hazel."

"No. But there's not likely to be another one like Fanny, either." Cole's pen scratched loudly in the quiet room as he signed another check. "I'm sure you'll work it all out. What are you planning to do with your night ashore?"

Henry scratched his head. "I thought I'd ask Fanny if she wanted to shoot some pool at the Rack Room. Now I don' know if it's wise, takin' her there lookin' like that."

"Why not?"

"I dunno. Some old boy might make a pass at her or somethin'."

Cole suppressed a grin. In his opinion, that might be just what Henry needed to spur him into action. "Well, then, why don't you take her out to dinner someplace decent?"

"Ya mean like a *date?*"

Cole could tell the old man found the concept alarming. "You don't have to call it that. It would just be two friends going out to dinner together." He creased the page of checks along the perforated line and ripped them out. He handed Henry his paycheck. "Fanny's been feeding your sorry hide three meals a day for the past two weeks. Seems like the least you could do is buy her dinner the one night she's not cooking for you."

Henry thoughtfully chewed his tobacco. "Well, I reckon that's true." He folded the check and stuffed it in his shirt pocket without looking at it. "What are you up to this evenin'?"

"Josephine and I have an appointment with a tailor.

She's got me ordering some custom-made clothes. Then we're going to the fanciest restaurant in town to practice all my fancy new manners by eating the most difficult food we can find."

Henry squinted at him. "When ya gonna tell me what's behind all them manners lessons?"

Cole glanced out the window. The sun was low on the horizon, turning the clouds in the west a shade of pink that reminded him of Josephine's lips. His fingers tightened on the pen in his hand. "Later."

"Why can't ya tell me now?"

" 'Cause I don't want to put up with you trying to talk me out of it."

Henry grinned. "Speakin' of talkin' ya out of somethin', have ya decided if you're stayin' shoreside after this run?"

Cole nodded. "For a while."

"A long while or a short while?"

"At least two months. I leased the *Chienne* this morning." Cole closed the large folder of commercial checks. "You and the rest of the crew are part and parcel of the deal, just like I promised."

"I wasn't worried 'bout that. I know you're a man of your word." The old man spit into his coffee can.

"I leased her to Brinway Shipping. You know Paul Brinway. He should be an easy enough man to work for."

"Yeah, Paul's okay." Henry wiped his mouth with the back of his hand. "He's not you, though. It won't seem right, not havin' you aboard." The old man regarded Cole thoughtfully. "Whatever you're up to, I hope it don' take too long."

It had already taken too long, Cole thought, staring out at the river. He'd waited sixteen years to get back at Robert McAuley, and now that he had his plans in motion, he was chomping at the bit to finally taste revenge. He couldn't wait to see McAuley's face when he found out his fiancée had dumped him for Trash Boy. He intended to find the most public, most humiliating way possible to make the announcement.

"Does Josephine have anything to do with your decision?"

Cole glanced up at his first mate. "Why would you ask a thing like that?"

Henry shrugged. "Jus' wonderin'. She's not the type o' woman you usually get involved with, ya know." The old man looked at him intently. "Are things okay with you two?"

Cole glanced at him sharply. "What do you mean?"

Henry's bony shoulders lifted again. "I dunno. Seems like you've been keepin' your distance from her lately. You two aren't nearly as touchy-feely."

Damn. He hoped no one else had noticed. The leather chair creaked as Cole rose from it and strode across the pilothouse. Ever since the night of her nightmare, he hadn't trusted himself to touch Josephine, not even in public. Just the memory of how she'd looked and felt and tasted was enough to work him into a lather.

Pulling a key from the pocket of his jeans, Cole unlocked a file drawer, stashed the checkbook inside, then carefully relocked it.

"The boys have commented on it," Henry continued. "Hambone said you never go to your cabin till way after midnight. Mentioned he saw you workin' out on that weight machine for three hours straight the other night and thought it a mite strange." Henry rose from his seat at the chart table. "He an' Junior was even wonderin' if Josephine might be up for grabs on the trip back."

Cole turned toward Henry, his muscles tensed. "You tell those morons no one but me is gonna be grabbing Josephine. And it's none of their business when or how I do it."

Henry gave a raspy chortle. "Yes, sir. I'll be sure an' tell 'em." He picked up his can and loped to the door. "Well, now, you two have a nice evenin' on the town."

"Same to you and Fanny." The door closed behind Henry with a loud metallic click.

Cole gazed out at the river, his lips pressed in a hard, tight line. *Dadblast it!* He'd been considering trading cabins with the cook for the downriver portion of the trip, but to do so now would invite all kinds of trouble.

Hell. It was torture, trying to sleep with Josephine in the room with him. If he could just make love to her, he was sure he'd get over this burning obsession. It wasn't like him to be so noble. But it wasn't in him to take advantage of a woman, and that was just what he would have been doing if he'd made love to her the other night. The wisest course of action was to keep his distance from her, but it was damn hard to do when she slept right over his head.

The tuxedoed waiter inclined his head solicitously. "Is the wine to your liking?"

Cole lifted his glass of sauvignon blanc. "It's excellent."

"And the escargots are wonderful," Josephine added, daintily spearing another morsel with her seafood fork. With a satisfied smile, the waiter scurried away.

"If you ask me, they taste like rubber dipped in garlic butter," Cole remarked, stabbing one with a fork scarcely larger than a toothpick. "Hardly worth the effort it takes to get at them."

"Well, you look like you've been eating them all your life. You're handling them very well."

I'd rather be handling you. Cole thought lustily. He was having a hard time pulling his eyes away from her long enough to even look at his plate.

Henry had mentioned that Fanny had gotten all gussied up, but he'd said nothing about Josephine. When Cole had walked into the cabin and seen her this evening, he'd frozen in the doorway and gaped like a frog. She was wearing a sleek black dress that flattered her every curve, and her hair swung loose and free around her shoulders. Her eyes and lips were artfully accented, her long legs were sheathed in shimmering stockings, and shiny gold earrings caught the light with every twist of her head. She was a class act, as always, but she was no longer low-key. It was as if she'd been in black and white, and now she was full color. She was drop-dead gorgeous. And judging from the furtive glances she was receiving from the other men in this overpriced French restaurant, he wasn't the only one who thought so.

"Have I mentioned that you look wonderful tonight?"

Josephine's lips curved in a shy smile. "About a dozen times."

"Well, it bears repeating. You look terrific."

He loved the way the color heightened in her cheeks. She muttered a soft thank-you and looked away. "Speaking of terrific, I think you selected some terrific suits."

"*You* selected them," Cole reminded her. "I just stood there and got measured."

"Well, they're going to look great."

"I'll take your word for it. I had a hard time visualizing a finished suit from a three-inch square of fabric. Why couldn't I have just gone to a department store and shopped like a normal person?"

Josephine smiled. "Because Prince Dumanski wouldn't be caught dead wearing off-the-rack."

"Most people wouldn't know the difference."

"Maybe not. But Alexa would."

The mention of Alexa was an unwelcome intrusion. Cole was relieved when the waiter reappeared and deftly removed their plates, then placed two beautifully garnished bowls of gazpacho before them. Cole lifted his spoon and took a sip, then made a face. "It's cold!"

"It's supposed to be."

"You mean some people actually *like* cold soup?"

"Well, if it bothers you, don't think of it as soup."

Josephine sipped a spoonful. "Think of it as chilled pureed vegetables."

"That's even more unappetizing."

"All right, then. Think of it as salsa without the hot peppers."

"That would be great, if I were in the habit of drinking an entire bowl of salsa."

Josephine smiled. "Hmmm. Well, how does chunky V-8 juice strike you?"

Cole grinned. "As only slightly less repugnant than what this stuff really reminds me of."

"Which is?"

"Tomatoes strained through Junior's teeth."

Josephine erupted in laughter, nearly choking on a mouthful of gazpacho in the process. Her cheeks blazing, she hid behind her napkin as she collected herself. Cole rested his wrists on the table, inordinately pleased. "Why, Empress. I do believe I'm starting to be a bad influence on you."

Josephine reached for her glass of wine and took a sip, her eyes gleaming softly over the rim. She set the glass back down. "I disagree. Overall, I think you've been a very positive influence."

Cole's heart slammed hard against his chest. "Is that a fact?"

She nodded. Her eyes held a warmth, a depth he'd never seen before. Her expression grew serious. "You helped me a lot the other night when I had that nightmare."

Cole shrugged. "Glad I could be of service."

"I mean it." The candlelight flickered over her face, making her eyes shine like faceted sapphires. "I'd been viewing life as a perpetual penance and didn't even realize it. You made me stop and think about things."

"What kind of things?"

"About what I believe, about what I want. I guess it's the kind of thing most people figure out in their teens, but I never did. It's as if that accident stunted my growth, or even killed part of me—the part that felt free to make choices. I've been terrified of making of another mistake, afraid to trust my own judgment." Her eyes were warm and soft. Her gaze fell over him like a snug blue blanket. "The things you said helped me see that."

His chest felt tight and hot. He was out of his depth here, swimming in unknown waters. He cleared his throat and searched for the firm footing of a more concrete topic. "You said you'd been thinking about what you want. Does that mean you've decided what you're going to do once you get back to New Orleans?"

"Yes." She took another sip of soup.

"Are you going to tell me, or do I have to guess?"

She looked up. "I'll tell you, but you've got to promise not to laugh."

"Oh, no. Don't tell me you're going to look for another job as a cook."

Josephine grinned. "You'd be surprised how much my cooking has improved since Fanny's been giving me lessons. But no, that's not it. It's something I'm much better suited for than cooking."

"Belly dancing?"

Josephine laughed. "Not quite."

"Hmm. Well, it can't be sumo wrestling. Perhaps a career as a tattoo artist?"

"Nothing nearly so exotic."

"You're taking up pig farming?"

Josephine laughed again. "No, but thanks for making my plans not seem so outlandish."

He grinned. "So what are they?"

She drew a deep breath. "I'm going to open my own etiquette school, but not the kind that teaches debutantes how to curtsy. I'm going to offer courses in executive manners."

"Executive manners?"

Josephine nodded, her eyes sparkling with excitement. "I plan to market it to corporations."

"Hmm. What would you offer?"

"The same kind of thing I've been teaching you." She leaned forward. "I think there's a real market for it. Aunt Prudie was once approached by one of the major New Orleans hotels. They wanted to know if she'd be interested in conducting an etiquette seminar for their executive staff, but she turned it down. She said she didn't want to do anything so commercial."

"Of course not," Cole said dryly. "The old gal wouldn't have wanted to have dealt with anything as crass as money."

Josephine smiled. "You sound like you knew her."

"I almost feel like I did."

Josephine sat back in her chair. "I tried to talk her into it. I'd read an article in a business publication about how corporations spend millions of dollars for executive training on all kinds of issues—sensitivity training, creative thinking, travel safety, international protocol. . . . It just seemed to me that executive etiquette would be a logical topic. I'm sure there's a market for it in New Orleans."

Cole thoughtfully nodded his head. "You just might be on to something."

"I think I might be, too. I'm excited about it."

And I'm excited about you, Cole thought as the waiter returned and swept away their soup bowls. Everything about her tonight was sexy as hell—the soft scent of her new perfume, the way she crossed her incredible legs, the way she rested her hand on his arm when she laughed at something he said.

She reached out and flicked a piece of invisible lint away from his sleeve, her hand lingering on his. He looked at her, and she gave a slight smile, holding his gaze a beat longer than expected. With any other woman, he'd think she was coming on to him.

Cole reached for his glass of water, disconcerted. There was something different about Josephine tonight, something besides her dress and hair and makeup. She was sporting a new attitude, a new confidence, a new . . . flirtatiousness.

That was it, Cole realized suddenly. Josephine was flirting with him.

And just what the hell was he supposed to do about it? Cole scowled as the waiter set his entrée before him. Ever since the night of her nightmare, he'd deliberately kept his distance. Josephine had made her feelings very clear. She didn't want to become his lover while preparing him to seduce Alexa. He could understand that. He didn't like it, but he could accept it. He *had* accepted it. So why the hell was she flirting with him?

The question preyed on Cole's mind throughout the rest of the evening. It was almost a relief when the cabdriver dropped them off at the wharf and they reboarded the boat.

"Thank you for a wonderful evening," she said as he opened the door to their cabin. She flipped on the bathroom light, then pulled the door partially closed so that soft light spilled faintly into the room.

"Thanks for helping me pick out the new duds." He stood in the doorway and watched her take off her earrings. Something about the way she was looking at him made his blood race. He took a step back. "Well, I'm sure you need some sleep."

She looked him straight in the eye. "I need something else a whole lot more."

His mouth went dry, and his hand tensed on the doorknob. "Josephine, don't play games with me. You've been flirting with me all evening, and I don't know what to make of it."

She placed a hand on her hip. "You don't?"

Tension coiled all through him. "Just because I'm pretending to be a gentleman doesn't mean I really am one.

295

I'm warning you—don't start anything you don't intend to see all the way through."

"I'm not."

"You're not what? Starting something?"

"No. I'm not going to want to stop."

The words were spoken softly, but they hit him hard. He stood stock-still, his heart pounding, then stepped into the room and closed the door behind him. "If you're coming on to me, Josephine, you're going to have to tell me in a way that is unmistakably clear."

Her hands reached behind her neck. He heard the hiss of a zipper. Dropping her arms, she slowly stepped out of her dress. She stood before him, wearing only a lacy black teddy and thigh-high black stockings. Her dress dangled from one finger. "Is this clear enough?"

He swallowed hard. Good God, but she was gorgeous. His gaze moved over her, taking in the row of ribbons that tied the gossamer fabric together down the center of the teddy, revealing enticing tidbits of skin. His gaze paused on the deep shadow between her breasts, then shifted to the delicious flash of white thigh gleaming above the top of her silk stockings.

She shivered as his gaze licked over her. She felt bold and scared, vulnerable and wanton, all at the same time.

He reached behind him and locked the door, never taking his eyes off her. "I believe I've gotten your message."

Josephine's heart hammered hard as he slowly walked toward her. He reached out and gently lifted one black strap of her teddy, his finger grazing her shoulder. "I had no idea you had such exotic taste in underwear."

Tension stretched inside her like a taut rubber band. "Do you like it?"

"Oh, yes. Yes, indeed." His finger slowly slipped the strap off her shoulder. "But I like what's in it even better." A shiver chased through her as he bent his head and kissed her now-naked shoulder. Her skin quivered as his lips slid slowly, gently, to the side of her neck.

His breath sent puffs of heat against her skin, and his clean-shaven jaw rasped the vein where her pulse thrummed wildly. Her dress fell from her finger to the floor. The next thing she knew, she'd been literally swept off her feet. One arm under her knees, one under her back, Cole picked her up and carried her to his bed.

She felt the give of the mattress against her back, felt the softness of a pillow under her head. But mostly she felt Cole, leaning forward to claim her lips. His mouth was warm and demanding, and she moaned as it moved over hers. She welcomed the invasion of his tongue, welcomed the roughness of his jaw, welcomed the weight of his chest against hers. She even welcomed the harshness of his wool jacket against her skin, but the need to feel his naked chest against her was overpowering. She pushed his jacket off his shoulders. He struggled out of it, never losing contact with her mouth. She reached up and undid the buttons on his shirt. He shrugged that off as well, flinging it to the floor.

Her hands splayed across his naked chest, through his thicket of masculine hair, across the granite plane of his muscles. She tentatively touched a flat brown nipple, causing it to harden and rise.

"Good God, Josie," he murmured, straddling her on the bed.

He nibbled his way down her neck to the hollow between her breasts and tugged at the ribbon with his teeth, unfastening the bow that held the fabric together. Her nipples tightened and puckered as the black lace fell away, exposing them to his view. Slowly, achingly slowly, he took one in his mouth and suckled. Josephine let out a throaty moan. Cole took his time, lavishing attention on first one, then the other, inciting her with his tongue, stoking a fire within her. Heat shot through her, radiating out and down, pooling into white-hot need between her thighs. She arched against him, wanting, needing closer contact.

"Stay right there," he whispered. "Don't move." He

pulled away. The absence of his warmth left her aching and bewildered, until she realized he was shucking off his slacks and briefs. He pulled something from a dresser drawer, then returned to kneel over her.

"Now. Where were we?" He grinned down at her, tracing a circle around her breast.

He was completely naked. Josephine couldn't help but stare, her eyes widening. She'd never known that the male anatomy could be so . . . imposing.

"You're already . . . " She swallowed hard and tried again. "You're already ready."

"Hell, darlin'," Cole said in a growl, his mouth back on hers. "I've been ready since you came aboard. Just thinking about you makes it difficult to walk upright."

His response left her puzzled. "If you're ready, then we'd better hurry."

"Hurry?"

"You know. Before it—you know—goes away."

"Goes away?" Cole pulled back and stared down at her, his expression perplexed. His eyes suddenly softened. "Ah, sugar. Is that what used to happen with Wally?"

Josephine looked away, mortified that he'd discovered the truth. She felt Cole's finger on her chin, tipping her face back toward him. "Is it?"

Josephine nodded miserably. Better to go ahead and admit it than to have Cole discover it all on his own. He was bound to find out anyway. "I-I'm afraid I'm not very good at keeping a man aroused."

Cole's eyebrows shot up. "That jerk told you that?"

Josephine closed her eyes, too ashamed to answer.

Cole swore softly. "Sweetheart, the only thing you're not good at is picking men to get involved with."

She opened her eyes. The hopefulness in her expression did something funny to Cole's chest.

"You've got me so aroused I can hardly stand it. I'm throbbing like a toothache for you. There's only one way to get me out of this condition. Believe me, sweetheart, nothing's going away until we're both good and ready."

"Really?"

This Wally creep was even more of a loser than he'd imagined. Cole nodded. "We've got all night, Josie. There's no need to hurry." His lips nipped at hers, then settled in for a long, languorous kiss. His pelvis rocked against hers, and she instinctively responded in kind. He let out a murmur of pleasure. "Unless, of course, you keep doing that."

Delight, pure and bright, beamed from her eyes. A peculiar warmth unfurled deep within him. He bent his head and kissed her breast, pulling the nipple into his mouth and grazing it with his teeth. Her hand played across his chest, tracing the line of crisp curls across his belly, moving low, then lower, until he moaned with pleasure.

"Maybe we could hurry just a little," she whispered.

Her eagerness excited him almost beyond endurance, but he forced himself to take it slow. He was determined to make it good for her.

"You bet," he whispered, lowering his head and unfastening another tie on her teddy with his teeth. His hands moved to her inner thigh, to the soft white flesh that stood out in such erotic contrast to the black silk of her stockings. His lips slid down her belly, untying each and every fastening with deliberate slowness as his hands slipped up her legs. She was breathing hard and fast by the time the last tie was unfastened. Only a triangle of lace remained.

Softly, gently, slowly, his mouth slid down that triangle while his hands moved up. "Oh, please," she murmured, her head thrashing on the pillow. "Please."

His fingers found three snaps at the teddy's most intimate opening. Deliberately, carefully, he unfastened them, one by one. His lips moved down over dark blond curls, lower and lower. He felt her gasp and tremble. His fingers moved higher, gently stroking the spot he ached to stroke in another way. He heard her cry out, felt her shudder, felt her implode.

A sweet, warm emotion flowed through him, settling into a lump in his throat. "That's it, sweetheart," he murmured, his voice a low rasp. "That's it."

His voice filtered through her consciousness as she drifted back to earth on a cloud of pleasure. She was vaguely aware that he reached for something on the nightstand. She heard the rip of paper, the crinkle of foil, and then he was hovering over her. She pulled him down into a deep kiss, her hands clutching the hard muscles of his back.

"I want you so bad," he mumbled against her ear.

"Then take me," she whispered back.

He'd already taken her heart. Her soul was filled with tenderness for this fierce, unruly, impossible man, this man whom she loved.

He filled her slowly, giving her time to adjust to his size, then thrust against her in a rhythm as ancient as life. She clung to him tightly, reveling in the femininity that allowed her to hold him inside her, to love him with her body as well as her soul.

He was hard and hot and delicious. Despite the fact that he'd just given her a banquet, she found herself craving seconds. She wanted another ride to the stars, another glimpse of heaven. Before she knew it, he'd catapulted her there—up and over that rainbow, up to the ozone. He followed right behind. They burst through the stratosphere, up to where blue sky met all eternity. And for a moment, a blessed, sacred moment, she held him for all time.

Chapter Sixteen

Fanny's face creased in a knowing grin when Josephine walked into the galley the next morning. "Well, well, well! Looks like somebody had a late evening last night. You slept all the way through breakfast and halfway to lunch."

Josephine glanced at the clock on the wall. *Dear heavens*—it was a quarter to eleven! Judging from the fragrant aroma of Italian spices that filled the galley, Fanny was already preparing lunch. Josephine sheepishly reached for an apple from the fruit bowl on the counter.

Fanny spooned another dollop of meat sauce on the pan of lasagna she was assembling, her grin widening. "I take it your plan worked."

"I suppose you might say that."

"Ain't no supposin' about it."

Josephine smiled. It had worked, all right—beyond anything she'd ever imagined. She and Cole had made love most of the night. She'd never known that lovemaking could be so varied, never known that a lover could be so tender and imaginative and intense all at the same time.

"I can't get enough of you," Cole had murmured that morning, drawing her to him yet again before he rose to shower and dress.

A dreamy smile curved the corners of Josephine's mouth as she rinsed the apple in the sink. Cole had certainly put to rest any doubts about her ability to arouse a man.

She flipped off the faucet and reached for a paper towel, only to find Fanny watching her, an amused twinkle in her eyes. Josephine quickly looked down and busily rubbed the apple. "I'm, uh, sorry I missed my cooking lesson this morning."

"That's quite all right, honey. I'm sure you were gettin' lessons of a whole other kind."

Josephine met Fanny's impish gaze and laughed. "What about you? How was your evening with Henry?"

"Nothin' like your evenin' with Cole."

Josephine watched the older woman spread a layer of ricotta cheese over the meat sauce. "Well, you look wonderful this morning, Fanny. I love your hair brushed forward like that. And that red sweater really brings out your eyes."

Fanny looked down at her voluptuous chest and made a wry face. "That isn't all it brings out."

Josephine grinned. "What did Henry think of your new look?"

Fanny rotated the pan of lasagna and worked on the other side. "To tell you the truth, I think I scared him to death." Fanny picked up a handful of shredded mozzarella cheese and sprinkled it over the pan.

"What happened?"

"Well, at first he just stared at me like I'd gone out and rolled in a pile of manure or somethin'. He wanted to know what I'd done to myself. Then he got all poker-faced and quiet-like." She grinned. "But he shaved before he took me out to dinner. An' he took me to a right nice restaurant.

302

An' during dinner, I caught him lookin' at me in a way that nearly made me slap his face."

Josephine laughed.

"Afterward, we took a long walk. We had a lot of laughs, and it was a real good time. Then we got back to the boat, an' he got kinda quiet, and for a moment there, I thought he was actually gonna kiss me."

"Then what happened?"

Fanny gave an exasperated sigh. "Nothin'. Not a darn thing. One minute he was lookin' at me all frisky-eyed, and the next he was hurryin' off to his cabin, mumblin' 'bout an early mornin'." She tossed a final handful of mozzarella on the pan, then turned and wiped her hands on a blue dish towel. "To tell you the truth, it made me feel kinda funny, havin' him look at me that way. I'm used to gettin' all prickly when a man does that. Too many years of jerks makin' jokes about my chest, I guess."

"Henry's not like that."

"I know." Fanny self-consciously smoothed her sweater. "The problem with wearin' a getup like this is that Henry's not the only one who notices. I caught Hambone starin' at me all googly-eyed this mornin'. An' ya know what that varmint said? He said he didn't know I was totin' such a fine rack under those gunnysacks I wore."

Josephine nearly choked on her bite of apple.

Grinning, Fanny pulled a roll of aluminum foil out of a drawer and ripped off a length of it. "I thought Henry was gonna strangle him."

A loud clamor sounded outside the galley door. "Speak of the devil," Josephine murmured as Henry sauntered into the galley.

Fanny whipped back around, her back to the door, and industriously smoothed the foil over the pan.

Josephine smiled at the first mate. "Good morning, Henry. My, don't you look handsome without your beard!"

Henry self-consciously rubbed his jaw, his eyes darting to Fanny. He looked back at Josephine. "You okay this mornin'?"

Josephine found herself blushing at the oddly worded question. "I'm fine. Why?"

"When you didn' come down to breakfast, I got to worryin' that you might be feelin' under the weather."

"Oh, I'm fine. I just overslept. I didn't get much sleep last night." From the corner of her eye, Josephine saw Fanny's amused grin. She gave the older woman a surreptitious elbow in the ribs. "Would you like a cup of coffee, Henry?"

"Sure would. That happens to be what I came down to fetch."

Josephine pulled down two cups and splashed hot coffee in them. She passed one to Henry and picked up the other. "Here you go. Well, if you two will excuse me, I'll take this up to Cole."

Fanny slid the lasagna in the oven, then turned around, her heart pounding. It was ridiculous, getting all worked up over a man at her age. Yet every time she found herself alone with Henry, she felt nervous as a schoolgirl.

"What's up with her?" Henry asked, hooking a thumb in the direction of the door Josephine had just gone through. "She's all lit up like a Christmas tree."

Fanny opened the refrigerator and pulled out a plastic bag full of fresh string beans. "She's just realized she's in love."

Henry frowned. "With the cap'n?"

A surge of irritation flashed through Fanny. Henry could be thicker than a fire wall sometimes, especially when it came to women and emotions. Fanny shot him a scathing look. "It sure ain't with Junior."

Henry grinned and ambled around the counter, carrying his coffee. "Well, I jus' hope Josephine doesn't end up all heartbroken."

304

"You think the captain's gonna hurt her?" Fanny bent and pulled a colander and a large bowl out of a low cabinet.

Henry noisily swallowed a mouthful of coffee. "Not intentionally."

"But you think he will all the same." Dumping the beans in the colander, Fanny rinsed them under the faucet.

Henry's bony hip rested against the cabinet. "Well, now, I think of Cole like a son, so don' git me wrong, but there's a lot of anger and turmoil inside him, and I don' think it leaves much room for lovin' a woman." Henry rubbed the handle of the coffee mug with his thumb. " 'Asides he's not a settlin' down kinda guy. He's too restless. Just like me."

"You weren't always too restless," Fanny observed, shutting off the faucet. "You were married once."

"Yeah. But I was a different man when Hazel was alive." He watched Fanny pull out a bean and snap off the end. "A better man."

"You seem just fine to me now." Fanny dropped the bean into the bowl.

A warm feeling curled inside Henry like a shot of whiskey. He threw her a curious gaze. He liked her hair that way, those little wisps framing her face all soft-like. And that nubby-textured ruby sweater wasn't tight, but it sure showed off her figure. Up until yesterday, he'd kinda thought she was big all over, but in this outfit, he could see that she wasn't. Her hips and waist were right slim. Dadburn if Fanny wasn't flat-out attractive. "How come you never married?"

Fanny lifted her shoulders. "The right man never came along, I guess."

"You're a nice-lookin' woman."

Fanny's eyes flew wide in surprise.

Henry felt his face heat. He wasn't trying to flatter her, just stating the facts. He set down his coffee mug and self-consciously rubbed his jaw. "I mean, you must have had your chances."

He was relieved when she turned her attention back to snapping beans. "Oh, there were men. But I never could tell if their interest was in me . . . or just part of me." She snapped a bean right in two, making a loud cracking sound that reverberated through the room. "You know, it can be burden, bein' built like this. You get all kinds of unwelcome attention." She snapped another bean loud enough to sound like a cracking timber.

Henry guiltily forced his gaze away from her chest and reached for a bean. "Were ya ever in love?"

"Yes." Fanny's hands stilled. "Only Mr. Right turned out to be Mr. Dead Wrong."

"Oh, yeah?" Henry snapped off the end of the bean and dropped it in the bowl. He reached into the colander for another. "What happened?"

The rhythmic snapping of beans filled the room. "Oh, it was back when I was young—in my early twenties. I was workin' in a café in Shreveport. The place specialized in fried catfish. Thinkin' back on it, I can still smell it. Seemed like the smell of it clung to everything." She reached for another bean. "I was waitressin' there, trying to put my two youngest brothers through college, sick to death of catfish an' grease an' waitressin'. This feller walked in one day. He was the finest-lookin' man I'd ever seen. Jet black hair and straight white teeth and a smile that made you want to reach for your sunglasses. Lordy, but he was fine. He was from California, and he said he was a talent scout. He was in Shreveport for three weeks, visitin' his brother. Said his job was lookin' for new talent for the movie studios, an' he thought I had what it took. Oh, but he had a fine line of fancy talk. Said I was attractive in a girl-next-door sort of way, that I had a believable kind of beauty."

Fanny shook her head ruefully, her gaze far away. "I

told him I wasn't interested in being a movie star, but he wouldn't take no for an answer. He took me out and bought me flowers an' flattered me like no one ever had. He filled my head with all kinds of promises—promises about the movies, promises about the two of us. He said we were like two peas in a pod. Said he'd been dreamin' of a gal like me, said I was just the type he wanted to marry and settle down with. I fell head over heels. I thought the sun and the moon rose and set in this guy."

"What happened?"

"He wanted to take some pictures of me. For the studios, he said. First he wanted to take some of me in a dress, then in a low-cut dress, and then without the dress. . . . Well, you get the idea."

Henry felt the muscles knot in the back of his neck.

"He went back to California, promisin' he'd call, and I never heard from him again. I wrote him letters, but they came back undelivered. I tried to call, but he'd given me a bogus phone number. Then two months later, those pictures he'd taken came out in a cheap girlie magazine. A customer at the restaurant had a copy. He passed it around to everyone."

"Lord have mercy!"

"I thought I was gonna die. But that isn't the worst of it." Fanny picked up another handful of beans. "I was pregnant. I found out right after those pictures came out." Fanny continued to snap the beans.

"Oh, Fanny! What did ya do?"

"Well, I was gonna have the baby. I gave notice at my job and was all set to move to Mississippi, where I didn't know anybody. Back in those days, havin' a baby out of wedlock was about the worst thing a gal could do. Near the end of the third month, though, I miscarried. My brothers said it was a blessing, but I never saw it that way."

"Ah, Fanny." Henry's heart felt heavy. "The whole thing's a damn cryin' shame."

"Shame's the word for it, all right. I was so ashamed I wanted to die. I didn' want anyone to even look at me. I stopped wearin' makeup and fixin' my hair and started dressin' to hide my chest, an' I started workin' in the kitchen instead of out with customers. I pretty much kept to myself after that."

Henry found it hard to speak. Even if he could, he didn't know what to say. Feelings rumbled and stirred inside him like aggregate into concrete. He settled for shaking his head.

"It's hard to believe I was ever stupid enough to fall for such a shyster. Especially since I never cared a fig 'bout all that Hollywood stuff he was promisin'. All I ever wanted was to be loved—to have a husband and a family and a home." She glanced at Henry, then looked back down at the beans. "Like your Hazel. I'd say she was one lucky woman, bein' loved by a man like you."

The air seemed to thicken and gel around him. Henry swallowed, his chest tight with emotion, a familiar lump in his throat. This time, though, the emotion churning inside of him wasn't over Hazel.

The realization alarmed him. *Jiminy Christmas*; he couldn't start somethin' with Fanny! He cleared his throat, trying to clear his mind. While he was at it, he'd best clear the air as well.

"I was the lucky one. There'll never be another woman like Hazel. I'll never love another woman like I loved her."

"No, I'm sure you won't. But you could love someone different in a whole different way." A bean snapped softly in the silence. "If you let yourself."

The lump in Henry's throat grew until it felt like a boulder. Something akin to terror shot through him. He dropped an unsnapped bean on the counter and grabbed his mug of coffee. "Well, I'd better go see what my two stooges are up to. See ya in an hour or so."

He hurried out the door before Fanny could respond.

She was scaring him to death, and for the life of him, he didn't know why.

Cole's heart gave an unaccustomed lurch as Josephine let herself into the pilothouse.

"I brought you some coffee," she said, closing the door behind her.

"Thanks. Put it in my cup holder, would you? I've got my hands full right now, steering around this bend." He smelled the soft scent of her perfume as she drew close. Her hair brushed his neck as she leaned forward and placed the cup in the armrest of his chair. A tumble of confused emotions raced through him. Last night had been incredible—beyond incredible. He'd been thinking about her all morning. Usually he separated his work from his personal life, but Josephine crossed all boundaries.

He pulled on the sticks, steering the long line of barges around the bend. While he maneuvered the turn, Josephine scooted up a chair. When he'd aimed the barges into the center of the river for a straight stretch, he turned and glanced at her.

Fine lines radiated out around her eyes, and her mouth was pressed in a tight line. Uh-oh—something was on her mind.

It didn't take her long to get right to the point. "I want to talk to you about last night."

Cole's hand tensed on the lever. Here it came—the inevitable morning-after discussion. Why did women always have to make sex so complicated?

Cole braced himself, wondering what kind of emotional luggage Josephine was about to unpack. Recriminations? Regret? *Oh, criminy*—what if she wanted to talk about long-term commitment? A nerve jumped in his jaw.

"What about it?" he asked cautiously.

"It was wonderful."

"Yeah. It was." Amazingly wonderful. Josephine was

incredibly responsive, intuitively sensuous. She'd made him feel . . . Hell, he didn't know what it was she'd made him feel, but he'd felt it down to his very bones. Just thinking about it gave him a fresh stirring of arousal.

She leaned toward him. "I thought you might be worried about things, since you know how I feel about relationships and commitment."

Just as he'd feared—the dreaded *C*-word! The muscles in Cole's shoulders tightened.

"I just wanted to let you know that I know what last night was, and I'm okay with it," she said softly.

That put her several steps ahead of him, because he was completely in the dark. "You do?" he asked warily. "I mean, you are?"

Her head bobbed. He waited, but no further explanation was forthcoming.

"Okay, I'll bite." He waited, but she just looked at him. "What was it?"

"Why, temporary, of course."

Cole knew he should probably feel relief, but instead he was gripped by anxiety. What the hell was she getting at? Was she saying that last night was all there was going to be? Surely she wasn't proposing that they revert back to chaste cohabitation! He picked his words carefully, as if he were picking his way across a field of land mines. "How temporary?"

"The rest of the trip. I mean, I know that once we get back to New Orleans, you're planning . . . " Her voice faltered.

Alexa's presence swirled out of her unspoken words, until she seemed to stand like a ghost between them. Cole stared out at the river, chagrined.

Josephine nervously licked her lips. "I want you to know that I don't expect anything long-term. I initiated things last night, and I knew it would be temporary when I did."

Oh, jeez. Why did he feel so lousy, hearing her say the very things he wanted her to say?

"So I think we should just enjoy ourselves and each other and not turn this into anything heavy." She drew a deep breath. "Okay?"

Damn it, he should feel relieved, but he didn't. His chest felt hot and tight, and his spirits felt lower than a bottom-feeding catfish. "Okay."

"All right." She rose from her chair.

He couldn't let her go like this. He needed to touch her, to get a reaction from her, to affirm the connection between them. "Not so fast." He reached out and pulled her onto his lap. He was relieved when she smiled and wound her arms around his neck.

"Isn't there some sort of Coast Guard regulation against this?" she asked, kissing him softly on the lips.

"Only if you handle the sticks."

She laughed. The sound lightened his heart. "I'll save that for tonight, then."

He nuzzled her neck, keeping one eye on the river. "You'd better." He reluctantly turned her loose as another towboat cruised around the bend ahead.

Josephine rose and tucked her long-sleeved T-shirt into her new pair of jeans. Funny how she could make a regular pair of Levi's look expensive, Cole thought. Everything about her reeked of class.

Which was why he had hired her, he reminded himself. To acquire some of that class for himself. "What kind of lesson do you have planned for me today?"

He thought her face fell slightly, but her smile was back so quickly he couldn't be sure. "German wines. A Romanian prince would surely be familiar with them."

He nodded.

"We also need to practice your dancing." She headed for the door. "We didn't get very far with your waltz lesson last time."

Cole grinned. "I don't expect we'll get much further tonight."

Josephine smiled back. It was a slow, sexy smile, a smile full of promise, and Cole thought it was the most seductive thing he'd ever seen.

"No, I don't expect we will." She pulled the door closed behind her. Cole turned his attention back to the river, but his thoughts stayed on Josephine. Regardless of her words, he didn't think she was the kind of woman who could live in today without thinking of tomorrow. And she knew Alexa lurked in tomorrow.

The thought made his stomach twist. He'd waited years to get even with McAuley, and he couldn't stop now that he was within striking distance. He didn't want to hurt Josephine, but he was afraid it was already too late.

"One, two, three, pause. One, two three, pause." Josephine pulled away from Cole and looked up at him. She tried for a stern frown, but he was so handsome in the flickering candlelight that she could manage only to tone down a smile. "I've been trying to teach you to waltz for seven nights in a row now, and we haven't yet finished a single dance."

"That's because you keep distracting me." His hand moved low on her rump, across the denim of her short, fitted skirt. A shiver shimmied up her spine. "How do you expect me to concentrate when I've got you this close?"

Josephine was having the same problem. Cole's arms were strong and muscular, his chest warm and hard, and his hands repeatedly veered away from her waist. Worst of all, his pelvis kept bumping against hers in a most diverting manner. She deliberately stepped back. "Well, you'll just have to try harder. I'm not comfortable taking money from you unless I'm providing something of value in exchange."

His eyes twinkled mischievously.

She placed two fingers against his lips. "Don't you dare say it," she warned. "That's exactly what I *don't* want to be paid for."

Cole's gaze immediately grew somber. "Sweetheart, you know I'd never think that."

"All the same, I have certain standards." She stepped away and folded her arms over her chest. "I've never had a student fail my course, and I don't intend to start now. You're paying me good money to teach you how to behave in society, and that's exactly what I intend to do."

Cole ran a hand through his hair and sighed. "Okay. What have I got to do?"

"Practice the waltz. I want you to dance correctly through an entire song."

Cole cocked his head. "To do something that difficult, I'll probably need some sort of incentive."

She recognized the gleam in his eyes. A smile curved her lips. "What have you got in mind?"

His grin widened wolfishly. "Well, if I follow your instructions, then it seems only fair that then you should follow mine."

Josephine's pulse picked up speed. Over the past week, they'd made love dozens of times. He'd introduced her to a world of sensuality she'd never known existed, and in the process he'd completely, utterly, irrevocably stolen her heart. She didn't know how she would stand it when their time together was over.

The thought formed a lump in her throat. She swallowed it down, silently repeating the phrase that had become her private mantra, the phrase she used to shield herself from dwelling on the inevitable hurt ahead: *Live this moment to the fullest*.

She was certain she'd never love another man as she loved Cole. And since she'd never love this way again, she needed to savor every second, to memorize each minute, to press each experience into her heart like flowers in a heavy book. Later, when she was alone, she could pull out the memories and linger over each one, like an old woman sorting through the mementos of her long-lost youth.

Later. She would dwell on all that later. Right now she would make the most of the moment before her.

"Have we got a deal?" Cole asked, his eyes shimmering down.

"We do."

With a sexy smile, he crossed to his CD player and punched several buttons. A hauntingly lovely melody swept through the room and right into her soul. Cole held out his arms, and she stepped into them.

And then they were waltzing—moving as one, sliding, gliding, floating around the cabin. They danced effortlessly, as smoothly synchronized as the wings of an airborne bird. Cole held her against him, tightly enough that she could feel the muscles in his thigh, could thrill to the sensation of being guided exactly where she wanted to go. It seemed as if her feet never touched the ground, as if the music and the sheer magic of moving so perfectly in sync had suspended the law of gravity. Cole twirled her in a heady sweep as the music crescendoed, then fell to an aching close.

It took her a moment to realize the song was over. She gazed up into his face and vaguely blinked.

He gave his most charming smile. "Did I pass the exam?"

Josephine stepped back, her legs wobbly. "Wh-where did you learn to do that?"

"I used to know an instructor at a Fred Astaire studio."

An unreasonable burst of jealousy flared through her. *Know in the carnal sense?* She was about to ask him; then a sobering thought stopped her cold. She had no right to his past. She had no claim to his future. All she had was now.

Now. This moment.

She looked at him. "I thought you couldn't dance."

"I never told you that. You just made that assumption."

"But you let me give you lessons!"

"I let you *start* to give me lessons. We never actually completed a dance. Not till now." His smile would have charmed a voodoo queen out of her favorite gris-gris. "So how'd I do?"

He was maddening. He was unconscionable. He was . . .

"Magnificent." She heaved a defeated sigh and gave a reluctant smile. "You were magnificent, and you know it."

His grin widened. "Well, then, I guess that means I fulfilled my end of the bargain." He leaned close and kissed her neck. His hands slid down her back as his mouth slid up her throat. "Now it's time for you to fulfill yours," he murmured, nibbling on her ear.

The heat of his breath made her blood pump fast. "What do you have in mind?"

"I've been wondering all day what you're wearing under that skirt."

Josephine grinned. She'd bought seven pairs of panties at Victoria's Secret in Minneapolis—seven of the scantiest, most outrageous, most barely-there panties she could find. "I'm afraid we've come to the end of the lingerie show. All of my exotic undies are in the laundry."

"So what are you wearing?"

"Nothing."

Cole's eyebrows rose.

"Except for my panty hose, I mean. Dear heavens—you didn't think I'd been running around all day *completely* naked under this, did you?"

"It's a rather tantalizing idea." With a wicked grin, he pulled her to him and kissed her until her knees felt weak. "Hop up on the dresser," he instructed.

Josephine turned and eyed the waist-high piece of furniture, then looked back at him questioningly. Cole cocked an eyebrow. "You agreed to do as I say, remember?"

Josephine nodded, her heart rate accelerating. A shiver of excitement raced through her.

"Up you go." Putting his hands on her waist, Cole boosted her on top of the bureau. Candlelight flickered from two fat vanilla-scented candles burning on his desk.

"Now—hike up that skirt for me."

Josephine hesitantly hitched her skirt until it barely covered her upper thigh.

Cole watched approvingly. "Much better. But now you look like you're wearing too many clothes on top. You'd better balance things out by unbuttoning your shirt."

There was something undeniably sensuous about undressing for Cole. Josephine slowly unfastened the top button of her black knit shirt. "Seems to me it's only fair that you should do the same."

"It's my turn to call the shots, remember?"

She nodded and undid another button.

His eyes stayed on her like a bulldog's teeth on a bone. "But if it makes you feel more comfortable, why, I'll be happy to honor your request."

He quickly unbuttoned his shirt and stripped it off, his eyes never leaving her body. She slowly unfastened another button.

"Looks like you're having a little trouble there. Maybe I'd better come help."

"Maybe you'd better."

He stepped forward and freed her last two buttons, his warm hands brushing her belly. The next thing she knew, he was sliding the shirt down and off her arms. His gaze fastened on the sheer black bra she wore underneath. She knew the see-through fabric hid nothing, and her nipples puckered as his gaze settled on them.

He ran a finger lightly around the top of her bra, tracing the edge where it dipped between her breasts. She quivered. "It unfastens in the front," she whispered, dying for him to undo it.

"Oh, I'm not going to unfasten it," he replied softly. "Not yet, anyway."

He continued to taunt her with his finger, circling

under the curve of her breast then back on top, deliberately avoiding the sensitive peak in the center. Her skin felt as if it were on fire. Leaning back on her hands, she thrust her chest out, willing him to touch an aching nipple.

He took his own sweet time. Finally, when she was ready to cry out with frustration, he took her nipple in his mouth, fabric and all. The warmth of his tongue, the pressure of his gentle sucking, the slide of wet silk on her swollen flesh was exquisite. With a moan, she grasped at his shoulders.

"Lean back," he murmured. "Lean back and let me pleasure you."

She did as he said. She leaned back on her hands and let him suckle her breasts as heat, slick and needy, built to an inferno inside her.

She was relieved when his hands found their way to her inner thighs. Ripples of pleasure cascaded through her as his hands climbed higher and higher. A callus on his palm snagged on the smooth nylon of her panty hose, sending a secret thrill through her. He was so masculine, so much her opposite, so much her mate. An ache was building inside her, a throbbing need to be stroked and filled.

Cole dropped to his knees before her, his hands still on her thighs. "Now," he whispered in a ragged voice. "Let's see what's under that skirt."

Gently, slowly, he pried her legs farther apart, pushing her skirt up till it rode around her waist. She looked down, past the erect, wet, black-clothed tips of her breasts, to see Cole gazing at her most secret, most feminine spot. His eyes gleamed in the flickering candlelight. "You're beautiful," he murmured. "So very beautiful."

Slowly, excruciatingly slowly, he blazed a trail of kisses up her thigh, his tongue erotically tormenting her through the panty hose as it had through her sheer bra. She was ablaze, aflame. By the time he reached the inner seam of her panty hose, she was crying out in need.

"All right, sweetheart," he murmured, rising to his feet. "All right."

She felt a firm pressure, then heard a soft ripping sound. He was tearing her clothes right off her! The thought was startling and primal and thrilling. Her pulse thudded in her throat as he ripped her panty hose again.

She reached out for him, tugging at the zipper of his jeans. He quickly shed them, then stood before her—very male and very aroused. She reached out, laid claim to his hips and drew him to her, wrapping her legs around his muscled thighs.

He no sooner filled her than she was rocketing into space, past a million sparkling stars, into a brilliant, far-flung galaxy spinning wildly through the universe.

"Josie," he murmured. He grasped her bottom and tilted her more fully toward him, then slowed the pace until she was climbing the timeless spiral once again. She clutched him tightly, one arm around his back, the other on his rock-hard buttock, her calves twined around his still-standing legs. The tension built and grew to a single, cataclysmic moment, a moment when everything narrowed to a tunnel of light that burst around her and in her and through her. And in that moment, her whole world, her sole reason for being, was Cole.

She was vaguely aware of being lifted, of being borne in his arms. Still standing, he cradled her against him and drove deep. He gave a soul-felt cry, and his pleasure became her own.

He staggered to the bed, still holding her. He gently laid her on the mattress, then fell hard beside her. "Josie," he murmured, pulling her back in his arms. "My sweet, sweet Josie."

It was a moment of unadulterated bliss. She loved him. With every fiber of her being, she loved him. To have given and taken such pleasure from the man she loved filled her heart to bursting. She was glad, so very glad, to be his woman, to have Cole as her man.

Except he wasn't. The truth sent her plunging back to earth like a skydiver with a failed parachute.

She was his—there was no question of that. She'd given herself to him heart and soul, body and spirit—completely, thoroughly, irrevocably. But he was hers only on loan.

And the loan would be up in less than a week. They were already nearing Memphis, and the river was high and fast. They were heading downstream, running with the current.

And she was running out of time.

Her throat tightened with emotion. A tear slid from her eye, and she quickly wiped it away.

But not quickly enough. Cole's sharp eyes saw it. His finger traced its path along her cheek. "Hey—did I hurt you?"

"No." She turned her face to the wall as another tear slipped out. "No. I'm fine."

"If you're fine, then why are you crying?"

Josephine drew a deep breath. She was determined not to ruin their remaining time together. "Because you've made me so happy."

He tipped her face toward him and eyed her skeptically.

"You—you proved I'm not frigid," she said quickly.

He gave a wry grin. "You proved that yourself." He ran a hand over her hair. "It's hard to believe you ever thought you were."

"You introduced me to a whole world I never knew existed." Josephine reached out and touched his face, wishing she could touch his heart as well. "And you helped me believe in myself. But most of all, you helped me come to terms with my past. You helped me forgive myself." She rolled toward him and leaned up on an elbow, then gazed earnestly at him in the candlelight. "I just wish I could help you do the same."

"I don't need forgiveness," he said gruffly, rolling onto his back.

"I think you do. Deep down inside, I think you're blaming yourself for your foster mother's death."

"No. McAuley is to blame, and forgiveness is too good for him."

"But revenge won't solve anything. You told me yourself that what's done is done."

"This isn't done."

"Let it go," she whispered urgently. "Just forgive him and let it go."

"I can't. Forgiveness won't stop the burning I get in my gut whenever I think about what he did. Forgiveness won't erase the memory of how Mom's face looked when she thought I'd held him up." Placing his hands behind his head, he stared up at the ceiling, his jaw clenched tight. "I've tried to put it behind me for years, but I can't. I've come up with dozens of plans for revenge, but all of them could have landed me in jail. I made Mom a promise that I wouldn't do anything illegal, and I intend to keep it."

Josephine's heart turned over.

"That's what so perfect about this plan. I've got nothing to lose."

"What if doesn't work?"

"At least I will have tried." He sat up in bed, his eyes intense. "It's the perfect punishment. McAuley's pursued Alexa for years. She's the one thing he wants that his money couldn't buy. Just when he thinks he's finally about to win her, just when he thinks he's finally acquired the ultimate status symbol, I'm going snatch her away and make him look like a fool." He rolled out of bed, planting his feet on the floor. "And you know what? I can't wait."

Josephine turned to the wall. She felt his hand on her head.

"Hey—Josie, are you crying again? This has nothing to do with you—with us."

There was no "us"—not past the end of the trip. Josephine had known that from the very beginning. But it didn't make it hurt any less.

"Ah, hell. I never meant to hurt you," he said softly,

stroking her hair. "It was selfish of me to have ever gotten involved with you."

Josephine called upon all her inner strength. She wouldn't spoil the few nights they had left together. She wouldn't leave him with a fresh load of guilt. After all, she was the one who'd initiated their lovemaking.

She drew a deep breath, wiped her face on her pillow, then turned toward him, forcing a soft smile. "I wouldn't have missed being with you for the world. You've taught me more than you'll ever know."

She sat up and kissed him, letting her hand slide down his bare chest, down his flat belly. Her hand slipped farther as she deepened the kiss. She was pleased when she felt his jolt of response. "In fact," she whispered, "I'm ready for another lesson."

Chapter Seventeen

Four nights later, Fanny had just turned down the covers on her bed when a tentative knock sounded on her door. "Josie?" she called.

"No, it's me."

Henry. Fanny's heart skipped a beat. She started to grab her old plaid flannel robe and pull it over the red silk night-gown Josie had talked her into buying in Minneapolis, then thought better of it.

What the heck. It wouldn't hurt that stubborn old mule to see her looking like a woman. She knew he was attracted to her. She'd seen the way he stared at her when he thought she wasn't looking, but she was beginning to give up all hope that he'd ever do anything about it. Only three more days remained until they docked in New Orleans.

Despite her decision not to wear her robe, Fanny couldn't keep from placing her hand over the gown's scooped neckline as she cautiously opened the door. "Yes?"

"I've, uh, got somethin' fer ya."

He was clean-shaven, and he smelled faintly of Old Spice. Fanny's galloping heart picked up speed. "How nice." She opened the door wider. "Would you like to come in?"

His face turned ruddy as he nodded. "It's not somethin' I'd want to give to ya out in the hall."

"Come on in, then." She stepped back from the door.

Henry shuffled into the cabin, his face reddening even more, his posture stiff. Fanny caught him glancing at her décolletage, then averting his eyes. Twice.

She nervously moved to the back of her room and perched on the edge of her bed. "This is a pleasant surprise."

"I've, uh, got somethin' that belongs to you, an' I figured you'd want it back." Henry nervously unbuttoned the bottom of his plaid flannel shirt and pulled something out.

Fanny gasped as she recognized her new red lace bra and matching silk panties. "Where did you find those? I thought the washing machine ate them."

"Wasn't the washin' machine." Henry's eyes nervously darted from Fanny to the undergarments and back. He cleared his throat. "It was Hambone."

"Hambone?"

Henry nodded. "I found 'em in his cabin. I had to go in there to wake him up for his shift this evenin' and I found them hangin' out from under his pillow. Don' know what he's been doin' with 'em. Don' wanna know. Ya prob'ly oughta wash 'em though."

"I'll do that." Rising, Fanny laughed, gingerly took the undergarments and placed them on her dresser. She shook her head. "Stealin' underwear. I swear, that Hambone is one sick puppy."

"You got that right." Henry stuck his hands in his pants pockets. "Well, I figgered you'd want 'em back. When I saw 'em, I knew they were yours."

Fanny glanced at the enormous bright red bra and

grinned sheepishly. "I don't have to ask how you knew that."

Henry grinned, too, his face coloring even more. "Well, I gotta tell you, seein' your underwear in Hambone's bed upset me somethin' fierce."

"It did?"

Henry's Adam's apple bobbed in his neck. "I knew you wouldn't—that you an' he wouldn'—hadn'—ah, hell, you know what I mean. I knew ya didn'. But seein' him with somethin' so personal of yours made me fightin' mad. I punched him but good."

"You didn't!"

"I did. An' he's got the black eye to prove it."

Fanny's heart did a back flip.

"It's been botherin' the bejesus out of me, watchin' Hambone ogle ya like he's been doin'. An' findin' these undies in his cabin was the last straw."

A long, awkward silence stretched between them. Fanny's mouth went dry. She cleared her throat and stared down at the dresser top. "You probably think it's foolish, a plain gal like me wearing fancy underclothes like that."

"No. I don't think it's foolish at all. I think it's—" Henry stopped.

"What?"

Henry's Adam's apple jerked once more. He cleared his throat. "I think it's downright sexy."

Fanny's heart pounded so fast she thought she might pass out.

Henry shifted his feet, pulled his hands out of his pockets, then shoved them in again. "Fanny, I've been thinkin' 'bout what you tol' me the other day. It's been preyin' on my mind how that no-good Hollywood scoundrel done ya bad, and made you not trust men and end up all alone. An' then I got to thinkin' 'bout what you said about Hazel an' me. An' I got to thinkin' that because she was so wonderful, I've hid out from other women, and I'm all alone, too. An' thinkin' of it like that, it didn' make a lick o' sense."

Fanny fanned herself with her hand.

"All these years since Hazel passed on, I been thinkin' no one could replace her, so I haven't messed with women. But what you tol' me the other day set me to thinkin'. You said somethin' about maybe carin' about someone different in a whole different way. It wouldn' be replacin' Hazel, 'cause she'll always have that part of my heart. But maybe someone else could have a whole different part."

Fanny held her breath. Henry looked at her. His eyes were blue, blue as the sky, blue and intense. His face was weathered, but his eyes were young, and looking in them somehow made her feel young again, too.

"Now you an' me, we get along jus' fine. I like your cooking an' your card playin' an' your jokin', and I like the way you say things straight out. An' I gotta admit I'm real partial to the way ya look." Henry stopped and swallowed again. "An' when I saw your undies in Hambone's bed, well, I got jealous as a gelding at a stud farm. An' I decided it was high time to quit lollygaggin' and to come see ya and speak my piece. So . . ."

He hesitated. The very air around them seemed to hold its breath. "Damn it, Fanny, can I give you a kiss?"

Fanny's heart soared through the ceiling, up two decks and into the starry night. She could barely hear her own voice over the roar of her pulse thundering in her veins. "Henry, you old fool, I thought you'd never ask."

The next sound she heard was Henry's foot kicking her cabin door closed. Then she was in his arms, and finally, finally, she was in the place she'd spent her whole life seeking, the only place she'd ever wanted to be, the home she'd at long last found.

"Hard to believe we'll be in New Orleans by mornin'." Henry neatly wiped his mouth with his napkin and smiled across the table at Fanny. "Seems like the shortest trip I ever took."

"Lasted darn near forever, if you ask me," Hambone

muttered, blinking the eye that wasn't swollen shut.

"Yeah." Junior crammed an enormous forkful of peach cobbler into his mouth. "Guess this'll be our last manners lesson, huh?"

And my last night with Cole. Josephine's heart felt heavy and tight, as if the towboat's anchor were wrapped around it. She forced a smile and looked around the table, her gaze beginning and ending with Cole. Every time she looked at him, she wanted to burst into tears, yet he drew her gaze like a sore tooth drew the tongue. "Yes. And all of you have made wonderful progress. I'm very proud of you."

Hambone puffed out his chest. "Really?"

"Yes. You've made more progress than any class I've ever taught."

Cole grinned at her from the opposite end of the table, and she knew he was reading between the lines: she'd never taught a class with so much room for improvement. The crew was far from perfectly mannered, but at least they no longer ate with their fingers, belched at the table or grabbed food off each other's plates.

"Who's done the best?" Hambone prodded.

"You've all done very well."

"It's impolite, *mon ami,* to ask a question that puts a lady on the mark," Gaston chastised Hambone.

"I think you mean on the spot." Josephine smiled at the engineer. "And you're absolutely right, Gaston."

The Cajun flashed a bright grin and lifted his water glass. "*Merci, chérie,* for making us gentlemen. It's sure to be a big help with zee ladies."

Cole lifted his glass as well. "Here's to Josephine, who turned a boatload of sows' ears into a bunch of silk purses."

"Hear! Hear!" Henry raised his glass.

Cole took a long sip, his eyes fixed on Josephine. Her heart thudded painfully in her chest. She loved him. With her heart and soul and all her being, she loved him. And it was time to let him go. It was hard to smile while her heart was crying.

She was relieved when Cole turned to Fanny and again lifted his glass. "And here's to Fanny—the best cook ever to grace our galley."

"I'll second that!" Henry said.

"Yeah!" Hambone, Junior and Gaston chorused.

Fanny blushed furiously, but her round face shone like the moon.

"You outdid yourself tonight, Fanny," Cole said. "The pot roast was delicious."

Fanny shot Josephine a sly grin. "I'm glad you liked it, but I didn't cook it."

"You didn't?"

"No. Josephine did."

"No kiddin'?" Junior asked, his eyes wide.

"No kiddin'. I've been giving her cooking lessons, and she fixed the whole meal tonight as her graduation exercise."

"Wow! Beats the heck out of what she served us going upriver," Hambone exclaimed.

"No joke! Remember that globbed-up rice and those awful beans?" Junior remarked.

"Everyone seems to have learned something on this trip." Cole lifted his glass again. "Here's to the completion of a successful voyage, and to good luck in all our future endeavors."

Everyone murmured agreement.

"Can't believe you're gonna stay ashore in New Orleans, Boss," Hambone said.

"It's just for a while. I have a piece of business to attend to."

The knot in Josephine's throat swelled like wet rope. She knew all too well what—or rather *who*—Cole's piece of business involved. She'd done her best not to think about it, to chase the thought from her mind every time it surfaced, but she could avoid it no longer. It was time to pay for all the joy she'd experienced with an equal amount of pain.

The conversation shifted to other topics; then the meal was mercifully over. Josephine ducked her head and began gathering up empty plates as the men straggled from the galley.

She looked up to find Cole at her side. "Henry will help Fanny clean up. I'm sure they'd rather be alone, anyway."

Josephine nodded, her throat tight. Fanny had been walking on air the past few days, and Henry had been strutting about like a banty rooster. The pair was virtually inseparable, and everyone on the boat knew that Henry had moved into Fanny's cabin.

"I'd like some time alone with you."

Josephine tried to muster a smile, but her lips trembled. *Oh, dear heavens*—how was she going to make it through tonight, knowing it was her last with Cole?

He held the door to the galley open for her, then did the same with the hatch that led to the deck. The wind was soft and warm on her face. She could tell they were close to New Orleans. The air in southern Louisiana had a different feel, a heavier, silkier texture than anywhere else on earth.

Cole took her elbow as they strolled the narrow deck. "I haven't seen much of you today."

Josephine bravely strove for a light tone. "Well, I've taught you all I know, so there was no need for any further lessons. Besides, I was busy cooking dinner."

"And you did a great job. If you ever want to apply for a job as a cook again, I'll hire you in a minute."

"If I promise not to serve blackened green beans?"

The corners of Cole's eyes creased in a devastatingly attractive fashion as he smiled. "Well, yes. We'd have to make a few stipulations."

Cole led her to the aft deck, to the spot where they'd

shared so many special moments. Josephine's heart ached with nostalgia, and she wasn't even gone. She walked to the railing and gazed out at the churning water, her insides churning, too. Cole leaned on the rail beside her.

"Thanks for making those calls for me this morning," he said.

"You're welcome." Posing as the attaché for Prince Dumanski of Romania, Josephine had helped him put his plan into action. She'd called the Windsor Court Hotel and reserved the five-star establishment's most elegant suite, ordering it stocked with fine wines, cigars, fresh fruits and caviar. She'd made an issue of the fact that the prince preferred to remain anonymous during his stay, which almost certainly ensured that the public relations director would contact the gossip columnist for the *Times-Picayune* as soon as Cole checked out.

She'd also made an appointment for Cole to have his hair cut by the city's most exclusive hairdresser, a garrulous nymph of a man who cut the hair of anyone who was anyone and traded in gossip as if it were blue-chip stocks. She'd sworn him to secrecy about Cole's title, explaining that Cole preferred to remain incognito. The fact that she'd asked him to remain silent guaranteed that the news would be spread far and wide.

"You make a very convincing attaché."

Josephine's fingers tightened on the metal railing. "Just doing my job. After all, I was hired to turn you into a prince."

"And how do you think you did?"

She bravely tried to smile. "Exceptionally well. You act like a prince, you talk like a prince, you look like a prince. You even have the newly tailored wardrobe of a prince waiting for you in New Orleans."

He had everything he required. He had no more need of her. She blinked hard, trying to hold back the tears that suddenly threatened to fall.

"I can't thank you enough for all you've done."

"It was my pleasure." She kept her head averted, trying hard to gain control of her emotions.

After a long moment his arm reached around her. "You're awfully quiet. What are you thinking?"

Josephine kept her gaze on the smokestacks of a brightly lit refinery on the shore. "About everything I need to do to get my business started. I want to hit the ground running."

"What are you going to do first?"

"Get a brochure printed. I've already sketched one out."

"Atta girl!"

The simple encouragement brought fresh tears to her eyes. She blinked them away. "Then I intend to contact every businessman Aunt Prudie or I ever knew and set up an appointment to make a sales pitch. And I hope to get each of them to recommend me to another business while I'm there, so I don't have to make cold calls."

"You've really thought this out. I'm impressed." Cole tipped her face toward him. "But I'm not surprised. You're really something, you know it?"

His eyes were warm and sincere and full of affection. The very tenderness she saw there cut her to the quick.

She knew he didn't want to hurt her. She knew he cared for her. But she also knew he would never love her—not in the way she longed to be loved. She wanted forever. He could offer only a little while. He'd told her as much, and his plans confirmed his words.

His features started to blur as her eyes filled with unshed tears, but not so much that she couldn't see the remorse in his eyes. She turned her gaze back to the shoreline.

"I'm going to miss you," he said softly, slipping his arm around her waist.

Josephine drew a deep breath, willing herself not to cry. He'd helped her overcome a burden of guilt. She didn't want to leave him with a burden similar to the one he'd helped her discard.

His hand drifted up her back and sifted through her hair. "After I finish, I'll call you."

Josephine swallowed hard. She knew him well enough to know he could handle anger better than guilt. Guilt was a slow, painful toxin. Anger would burn hot and fierce, but it would burn only his heart, not his soul. And after a while, it would burn itself out.

It was time for the performance of her life. Time to muster everything she had. It would be better for him to hate her than for him to hate himself.

She tightened her grip on the railing, trying to grip her self-control as well. "It would probably be better if we didn't see each other in the future."

"What?"

She forced a light tone to her voice. "Well, we've helped each other achieve our goals. It's time to move on."

Cole's gaze seemed to cut right through her. "Move on?"

She nodded. "Let's face it. There are a lot of differences between us."

"I know." With a sensuous smile, he moved his hand to her bottom. "I've always loved those differences."

Josephine shifted away, out of his grasp, her heart breaking. How, oh, how could she do this?

How, oh, how could she not? She drew a deep breath and forced herself to adopt her coolest demeanor, the one she'd perfected over all the years she'd spent masking her true emotions. "I've enjoyed our time together. You helped me tremendously. And I'll never forget all that you've taught me."

Cole reached for her again. "I thought you were the one doing the teaching."

"It was a reciprocal arrangement, don't you think? I taught you about manners, and you taught me about sex. It's time for both of us to move on and use what we've learned."

Cole looked as if she'd struck him. He stepped back and his eyes narrowed. "And how, exactly, do you intend to use your new knowledge?"

She turned her eyes to the shoreline. "To find a suitable mate."

"Suitable?" He spit the word out like a piece of rotten fruit. She could feel his hot, angry gaze on her, but she continued to stare across the river. "Isn't that the word you used to describe Wally?"

Pain pierced her heart like a spear. She made herself press forward, made herself see this through. Inhaling deeply, she forced herself to turn and face him. "Come on, Cole. We've never pretended this was a long-term thing. It was great while it lasted, but now it's over. It's time to go our separate ways."

His gaze was cold, his eyes as hard and impassive as chunks of coal. "Because I'm not suitable."

Oh, dear God—it would hurt less to sever her own arm than to do this! But she had to do it. It was her ultimate sacrifice, her final gift—one he would never even know she'd given him, one he would never understand.

She loved him enough to allow him to hate her. She closed her eyes for a long second and drew a deep breath. "We come from entirely different backgrounds. I'm sure that when you think things over, you'll agree that I'm right."

"I don't need to think things over, Empress." The tender lover she'd known was gone. In his place was the man she'd first met—a hard, dangerous stranger with cold eyes and a contemptuous gaze. "You know, you had me fooled for a while there. I thought you were different, but you're just as shallow as Alexa and McAuley and all the rest of your kind."

Inwardly she cringed, but outwardly she maintained her calm.

"Well, I won't inflict my unsuitable presence on you any

longer. I'll spend the night in Henry's cabin." He turned to walk away, then whipped back around. "I trust I'm paying you enough to keep your mouth shut about my plans?"

His words struck her like a blow. "You—you don't have to worry."

"Well, I'll add a little extra hush money as an added incentive. Henry will give you your check first thing in the morning."

He turned and strode down the deck, his dark hair whipping in the wind. The tears that she'd held in check all day coursed down her cheeks as she watched him walk away, taking her heart with him.

Chapter Eighteen

Three weeks later, Josephine found herself in the back of a hotel limousine, headed to the symphony benefit ball at the Grand Regent Hotel. She smoothed the skirt of her champagne-colored gown and glanced over at the handsome man seated beside her on the leather seat. The owner of the hotel that was hosting the ball, Elliott Geraud, had impeccably groomed blond hair, a fit physique and a nose so aristocratic that Josephine suspected it was the work of a plastic surgeon. Wealthy, well connected and well-bred, Elliott was considered one of the most eligible bachelors in New Orleans. Just the mention of his name was enough to make most well-heeled New Orleans women sigh.

Unfortunately he made Josephine sigh only with boredom.

"I'm glad you finally agreed to go out with me," he said, stretching his arm across the back of the leather seat and giving a brilliant smile—a smile Josephine was sure was well practiced. "You're a difficult lady to pin down."

"I've been rather busy." Which was true. In the three

weeks since she'd disembarked the *Chienne,* Josephine had thrown herself into a whirlwind of activity. She'd not only produced a brochure and made dozens of sales presentations, but she'd already conducted seminars for five companies and booked fifteen more. At the same time, she'd rented an apartment in the warehouse district and was in the process of furnishing it with finds from flea markets and antique stores. She stayed busy from the moment she awoke until she finally climbed into bed around midnight.

And then, no matter how tired she was, the memories she frantically kept at bay during the day overwhelmed her. Memories of Cole's eyes as he leaned in for a kiss. Memories of his lips brushing hers. Memories of his wounded, angry expression the last time she'd seen him.

An emptiness as brown and vast as the waters of the Mississippi would flow over her until she thought she'd drown in despair. He'd never even told her good-bye. He'd sent Henry with her paycheck the next morning, along with instructions to escort her off the boat. She'd bidden a tearful farewell to Fanny, who'd taken down the address and phone number of her school and promised to stay in touch. Fanny had called her daily until last week, when she and Henry had set out on another trip upriver on the chartered towboat.

"I hope all your busyness means that your business is doing well," Elliott remarked.

Josephine forced her attention back to the man beside her. "Very well. I can't believe how rapidly it's taking off."

"Well, I can. The seminar you presented at my hotel was excellent."

Josephine gave him a grateful smile. "I appreciate the reference you gave me. It's been a big help in getting other clients."

"Every word was true. I'm glad things are working out for you."

And on the surface, they were. Her career was taking off, her money troubles were rapidly evaporating, and one of the most sought-after bachelors in New Orleans was pursuing her. But inside, where it counted most, she felt as dry and lifeless as a dead leaf.

She stared out the rain-streaked limo window. It probably had been a mistake to agree to come on this date with Elliott, but he'd worn her down with his persistence. And as he'd pointed out, networking was essential to her business. Attending a symphony ball was the perfect way to meet potential new clients.

The limo turned onto Decatur Street. Elliott touched the delicate diamond-and-ruby bracelet on Josephine's arm. "What an exquisite piece."

"Thank you. It was my mother's."

"It looks lovely on you." His eyes roamed over her appreciatively. "And so does that dress. You look wonderful."

Josephine smiled. Before her trip up the Mississippi, she would have been thrilled to receive this type of attention from Elliott. Now, however, it simply made her miss Cole.

"This is supposed to be a rather lively gathering tonight," Elliott remarked. "I heard that that prince fellow is supposed to be here."

Josephine's heart skipped a beat. "Prince?"

"You know. He's been mentioned a couple of times in the 'About Town' column of the *Times-Picayune*."

Josephine nervously fingered the heirloom bracelet on her arm. She'd seen the newspaper items, of course. In fact, she'd committed them to memory: *The Windsor Court Hotel played host to royalty last week when Prince Cole Dumanski made the five-star hotel his temporary abode. Rumor has it that the dashing Romanian prince, who prefers to remain incognito, is planning to make New Orleans one of his many homes away from home.*

And then, last week—*Sources tell us that a certain estate in Audubon Place has been purchased by a dashing*

*prince who insists on keeping his royal status anonymous.
I can't say who, but astute readers will remember reading
about him in last week's column.*

Elliot looked at Josephine curiously. "I heard he bought
your aunt's old house. Have you met him?"

Josephine wound her fingers together tightly in her lap
to keep them from shaking. "No. I wasn't involved in the
sale. The bank handled all that."

"Well, I understand that this fellow is supposed to be the
next in line to assume the throne if Romania ever reverts to
a monarchy. Jason Willis's wife says her sister met him at
an embassy function in Washington a few years ago."

Josephine blinked, trying hard not to show her astonishment. The gossip mill was not only churning, it was taking
on a life of its own. "Is that a fact?"

Elliott nodded. "Jason says his sister-in-law found him
very charming."

"How interesting." Josephine's heart pounded erratically. She was still trying to digest the fact that Cole was
going to be at tonight's event. For some reason, the possibility of running into Cole in New Orleans hadn't occurred
to her. How would she manage to see him again and not
fall apart?

She would somehow have to, she told herself sternly.
She couldn't let on that she even knew him, much less how
much she missed him. For his sake, she needed to act as if
she'd moved on with her life.

And Elliott would serve as the perfect foil. She glanced
at the man beside her, then gave a wan smile as he reached
for her hand.

Cole spotted Alexa the moment he strode into the hotel
ballroom. She was easy to pick out—she was the tall
brunette in the red sequined gown holding court near the
dance floor.

His stomach tightened, but not from desire. He stood by
the foyer and watched her dispassionately, viewing her

with the same detachment with which he might admire a beautiful painting. Her hair fell around her shoulders like black satin, her face was exquisitely made up, and her stylish dress was daringly cut to flaunt her stunning figure. She was attractive—there was no denying it. But she no longer appealed to him in the slightest.

Compared to Josephine, Alexa looked hard-edged and cold. Everything from the way she stood with one hand on her hip to the length of her bright red nails seemed calculated for effect. Josephine's beauty was uncontrived and subtle, while Alexa's was posed and deliberate.

Not that appearances meant anything. Josephine's heart was just as hard as Alexa's, Cole thought bitterly. With Alexa, at least, a man knew exactly what he was getting from the very beginning.

Josephine had sucked him in and played him for a fool, and the damnedest part of it was that he didn't know how it had happened. She'd annoyed him, then she'd intrigued him. She'd made him want to break through her wall of reserve. But somehow, when he wasn't looking, she'd managed to break through his walls instead.

He'd fallen for her hard, and he'd thought she cared for him as well.

Not that it should matter, he told himself. He hadn't been prepared to offer her a future. Hell, he couldn't even envision a future for himself, beyond carrying out his current plans.

Besides, he hadn't come here tonight to think about Josephine, he thought sternly. He'd come here to set his plan in motion. In the last three weeks, he'd finalized his purchase of Aunt Prudie's house and opened an office in the World Trade building. When he'd discovered that Alexa was chairing the symphony ball, he'd immediately called and offered an enormous donation, claiming a great fondness for music. As he'd hoped, she'd insisted that he sit at her table tonight.

He watched the young woman who'd taken his name at the door approach Alexa and whisper something in her ear. Alexa immediately turned and looked toward the door.

Smiling broadly, Alexa sauntered toward him, her hips swaying seductively. He held his breath. This was the moment of truth. If she recognized him, his plans would be ruined.

"Prince Dumanski! I'm so delighted to meet you." Alexa stretched out her hand. "I'm Alexa Armand."

Cole smoothly bowed over her hand. "The pleasure is mine." He straightened and stepped close. "But please, just call me Cole."

"Oh, of course." She tipped her head, giving him a coy look. "I understand you prefer to remain incognito."

"Titles are such a bore, don't you think?"

"Actually, I find them rather fascinating." Alexa's smile clearly said she found *him* fascinating. "But if you prefer first names, then you must call me Alexa."

Cole tightened his grip on her hand. "Alexa. A beautiful name for a beautiful woman."

Alexa's fingers squeezed his palm. "You flatter me, Your Majesty."

"Just Cole. Please."

"I'm sorry." She smiled up enticingly. "Cole."

She didn't recognize him, he thought with relief. And just as he'd hoped, she seemed enamored with the idea of mingling with royalty. He released her hand, noting that she let her fingers slide slowly down his palm.

"I've arranged for you and your date to sit at my table." She tossed her hair in the seductive manner he remembered from high school.

"That's very kind of you, but I'm afraid I'm alone this evening. I hope that won't spoil your seating arrangements."

She moved closer, so that her breast brushed his sleeve. "Oh, not at all."

Cole resisted an impulse to step back. "I don't suppose I'd be lucky enough to discover that a lady as lovely as yourself is unescorted this evening?"

She smiled ruefully. "I'm afraid I'm with someone."

"A husband?"

"Oh, no. I'm not married."

And not giving any indication that you're engaged, either, Cole thought dryly. This was going to be easier than he'd imagined. Cole leaned closer. "I'm very glad to hear that."

"Alexa, darling—there you are." A heavyset man with a ruddy complexion and russet-colored hair swaggered up, reeking of bourbon.

Every muscle in Cole's body stiffened. Robert McAuley. The hatred Cole had felt for the man for years boiled up inside him. It was hard to disguise it now, seeing him in person again.

He carefully kept his face expressionless as Robert placed a proprietary hand around Alexa's waist and moistly bussed her on the cheek. Cole noted with interest that Alexa seemed less than thrilled by Robert's arrival.

"You must be that prince everyone's talking about," Robert said, eyeing him curiously.

"Yes, but he's very modest about his title," Alexa explained. "He prefers simply to be called Cole Dumanski."

Cole forced himself to smile and extend his hand. The redheaded man took it. "I'm Robert McAuley. Alexa's fiancé."

Alexa continued to smile, but her eyes narrowed in annoyance.

"Congratulations," Cole said smoothly, resisting the urge to crush Robert's fingers as he shook his hand. "You're a fortunate man to have won the heart of such a beautiful woman."

Robert's chest puffed out in pride. "She's quite a prize,

isn't she?" His small, pale eyes raked over Alexa possessively. "I've been chasing her since junior high. It took me nearly twenty years and half a million dollars in jewelry, but I finally convinced her to say yes."

Cole was certain it would ultimately cost McAuley far more than that. Rumor had it that Alexa had consented to marry McAuley only after a published report ranked him as the wealthiest man in Louisiana. Cole smiled politely. "You're a lucky man."

The sly smile Alexa shot him gave every indication that Cole could easily get lucky, too.

Robert peered at Cole closely. "You know, something about you looks familiar."

Cole's heart froze. If McAuley recognized him now, the game was up.

Alexa tossed her hair. "He's royalty, Robert. I'm sure you've seen his picture in *Town and Country* or *People* or somewhere."

Robert leaned close, close enough to blow bourbon fumes in Cole's face. "No, I'm sure we've met. Do you play polo?"

"Not well," Cole hedged.

"Me neither, so I've gotten pretty good at cheating." Robert laughed as if he'd said something extremely witty. Cole was fairly certain he was merely stating the truth.

"Did you play in the Houston match last spring?" Robert pressed.

"I'm afraid I didn't make that one."

"Hmm. Well, I'm sure we've played against each other somewhere. I never forget the face of an opponent."

Me neither, Cole thought grimly. *Me neither.* He pulled his lips into a smile. "Perhaps we can arrange a rematch in the near future."

"Maybe so. But if you want to win, you'd better play on my team." McAuley laughed and tightened his grip on Alexa. "Isn't that right, sweetheart?"

Cole gave a polite smile, gritting his teeth behind it. McAuley hadn't changed a lick since high school. Alexa hadn't, either. She had no more affection for the man she was about to marry than she'd had for him at sixteen.

Well, one thing was for sure, Cole told himself grimly—he'd chosen an excellent avenue for revenge. McAuley was still obsessed with Alexa. She represented all the beauty and acceptance that Robert's rich daddy had never been able to buy for his unpopular, homely son. Cole couldn't wait to see the SOB's face when he found out he'd not only lost the woman he'd pursued for twenty years, but lost her to the only boy at St. Alban's who'd been more despised than he was.

It was the most tedious dinner of Cole's life. He hated sitting at a table with the man responsible for Mom Sawyer's death, hated having to smile and act pleasant and make small talk. His only outlet was to subtly flirt with Alexa, who not-too-subtly flirted back. Cole was pleased to note that Robert looked increasingly aggravated as the night wore on.

He was relieved when the waiter finally cleared the dessert plates and the orchestra began tuning up.

Alexa turned to Robert. "I really ought to introduce Cole around."

Robert picked up his drink and lurched out of his chair. He shot Cole a dark look. "I'll come with you."

And so the three of them made the rounds of the ballroom tables. At each stop, Alexa introduced Cole, never failing to mention his royal status despite his repeated protests.

They'd nearly completed a full tour of the room when Cole spotted a familiar figure. He inadvertently stopped in his tracks, his heart beating hard and fast.

Robert followed his gaze. "Hey, who's the babe with Elliott?" he asked Alexa.

Alexa looked where he pointed. "Good heavens. Why, I believe that's Josephine Evans!"

Robert let out a low whistle. "Wow. She's really blossomed since that old aunt of hers kicked the bucket."

Cole's heart thundered against his wing-collared shirt. It was Josephine, all right—looking like a golden vision in a long, fitted dress almost the exact color of her hair. Golden threads woven through the champagne fabric glimmered like the highlights in her hair under the low lights of the chandeliers. Cole felt as if he'd been socked in the gut.

"I'm surprised to see her. I heard she'd left town," Alexa remarked.

"Well, looks like she's back. And from the way Elliott is staring at her, I'd say he's more than a little smitten."

Alexa headed directly toward the couple, tugging Cole along. The tall man rose from his chair and smiled as Alexa approached.

"Hello, Elliott," the brunette purred, kissing him on the cheek. Cole stared down at Josephine. She stared back, her eyes huge, her face pale. Cole's stomach tightened like the lead line on a pier post.

Alexa pulled on his arm. "Cole, I'd like you to meet Elliott Geraud. Elliott owns this hotel and has generously provided the ballroom and dinner for tonight's benefit. Elliott, this is Prince Cole Dumanski."

"Please—no title. Just call me Cole." He woodenly shook the man's hand, trying hard to keep his eyes away from Josephine. His mind had gone blank, and it took an effort to think of an appropriate remark. "Your hotel is beautiful. And the dinner was superb."

"Thank you. It's an honor to have you here." He turned to Josephine. "May I present Miss Josephine Evans."

Cole had no choice but to take Josephine's hand in his. Her hand was warm and soft, and he thought he felt it tremble. A current shot through him, a current charged with heat and emotion and memories. He remembered that

343

hand running over his body, remembered how it clutched his back in the throes of passion. He remembered, and the memory burned like acid.

Josephine gazed back at Cole, trying not to drown in memories of her own. This was the man she loved, the man who held her heart, the man who owned her soul.

He was handsome, more handsome than she remembered. The custom-made tux she'd helped him order in Minneapolis fit him exquisitely, and his new haircut only accentuated his tanned skin and chiseled features. He looked every inch a prince. Judging from the way Alexa was looking at him, Josephine wasn't the only one who found him attractive.

A stab of jealousy, sharp and fierce, cut through her.

"Josephine's late aunt was an old friend of my family's," Alexa was saying.

"Very nice to meet you." Cole's words were warm, but his gaze froze her to the bone. Another bayonet of pain pierced her heart. He hadn't forgiven her for the way she'd left him.

"You look wonderful, Josephine." Robert stepped forward and kissed her cheek. "Your dress is stunning. And so is your jewelry." He took her hand and studied her bracelet. "A gift from an admirer?"

"Oh, no." The question left Josephine flustered. "It was my mother's."

Alexa's lips curled in a catty smile. "I'm surprised to see you, dear. I heard you left town after your aunt's . . . death." The pause indicated that something far worse than death had actually transpired.

Josephine pulled her spine to its straightest posture. "I was gone for a while, but now I'm back."

"Oh? Did you go anyplace interesting?"

Josephine glanced at Cole, then looked away. She had to be strong. She couldn't let on that she cared. Indifference—that was the attitude she needed to project. For his sake, she needed to act as if their time together had meant nothing. For the benefit of the others, she needed to act as if she didn't know him at all. "Just Minneapolis and back."

Elliott gestured to several empty seats at his table. "Would you care to join us?"

"Sure." Robert was already lowering himself into a chair. "I could use a drink."

A nearby waiter produced a fresh bottle of champagne. When everyone was seated and served, Elliott raised his glass. "To old friends and new acquaintances." He smiled at Alexa and Robert, then glanced pointedly at Josephine. "And new loves."

Across the table, Cole's face hardened. Josephine forced a smile, then reached for her glass. She normally didn't drink, but tonight she needed fortification. The relaxing warmth spread down her throat and through her chest. Josephine took another deep sip, and the waiter refilled her glass.

Elliott leaned toward her. "Would you like to dance?"

Josephine felt the beginnings of a pleasant buzz. Dancing with Elliot would be a way to escape the table—and maybe, just maybe, give Cole a dose of his own medicine. It stung like a manta ray, seeing him with Alexa, knowing he was trying to win her heart.

She smiled up at Elliott. "Why, yes." She took another long sip, then let him lead her to the dance floor. She saw Cole scowling at her from the table as she stepped into Elliott's arms.

Good. Josephine clung to Elliott a little more tightly than necessary as the handsome hotelier led her in a graceful turn. When she spun back around, Cole's and Alexa's seats were empty and Robert was now scowling at the dance floor. Josephine turned in the direction of Robert's gaze and saw Cole and Alexa step onto the dance floor.

Cole placed his hand on Alexa's waist, and Josephine's stomach suddenly felt as if she'd gone over a bump at high speed. She stumbled, causing Elliott to step on her foot. I'm so sorry," he murmured. "Did I hurt you?"

"No." *Not nearly as much as the sight of Cole with another woman in his arms.*

Josephine watched Alexa's hand slide from Cole's shoulder to his neck, watched her fingers slip above his collar into his hair when he spun her away from Robert. Her stomach knotted as Cole's hand moved low on Alexa's hip.

Cole executed a perfect turn, and Josephine realized that his eyes were on her, his mouth flattened in a hard, displeased line. She moved her own hand to Elliott's neck, imitating Alexa's move. She was gratified to see a muscle twitch in Cole's jaw.

Elliott guided her to the other end of the dance floor, and she was mercifully unable to see Cole any longer. She was relieved when the song was over and Elliott took her back to the table. He pulled out her chair.

"If you'll excuse me for a moment, I need to have a word with my banquet manager."

"Of course."

Elliott strode away, and Josephine took a long drink of champagne. Robert leaned forward. "It looks as if Alexa and the prince are staying on the dance floor for another number. Would you care to dance?"

If Cole had been bothered when she danced with Elliott, how would he react to her dancing with Robert? She smiled at the prospect. "Why, yes. I believe I would."

She let him lead her to the dance floor.

"So what do you think of the prince?" Robert asked as he took her hand.

"He seems very nice."

"Hmmph." Robert pulled her close. His boozy breath made the hair stand up on the back of her neck. "I think he's a worm."

"Why?"

"He's trying to move in on Alexa."

Josephine looked away, her stomach suddenly queasy. "Oh, I'm sure he's just being charming."

"Yeah, well, I'd like to kick his charming ass back to

346

Romania or New York or wherever he came from." He gave her a smarmy smile. "I've got a proposition for you."

A burst of alarm shot through her. "A . . . proposition?"

Robert's small, orthodontically perfect teeth flashed in a cold smile. "I want to send Mr. Prince packing. And I understand that your old aunt left you a little strapped for cash. Maybe you and I can help each other out."

A curl of dread tightened in her stomach. "What do you have in mind?"

"I want you to slip that bracelet of yours in Mr. Fancy-pants's pocket, then announce that it's been stolen. That's all you have to do. I'll handle the rest."

Josephine's blood ran cold. Robert was despicable. Below despicable. He'd framed Cole as a boy, and he was about to do it again. And this time he wanted her to help.

"I'll pay you ten thousand dollars."

"Oh, Robert, I can't—"

"I'll make it twenty."

An idea hit. Maybe it was the champagne, maybe it was seeing Cole again, maybe it was the pain of having him look at her so coldly—Josephine didn't know. She knew only that she was suddenly sure of what she was going to do.

"How . . . how would I get it in his pocket?" she asked hesitantly.

Robert's low, evil chuckle made Josephine's blood run cold. "Drop it in while you're dancing with him."

"What if he doesn't ask me to dance?"

"He will. I'll make sure of it."

As the song mercifully drew to a close, Josephine silently slipped the bracelet off her arm and into her hand, ready to do what had to be done.

Cole pulled out Alexa's chair, then seated himself next to her. He'd just taken a sip of champagne when Robert leaned across.

"Josephine was just telling me how much she wants to

dance with you," Robert said.

Cole glanced over at her, trying to hide his surprise. He saw Josephine's face flame.

McAuley grinned. "She said dancing with a prince would make her feel like Cinderella at the ball."

Unless he wanted to look like a heel, Cole had no choice. He stiffly rose from his chair and inclined his head toward her. "Well, then—may I have this dance, Miss Evans?"

Josephine gave a tremulous smile. "I'd be honored."

Cole led her to the dance floor, trying to ignore the way her hand felt in his, wishing his heart weren't racing so hard. "What the hell are you up to?" he said in a growl.

"I'm not up to anything."

"Then why did you get McAuley to con me into asking you to dance?"

"I didn't. He did it on his own."

Damnit, why did she have to feel so good in his arms? Holding her like this reminded him all too clearly of things he was better off forgetting. Cole scowled. "Why the hell would he do that?"

"Because he's angry that you're flirting with Alexa."

So McAuley wanted to get Alexa away from him— probably to give her a good scolding. Cole smiled. "Good. That's the whole idea."

"You don't understand." Jospehine's brows knit together as she looked up at him. Her eyes looked soft and worried, and he steeled himself against the pull of affection he felt for her. "McAuley's dangerous. You need to watch him."

"Your concern is touching."

"I know you're angry at me, but I want to warn you. . . ."

Damnit, why did she have to look so sincere? If he didn't watch himself, he'd fall back into the trap of believing she was different from all the rest. "I've already paid you for your services," he said coldly. "They're no longer needed."

Her back straightened so stiffly he felt as if he were dancing with a broom. "I suggest that you save all of your personal interest for that hotel man with the blow-dried hair," Cole added. "He seems a far more *suitable* recipient of your concern than me."

The rest of the dance was completed in silence. Cole tried desperately to pretend he was holding someone else, someone who didn't make his blood heat and his senses reel, but it was a lost cause.

Thirty minutes later, everyone gathered back at the table while the band took a break. Cole saw Robert glance at Josephine's wrist, then widen his eyes.

"Josephine—where's that lovely bracelet you were wearing?"

Something about the look on Robert's face sent a frisson of alarm racing up Cole's spine. He watched Josephine look at her naked arm. "Oh, dear—it's gone!"

"Maybe it fell off," Elliott said. "Let's check around the table." Everyone scooted back their chairs and looked on the carpet. When that produced no results, Elliott called over a waiter and instructed him to search the dance floor.

"Perhaps it's been stolen," Robert said when the waiter returned and reported no luck.

"Oh, come on, Robert." Alexa examined her manicure. "This is a five-hundred-dollar-a-plate symphony benefit. It's not exactly a crowd of pickpockets."

"No." Robert cut a glance at Cole. "But there are some people here we really don't know."

A feeling of déjà vu washed over Cole in a cold, sickening wave.

Alexa gave a disinterested shrug. "Josephine can just turn it in on her insurance and buy something new."

"I . . . I'm afraid I no longer have any insurance," Josephine said ruefully. "Even if I did, it's irreplaceable. It's a family heirloom."

Elliott patted her hand. "I'll call security and have them come up to take a report," Elliott said. "In the meantime, I'll have the band announce that it's missing and ask anyone finding it to return it."

Half an hour later, the thin, middle-aged director of security closed his notebook. "Well, I think I have everything I need."

"What are our chances of recovering it?" Elliott asked.

The security man shook his head. "If we don't find it tonight, I'm afraid they're not very good."

Robert leaned forward. "I saw a TV show a few months ago that said jewel thieves often attend functions like this looking for victims."

"How in the world would a thief get it off her arm?" Alexa asked.

"While he was shaking her hand or dancing with her, most likely." Robert cast another look at Cole that made his blood run cold.

Good God—surely McAuley wouldn't frame him again! In an instant, he knew that he would.

That he already had. A chill raced up his spine.

"I really don't know what we can do, short of frisking everyone as they leave the party," the security man said.

"Maybe that's what we ought to do," Robert said.

Cole gripped his glass of champagne so hard he nearly snapped off the stem, his blood freezing in his veins. *Not again. Not again!*

"Oh, come on, Robert," Alexa said. "I'm chairing this event, and I'm not going to have my donors treated like common criminals."

"Maybe we don't need to check them all."

Elliott leaned forward, his forehead creased. "What are you saying?"

"I'm saying only three of us have danced with Josephine this evening." He looked straight at Cole. "Perhaps the three of us should empty our pockets."

350

"Oh, honestly, Robert—surely you don't think Elliott or the prince stole Josephine's bracelet!" Alexa's voice carried loudly enough to be heard by the next table. A murmur rippled through the ballroom; then the room fell eerily silent. All eyes turned to their table.

"I'm not saying that. I simply think we should eliminate all doubt."

The blood drained from Cole's face. He knew a setup when he saw one, and he was definitely being set up.

He'd try to bluff his way out of it. His glass clinked as he set it down hard on the linen tablecloth. "It's clear what you're trying to insinuate, Mr. McAuley. I've never been so insulted in my life."

"Robert doesn't mean to insult you," Alexa said, her hand on Cole's arm.

"No. I simply want to clear your good name." The smirk on Robert's face was exactly the same as the one he'd worn fourteen years ago while the cops searched Cole's room. "If you've got nothing to hide, why, it shouldn't bother you to empty your pockets."

The two men stared at each other, the tension between them almost palpable.

Elliott rose to his feet. He gave a small chuckle, obviously trying to break the tension. "Well, this is embarrassing to all of us, but I'll gladly comply." He removed his jacket and passed it to the security chief. The chief patted it down and handed it back. Elliott then turned his pants pockets inside out, showing nothing but lining.

Elliott gestured to Robert. "Your turn."

"After Mr. Dumanski."

Cole slowly rose to his feet, feeling like a condemned man. He was certain Robert had planted the bracelet on him, but a refusal to follow Elliott's example would be the same as an admission of guilt. By complying, though, he was falling into Robert's trap. The gleeful sneer on the man's face told him as much.

Cole glanced at Josephine. Had she been trying to warn him about this earlier? She slightly, almost imperceptibly, nodded at him, her eyes reassuringly fixed on his. Something in the tiny gesture and the steadfast look in her eye strangely emboldened him.

He slowly removed his jacket and passed it to the security guard. The guard patted it down, then reached into the breast pocket. Cole held his breath.

The officer's hand reappeared, holding a packet of condoms. Laughter rippled through the ballroom.

The officer's face turned red. "Sorry," he muttered, jamming the foil packet back in the pocket.

Drawing a deep breath, Cole thrust both hands deep into his pants pockets. He exhaled with relief when he pulled out nothing but the black silk lining and his money clip. He handed the clip to the officer, who quickly looked through it and returned it.

The tightness in his chest loosened and eased. He turned to Robert, whose face was a mottled red. "Your turn."

Robert abruptly rose and angrily yanked off his jacket. As he did, something that sparkled fell from its pocket.

The crowd let out a collective gasp, then burst into an excited murmur.

Robert stared at the bracelet lying on the ground. "How the hell did that get there?" he demanded.

The security director frowned. "Perhaps you can tell us."

"I-I have no idea." Robert looked at Josephine, his eyes murderous, a blue vein bulging in his forehead.

And in that second, Cole knew: Josephine had planted it. She'd somehow learned of Robert's plan and thwarted it. A rush of tenderness surged through him like a warm wave.

All eyes turned to Josephine. She bent and picked the bracelet off the floral carpet, then gracefully straightened. "It must have fallen off my arm while we were dancing.

I'll have to have a jeweler check the catch." She smiled at Robert. "Thank you for finding it for me."

The security officer looked at Robert, his eyes narrowed, then looked back at Josephine. "Do you want to press charges?"

Cole held his breath. Josephine's eyebrows rose. "Whatever for? The latch came loose, that's all. I'm so glad it landed someplace safe."

"Me, too," said Elliott, obviously eager to put the incident behind them. "What do you say we all have another round of champagne?"

Half an hour later, Cole surreptitiously dropped a note in Josephine's lap as he excused himself from the table. Josephine headed to the ladies' room, where she unfurled the folded scrap of paper.

Must talk to you. Meet me in room 1009 ASAP.

Josephine's heart drummed wildly. Without giving herself time to think better of it, she hurried to the elevator and rode up to the tenth floor.

The door slid open on the lushly appointed concierge level. She followed the numbers to the end of the hall, to the large double door of what was obviously one of the hotel's finer suites.

Her mouth went dry as Cole answered her knock. "Come in."

She stepped into a luxurious living area dominated by an enormous marble fireplace with a heavy black clock on the mantel. Two gold damask sofas, a pair of floral wing chairs, an Oriental rug and an enormous mahogany and glass coffee table filled one end of the room. At the other end stood a long mahogany dining table surrounded by ten chairs upholstered in a rich silk stripe. She looked around. "I thought you'd already moved into your new home."

"I have. I only rented this suite for tonight."

Because of Alexa. He had prepared to seduce her tonight, if the situation warranted. Another piece of

Josephine's heart cracked and broke off.

Cole motioned to one of the sofas. Setting her purse on a side table, Josephine hesitantly lowered herself onto it. Cole sat beside her and stretched his arm along the back. "I owe you an apology."

"It's okay."

"No, it's not. You were trying to tell me what Robert had planned, and I wouldn't listen." His eyes fixed on hers. "In addition to an apology, I owe you a huge debt of gratitude. What happened?"

Josephine stared at the fireplace. "Robert asked me to put my bracelet in your pocket. I, um, decided to put it in *his* pocket instead."

Cole grinned, his white teeth flashing. "I never knew you were so devious."

She grinned back. "I didn't, either." Her smile faded as her heart filled with emotion. "I just knew I couldn't let him do that to you. Not again."

Cole's gaze locked on hers. For a long, silent moment, they simply looked at each other. The air between them seemed to heat and expand. Tension hummed back and forth, vibrating like the taut string of a violin.

"How can I thank you?" Cole asked at length.

The look in his eyes made Josephine's heart slam against her ribs, knocking her breath away. When she finally found her voice, it was only a throaty whisper. "You'll think of something."

And then she was in his arms and his mouth was on hers, and he was holding her as if there were no tomorrow. He kissed her greedily, like a man who'd been too long deprived of life-giving sustenance. She clung to him and kissed him back, giving as good as she got, kissing him as if she were reclaiming her soul.

"Josie," he murmured. His hands moved down her back, pulling her close against him. Hot chills raced through her as his lips slid to the side of her neck, to her ear, then across her cheek. She pressed herself against him, her fingers feathering through his dark hair as he pulled her down on the sofa.

A deep chiming sound thrust its way into her consciousness. Startled, Josephine turned toward the mantel.

"It's just the clock," Cole whispered. "It's midnight."

Midnight—the magic hour.

"Robert was right about one thing." She gently touched Cole's face, the face that filled her dreams. "You *do* make me feel like Cinderella."

"Just don't turn into a pumpkin," he murmured, lowering his head to kiss her again.

But the spell was broken. As the clock continued its deep, somber chiming, every gong reminded her of the relentless crusade of time, of the unstoppable march into the future.

A future where Cole would hold Alexa.

The clock pronounced its final bong. The note hung in the air, suspended like thick fog.

Tears welled in Josephine's eyes. She pulled away. "It . . . it's late. I have to be getting back."

She turned, grabbed her satin purse from the table and headed for the door.

"Josephine!" Cole called.

She forced herself to ignore his voice, forced herself to ignore her own heart's pleading, forced herself to walk through the door and close it behind her. She didn't dare stop, didn't dare look back. It was over.

Everything was over, except for the pain.

Chapter Nineteen

Josephine pulled a cream-colored satin suit off the rack at the House of Breaux Bridal Salon on St. Charles Avenue two weeks later and handed it to Fanny. "This one would be perfect for you."

Fanny held it up against her chest in the three-way mirror. "Oh, it's beautiful! I love the little pearls embroidered on the jacket." She paused and looked at Josephine uncertainly. "But it looks so bridelike!"

"That's the whole idea," Josephine said teasingly.

"Are you sure it's not too young-looking for me?" Fanny turned sideways and frowned at her reflection.

"I think it's perfect. And I'll bet Henry will, too."

Fanny grinned. "Henry doesn't care what I wear. He said he's only interested in getting me out of it after the wedding."

Josephine laughed. "You've got that man acting as young as Junior."

"He sure makes me feel that way," Fanny admitted.

"Well, being in love agrees with both of you. You look

wonderful. And I've never seen Henry look better than he did last night."

After the *Chienne* had docked in New Orleans yesterday, Fanny had called and invited Josephine to join her and Henry for dinner, saying she had exciting news. The news that the couple planned to marry had come as no surprise to Josephine. The transformation in Henry, however, did. Not only was he sporting a new haircut, new clothes and a clean-shaven face, but he'd traded in his chewing tobacco for Wrigley's Big Red chewing gum.

"I want to enjoy a long life with Fanny, so I figgered I best give up my unhealthy ways," Henry had explained.

"I've never been happier," Fanny confessed, running a finger over the glossy pearls on the front of the jacket. "I thought I was destined to be an old maid. I can hardly believe I'm about to be married!"

"I can hardly believe you're going to do it in just three days," Josephine said wryly. "Most people plan these things months in advance."

"Well, Henry wanted Cole to stand up for him, and I wanted you as my maid of honor, so that meant we had to wait till we got to New Orleans. And we both want to get married aboard the boat. Since it's chartered out for another run up the river, we have to hurry." Fanny's eyes grew warm and concerned. "I just hope it won't be too hard on you, seein' Cole again."

Last night at dinner, Josephine had told Fanny and Henry the whole story about Cole and his scheme to get even with McAuley. Not wanting to cast any clouds over the couple's joy, she'd downplayed the way it was affecting her, but she was afraid Fanny and Henry had seen through her act of indifference.

Josephine pasted on another brave smile now. "I'll be fine."

"Maybe you should bring that fellow you're dating. It might make things easier on you."

"Maybe I will." Although it was questionable whether

having Elliott along would make things easier or not. Elliott had become increasingly dissatisfied with the quick good-night pecks Josephine gave him before darting inside her apartment at the end of an evening. He'd invited her to go away with him for the weekend, and he was beginning to press the issue.

"I care about you, Josephine," he'd told her the other night. "I'm ready to take our relationship to the next level. If you need some sort of commitment from me before that happens, well, I'm ready to make one. We haven't dated all that long, but we've known each other a long time, and I think we're perfect together."

It was the right offer from the wrong man. If Elliott had shown this type of interest in Josephine a few months ago, she would have been elated. But that was B.C.— Before Cole—and Cole had changed her life.

It was a cruel irony, Josephine thought dejectedly. Because of Cole, she'd blossomed into the kind of woman who could attract one of the city's most eligible bachelors. Yet because of Cole, she could muster no interest in him.

She'd tried to care for Elliott. She'd told herself that she was being ridiculous, that it was time to move on with her life. She'd known from the beginning that her time with Cole was limited. It was ridiculous to pine for a man who had no interest in a long-term relationship—a man who was intent on seducing someone else, for heaven's sake! She'd told herself that Elliott was kind and attractive, and she'd be a fool not to encourage his attentions.

She'd told herself, but her heart hadn't listened.

She was seeing Elliott tonight. She'd been in the middle of a meeting when he'd called to ask her out, so she hadn't gotten all the details about where they were going. "Wear something special," Elliott had told her. "It should be a night to remember."

She had the awful feeling he was going to propose. She didn't want to tell him no, but she knew she couldn't tell him yes. The best she could hope for was to buy some

Elliott shook his head. "Thank you, but I'd better take her home. I've already called a taxi."

"Well, at least come in and greet our guest of honor."

Alexa ushered them into the living room. Josephine's heart lurched in her chest at the sight of Cole on the far side of the room. His back was to her, but it was almost as if he felt her presence. He turned toward her, and his gaze collided with hers.

Josephine felt as if all the air had been squeezed out of her lungs. Cole froze, a glass of champagne in his hand.

Alexa sidled up to him. "Cole, darling—I'm sure you remember Josephine and Elliott."

Cole gave a slight bow, his expression now carefully obscure. "Of course. It's nice to see you again."

"Elliott was just saying that they're not going to be able to stay. Josephine isn't feeling well."

"I'm sorry to hear that." He stiffly addressed Josephine. "Is there something I can do?"

Yes. You can tell me that you're calling off this ridiculous plot, that you can't live without me, that you love me and want to be with me always.

It was killing her, seeing him again. Josephine wrenched her eyes away from him and turned to Alexa. "If you don't mind, I think I'll take you up on that offer to rest in the library until the taxi gets here."

"Of course. It's this way." Alexa began to lead her away.

Elliott started to follow. Josephine placed a hand on his arm. "Have a drink and enjoy yourself. I'll be fine."

"Are you sure?"

"Yes."

Elliott watched Alexa lead her away. Cole's eyes followed, too. He cleared his throat. "Too bad she's not feeling well."

"No one's more disappointed than me," Elliott confided. "Can you keep a secret?"

The corner of Cole's lip lifted. "I've been known to keep one or two."

Elliott chuckled. "I'd planned to take Josephine out in Alexa's rose garden and propose tonight. All of our friends are here, and I thought it would be exciting to come back in and announce our engagement."

Cole felt as if he'd been poleaxed. He forced his lips into an upward curve. "I didn't realize things were so serious between you two."

Elliott grinned. "Josephine's an old-fashioned kind of girl. It's either serious or it's not at all, and I'm getting tired of not at all, if you get my meaning."

It was hard to form a smile when he was gritting his teeth so tightly, but Cole did his best. "Have you two been dating long?"

"No, but we've known each other for years. When Josephine came to see me about conducting executive etiquette classes for my staff, something just clicked. I hadn't seen her in quite a while, and well, she just blew me away." Elliott accepted a glass of champagne from a passing waiter. "She's everything I'd ever want in a wife."

Cole felt as if his face would break from the effort of continuing to smile. "Well, I wish you all the best," he ground out.

What he really wished was that Elliott would strangle on his own spit. The thought of Josephine in this man's arms, bearing this man's babies, was enough to make him want to castrate the SOB.

A portly, gray-headed man walked up and slapped the hotelier on the shoulder. "Elliott! How's the hotel business?"

Cole used the interruption as an opportunity to escape. Politely excusing himself, he headed off to find Josephine. He didn't know what he was going to say. He only knew he had to see her.

Unfortunately, he was intercepted by Alexa before he made it to the foyer. "Cole—there you are! Would you like

o see the rest of the house?" She took his arm, pressing
ier breast against it. "The upstairs is particularly interest-
ng."

There was no mistaking her meaning. It was the oppor-
unity he'd been waiting for. Yet all he could think about
vas Josephine. "I'm sure it is," he hedged. "But what
ibout Robert?"

Alexa gave a self-satisfied smile. "I sent him out for
nore liquor. He'll be gone for at least half an hour." She
ugged on Cole's arm. "Let's not waste a minute."

Cole reluctantly followed her down a hallway to the
)ack stairs. This was the culmination of his entire scheme.
Ie couldn't have planned it better. If he played his cards
ight, Robert might actually discover him with Alexa. But
nstead of thinking about how close he was to victory, all
ie could think about was Josephine.

He couldn't stand the thought of Elliott touching her. Of
ier touching Elliott. Of the two of them together.

It's not my concern, he silently argued with himself. *She
›lew me off to find someone suitable. She made it clear she
vanted nothing more to do with me.*

And yet, there had been something in her face tonight as
;he'd looked at him across the room—something that had
·eached out and squeezed his heart like cardiac massage.
³or a moment, he'd seen her as she'd been on the boat—
)pen, giving, accessible, loving.

Loving. That was the word for it. Josephine was loving.

Did she love him? The thought was startling. And yet it
it with what he'd seen in her eyes.

Trying to thrust the disturbing concept from his mind,
²ole resolutely followed Alexa up the stairs, down a long
iall, and into a lush room that looked like a bordello. A
arge canopied plantation bed draped in scarlet velvet
lominated the room. An enormous mahogany bureau, an
:laborately carved chest of drawers and an oversize mir-
·ored armoire flanked the walls. A scarlet chaise longue
ingled into the room from one corner, and a freestanding

cheval mirror stood at another. Knowing Alexa, she'd probably lined the underside of the antique canopy with a mirror.

It wouldn't even surprise him if she kept an assortment of chains and handcuffs in her bedside dresser. After all, she seemed to take such pleasure in knowing she was causing pain.

And he wasn't any better. The realization stung like the tail of a whip. The only reason he was here now was to hurt Robert.

Alexa closed the door. With a slow, seductive smile, she deliberately turned the lock, then moved toward him, fingering the deep décolletage of her dress. "Tell me what you'd like." Her voice was a deep purr. "I'll do anything you want."

"Anything?"

"Anything."

"All right. I want you to go downstairs and tell Robert you're breaking your engagement. I want you to tell him that you and I are lovers, and that you're going to be my wife."

Alexa's arm fell to her side. "You're joking."

"Not in the least."

"Are you—are you proposing to me?"

"I am."

She stared at him, her lips parted. "I knew you were attracted to me, but I didn't know . . . " She paused. Her eyes narrowed, then grew bright and glassy. Her lips tilted up. She stared at him as if he held the key to her heart's desire. "Would I be a princess?"

Just as he'd figured: she was enamored with the idea of being a real live princess. But he failed to feel the sense of triumph he'd anticipated at how easily she was falling into his trap. "You'd be as much a princess as I am a prince."

He could practically see the wheels spinning in her mind. She could marry him and acquire a title. If it didn' work out, she could always get a divorce, and for the rest of her life, the upper crust of New Orleans would still no doubt refer to her as the Princess.

She probably thought she had nothing to lose. She no doubt figured Robert would always be available. After all, he always had been. All she'd have to do was crook her little finger and he'd come running as he always had.

"So will you?" Cole pressed. Too late, he realized he wasn't proposing in a very princely manner.

But it didn't seem to matter. Alexa's eyes were raptly fixed on the crown she imagined herself wearing.

"Yes. Yes!" Alexa flew across the room as rapidly as her high heels would permit. Flinging herself at him, she kissed him deeply. He resisted the urge to wipe his lips with the back of his hand when she finally came up for air.

Her hands impatiently pushed off his jacket, then clutched at his back. Her nails softly raked his skin through the cotton of his shirt. Her long, red nails suddenly struck him as bearing an uncanny likeness to the blood-covered talons of a vulture. He'd thought he'd take satisfaction from having the woman who'd rejected him as a youth want him as a man, but instead he felt a cold wave of revulsion. He felt as though he were in the clutches of some flesh-eating predator.

He eased away from her. "Perhaps we should talk to Robert before we take things any further. The honorable thing to do would be to end your engagement to him first."

"As far as I'm concerned, it's already ended." She stepped closer and ran the pad of her finger lightly down the side of his cheek. Her lips drew into a wicked smile. "And I can't wait to take things further. I've wanted to get you in bed since the first moment I met you."

He wanted to hurt Robert. That was the whole idea. And Robert would be hurt the most by knowing Alexa had betrayed him. That had been the plan from the beginning, the whole reason he'd hired Josephine.

So why couldn't he stop thinking about her now that he

was about to accomplish the goal he'd hired her to prepare him for?

The thought made him angry. Damn it, he hadn't gone to all this trouble to stop now. By God, he'd see this thing through.

"All right, then," Cole said gruffly. "Take off you clothes."

Alexa reached behind her neck. The zipper hissed open and Alexa stepped out of her dress. She thrust out a hip and stood before him, wearing a black satin thong, a black garter belt, sheer black stockings and a black underwire bra. Her large brown nipples shone through the sheer shiny fabric like headlights through a fog.

She cocked her head and gave the slow, provocative smile of a woman sure of her own beauty. "What do you think?"

"You're beautiful." And she was. Her breasts were lush and high, her waist narrow, her hips and thighs exquisitely shaped. Her skin was smooth and lightly tanned. She was as lovely as any of the airbrushed beauties in Hambone's or Junior's magazines.

But Cole didn't feel the slightest twinge of desire. "Keep going," he ordered.

Alexa cocked her head saucily. "Aren't you going to undress, too?"

"Not yet."

She looked as if she were about to protest.

"You said you'd do anything I want," he chided. "And what I want is for you to take off your clothes. Now."

"All of them?"

"Every last stitch."

She smiled that smile again. "As you wish." Moving with deliberate, seductive slowness, she unfastened her bra. Her large breasts bounced free of their satin slings.

They were large. They were lush. They were perfectly shaped. But they weren't Josephine's, and they left him completely cold.

He watched as she unfastened the garters from her right

ocking, then sat on the edge of the bed and provocatively
olled it down. She stood and unfastened the garters on her
eft leg, this time turning around to give him a clear view
f her thong-exposed backside. Slowly, slowly, she unfas-
ened the hook and eye at the back of the lace garter belt
nd let it drop to the floor. Her bare buttocks glimmered in
he lamplight. She turned around, taking her time. Then,
ooking him dead in the eyes, she peeled off her scant
anties.

She was completely naked. She made a slow pirouette,
aking sure Cole could see her from all angles. It was an
xpertly executed maneuver, one she'd evidently practiced
a front of a mirror—and in front of God only knew how
any men. She was gorgeous, and she knew it.

He didn't feel the least stirring of desire.

She's not Josephine.

Alexa slunk across the room, seductively swaying her
ips. As she drew closer to Cole, the walls seemed to close
a, squeezing tighter and tighter until it felt as if the very
ir had been pressed into a substance too thick and heavy
o breathe.

All of these years, he'd thought he wanted revenge.
le'd thought he wanted to make the woman who'd
ejected him want him, he'd thought he wanted to get back
t the man who'd hurt him, he'd thought he wanted to
venge Mom Sawyer's death. But he'd been wrong.

All of these years, he'd really wanted something far dif-
erent. He could suddenly see it. It was suddenly right in
ront of him, like a long-buried treasure that had just
vashed ashore.

All of these years, what he'd really wanted was to get
ack what he'd lost when Mom had died—someone who
new him and accepted him as he was. Someone who
elieved in him. Someone who loved him. Someone whom
e loved in return.

Josephine. He closed his eyes, and he saw her face as it
ad looked when their gaze collided across the living room

earlier that evening.

He wanted what he'd seen in her eyes. He wanted more than revenge, more than money, more than any damn person or any damn thing in the world. He wanted *her*.

He loved her.

She'd said she wanted someone suitable. Well, b damn, *he* was suitable—a lot more suitable than that stiff necked jerk who wanted to marry her. And when he g out of here, he'd find a way to convince her of that fact.

But first he had to get out of here. Alexa's hands sli down his chest until her fingers reached the cummerbun of his tuxedo. Cole's hands clamped on top of hers, stop ping her.

"Before you do that, maybe you'd better learn a littl more about who you're undressing."

"I know all I need to know," she murmured, rubbing he naked breasts against the studs of his shirt.

"I don't think you do." He held her hands by the wrist "I don't think you're aware we knew each other year ago."

Her eyes flew wide. "We did?"

Cole nodded. "Fourteen years ago, to be exact. Bac then I was known as Collin Sawyer." His mouth twisted "You used to call me Trash Boy."

Alexa's lips parted. Her eyebrows pulled together, the rose in shock. She stared at him, wild-eyed. "But . . . bu you can't be. You're a prince!"

Cole gave a mirthless grin. "I never claimed to be prince."

Her mouth fell open. Her eyes registered disbelief. "Bu it was in the paper! And so many people know you name!"

Cole released her hands and stepped back. "Interestin phenomenon, isn't it? They're no doubt remembering m father. He killed four people and shot a cop twenty year ago, so he was pretty notorious." He grinned, enjoying he horror-stricken expression. "I seem to recall you were fa

368

cinated by it. For some strange reason, it used to turn you on."

Alexa backed away, attempting to cover herself with her arms. "Wh-what are you doing here?"

"I came to get even."

The color drained from Alexa's face. She grabbed a pillow and held it in front her, covering her nakedness. "It—it was all Robert's doing," she rapidly explained. "It was his idea, planting those things in your room. I didn't want to do it, but he told me if I didn't, you'd ruin me."

Cole's heart stood still. *Alexa* had planted the things in his room? He carefully disguised his surprise. "I've always wondered how you got in and did that without awakening me."

"You weren't home. You were waiting for me in the park."

A cold wave of comprehension washed over him. That evening fourteen years ago had been a setup from the very beginning. All this time, he'd thought McAuley had somehow sneaked into his room and planted those objects after their fight. He'd always wondered how McAuley had managed to place those things under his mattress while he slept on top of it. He'd marveled at what he'd thought was McAuley's incredible nerve.

But McAuley had never even been in his room until he showed up with the cops. The person with the nerves of steel was Alexa.

"You'd become so persistent. I was afraid you'd spoil everything." She gnawed her bottom lip, raking her lipstick off with her teeth.

Spoil. What an inadequate word to describe what she'd done to his life. "I went to jail because of your little stunt," Cole said coldly. "And as a result, my foster mother died of a heart attack three days later. She *died,* Alexa. All because you didn't want anyone to find out you'd been hanging around with the likes of me."

Alexa's knuckles turned white against the burgundy pillow she clutched in front of her. "If you try to make trouble, I'll tell everyone you're an impostor."

"Go right ahead. You're the one who threw this enormous party and insisted on introducing me to all your friends. You're the one who'll end up looking like a fool."

He saw her throat convulse as she swallowed. "I-I'll tell Robert," she warned.

Cole folded his arms over his chest, his lips curling into a smirk. "I'd love to know what you plan to tell him. That you were going to jilt him for me? That we used to be lovers?"

"He'd never believe you."

"He might if I give him a few personal details—like describing that little mole on your backside. Or mentioning a few of the more colorful words you use during sex."

Alexa's eyes narrowed like a cornered cat's. "Wha-what are you going to do?"

"Well, now, that's a good question. I'd planned to get you to publicly break your engagement to Robert and announce your engagement to me, but once you agreed to it so easily, it lost all its appeal." His gaze raked over her still-naked body. "Just as you have."

He moved toward the door. She ran after him. "Wait! You can't go without telling me. What are you going to do?"

Cole hesitated. *What, indeed?*

The answer was suddenly as clear as lightning in a night sky. *Nothing.* He'd do nothing at all. He'd let her squirm and worry. Let her spend her entire life waiting for the other shoe to drop. Let her go ahead and marry Robert.

Which would be the best revenge of all. Because Alexa and Robert would no doubt end up inflicting more pain on each other over the course of a marriage than he could ever inflict on either one.

He opened the bedroom door. "You'll just have to wait and see, won't you?"

He strode out of the room, down the hall, down the stairs

and out the front door. The humid night air was heavy with the scent of night jasmine, sweet olive and honeysuckle. He inhaled deeply and firmly closed the door behind him.

It was a door he should have closed long ago. He drew another breath, this one the breath of a free man.

Chapter Twenty

Soft afternoon light filtered through the porthole in the cook's cabin as Josephine fastened the strand of pearls around Fanny's neck the next day. She stepped back, her hands clasped at her chest, and gazed at the older woman. "Oh, Fanny," she exclaimed. "You're beautiful!"

She watched her friend smile at her reflection in the dresser mirror. The deep cream wedding suit was bridelike and feminine, its tailored lines flattering to Fanny's figure. Her face was softly made up, her hair swept into loose, casual curls. But the expression in her eyes was what transformed her from attractive to radiant. She looked as if she were all lit up from the inside out.

"I've never seen anyone look so happy," Josephine said.

"I've never felt so happy," the older woman admitted. "This is the best day of my life." She reached out and patted Josephine's hand, her brown eyes warm and wistful. "I just wish you were happy, too."

Josephine smiled, not wanting to put a damper on her friend's wedding day. "Everything's looking up. My business is going well and my money troubles have all but disappeared."

The look Fanny shot her clearly said she wasn't a bit fooled. "Are you still seeing that hotel owner?"

Josephine picked up the bridal bouquet from the dresser. "I broke up with him last night," she said, keeping her tone light.

"Oh?"

"Yes." She fussed with the long silk ribbon that trailed from the arrangement of gardenias, white roses and baby's breath. "He was getting way too serious, and I'm not ready to make a commitment."

"To him, you mean."

There was no use trying to put up a pretense with Fanny. One of the things Josephine loved about the woman was her blunt way of cutting right to the heart of a matter. Josephine sighed and put down the bouquet. "Oh, Fanny— it's bad enough that I have to see Cole and Alexa everywhere I go and pretend that everything's all right. But it's too much, trying to pretend I care for Elliott, too. I tried to care for him, I really did, but I just don't feel anything. It wasn't fair to him to let him think I did. So I told him I thought it was best if we didn't see each other anymore." Josephine stared down at the flowers and sighed. "This whole business of Cole and Alexa is killing me. I wish I could just go away for a few weeks until it's all over."

"Do you mean that?" Something in Fanny's voice made Josephine look up. " 'Cause if you do, I've got the perfect solution."

"You do?"

Fanny nodded. "The man who chartered this boat, Captain Paul, is still looking for a cook to replace me while I'm on my honeymoon. Evidently towboat cooks are harder to find than crawfish feathers." Fanny regarded her warmly. "It would do you good to get away. Besides, there's something therapeutic about cookin'. Whenever I've been at my lowest, I've always found cookin' for a big bunch of folks somehow nourishes my soul. I know I taught you enough to handle it."

Josephine fingered her mother's bracelet on her arm. It was certainly tempting. She was sick of networking, sick of seeing the same faces everywhere she went, sick of having to smile when her heart was breaking.

She sighed. "I'd love to, Fanny, but I can't. I've got several corporate etiquette seminars scheduled."

"So? Reschedule them."

"Just like that?"

"Why not? The big companies who've hired your services have gotten along all this time without any etiquette courses. Surely they can wait a few more weeks."

Josephine opened her mouth to protest, then abruptly clamped it shut. *Why not, indeed?* None of her clients had seemed in a hurry for the seminars; she was the one who'd insisted on conducting them as soon as possible. Postponing them a few weeks shouldn't pose a problem.

It was high time she started taking care of her own needs as well as she'd always taken care of everyone else's. Pressing her lips into a decisive line, she nodded. "All right. If you think Captain Paul will hire me, I'll do it."

Fanny gave her a hearty pat on the back. "That's the spirit! And don't you worry. He'll jump at the chance to sign you on. I'll introduce you to him at the reception and tell him I trained you myself."

Josephine glanced at her watch, then looked up and smiled. "Before you do that, there's a little matter you need to attend to first. There's a man upstairs chomping at the bit to make you his wife."

Fanny grinned. "Well, then, I'd better not keep him waiting."

Two hours later, Fanny gazed up at Henry as they two-stepped around the sawdust covered floor of the old wharf-side bar they'd rented for their wedding reception. The view out the window looked like a photo on a tourist post-card, but Fanny had eyes only for her new husband.

Henry smiled down at her. "You look too nice for words, Mrs. O'Shea."

"Mrs. O'Shea," Fanny repeated softly. "I can't tell you how much I like the sound of that."

"Well, that's a good thing, 'cause you'll be hearin' it the rest of your days."

Fanny snuggled happily in his arms.

"I don' mind tellin' ya, Fanny, I dang near dropped my teeth when you walked out on that deck lookin' like that. You're purtier than a dressed catfish with a side o' hush puppies."

Fanny laughed. "Knowing how you like catfish, that's mighty high praise."

"It was meant to be."

Fanny grinned. "You look mighty handsome yourself. Where'd you get that suit?"

"Cole dragged me to one of them fancy stores and helped me pick it out."

The mention of Cole's name made Fanny frown. "Where is that man, anyway? He disappeared after the ceremony. I need to have a word with him about Josephine."

Henry's brows pulled together. "Now, Fanny—we aren't supposed to know anything about what he's up to. We promised Josephine, remember?"

"I'm not gonna mention that. I'm just gonna tell him he's a darned fool, lettin' Josephine get away."

Henry shook his head. "Ya shouldn't go meddlin' in other folks' affairs. Remember what happened last time you stuck your nose into their business, thinkin' Josephine had STVD or whatever it's called?"

"You're the one who started that whole story."

"That don' make no never mind. What I'm sayin' is it's not your place to go interferin'."

"I'm not gonna interfere. I just intend to pass along a little information." Fanny looked up to see Cole working his way toward them. "And here he comes now."

"Hey there, Henry." Cole tapped his first mate's shoulder. "Sorry to cut in, but it's time to let the best man have a dance with the bride."

Henry scowled. "What am I supposed to do in the meantime?"

"Go dance with the maid of honor," Cole suggested.

"Ya mean Josephine? Seems to me you're the one who should be dancin' with her."

Cole smiled, but it didn't reach his eyes. "I tried, but she won't even talk to me."

Fanny dropped her new husband's hand. "Go on, Henry. Cole and I have a few things to discuss."

Henry cast her a worried look, then walked away, wagging his head.

"What's with him?" Cole asked, taking Fanny's hand.

"He thinks I'm gonna meddle. He knows I want to talk to you about Josephine."

"Well, it just so happens I want to talk to you about the same thing." Cole placed his hand lightly on her waist and began guiding her around the floor to the beat of "Boot Scootin' Boogie."

"Really?" Fanny cocked her head to the side. "Go right ahead."

"No. Ladies first."

"All right." Fanny drew a deep breath and said a silent prayer that she wouldn't step on Cole's toes too badly. At least, not any that weren't in her path on the dance floor. "I know you're the captain and Henry's and my boss an' all, and in most things I think you're real smart—but you're missing the boat when it comes to Josephine."

"I know."

Fanny's brows rose in surprise. "You do?"

Cole nodded grimly. "What's the story with her and that hotel guy?"

"She broke up with him last night."

Something deep in Cole's chest unwound and relaxed. His face pulled into the first honest grin he'd given since Josephine left the boat. "Is that a fact?"

Fanny nodded. "She never gave a seagull's squawk about that man." She looked Cole straight in the eye, her expression stern. "In case you've overlooked the obvious, I'm going to tell you an important fact about that gal. She's so head over heels in love with you she can't see straight."

Cole's heart pounded hard. "She seemed to think she could do better than me when she left the boat," he said cautiously.

Fanny snorted. "That was all hogwash, and if you had a lick of sense, you'd know it. She only told you that 'cause she didn't want you feelin' bad about dumpin' her when you set out on this cockamamie plan of yours."

"She told you about that?"

Fanny looked sheepish enough to grow wool. "Ah, Captain, don't be mad at her. I dragged it out of her. She didn't mean to tell me."

Cole waved his hand impatiently. "I don't care about that. I just need to know. What exactly did she say?"

"She didn't want you to feel bad. She said she figured you could handle bein' mad better than you could handle feelin' like you'd hurt her. She loves you."

"She told you that?"

Fanny shot him a reproving look. "She didn't have to say it for me to know it. Any fool could see it. But yes, she told me." The directness of Fanny's gaze added to the impact of her words. A jolt of joy shot through Cole as if it had been injected directly into his veins. "This get-even scheme of yours damn near broke her heart. But that's not the only way you've hurt her."

He'd hurt her. Oh, damn, he hadn't meant to. Guilt twisted Cole's gut, adding to the maelstrom of emotions pitching around inside him. "What do you mean?"

"I mean if you'd been able to see her, really see her, without lettin' your prejudice against uptown folks cloud up your view, you'd have known she wasn't the kind of woman who'd judge you by anything but your heart."

Damn. Fanny was right. A sense of shame socked him right in the gullet. He'd let pride and anger distort his vision. He'd been so obsessed with the prejudice he'd endured that he hadn't realized how prejudiced he'd become himself. He'd been so focused on old hurts and past resentments that he hadn't been able to see that the thing he wanted most was being offered right before his eyes.

He glanced around, looking for Josephine. He finally spotted her through the rusty screen door that led to the pier, sitting at a cheap green plastic table with Gaston, Hambone, Junior and Henry. His gaze flew to her like a homing pigeon. Dressed in a blush-colored bridesmaid's gown with her hair swept up in a tousle of curls and her mother's diamonds sparkling at her wrist, she looked like she belonged in a fairy tale.

Yet she seemed perfectly at ease right here—on an old run-down pier at an old run-down bar, in the company of rowdies, her feet propped on a chair, a beer bottle in her hand and her head thrown back in laughter.

Cole's heart swelled with an odd mix of love and pride. Josephine might have molded him into the likeness of a prince, but by golly, he'd had just as profound an influence on her.

Who would have guessed that the prissy woman who'd hit his truck in March—the woman with the prim lips, the uptight attitude and the tightly bunned hair—would be sitting here in May, looking like an angel and acting like a deckhand?

For that matter, who would have thought that Henry—his hard-nosed first mate, who was never without his chewing tobacco and hadn't even looked at a woman in twenty-some-odd years—would have traded in his Red Man for Big Red and would be getting hitched?

This love business was amazing, all-powerful, transforming stuff, Cole reflected. It didn't confine itself to people who wanted it or even knew they needed it. Like an oil spill, it started with a drop and sprawled out, coating everything in sight, spreading in a never-ending, ever-widening circle.

Hell. Who was he to fight it?

"We're supposed to be dancing," Fanny prompted gently.

Cole realized he'd stopped in his tracks, right in the middle of the dance floor. He gave a wry grin and resumed moving his feet to the music. "So tell me, Fanny—what can I do to win her back?"

Fanny eyed him warily, like a mother bear defending her cub. "Depends on what you want her back for."

"For forever." The moment he said it, he knew it was true. "I want her back for forever."

"You're finished with all that nonsense with that other woman?"

"There's no woman in my life but Josephine."

Fanny face melted into a grin. "Well, then, that's more like it."

"So what do you suggest?" Cole prodded.

"It's simple. Just tell her how you feel."

"I'm afraid that's not so simple. She won't talk to me." Cole's gaze again drifted to Josephine. He wasn't sure, but it looked for all the world as if she and his deckhands were having a spitting contest off the pier. He grinned proudly, his heart expanding until it felt like it might burst in his chest.

He looked down at Fanny. "She said we have nothing to talk about. She told me in no uncertain terms to leave her alone. She said she didn't want to cause a scene at your wedding, but if I approached her again, she would."

Fanny chortled. "She's a spunky little gal, that's for sure."

"Among other things." Cole's wry smile darkened into a troubled frown. "Honestly, Fanny—I don't know what I can do, short of tying her up and forcing her to listen to me."

Fanny's eyes glimmered mischievously. "Maybe that's just what you need to do."

"What?"

"You need to get her in a situation where she has no choice but to hear you out." Fanny's lips pulled into a sly smile. "And I've got the perfect idea."

It was still dark when Josephine flipped on the light in the cook's cabin aboard the *Chienne* the next morning.

Captain Paul, a garrulous, gray-haired man who loved to talk about his Mardi Gras Krewe nearly as much as he loved to talk about his six grandchildren, set her heavy suitcase just inside door. "Make yourself at home, Josephine. We're awfully glad to have you aboard."

Josephine smiled. "Thank you."

Captain Paul rubbed his potbelly, rumpling the fabric of his purple-green-and-gold-striped Mardi Gras shirt. According to Fanny, the captain wore Mardi Gras colors all year long. "We'll cast off in a few minutes. The deckhands have finished lashing the tow and are checking it over now. You get settled in and let me know if you need anything. We've all had breakfast, so you don't have to worry about that."

"Okay. Thank you."

The captain pulled the door closed, and Josephine looked around. She'd been in Fanny and Henry's cabin when she'd helped Fanny get dressed for her wedding, but the changes in the decor stood out more prominently now that she was alone. The cabin was a far cry from the gray, dingy quarters she'd occupied when she'd first come aboard the boat in March. Henry had painted the room a sunny yellow, and a built-in double bed now occupied the end of the room under the porthole. The bed was covered with colorful quilts and pillows. A piece of Fanny's needlework hung on the wall, proclaiming *Home is where the heart is.*

Josephine stared at the framed handiwork as she sank to the bed. If home was where the heart was, she thought despondently, then she was destined to be homeless. She'd given her heart to a man who had no use for it.

She turned and gazed out the porthole, studying the lights across the river and their reflection on the murky water. A sense of despair as vast and endless as the waters of the Mississippi swirled over her, threatening to pull her under.

Maybe this hadn't been a good idea after all. She'd thought that getting away from New Orleans would help her get over Cole, but being here on his boat only made her miss him all the more.

She sighed and rose to her feet, unzipping the suitcase she'd placed on the bed. Seeing him at Fanny and Henry's wedding yesterday had been harder than she'd ever imagined. Maybe it was because he'd been in the setting and among the people where she'd grown to love him. She hadn't dared to talk to him; she'd been afraid she would break down and cry, and she was determined not to do that in front of him.

She wondered how his plan to win Alexa was progressing. From what she'd seen the other night at the party, it was going very well indeed. The woman had been eyeing him like Junior eyed Fanny's chocolate cream pies.

She wondered if Cole was happy. She wondered if bringing closure to his past would bring him peace.

She wondered if she would ever have any closure or peace herself.

"Remember the good parts," she reminded herself. She'd known when she'd entered into the affair with Cole that it couldn't last, but she'd made the decision to do it anyway. And no matter how it hurt now, the good still outweighed the bad. He'd freed her from the tight, overly

structured, self-imposed prison that had held her captive
for so many years. He'd taught her how to laugh and love
and live. And if the price for that was to long for him for
the rest of her life, well, she'd just have to pay it. It was
better to have loved and lost than to have never loved at
all.

The room suddenly seemed too confining. She'd unpack
later, she decided. Fanny had said that cooking nourished
the soul, and by golly, her soul could do with some nour-
ishment. She wasn't officially in charge of a meal until
lunch, but the crew would probably want a fresh pot of
coffee when the boat finally got under way.

She made her way down the stairs to the galley, then
stopped short just inside the door. *Good heavens*—the
room had been completely redecorated! Everything about
it seemed new and fresh. The dark paneling had been
painted a crisp white, the dining table sported a new tablecloth, pictures decked the walls, and Fanny's pots and
pans—the ones she'd brought with her when she'd
boarded the boat—now hung from a metal rack above the
stove. The galley even had a fresh, new lemony scent. It
was entirely different from the kitchen and dining room
Josephine had walked into two months ago.

But then, she was different now, too, Josephine realized.
She was no longer a straitlaced, repressed, younger version
of Aunt Prudie. She was her own woman. A woman who
knew that no matter what life threw her way, she could
deal with it. A woman who could look the world in the eye
and not back down.

A woman who even knew her way around a kitchen.
Smiling at the thought, Josephine pulled a coffee filter
from the cabinet and retrieved the bag of chicory-laced
coffee from the refrigerator.

She'd just finished measuring out the grounds when the
floor shuddered and thundered beneath her. Despite her
misgivings about being here, the same feeling of excite-

ment that had overtaken her that first day raced through her again. There was something thrilling about new beginnings, about setting out on a new adventure.

A loud crackling boomed over the intercom. "Cast off the forward line," a deep voice intoned.

A shiver chased up her spine. The voice certainly sounded familiar. But then, she reasoned, all voices probably sounded alike over the rusty intercom.

"Cast off the aft."

It sure sounded like Cole. Nostalgia, aching and intense, washed over her. Determined not to let her feelings overwhelm her, Josephine finished pouring the water in the coffeemaker, placed the pot on the burner and flipped on the machine.

"All gone!" the voice announced.

The engines rumbled even louder, and the view out the porthole shifted. They were pulling away from the dock. Josephine hurried to the window and peered out, then blinked in shock.

A gray-haired man in a purple-green-and-gold-striped Mardi Gras shirt was striding down the wharf, away from the boat. It looked for all the world like Captain Paul.

But it couldn't be. He was up in the pilothouse.

Wasn't he?

Josephine hurried out the galley door to the hallway, then tugged free the hatch to the deck. She stepped outside just as the man turned and waved.

"Captain Paul!" she yelled.

What was he doing on the dock? How could the boat cast off without its captain?

She stared at the gray-haired man as the boat pulled into the middle of the river, her heart pounding furiously. Perhaps she'd misunderstood. Perhaps Captain Paul was merely chartering the boat and he'd hired someone else to captain it. Perhaps.

But she knew in her bones that wasn't the case. Something was wrong—terribly wrong. Who was in charge of the boat? Whose voice had called those orders over the loudspeaker?

Slamming the hatch closed, Josephine bounded up two flights of stairs, taking them two at a time. She strode to the door of the pilothouse and yanked it open. It was a good thing she was gripping the doorknob with her hand, for her knees suddenly went weak beneath her. Seated in the leather captain's chair, his hands on the steering sticks, was an all-too-familiar, all-too-handsome man.

"Cole!" she gasped.

He turned and flashed her a blinding grin. "Come right on in, Josephine. Pardon me if I don't stand up to greet you, but I'm a little busy at the moment."

Josephine's blood roared in her ears so loudly that she couldn't hear herself think. Her fingers clenched the door-jamb so tightly her knuckles ached. "What are you doing?"

"What does it look like I'm doing? I'm piloting the boat."

"I see that. I want to know why."

"Well, sugar, if I don't, the boat is likely to hit some-thing, and the Coast Guard tends to frown on that."

A vein throbbed in Josephine's temple. "That's not what I mean, and you know it." She stepped into the pilothouse, letting the door close behind her. "Where's Captain Paul? This boat is supposed to be chartered to him."

"It is. And don't you worry about him. He's going to make the profit off this little run."

She jabbed her fists onto her hips. "So what are *you* doing here?"

"Well, I couldn't get you to listen to me on land. So when Fanny told me you'd signed up as cook, why, I thought I'd come along, too. I figured it would give us a chance to have a little talk."

Josephine's head swam. "We have nothing to say to each other."

"Oh, we most certainly do."

A feeling of panic, of being cornered, rushed through her. "I want off this boat."

"Sorry, sweetheart. I'm afraid you're stuck."

He couldn't do this to her. She wouldn't stand for it. "I demand that you pull ashore and let me get off this boat," she said through gritted teeth.

"Sorry, darlin'. No can do."

Anger, hot and fierce, boiled in her blood. It was bad enough that the man had broken her heart. She wasn't going to sit by and let him stomp on it, too. "So help me, if you don't let me off this boat, you're going to regret it."

"What are you going to do? Call the cops?"

"Good idea." Lurching forward, she grabbed the intercom mike from its cradle above his head.

"Hey!" Cole grabbed at it, but Josephine jumped back, stretching the long, coiled cord out of his reach. She pressed the button on the mouthpiece. "Help! Help!" she yelled. The sound bleated through the loudspeakers outside the boat like a surreal echo.

"Are you crazy?" Cole demanded. He looked like he wanted to strangle her, but the traffic on the river constrained him to his seat. Another towboat was approaching, a tanker was behind him and a Coast Guard cutter was pulling away from a dock just ahead.

He held out his palm. "Give me that thing."

Holding the microphone with both hands, Josephine stepped farther away. "Not until you stop this boat and let me off."

"I can't do that."

"All right, then. You asked for it." Glaring at him, she pushed the button and shrieked into the mike. "Mayhem! Mayhem!"

Cole scowled like a pit bull about to pounce. "*Mayhem? What the hell kinda call is that?*"

"Mayhem! Mayhem!" she yelled again.

His eyes blazed with annoyance. "I think you mean Mayday."

"Oh. Thanks." Josephine pressed the button and called again. "Mayday! Mayday!"

"Are you out of your friggin' *mind?*" Cole said in a hiss. "The Coast Guard's up ahead and they don't take kindly to false alarms. You're gonna get me arrested."

"Good!" Spotting the Coast Guard boat, she waved her arm and shouted into the microphone, "Mayday! Kidnapping! Help!"

Cole slapped his forehead with the flat of his hand.

Josephine was pleased to see an officer on the deck of the cutter train a pair of binoculars in her direction. She waved again. The boat turned toward them.

"Are you in trouble?" bellowed the loudspeaker on the Coast Guard boat as it pulled alongside.

"Stop foolin' around, Josephine," Cole ordered. "Give me that thing!"

Josephine shot him her most belligerent look. "Mayday! Mayday!" she yelled into the mike.

The Coast Guard vessel drew abreast of the towboat. "Stop your craft, Captain," the Coast Guard loudspeaker ordered. "We're coming aboard."

"Damn it, Josephine, you've done it now!" Cole pulled back the throttle, forcing his boat to tread water against the current.

A tall, uniformed Coast Guard officer leaped from the deck of the cutter to the deck of the *Chienne*, a rope in tow. A moment later, the two boats were lashed together, and two other officers had scrambled aboard. In less than a minute, they all burst into the pilothouse. Pete, Cole's relief pilot, was right behind them.

"What's going on here?" a balding officer in a crisp white uniform demanded.

"This pirate is holding me captive." Josephine pointed at Cole.

"I am not!" Cole protested. "She signed on as the cook."

Josephine glared at Cole. "He's not even supposed to be on this boat. He threw the regular captain off it and just took over."

"He hijacked this vessel?" the tall officer inquired incredulously.

Cole's mouth twisted in a scowl. "How the hell can I hijack my own damn boat?"

The officer looked at him sternly. "Hold your tongue, there, son. We're trying to get to the bottom of this."

Cole let out a low, muttered oath. Josephine pulled herself to her tallest posture and summoned her most commanding tone. "The thing that's important here, officers, is that he's holding me against my will."

"Who's in charge of this vessel?" the tall officer asked.

"I am," Cole said.

"But he's not supposed to be," Josephine stated hotly.

Cole muttered another oath. He motioned to Pete. "This is the relief pilot. Why don't you take over, Pete, while I straighten this out."

Pete slipped into the captain's seat as Cole eased out.

The tallest Coast Guard officer looked from Cole to Josephine. "Just what the heck is going on here?"

"It's like I said," Josephine said. "I'm being held against my will."

Cole glowered at her. "You are not!"

The balding officer glanced at the tall one. "I don't know what this is all about, but I don't like it."

The tall one nodded. "I think we'd better take them both off the boat until we get this settled."

"Yeah," chimed in the shorter, stockier officer. "And give 'em Breathalyzer tests."

"Good idea," the first officer said.

"Why?" Cole demanded. "We haven't done anything wrong!"

"A Mayday call was sent out. We're required to investigate all calls for help," the tall officer replied.

387

Robin Wells

Cole waved his hand. "It wasn't a serious call. It was just an accident."

"It wasn't an accident!" Josephine exclaimed.

Cole shot her a look that would have silenced most sane people. "I apologize for the unruly behavior of my cook. I accept full responsibility. If there's a fine, I'll gladly pay it."

"Wait a minute!" Josephine interjected. "*You* can't accept responsibility. *I'm* the one who sounded the alarm!"

The look Cole shot her was sharp enough to draw blood. "Will you just be quiet, Josephine, and let me handle this?"

"I most certainly will not." She tilted up her chin and glared at him defiantly. "I happen to be quite proud of my actions. I finally broke some rules—broke them big-time. I even broke the law!" It was a personal victory, a rite of passage, and she wasn't going to let him take it away from her. "I insist on taking all the responsibility."

The tall officer glanced at the balding one. He pointed to his head and drew a tiny circle in the air with his finger. They both looked at Cole and Josephine, then exchanged a meaningful glance.

"All right, you two," the taller one ordered. "We don't know what you've been drinking or smoking, but a blood test should sort it all out. Come on."

"Where are we going?" Cole asked.

"You're going to take a little ride back to headquarters with us. Your pilot here can take the boat back to the wharf until we get to the bottom of this."

The next thing Josephine knew, she was being escorted off the *Chienne* and onto the Coast Guard vessel as a Coast Guard helicopter buzzed overhead. The officers led Cole and Josephine down a set of steep gray steps to a narrow room. It was vacant except for a long, built-in bench that lined the wall. The single window at the end was covered in thin bars.

The tall officer handcuffed Josephine's hands behind her back, while the balding one did the same with Cole.

388

The short one waved his hand at the bench. "You two cool your heels in here. We're going to collect the records off your boat; then we'll take you ashore and get this thing settled."

The officers left the room, closing the door behind them. Cole heard the lock click into place, then footsteps receding in the distance.

Josephine turned and glared at him. "Well, I hope you're satisfied."

Oddly enough, *satisfied* was just the right word to describe how he felt. "As a matter of fact, this is just about perfect." Cole grinned at her, which seemed to infuriate her all the more. "I've finally got you in a spot where you have no choice but to sit still and listen to me."

Josephine sniffed haughtily. "If this makes the newspaper, it's going to be rather hard for you to explain it all to Alexa."

"Alexa's opinion doesn't matter in the least."

Josephine looked at him. For a moment her haughty air slipped away, and he saw beyond the facade to the woman he loved. Just as rapidly, it reappeared. She tipped up her chin. "Well, an arrest certainly won't reflect well on Prince Dumanski."

"The prince is no more."

Josephine froze. "What do you mean?"

"I realized that the worst revenge I could ever wreak on Alexa or Robert would be to let them marry each other. Those two will inflict more pain on each other than I ever could."

Josephine stared at him, her eyes huge. A myriad of emotions played over her face, though he could tell she was struggling to contain them. "What happened?" she finally asked. "Did your plan fall through?"

Cole shook his head. "Actually, everything went better than expected. Alexa was ready to publicly cancel her engagement to Robert and announce she was going to marry me."

389

Josephine's neck moved as she swallowed. She looked away. "Congratulations."

"I said she was ready to. I didn't say she did." Cole shifted on the bench, turning toward her. "Here's the interesting part. When it came right down to it, I couldn't bring myself to touch her."

Josephine hesitantly glanced over. He caught her eye and held her gaze. "You see, I realized I'd fallen for another woman. A woman who'd taught me all about love and forgiveness, a woman I just couldn't get out of my mind. In fact, this woman seems to have spoiled me for every other woman out there."

Josephine stared at him, her eyes large blue pools. In their depths, he saw all of the hurt he'd caused her, all of her fear that he was about to cause her more. He saw wariness and caution.

And hope.

A lump formed in his throat. He cleared it and forced a casual tone to his voice. "What about you? Where's your hotel tycoon?"

Josephine's heart pounded like the piston in a boat engine. "I broke up with him."

Cole cocked an eyebrow. "Oh? I thought he was just what you wanted in a man."

It was time to drop the pretense. Time to bare her heart, to strip to her soul, to stand completely naked before him. "I want someone who sets his own rules instead of just following everyone else's." Her voice was barely above a whisper. "Someone who knows that the best things in life don't come on a silver spoon, who knows that love and trust are the most valuable commodities of all." She drew a shaky breath. "I want someone who's not afraid to risk his heart, even though he knows it's the biggest risk of all."

Cole looked at her for a long, emotion-charged moment, a moment in which she swore she heard his heart beating in time with her own.

"I'm game," he murmured, his voice deep and low.

She was afraid to believe what she thought her heart had heard. She forced the question from the depths of her soul, knowing that her future, her very life hung on his answer. "Game for what?"

"For forever." His gaze poured over her, as warm and sweet as hot chocolate. He lowered himself from the bench and knelt on one knee before her, hands awkwardly locked behind his back. "Josie, I want you forever. I want you in my bed each night, and I want to wake up holding you each morning. I want you to share my name and my life. I want you to have my babies. And when I'm old and gray, I want to sit beside you in a rocking chair and swap memories of our life together. I love you, Josephine, and I want you to marry me." He paused and looked at her, and the tenderness in his eyes brought tears to hers.

"So what do you say?"

She couldn't say a word. Her heart was too full, her throat too choked with emotion. She could only nod.

"Atta girl." His lips curved in a rakish smile.

She smiled back, tears of joy welling in her eyes. Their hands were locked behind their backs, but their gazes met and held as surely as their arms ever had. Cole rose to his feet, then leaned down toward her.

Handcuffs and bars couldn't restrain Josephine's heart. It soared high and free as their lips met and their souls mingled. Josephine's last thought before she abandoned herself to pure sensation was that Cole had awakened her to what it meant to be truly alive.

And then she lost herself in his kiss—the kiss of true love from her very own Prince Charming.

SECOND OPINION

Evelyn Rogers

Lousy in bed, was she? What Dr. Charlotte Hamilton needs is a second opinion. Her ex-husband hurled the insult at her the moment their divorce was final, and the blow to the attractive doctor's self-esteem left her wanting to prove him wrong. Drowning her sorrows in a margarita, she finds herself flirting with a sandy-haired hunk at the bar. She isn't the one-night-stand type, but suddenly they are in a hotel room, where with his expert touch and stunningly sexy body, he proves her anything but lousy. But what she writes off as a one-night stand, Sam Blake sees as the beginning of something wonderful. In that one night, the handsome sportswriter is smitten. Sam will do anything to make the stubborn doctor his—even deny his own urges until she agrees to an old-fashioned date. And he is determined to give her the second opinion she really needs—not of sex, but of true love.

___52332-9 $5.99 US/$6.99 CAN

BODY & SOUL

JENNIFER ARCHER

Overworked, underappreciated housewife and mother Lisa O'Conner gazes at the young driver in the red car next to her. Tory Beecham's manicured nails keep time with the radio and her smile radiates youthful vitality. For a moment, Lisa imagines switching places with the carefree college student. But when Lisa looks in the rearview mirror and sees Tory's hazel eyes peering back at her, she discovers her daydream has become astonishing reality. Fortune has granted Lisa every woman's fantasy. But as the goggle-eyed, would-be young suitors line up at Lisa's door, only one man piques her interest. But he is married—to her, or rather, the woman she used to be. And he seems intent on being faithful. Unsure how to woo her husband, Lisa knows one thing: No matter what else comes of the madcap, mix-matched mayhem, she will be reunited body and soul with her only true love.

___52334-5 $5.50 US/$6.50 CAN

An Original Sin

Nina Bangs

Fortune MacDonald listens to women's fantasies on a daily basis as she takes their orders for customized men. In a time when the male species is extinct, she is a valued man-maker. So when she awakes to find herself sharing a bed with the most lifelike, virile man she has ever laid eyes or hands on, she lets her gaze inventory his assets. From his long dark hair, to his knife-edged cheekbones, to his broad shoulders, to his jutting—well, all in the name of research, right?—it doesn't take an expert any time at all to realize that he is the genuine article, a bona fide man. And when Leith Campbell takes her in his arms, she knows real passion for the first time . . . but has she found true love?

___52324-8 $5.99 US/$6.99 CAN

Something Wild

Kimberly Raye

Dependent only upon twentieth-century conveniences, Tara Martin seeks to make a name for herself as a top-notch photojournalist. But when a plea from her best friend sends her off into the Smoky Mountains to snap a sasquatch, a twisted ankle leaves her in a precarious position—and when she looks up, she sees the biggest foot she's ever seen. Tara learns that the big foot belongs to an even bigger man—with a colossal heart and a body to die for. And that man, who was raised alone in the wilds of Appalachia, will teach Tara that what she needs is something wild.

_52272-1 $5.50 US/$6.50 CAN

Dorchester Publishing Co., Inc.
P.O. Box 6640
Wayne, PA 19087-8640

Please add $1.75 for shipping and handling for the first book and $.50 for each book thereafter. NY, NYC, and PA residents, please add appropriate sales tax. No cash, stamps, or C.O.D.s. All orders shipped within 6 weeks via postal service book rate. Canadian orders require $2.00 extra postage and must be paid in U.S. dollars through a U.S. banking facility.

Name_____

Address_____

City_____ State_____ Zip_____

I have enclosed $_____ in payment for the checked book(s).

Payment <u>must</u> accompany all orders. ❏ Please send a free catalog.

CHECK OUT OUR WEBSITE! www.dorchesterpub.com

More Than Magic

Kathleen Nance

Darius is as beautiful, as mesmerizing, as dangerous as a m[an]
can be. His dark, star-kissed eyes promise exquisite joys, y[et]
it is common knowledge he has no intention of taking a wif[e.]
Ever. Sex and sensuality will never ensnare Darius, for he [is]
their master. But magic can. Knowledge of his true name w[ill]
give a mortal woman power over the arrogant djinni, and [an]
age-old enemy has carefully baited the trap. Alluring y[et]
innocent, Isis Montgomery will snare his attention, and th[e]
spell she's been given will bind him to her. But who ca[n]
control a force that is even more than magic?

___52299-3 $5.99 US/$6.99 CA[N]

HIGH ENERGY DARA JOY

Zanita Masterson knows nothing about physics, until a reporting job leads her to Tyberius Evans. The rogue scientist is six feet of piercing blue eyes, rock-hard muscles and maverick ideas—with his own masterful equation for sizzling ecstasy and high energy.

___4438-2 $4.99 US/$5.99 CAN

Dorchester Publishing Co., Inc.
P.O. Box 6640
Wayne, PA 19087-8640

Please add $1.75 for shipping and handling for the first book and $.50 for each book thereafter. NY, NYC, and PA residents, please add appropriate sales tax. No cash, stamps, or C.O.D.s. All orders shipped within 6 weeks via postal service book rate. Canadian orders require $2.00 extra postage and must be paid in U.S. dollars through a U.S. banking facility.

Name_____

Address_____

City_____ State _____ Zip_____

I have enclosed $_____ in payment for the checked book(s).

Payment <u>must</u> accompany all orders. ❑ Please send a free catalog.

CHECK OUT OUR WEBSITE! www.dorchesterpub.com

LOVE ME TENDER
SANDRA HILL

Once upon a time, in the magic kingdom of Manhattan, there lived a handsome designer-shoe magnate named Prince Charming, and a beautiful stockbroker named Cinderella. And as the story goes, these two are destined to live happily ever after, at least according to a rhinestone-studded fairy godfather named Elmer Presley.

___4457-9 $5.99 US/$6.99 CAN

Golden Man

Evelyn Rogers

Steven Marshall is the kind of guy who makes a woman think of satin sheets and steamy nights, of wild fantasies involving hot tubs and whipped cream—and then brass bands, waving flags, and Fourth of July parades. All-American terrific, that's what he is; tall and bronzed, with hair the color of the sun, thick-lashed blue eyes, and a killer grin slanted against a square jaw—a true Golden Man. He is even single. Unfortunately, he is also the President of the United States. So when average citizen Ginny Baxter finds herself his date for a diplomatic reception, she doesn't know if she is the luckiest woman in the country, or the victim of a practical joke. Either way, she is in for the ride of her life . . . and the man of her dreams.

__52295-0 $5.99 US/$6.99 CAN